P...
DIANA L. PAXSON

"As intricate and colorful as a Saxon brooch . . .
Paxson's words cast a shimmering light into [the]
somewhat dark and forgotten corner of myth."
Stephen R. Lawhead, author of *Avalon*

"Paxson brings her people and ideas to convincing life."
Publishers Weekly

"Few authors are as capable as Diana Paxson."
Jennifer Roberson,
author of *Chronicles of the Cheysuli*

"Beautifully written . . . exuberant, richly detailed
mythology . . . Paxson gives new form to classic legend."
Booklist

"Paxson brings new life to these heroic deeds, giving
them new meaning, humanizing them."
Locus

"[She] combines familiar legend and history with
remarkable grace."
Julian May, author of *Blood Trillium*

Other Books in
The Hallowed Isle series by
Diana L. Paxson

THE HALLOWED ISLE, BOOKS I & II:
THE BOOK OF THE SWORD AND
THE BOOK OF THE SPEAR

Wodan's Children *Trilogy*

THE DRAGONS OF THE RHINE
THE WOLF AND THE RAVEN
THE LORD OF HORSES

With Adrienne Martine-Barnes

MASTER OF EARTH AND WATER
THE SHIELD BETWEEN THE WORLDS
SWORD OF FIRE AND SHADOW

ATTENTION: ORGANIZATIONS AND CORPORATIONS
Most Eos paperbacks are available at special quantity discounts
for bulk purchases for sales promotions, premiums, or fund-
raising. For information, please call or write:

Special Markets Department, HarperCollins Publishers, Inc.,
10 East 53rd Street, New York, N.Y. 10022–5299.
Telephone: (212) 207–7528. Fax: (212) 207–7222.

DIANA L. PAXSON

THE HALLOWED ISLE

BOOKS III & IV

THE BOOK OF THE CAULDRON AND THE BOOK OF THE STONE

An Imprint of HarperCollinsPublishers

This is a work of fiction. Names, characters, places, and incidents are the products of the author's imagination or are used fictitiously and are not to be construed as real. Any resemblance to actual events, locales, organizations, or persons, living or dead, is entirely coincidental.

EOS
An Imprint of HarperCollins*Publishers*
10 East 53rd Street
New York, New York 10022-5299

Copyright © 2001 by Diana L. Paxson
Book III: The Book of the Cauldron copyright © 1999 by Diana L. Paxson
Book IV: The Book of the Stone copyright © 2000 by Diana L. Paxson
ISBN: 0-380-81759-4
www.eosbooks.com

All rights reserved. No part of this book may be used or reproduced in any manner whatsoever without written permission, except in the case of brief quotations embodied in critical articles and reviews. For information address Eos, an imprint of HarperCollins Publishers.

First Eos paperback printing: February 2001
First Eos trade printing: January 2000
First Eos trade printing: November 1999

Eos Trademark Reg. U.S. Pat. Off. and in Other Countries,
Marca Registrada, Hecho en U.S.A.
HarperCollins® is a trademark of HarperCollins Publishers Inc.

Printed in the U. S. A.

10 9 8 7 6 5 4 3 2 1

If you purchased this book without a cover, you should be aware that this book is stolen property. It was reported as "unsold and destroyed" to the publisher, and neither the author nor the publisher has received any payment for this "stripped book."

In Memoriam
Paul Edwin Zimmer

THE BOOK
OF THE
CAULDRON

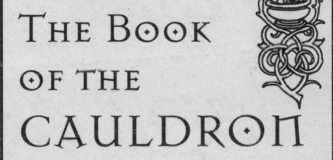

ACKNOWLEDGMENTS

My special thanks to Heather Rose Jones, who took time off from her doctoral studies in Welsh philology to advise me on the mysteries of fifth-century British spelling. For those who would like an excellent historical overview of the Arthurian period, I recommend *The Age of Arthur* by John Morris, recently reprinted by Barnes & Noble. I must also thank Caitlin and John Matthews for some of the insights in their book *Ladies of the Lake*.

Through the fields of European literature, the Matter of Britain flows as a broad and noble stream. In relation to this book especially, a major branch is Marion Zimmer Bradley's *The Mists of Avalon*. Therefore I offer this tributary with thanks and recognition to her and to all those who have gone before.

PROLOGUE

Life came first from the sea.

Cradle of creation and sheltering womb, it contained all elements. Dissolved and coalescing, joining, growing, the elements combined to become beings of ascending complexity.

Water is transformation.

Rising and falling, dying and rebirthing, it nourishes the world. Perpetually moving, it obeys the laws of moon and tide. Constrained, it grows stagnant and dies; free flowing, it renews the world.

Water is the blood of the Goddess, flowing through the streams and rivers that vein the land. In the lakes and pools, fed from the depths by bubbling springs, She pours out her blessings.

Water is woman's magic.

As the sea floods in answer to the moon so does her womb; each month she bleeds and is renewed. In blood she creates a child and bloody, she bears it; from her breasts springs sweet milk to be its food. Women seek the sacred spring and make offerings to the Goddess whose name means the power that wells up from the depths to the heights, knowing that her magic and theirs is the same. . . .

On an island in the ocean, nine priestesses serve a sacred shrine. As each moon waxes and wanes they praise the Goddess in Her times and seasons. But often, when the moon is full, the priestess who is their leader walks by the shore of the sea. Moonlight glitters silver on the waters. She stretches out her arms to embrace that splendor, but it flows through her fingers. She aches with yearning to hold the power by which she herself is held, and slowly, within the womb of her head a vision grows.

When the chieftains of her people come to make their offerings she requires of them silver. Piece by piece, she melts it together, beats it out into flat sheets, molded with images of the Goddess. Ready for love or armed for war, healing the sick or giving songs to the bard, milking a cow or hunting a deer or bringing a ship safe to land, nursing her child or bearing the soul of a dead man across the sea, the Goddess appears in all Her guises, blessing humankind.

Section by section the pieces are shaped, riveted and soldered until they are one. From hand and heart a great cauldron is born, silver as the moon. River pearls are set into its rim, gleaming softly. Then, singing, the priestesses bear it to the sacred spring. One by one, each priestess fills her chalice. She lifts it high to catch the radiance of the moon. Then she pours it into the cauldron, shimmering with silver light.

The song grows deeper, becomes a wordless humming, a vibration that shivers the surface of the water. From beyond this world come overtones and harmonies. A mist of radiance glows above the water, twines upward, shapes itself into the form of a woman. Turning, She opens her arms, Her voice joins in the singing, and shapes it into words. She dips liquid from the cauldron; into each chalice She pours Her blessings, and all are filled.

And when at last, the priestesses return to awareness of who and where they are, the Cauldron is empty. But every full moon when they fill it with water from the sacred spring, that water glows, and all who drink of it are renewed.

i

Birth Pangs

A.D. 487

Just before sunset, a wind came down from the heights to ruffle the water. The Lady of the Lake breathed it in gratefully, for the day had been warm, a promise of the summer season that Beltain would usher in. In the lands of men, the young folk would be going out into the woods to gather greenery for the festival, and if they took rather longer than was strictly necessary to cut the branches, and came back with their clothing awry, even the Christians would hardly dare chastise them on this eve. But on the Isle of Maidens there was no need to bring in the wilderness, for it was all around them. And while man and maid performed the old earth magic, she and her priestesses would invoke the magic of the waters whose power enabled all these green and growing things to survive.

Beyond the screen of willow and the silver sheen of the water, the mountain crouched like an old woman, cloaked and hooded in misty blue, hunched against the dimming sky. Igierne had seen it so when, as a girl, she first claimed this spot

7

as her private bathing place. Now she was an old woman herself. But the mountain remained the same.

She hung the rough towel across a branch and slid the cloak from around her shoulders, shivering a little at the touch of the air. For a moment she hesitated to remove her shift as well, but it was not going to get any warmer. Lips twisting wryly, she dragged it over her head and made her way down to the waterside.

White and wavering as a birch trunk, she saw her body reflected there. *I am a waning moon . . .* she thought wryly. Even her hair, once golden, was faded now to silver-fair. As a girl, she had spied on the older priestesses at their bathing and been astonished to find their bodies still so smooth. It surprised her still, looking down, to see her own shape so much younger than the face in her mirror. True, her breasts lay pendant upon her ribcage, and her belly had been stretched by the weight of two children, but her buttocks were round with muscle from walking, and her arms were firm.

If Uthir had been living, she would have rejoiced in his delight in her body, but he slept now beside his brother in the mound before the Giant's Dance. No longer was she high queen and his lady. Now it was her son Artor who ruled. When the princes of Britannia chose him, Igierne had offered to stay and manage his household, but the lords of Britannia, having accepted her son's right to rule them, wanted no motherly meddling in the process of turning him into a king. Even Merlin had been tolerated only grudgingly as his tutor, perhaps because they feared him.

And so she had returned to the Isle of Maidens to reclaim the role for which she had been born. She wrote to Artor with some regularity, seeking to supply the guidance she had not been allowed to give before, but increasingly her counsel came from her meditations as a priestess, rather than her memories of life as Uthir's queen. On the rare occasions when she visited her son, his court seemed like another world. These days, the health of her body mattered only because it served her soul. And that—she smiled down at the woman who looked back at her from the water—was still that of the maiden who had first bathed in these waters so long ago.

Still smiling, she stepped down the shelving strand into the water.

"Blessed be my feet, that I may walk in Thy ways . . . blessed be my legs, that I may stand before Thee . . . blessed be my womb, that I may be Thy shrine . . ." She scooped up water, purifying each part of her body, murmuring the words that would make her a fit vessel for the power of the Goddess to fill.

The Isle of Maidens lay hidden within the double enclosure of the Lake and its encircling hills. The Romans had massacred the Druid priesthood on the isle of Mona, and driven them from Afallon that men now called the Isle of Glass, but this sanctuary they had never found. In time its huts of daubed withies had been replaced by stone, but in some things the priestesses still held by the old Druid ways, and the most sacred of their rituals took place beneath the open sky.

If the island was doubly warded, the hazelwood formed the innermost barrier around its center, where a fissure in the island's rocky core had created a cave. The Sword-God's shrine had been a temple built by men, tolerated, but never truly belonging to the isle. The cave was its most ancient and original sanctuary. Three fires burned now before it, but the entrance remained in shadow.

Igierne lay back against the carved wood of her chair, willing her breathing to remain steady, waiting for her heartbeat to slow. Her pale hair lay loose upon her shoulders. For this ceremony her maidens were robed in white. Only she wore the black of the midnight sky, though her ornaments were of silver, set with moonstone and river pearls.

Overhead, a scattering of stars glimmered in the river of night. Long practice had taught her to sense the slow turning of the skies. The moon was in its third quarter, and would not rise till the night was half gone. Imperceptibly her breathing began to deepen. She straightened, hearing her own heartbeat echoed by the soft beat of a drum. Anticipation tightened her skin as the women began to sing—

> *"Thou art the source and the stream . . .*
> *Thou art the desire and the dream . . .*

that which is empty and that which fills,
that which receives and that which wills;
Thou art the part and Thou art the whole,
Thou art the body and Thou, the soul. . . ."

The mingled voices converged in a single note, sustained in a long vibration that thrummed in the still air. Elsewhere they called on the gods in other guises, and by other names, especially on this night, when the young God came forth from his leafy glades to couple with the Goddess in the fields. But here, at the heart of the isle, it was the Lady alone who ruled.

"Great Mother, be near us—" intoned Igierne.

"Hear us, be near us . . ." came the reply.

"Gateway to birth and doorway to death—" Ceincair's sweet voice rose above the rest.

"Hear us. . . ."

"Lady of hope and healing—" the litany went on, and with each salutation, the air seemed to thicken until it was difficult to breathe.

"Thou art the Cauldron of Changes, the Womb of Wisdom—" said Igierne, and at her words, Morut and Nest moved to the dark opening of the cave and began to pull the stones away. Beneath them was a wooden chest carved with triple spirals, and within the chest, something swathed in white silk which they set in the hollow of the stone before Igierne's chair.

As the cloth fell away, she felt her awareness shifting so that she saw with doubled vision the ancient cauldron of riveted silver plates on which goddess-faces and the images of strange beasts stood out in low relief, and a vessel of pure Light, outshining the fires.

A white-clad shape moved forward. From a silver pitcher, water poured into the cauldron in a glistening stream. The light grew brighter.

"I bring water from the ocean, the womb of the world. Receive the offering!" the voice was that of Nest.

Another moved into the radiance. "I bring water from the Tamesis, lifeblood of the land—" More water glittered through the air.

One by one the priestesses emptied their pitchers. The water they offered came from each of the great rivers that drained Britannia, and from the sacred springs.

"I bring water from the Isle of Mona . . ." chanted Morut.

"I bring water from the blood spring of Afallon . . ." sang Ceincair.

The light grew; glowing figures moved within a bright haze. Igierne stared into the glimmering depths of the Cauldron.

"Speak to us, Lady," she whispered. "In this moment when the doors open between the worlds, show us what is to be. . . ."

With that prayer, all other awareness became peripheral. The light welled up around her and she was free.

She saw Britannia laid out below her, picked out in lines of light as one Beltain fire signaled another across the land. Disciplines practiced for so long they had become instinct turned her mind toward those whose future she must see.

Beltain fires blazed on the hills above Isca. Igierne's gaze followed the flicker of light and shadow as men and women danced around them. Her son Artor was there, with Betiver and Cai, and that odd Saxon boy who they said was Hengest's grandson. Girls came to the king, laughing, and he kissed them and drank the mead they offered, but though many of his men allowed themselves to be led off into the leafy shadows, and Gualchmai was no doubt there already, Artor remained by the fires.

Is this how you honor the Goddess, my child? Igierne thought ruefully, and heard, as if in agreement, a ripple of silvery laughter. But Artor had grown up suspecting himself a bastard, she remembered with sudden pain. No wonder if he took care where he sowed his own seed.

He must have a queen to act as your priestess, Lady! she told the bright darkness. *Show me the woman who will share his bed and his throne!*

The image shattered. Colors ran in swirls of liquid light, painting a land of folded hills and peaceful woodlands, altogether a gentler country than the Demetian shore. In a sheltered valley the villa of a British prince lay dark while his tribesmen revelled in the meadow below. But at the edge of the firelight something stirred. Igierne's vision focused; she saw a slim girl-child with amber eyes and a cloud of red-gold hair clutching an old blanket around her as she watched the dancing. Even standing, she seemed to sway like a young tree in the wind. She would be beautiful in motion.

As the image dimmed, the Voice of the Goddess sounded in Igierne's awareness once more—*"She is Leodagranus' daughter. Her name is Guendivar . . ."*

She is young, yet, thought Igierne, *too young to understand what this means. I must find her and prepare her for her destiny.*

Images flickered before her: Guendivar grown, her bright hair crowned with flowers . . . laughing, dancing, racing through the woods on a grey dappled mare . . . and older still, her face racked by grief and looking for the first time like that of a mortal woman and not a maiden of faerie. Igierne strove to see more, but the vision became a blur that left her dazed and dizzy, floating in the void.

With an effort she regained her focus. To foresee fate did not necessarily show one how to change it, for the ancients held that it was always changing, and in seeking to avoid the end foretold many a man had instead been its cause. Better to seek knowledge of events nearer to hand, so that one might, if not prevent, at least prepare to meet them.

Morgause . . . With a regretful recognition that her concern sprang more from duty than desire, Igierne sought to see the outcome of her daughter's pregnancy.

On the height of Dun Eidyn the Votadini warriors drank to their king. She saw Morgause bearing the horn among them, too heavily pregnant for dancing. From time to time she would pause, biting her lip for a moment before continuing her round.

The child will come very soon, thought Igierne, *does she know it?* But this was Morgause's fifth pregnancy. She must know her own body's signals by now. It was stubbornness, not ignorance, that kept her on her feet this Beltain Eve. Igierne suppressed the irritation that thoughts of her daughter too often inspired.

Will the birthing go well? What will this child bring to Britannia?

Vision was dazzled by the blaze of morning light on water. But in the next moment a tide of red replaced it. A child's angry wail deepened into the battlefield roar of an army. Fear for her daughter gave way to a deeper terror as she saw Morgause, her features sagging with middle age and twisted by hatred, and beside her, a boy whose features were a younger, fairer reflection of her own, with a hint of someone else in the line of the jaw that Igierne could not quite recognize. Was it that which set something deep within to shivering, or was it the spark of malice in his eyes? Red darkness swirled across her vision: a raven banner tossed against a fiery sky. And then it was a flight of ravens, and a Voice that cried—

"He shall bring blood and fire and the end of an age . . . All things pass, else lack of balance would destroy the world."

Igierne writhed in soundless repudiation, knowing, even as she hated it, that this Voice also was divine. And then, like cool water, the Goddess as she had always known Her spoke in her soul.

"Fear not. While the ravens ward the White Mount, the Guardian of Britannia will remain. . . ."

She felt herself falling back into her body, starlight and firelight and the light of her visions shattering around her like a mosaic of Roman glass. Desperately she tried to fix the pieces in some pattern that would retain its meaning, but they were moving too fast.

"Merlin!" her soul cried, *"Merlin, hear me! Beware the child that is born the first of May!"*

Then it was over, though she ached in every limb. Igierne felt soft hands helping her to sit upright, heard a murmur of shock and concern.

"My lady, are you all right?"

"I will be . . ." she muttered. *Artor*—she thought, *I must speak with him soon.* Then she took a deep breath and opened her eyes to see the gibbous quarter-moon staring down at her from a sky that was already paling before the first light of Beltain's dawn.

At dawn on Beltain, Morgause went out with her women to bring water from the sacred spring. Before sunrise the air was brisk and Morgause was glad of the fleecy cloak she wore. Unbalanced by the great bulge of her belly, she moved carefully,

picking her way down the rocky path in the uncertain torchlight and the light of the waning moon that was more deceptive
still. From the group of maidens who walked with her came
laughter, swiftly hushed. The child in her belly stirred, then
stilled. Perhaps, she thought hopefully, the unaccustomed motion would lull him to sleep. He had kept her wakeful half the
night with his kicking, as if he could not wait for the womb to
open and set him free.

To walk from the fortress down to the base of the cleft below it and back could take half the morning, and the return
climb required considerable stamina. The women, eyeing the
queen's distended belly, had begged her to let one of the chieftains' daughters who attended her represent her in the ceremony, but Morgause refused. For a girl to take her place in
Leudonus' bed during her pregnancies did not threaten her position, but her condition had not permitted her to dance at the
Beltain fires. Morgause would allow no one to usurp any of the
other sacred duties of the queen.

"It will be safe enough," she told them. "The babe is not due
for another half moon." This was not quite true—she knew
very well that this child had been conceived in the rites at the
feast of Lugus, and so her pregnancy was now full term. But
her other children had come behind time, so she told the lie
without compunction.

Men might speculate, when the queen's sons were born
some nine moons after a festival, but those who did not follow
the old ways could never be certain they were not of
Leudonus' begetting. The majority of the Votadini tribesmen
believed, like Morgause, that her children were a gift from the
gods.

For a moment vision blurred; the torchlit darkness of the
road became the festival ground, and the chill of dawn the
warm summer night of Lughnasaid. The people were shouting,
a hero came to her in the darkness of the sacred enclosure,
filled with the god, and then the dark fire of the goddess reft
her own awareness away . . .

Morgause trembled again, remembering. It was only afterwards, listening to folk speak of the bull-fight and how the
young king from the south had saved the fallen priest of Lugus

and completed the ceremony, that she understood that it was Artor who had lain in her arms.

She had considered, in that moment of realization, seeking out the herbs that would cast the child from her womb. But the gods had willed that her brother's seed take root there. She did not dare deny them. Morgause was built for bearing, but a woman offered her life in childbed as a man marched into battle. Soon, now, the gods would judge both mother and child. And if such a child lived . . . surely he was meant for a mighty destiny.

A stone turned under her foot and she grasped at the arm of Dugech, who walked beside her.

"Lady, please, let me send for a litter to take you back to the dun!"

Morgause shook her head. To give up now would be an admission of weakness. She straightened defiantly.

"Then let us carry you down—"

Morgause started forward again without answering. The sky was growing lighter. The far side of the cleft stood in stark outline against that pallor; a gulf of darkness gaped below. *I am descending into the Underworld,* she thought, suppressing panic. For a moment she considered letting Dugech have her way, but now that the exercise had got her blood running, she felt better than she had before.

"The rite requires that I walk to the spring, and it will do me good. I have sat too long indoors. Only stay close so that I do not fall."

They moved on. The pallor above brightened to a pearly grey, and then, as the torch flames grew pale and the shapeless masses of shadow that edged the path became shrubs and trees lightened, with a hint of rose. They had reached the crossroads where the way that ran down the vale crossed the path that descended from the dun. Morgause turned. Behind the jagged peak of the Watch Hill the sky was beginning to flame with gold.

She tried to hurry then, ignoring the slow ache across her lower back. She wished now that she had called for the litter, but she had almost reached the spring. With relief she felt the pathway level out and took a deep breath of moist air. Beneath their mantles the white linen garments of her maidens glowed. Morgause paused to undo the pins that held her own cloak and straightened gratefully as its weight slithered to the ground. The flesh on her arms pebbled at the touch of the brisk air, but her blood was still heated from the walk and she did not mind the cold.

She beckoned to red-haired Leuku, who was carrying the bronze vessel, and strode toward the spring. To the east the sky was bright gold. Overhead the heavens glowed pale rose, but the scattered clouds, catching the sunlight, had hung out banners of flame.

The women stood in silence, watching that radiance intensify until the rock above was edged with a sliver of flame. As the sunwheel rolled up the sky, light blazed between the birches and sparkled on the waters of the well as if a fire had been kindled within. Pent breath was released in a shout—

"Water of life from the depths upwelling—" sang the queen.

"Bring us thy blessing!" her maidens chorused in reply.

"Fire of power from the heavens descending—"

"Bring us thy blessing!"

"Fire in the water kindling cool flame—" she sang then, and waited for the others to reply.

"Power we drink and protection we claim."

Carefully, she bent and tipped the rim of the kettle so that the glittering water trickled in. As she began to stand up, the ache across her loins became a sudden pang. For a moment Morgause could not move. When she could breathe again, she straightened, telling herself it had only been another preliminary pain. She had been having them for weeks, and knew them for the distant thunder that heralds the storm.

But with her next step, Morgause felt a trickle of warm fluid between her thighs, and understood that the time of waiting was done.

"My lady!" cried Dugech as the gush soaked the back of the queen's gown.

Morgause managed a smile. "The waters of my womb flow like those of the holy well. Let them be my offering. . . ." She held out the cauldron, and Leuku, her eyes wide, took it from her hands.

Without waiting for orders, Dugech whispered to one of the younger girls and sent her sprinting back up the trail.

"Let us spread our mantles to make a bed for you, lady, and you can lie down until the litter arrives."

Morgause shook her head. "I walked half the night to bear my first child. This labor will go easier if I get as far as I can under my own power." She knew that she was challenging the gods, but so long as she was moving, she could maintain the illusion that this process was under her control. Ignoring the shocked protest of the maidens, she started back along the trail.

From time to time a pain overwhelmed her and she would pause, gripping Dugech's shoulder until it passed. But it soon became apparent that this child was in a hurry to come into the world. By the time they reached the crossroads, the pains were coming swiftly. Morgause swayed, dragging in breath in hoarse gasps. The women were piling their cloaks on the grass beside the road. Dugech took one arm and Lcuku the other, and Morgause could no longer resist them. Biting her lip against the pain, she let them help her down to lie with her back braced against the bank where the pale primroses grew.

Her fingers clenched in the new grass as the muscles of her belly contracted and released again. She was aware that the litter had arrived, but by then things had gone too far for her to be moved.

She fixed her gaze on the hollow moon, sliding down the western sky like a rind of pearl. She could hear the girls whispering. It was not right that the queen of the Votadini should give birth like a beggar woman beside the road. And at a crossroads too! At Beltain, when the folk of faerie moved from their winter quarters to their summer homes, more might be passing along that road than men. Morgause shook her head, denying her own fear. This pregnancy itself had been a challenge to the gods—it should be no surprise that the birth was the same.

"Draw the circle of safety around me if you are afraid—" she grunted between pangs, "and then get ready to catch the babe."

The muscles of her belly writhed again, and she was unable to suppress a groan. Between birthings one always forgot the pain, but it seemed to her that the violence of the pangs that tore her now was greater than any she had known, as if the womb were trying to turn itself inside out in its haste to expel the weight it bore.

"Mother . . ." she whimpered, and then bit back the word. Blood trickled from between her thighs to stain the crimson gown. Igierne was not there—had never been there, really, when Morgause needed her, even when they were living in the same hall. Why should she call for her now?

Morgause had always taken such pride in her ability to bear sons. But women died in childbirth, and she was no longer in her first youth. *Am I dying?* Her thoughts circled in confusion. *Is the Goddess claiming my offering?* Shadows danced before her eyes like dark wings.

I am in Your hands, Lady . . . I offer my life if it will serve you, and that of my child. She let out her breath in a long sigh, feeling a dim sorrow, but no fear.

Then another convulsion took her and she cried out once more. The rolling ache became a wrenching agony.

"Warrior, and mother of warriors—now you shall fight for your life!" came a voice from within. *"Cast the babe from your body, now!"*

Morgause drew up her legs and dug her heels into the soft earth and pushed with all the strength she had. The pressure increased, as if she were being split in two. Again her muscles clenched and she bore down. She felt the gush of birthblood and a burning pain in her sex as the child's head crowned. Against her closed eyelids the sunlight was a whirl of red brightness. She sucked in air, and then with the last of her strength, pushed once more.

There was a moment of pulsing relief as the babe slid, warm and slippery, between her thighs. She gasped for breath, and in echo, heard his furious challenge to the world. The babe was still yelling when Dugech tied off and cut the cord and laid him on her breast.

Morgause lay in drowsy stupor, the contractions of the birth fading from her wracked body like the last tremors of love. She felt the warm seep of blood from her womb sinking into the thirsty soil and found it hard to care. Anxious voices twittered around her, but she ignored them. Only when hard fingers began to knead her belly did she open her eyes with a weak cry.

"My lady, the afterbirth must be driven forth—" said Leuku as the queen protested. The baby was still squalling.

"Set the child to the teat," someone said then.

There were a few moments of confusion as they undid her gown. Morgause felt the babe rooting at her breast, and then a sudden sharp pang that shocked through her entire body as he fastened onto the nipple and her milk let down. Through the convulsions that followed as she was delivered of the placenta he hung on. It was only when he let go at last that she saw blood flowing from her nipple along with the milk and realized that her son had been born toothed and ready to take on the world.

From nearby came the deep rumble of male voices. Morgause looked up and saw Leudonus' grizzled head above the others.

"You have a fine son, my lord, for all that he came early into the world—" said Dugech, leading the king into the circle of women. Morgause's lips twitched as the other woman bent to take the swaddled child from her arms.

Dugech knew perfectly well that this boy, like the others, was full-term. Even Leudonus, who had sired his share of bastards, must know the difference by now, but if so, he had his own reasons to uphold the fiction. He frowned down at the squirming bundle Dugech had handed him, and silence fell while men waited for him to acknowledge paternity.

"A fine boy indeed. He has your hair," he said finally. And then, holding him up, "Let him be called Medraut, of the royal kindred. Let the Votadini welcome a future warrior!"

This, if not explicit, was close enough to an avowal. The walls of the cleft echoed to their shout of welcome. Morgause smiled. *A warrior,* she thought, *and more than a warrior. I welcome a king!* She could sleep now, knowing others would guard her child. The moon had finally disappeared, but through her closing eyelids, she still saw the red glow of the Beltain Sun.

If she slitted her eyes just so, thought Guendivar, the reflections from the warriors' spearpoints merged into a single dazzle

of light. That was almost more fun than watching them throw
the spears, and certainly better than listening to them argue
about the casts. She had promised Telent that she would watch
him compete today. He was in Prince Leodagranus' guard, and
carried her around on his shoulders, though the last time she
asked he had said that at almost seven, she was too old.

Guendivar chewed on her lower lip, watching as he prepared
to cast anew. She knew that she was growing, but he was *very*
tall. Perhaps she would go away now, to punish him.

At the thought, she was already in motion, flitting past the
line of men like a white blossom before the wind. Her mother,
who had been dozing in the shade of the figured cloth, sat up
suddenly, calling, but by then Guendivar was halfway down
the field and could pretend she had not heard. Petronilla was
always trying to make her be polite and tidy; Guendivar had
learned the advantages of evasion early on.

She wanted to see the rest of the festival. At the edge of the
field, peddlers had set up their wares in bothies made of woven
branches and strips of striped cloth. There were only a few, and
their goods would have been considered paltry stuff when the
Romans ruled, but only the older people remembered those
days. In the old days they would probably have celebrated the
festival in Lindinis, her father's town, instead of spending most
of their time at the old villa in the hills. To the folk of the countryside, the red pottery oil lamps and the beads of Roman glass
seemed very fine. Guendivar wandered among them, admiring,
and one of the traders gave her a green ribbon to tie back her
hair.

The afternoon was waning when she saw one of her
mother's women advancing toward her with a decidedly repressive look in her eye. Rather suddenly Guendivar remembered that Petronilla had been quite explicit about the behavior
that was expected of a chieftain's daughter at this festival. She
knew that she had disobeyed, and she did not mind being pun-
ished once it was over, but the sun was still well above the
trees!

Before the woman could grab her, Guendivar was off again,
slipping behind a cart and then around the horse-lines and toward the protection of the trees. Perhaps her father's huntsmen

knew these woods better than she did, but Guendivar did not think anyone else could find her once she was among the trees. And even a woodsman might think twice about entering the tunnels that a small girl could negotiate with ease.

One of them brought her out into a small glade surrounded by hazels. The grass in the center was flattened, as if someone had been sleeping there, and hanging on one of the hazel twigs was a flower crown. Guendivar began to smile.

To watch the dancing last night had been exciting, with the drumming and the naked bodies shining in the light of the fires. She had not quite understood what those men and girls were seeking when they leaped over the flames or ran, half-embraced and laughing, for the forest, but she knew it must be something wonderful, part of the magic she felt pulsing from the land itself on Beltain eve.

Guendivar could still sense it, a little, here in the glade. She sat still, senses extended, feeling the warmth of the afternoon radiating from the grass. The sounds of the festival seemed distant, and as she continued to sit and her eyelids grew heavy, more distant still. She had not gotten much sleep the night before, and the day had been busy. The warm air caressed her and she curled drowsily down into the tangled grass.

It was the change in the light that roused her, a ray of the sinking sun that found its way through the tangle of branches to her closed eyelids. Still half-asleep, she scrunched them shut more tightly and turned her head, but the sun's angle let the last of its radiance pour through the trees. Sighing, Guendivar rubbed her eyes and slitted them open.

Within the glade, every stock and stone was glowing, and each leaf and blade of grass was edged with flame. *Pretty . . .* she thought, watching with half-focused gaze, and stretched out her arm. *Everything has light inside, even me. . . .* Beneath the scratches and the smears of soil and the scattering of golden freckles, her pale flesh shone.

A flicker at the edge of vision caught her attention. Her vision refocused; something was moving there. Bemused by beauty, she did not stir, even when her vision transmuted the spiraling sparkles into attenuated figures that danced and darted about the glade. At first they seemed tiny, but they seemed able to change their size at will, and they moved as if weightless, or winged. And presently she realized that the susurrus of sound was neither the wind nor music, but the chatter of high, sweet voices.

Fragments of old tales configured themselves into sudden certainty. Slowly Guendivar sat up, refusing to blink, lest the vision flicker away.

"I know you now . . ." she said softly. "You are faerie-folk. Have you just moved house into these woods today?"

For a moment even the motes of light seemed to stop moving. Then the air shimmered with faerie laughter.

"She sees us! She can see!" The faeries clustered around her in a glowing swirl. One of the figures floated upward to face her, expanding until it was as large as a child of three.

"Of course I can see you," answered Guendivar. "I have seen faeries before, I think," she added, remembering, "but they never talked to me."

"It is the moment between day and darkness, and in this child, the old blood runs true," said one of the others. *"But she will lose the vision when she is grown."*

Guendivar glared, but a new question was already on her lips. "Will you show me your country?"

"This is *our country—it is all around you, if you have the eyes to see—"* came the answer, and indeed, when Guendivar lifted her eyes, the familiar shapes of tree and rock seemed doorways to unguessed dimensions. But she dared not look too long, for fear that her new friends would flit away.

"Then will you give me a wish?" she asked.

"Our gifts can be dangerous . . ." the faerie responded, but Guendivar only laughed.

"Am I in danger here?" She grinned. "My wish is that my heart shall stay as it is now, and I shall always be able to see faerie."

"Are you certain? Folk so sighted may find it difficult to live in the mortal world. . . . "

Guendivar shrugged. "I think it is boring already. It will not matter to me."

"*It will matter . . .* " said the faerie, with momentary sadness. Then it, too, laughed. "*But we cannot refuse you on this day.*"

Guendivar clapped her hands, and as if on cue, the sun slid behind the hilltop and the light was gone. Her new friends were gone, too. For a moment she felt like crying, but it was getting cold, and she was hungry. She looked for the tunnel through the hazels, and found that to her altered vision, the world around her still shone from within.

The faerie had not lied to her. Laughing once more, Guendivar ran back to the world of humankind.

ii

A Shadow on the Moon

A.D. 489

 Just at dusk, on an evening when the first sliver of the first new moon of summer hung above the brow of the hill, Merlin arrived at the Lake. As always, he came alone and unheralded, appearing like a spirit at the edge of the forest. Igierne, on her way to the rock at the highest point of the island for her evening meditation, felt his presence like a breath of scent, which at first teases, and then releases a flood of memories. She stopped short on the path, so that Morut nearly ran into her.

"Go down to the landing and send the boat across to the shore. We have a visitor."

Morut's eyes widened, but she did not question Igierne's knowledge. Smiling, Igierne watched her go.

When she had first returned to the Lake to reclaim her role as its Lady, after Artor was made king, Igierne had felt herself half an impostor. The skills required of a bean-drui needed focus, application, constant honing. She was like a warrior taking down the sword he has allowed to rust on the wall. And yet her mental muscles, though stiff and clumsy, still remembered their early training, and in time she found that the passing years had given her a depth of understanding that had not been there when she was a girl. There might be others on the island to whom these skills came more easily, but none with her judgment regarding how and when they should be used. And after a dozen years as Tigernissa of Britain, Igierne found it easy to rule a gaggle of women and girls.

But Merlin, she thought as she watched him coming towards her, had wisdom of a different and higher order still. When she was a young woman, he had seemed much older than she, but from the vantage of fifty-two, a man in his early sixties was a contemporary. It was not age that set him so apart from other men, but an inherent wildness, despite all his years in the courts of kings.

He wore his accustomed wolfskin over a druid's white gown. Both were well-worn, as if they had grown to his gaunt frame. But he looked strong. Later, as she poured mint tea into his bowl from the kettle that steamed over her fire, she realized that Merlin was assessing her as well.

"I am no longer the girl you knew in Luguvallum . . ." she said softly.

"You are still beautiful—" he answered her thought rather than her words "—as the forest in autumn, when the nuts ripen on the trees."

Igierne felt herself flushing, and shook her head. "My moon has passed the full, but it is the sun we should be speaking of. When did you last see Artor?"

Merlin raised one bushy eyebrow in gentle mockery, but allowed her self-deprecation to pass. "Two, or nearly three moons past. He is rebuilding the fort at Isca. Castra Legionis, they call it. It will serve as a staging area for campaigns against raiders from Eriu. It was very crowded and full of soldiers. I did not stay long."

"That is the main threat, then? Not the Saxons?"

The druid shrugged. "At present. Artor has tamed Hengest's cub and set him to guard the sheep in Cantium, but the rest of the Saxon pack are still hungry. Ceretic sits in Venta, licking his chops and eyeing the lands around him, and the Anglians roam the fens. Artor will have to deal with them eventually. But why do you ask me? Does not he write to you?"

"From time to time—" She tapped the carved wooden casket where she kept Artor's letters. "But a druid's sight is different from that of a king."

"I cannot rule for him, Igierne," Merlin answered her, "nor can you."

She frowned, thinking of the advice she had been sending. Someone must speak for the Goddess, until Artor had a queen. "Is that why you spend so much time roaming the wilds?" she countered. "What if something happens? What if he needs you?"

"I will know." His voice was a subterranean rumble, as if he spoke through stone. "The stars have shown me that a crisis is coming. For good or for ill, it will settle things with the Saxons for a generation. When that time comes, it is ordained that I be there."

Igierne felt the truth of that in her bones. For a few moments there was no sound but the hiss of the fire.

"I too have searched the future," she said finally. "Two years ago, at Beltain. This year I dared not—I was afraid. I remember the terror, but of what I saw I know only that the Lady of Ravens was there, and red war coming, and a child."

"I know Her . . ." Merlin's face twisted with ancient sorrow. "Only the White Raven can stand against her when the war horns blow."

"But what of the child?"

"You called out to me in that vision, and I heard—" Merlin threw up his hands in exasperation. "But what would you have me do? Should I have counselled Artor to order every child born on the first of May exposed? Even Caesar would have been unable to enforce such a decree! Foreknowledge is a deceptive gift, Igierne, for our hopes and fears distort the shapes of what we see. When I was young I searched the heavens constantly, but the older I get, the less I seek to know."

"But if you foresee a danger, you can avoid it—" she exclaimed.

"Can you? The Greeks tell of a man called Oedipus, whose efforts to flee his fate instead fulfilled it."

Igierne glared at him. She knew that as women got older they often became stronger, more resolute, while many men grew gentler in old age. Certainly it was so with Merlin. He, who in their young days had been hard as the hills, seemed now as elusive as wind or water.

"If I see danger coming to my country or my child I will confront it," she told him, leaning forward with her hands on her knees. "And I will not cease to fight that fate while life shall last."

"Perhaps that is *your* fate, Igierne," Merlin said gently, and smiled.

"Mother, Aggarban is wearing my red belt!"

"Why can't I have it? You said you weren't taking it with you—"

Gwyhir's reply was muffled, as if he had decided to take matters into his own hands. Morgause sighed. She had been regretting Leudonus' decision to send her second son to join his brother at the court of Artor, but just at this moment she did not care whether he went to Castra Legionis or the Devil, if she could have peace in her house once more.

"Let him have it, Gwyhir," she snapped, thrusting aside the curtain between her closet-bed and the central common area around the fire. "You were telling me only yesterday that the belt is too small."

"But he should *ask*, mother," said Gwyhir, straightening to his full height. He had got man-high in the past moons, but was still growing into his bones. His hair, lighter than Gualchmai's, stuck out at odd angles, giving him the look of a young bird.

Aggarban still wore the belt, though he was flushed and rumpled where his brother had grabbed him. He was dark and stocky, not much taller than the fourth brother, Goriat, even though he was almost four years older. Morgause looked at them and shook her head. She was too young to be the mother of such a brood of big, boisterous boys. At the moment, she wanted to send them *all* to Artor; all, that is, except for her sweet Medraut.

Her youngest son was turned two this spring. She had

danced at the Beltain fires this year and gone into the woods afterwards with one of Leudonus' warriors. But she had not kindled. She told herself it meant nothing—there were three years between Gwyhir and Aggarban, after all, and four between Goriat and Medraut—but in her heart the fear was growing that Medraut would be her last child. Was he her punishment, or her key to greatness? She still did not know.

"Will you write and tell us all about Artor's fortress?" asked Goriat.

"I will be far too busy to write letters," answered his brother loftily, "riding, and training with the sword and spear. When I win my first fight I will let you know."

"And what if you lose?" Aggarban stuck out his tongue and darted out of the way of his brother's blow.

"Our brother Gualchmai is the greatest warrior the High King has," said Gwyhir. "He may beat me, but by the gods, nobody else will, once my training is done."

At least, thought his mother, he recognized that he still had a few things to learn. But in the long run, she shared his confidence. No son of hers could be anything but a champion.

"A fine lad," said Bliesbituth as they watched Gwyhir ride out with Leudonus and his men. He was a chieftain who often served as a courier between Fodreu and Dun Eidyn. "But why do you send him to the Romans? If you let him come to Pictland, we would marry him to one of our princesses and he might father kings." He smiled at his wife, a plump, pretty woman called Tulach, who was herself of the royal lineage.

"I have several sons," Morgause said diplomatically. "Perhaps one of the others—"

"You think I am flattering," said Bliesbituth, "but it is not so. Britannia was strong in the time of the emperors, but their time is ended. The Votadini should look northward. We were never conquered; our warriors never gave up their swords. If all the peoples who live north of the Wall were to unite, we would be a power to reckon with. The Romans call us the Picts, the painted people, but we are the Pretani, the true Britons of this isle. The south is exhausted—our time is coming now."

Morgause felt the blood of generations who had fought to

defend that Wall burning in her cheeks, but she held her tongue. From all accounts, Artor was keeping the Saxons and the men of Eriu in check; she was too tactful to remind Bliesbituth how her brother had dealt with the Picts three years before. The Romans, even at the height of their power, had been able to do little more.

Another thought chilled her suddenly. If all the might of Rome had been able to do no better, what did that say about the power of Alba? While Artor was young and strong, perhaps he could hold the north in check, but what about his successor? The lords of Britannia had refused to make her husband their king because his power was too far from the center of things, but in the time that was coming, it might be that only a king whose strength lay on the borders could hope to rule. *A king like my son . . .* she thought, smiling grimly, *my Medraut. . . .*

"And there is this to think on," said Tulach. "They say that the people of the south have abandoned their gods. The new religion teaches love, and peace. Is it any wonder that the empire has fallen? You think you keep the old ways here, my queen, but among the Pretani we have preserved the ancient traditions in all their purity. It is not only our menfolk who have power!" The silver ornaments clasped in the tight curls of her bronze brown hair chimed softly as she nodded.

Morgause smiled thinly. "It is true that there are many in Britannia who follow the Christos, but I am the daughter of the Lady of the Lake and the heir to its mysteries."

"No doubt, but there are things we could teach you, Morgause."

Morgause did not answer her. The dust of Leudonus' cavalcade was fading, and it was time to go in. She could not deny that for a moment Tulach's offer had tempted her. But the power that waited on the Isle of Maidens was bred in her, blood and bone. It had been too long since she had tasted its waters and breathed its air.

She should pay her mother a visit, she thought then, and take Medraut. It was time Igierne met her youngest grandchild.

"Well, Morgause, motherhood certainly agrees with you. You are blooming like a rose!" Ebrdila grinned toothlessly and patted the bench beside her. Behind her, the roses in Igierne's garden had been trained over an arbor. In this sheltered spot, the red blooms clustered in profusion, scattering bright petals upon the path.

True, thought Igierne, surveying her daughter with a more critical eye, *but this rose is beginning to look just a bit blown.*

Morgause still had a fine, full figure, but after five children, her breasts no longer rode high, and the muscles of her belly had not yet recovered their tone. But it was her face that had prompted the observation, as Igierne noted the permanent high color in the cheeks, and around the mouth, the first faint lines of discontent. Ebrdila's old eyes might not be able to see it—but then Morgause had been her special pet since the days when Igierne, newly married to Uthir, had left the girl in her care.

"Oh, I am very well!" Morgause gave the old woman a swift hug as she sat down beside her, "and so is my baby. Is he not a fine boy?" She smiled complacently at the child who was playing with the rose petals in the path.

"He is indeed," answered Ebrdila, "just like his mother!"

Igierne had to admit the boy was handsome, though most children, however ugly as babies or gawky as they grew, were plump and rosy at this age. Had Artor been so sweetly rounded when he was two, so seriously intent upon the wonders of the world? Regret for the lost years ached like an old wound in her breast. This boy's hair shone like burnished bronze in the sunlight—Morgause had been the same—but when he looked up, Igierne found herself disconcerted by his considering stare. Then he grabbed for another rose petal and laughed, and the odd moment was gone.

Igierne cleared her throat. "And how is Leudonus?" For a moment Morgause simply stared at her. *Your husband,* thought Igierne, *surely you remember him, even if he is not the father of this child.*

"He is in Isca with Artor," Morgause answered, a little defiantly. "He took Gwyhir into his household with Gualchmai. But surely you knew that—do not you and your son correspond? I thought he asked your advice every time he wiped—"

"Morgause!" Ebrdila chided gently, "There is no need to be coarse."

She had not criticized the content of the remark, only its expression. But at least Igierne now knew that the jealousy Morgause had felt for her brother when she was a girl was still there.

"And did Leudonus suggest that you spend his absence here?" she asked, trying to keep her tone from becoming sarcastic. "It has been a long time—"

Morgause frowned. "I found myself missing the Lake, and all those I love here," her daughter said then. "I did grow up here, after all."

"Indeed you did!" Ebrdila smiled happily and patted her hand.

I feel ill, thought Igierne, but she managed a smile as well. Whether she liked it or not, Morgause was born of the old blood. The Isle of Maidens was her heritage.

"Tonight the moon shines full, and we will honor her. It will be good to see you in the circle once more."

"Not the ritual on the hilltop, I hope—" said Morgause.

"But of course. The night will be clear," her mother replied.

Morgause grimaced. "I had hoped to see the Cauldron again. Artor bears the Sword, but the Hallow that remains on this isle is its equal in power. I am surprised you do not make more use of it!"

Igierne lifted one eyebrow. Was *that* why Morgause had come? "Would you take a war-axe to slice cheese? Neither Sword nor Cauldron are to be used unless need compels."

"True, but unless you practice with a weapon, you won't know how to use it when the need does arrive. Your son bears the Sword, but the Cauldron is my inheritance. Is it not time I began to learn its mysteries?"

From the look on her daughter's face, Igierne feared she had not been able to conceal her instinctive alarm.

"Not while you are still a mother and a ruling queen." She kept her voice even with an effort, wondering why she felt so reluctant to let her daughter anywhere near the Cauldron, since what Morgause had said was quite true. "I myself did not even begin to understand it until I was done with all that and retired to the Lake to give my whole heart to its Mysteries."

"No doubt you are right." Morgause shrugged dismissively. "And I am sure the ceremony on the heights will be very beautiful. It has been some time since I did much climbing, but if you can get up the mountain at your age, I should be able to manage as well."

"No doubt—" Igierne echoed with an edged smile. She had better walk by the lake this afternoon and meditate, she told herself, to clear her mind of anger before the ritual.

> *"Lady of the Silver Wheel,*
> *Lady of the Three-fold Way,*
> *Dreams and Destiny you deal,*
> *Hear us, Goddess, as we pray . . ."*

Women's voices echoed, soft and sweet across the water as the procession followed the path by the shore.

> *"Lady of the shining road,*
> *Lady of the sacred round,*
> *Holiness is your abode,*
> *Help and healing there abound."*

Breath shortened as the trail turned from the lake and began to wind up the hillside, but still the priestesses sang. Cupped by its encircling mountains, the island on the lake contained powerful magic, but by the time the full moon breasted those heights, it was high in the sky. The priestesses used the meadow where lay the circle of stones, where they could observe the moment she lifted above the horizon, to honor her.

Igierne felt the blood sing in her veins as the exercise warmed her, and smiled. Ebrdila no longer made this journey, but she herself could still keep up with the youngest of her priestesses. It was Morgause whose face was growing red with exertion as they climbed.

> *"Lady of the starry sky,*
> *Lady of the sparkling sea,*

Queen of all the hosts on high,
And the deeps of memory—"

They reached the summit at last, their shadows stretching black across the grass as the sun sank behind them. Northward, a cloudbank still hung in the heavens, but in the east the sky, tinted a pearly pink by sunset, was clear. Igierne could hear her daughter's harsh breathing ease as they spiraled around the slab of stone that lay on the grass. Cup and ring marks had been carved into its surface by some people long forgotten. Several still held a little water from the morning's rain.

"Lady of the moon's red tide,
Lady of the flowing breast,
Ever-changing, you abide,
Grant us motion, give us rest."

As each woman passed the stone, she bent, touched fingertip to the water and blessed herself, belly and breast and brow. Igierne felt her knee joints complain as she took her turn, and her sight darkened for a moment as she straightened again, but she kept her balance and moved on. She shook her head in self-mockery, knowing that if Morgause had not been there she would have stopped a moment to catch her breath at the top of the hill.

Eastward, the hills fell away in long folds to a dim haze that hid the more settled lands. And there, at the limit of vision, a luminous pallor was beginning to suffuse the sky. The priestesses waited, humming softly. The air brightened suddenly as the sun hung for an instant on the rim of the hills behind them. Then it was gone, and the world was lit by a gentle afterglow. Silently Igierne began to count, knowing that beyond the mountain the sun was still sinking towards the distant sea. The colors of the sky above deepened, the clouds catching the light in bands of gold and rose. She heard her own indrawn breath repeated around the semicircle, and they began to sing once more.

"Radiant Lady, bless the night,
Bless the waters and the skies,

Bless the world with silver light,
We summon you—arise, arise!"

Every month they honored the full moon, on the Isle when the weather was cloudy, and on the heights when the sky was clear, yet the hair lifted on Igierne's neck as a growing glow silhouetted the shape of a distant hill. And then, as if in answer to the compulsion of the song's final line, they saw the hill edged by a rim of blinding silver, and the huge, wonderful disc of the moon rose suddenly into the eastern sky.

Without thought she found her own arms rising with those of the others, as if to lift that bright orb into the sky. Swiftly the moon mounted the heavens, until the women stood with arms stretched high in adoration, hailing the Goddess with a wordless ululation of pure sound.

Gradually the human song faded until only the jubilant chirring of crickets could be heard. Some of the priestesses remained standing with uplifted arms to pray silently while others sank to the earth, sitting cross-legged with their hands open upon their knees. Igierne stayed where she was, staring at the moon's brightness until vision was overwhelmed by light.

Lady, hear and help me! her heart cried. *Here stands the child of my body—why do I find it so hard to love her? She is my daughter, not my enemy!* She heard the harsh rasp of her breath and stopped, willing the inner babble to still, remembering the many times she had told young priestesses that it did no good to ask the gods questions if you were not willing to listen for the answer.

She could hear Morgause breathing beside her. After a time, she realized they had found the same rhythm. She felt ashamed that she should be so surprised.

Is that Your answer? She stopped the thought, concentrating on her breathing, waiting. The moon was halfway up the sky, its color changing from the warm pearl glow of the horizon to a pure silver light. Listening, she heard Morgause's steady breathing grow ragged, as if she were trying to hold back tears.

What does she have to cry about? was Igierne's first, swiftly suppressed response. If this woman whose arrogance had irritated her so this afternoon was weeping, her sorrow must be all the greater for being hidden. There were those who must have thought the same of Igierne herself, in the days when she mourned secretly for her lost son while all men hailed her as Uthir's queen.

Ah, child, there was a time you would have brought your trouble to me and wept in my arms. How have we become such strangers? She turned to her daughter, intending to offer comfort. As she met Morgause's eyes, the younger woman's gaze grew stony and she turned away, but not before Igierne had seen upon her cheeks the silver track of tears.

Igierne stared at her back, feeling the tears start in her own eyes. *Sweet Lady, help her! Help us all!* came her heart's silent cry.

In the next moment a breath of wind stirred the grass and gently touched her hair. As it dried her cheeks, she thought that with it came a whisper, *"I am with you, even in your pain. . . ."*

As the harvest moon waned the north lay at peace. The grain was ripening, and on both sides of the Bodotria estuary, men labored to reap the golden sheaves. Braced against the side of the boat that was carrying her over the water, Morgause turned her face to the sea wind and breathed in freedom.

Leudonus was still in the south with Artor, and when Morgause announced her intention to visit the lady Tulach in Fodreu, there was no one in Dun Eidyn with the power to say her nay. Medraut had screamed when she detached his little hands from her gown and handed him to his nurse, but even his cries had no power against the imperative that ever since her visit to the Lake had beat like a drum in her brain—

My mother still loves Artor more! She will never share her secrets. Whatever magic I wield must be my own!

The land on the Pictish shore of the estuary was much the same as the country around Dun Eidyn. Why, she wondered, did the air seem fresher, and the colors more intense, on the other side? It was not only the change of scene that excited her, thought Morgause, for the Lake Country that surrounded the Isle of Maidens was a different land entirely, and she had only felt more constricted there. Perhaps it was because among the Picts she was bound by no ties of love or duty, only by whatever mutual obligations she should agree to in her search for power.

Tulach was waiting for her on the shore, accompanied by a half dozen tribesmen wrapped in tattered plaids and two older women in dusty black robes. They had enough ponies for the Votadini as well.

"Are you taking me to Fodreu?" asked Morgause as she mounted the shaggy little mare they had brought for her. Her own escort eyed the Pictish warriors uneasily, but with or without the consent of kinfolk, there had been marriages enough across the border that half of them had relations on the other side. As they moved out, their suspicions began to submerge in a murmur of genealogical comparison.

Tulach shook her head. "The place for the ritual I have in mind for you lies farther up the coast. We should reach it before nightfall."

"What is it?"

"A place of the old ones, who were here before Roman or Briton. The Picts are partly of that blood. You have such circles in the south as well, but you have forgotten how to use their magic. The old powers are still there, if you know how to call them. You will see."

Merlin knows how to call them, thought Morgause, remembering stories she had heard. Did she truly want to wield that magic, so ancient it seemed alien to her kind? But she had come too far to turn back now.

Her mother would never dream of challenging Merlin. Her mother, she reflected bitterly, was content to follow a woman's traditional path, supporting, encouraging, waiting in the shadows. Did Artor even bother to read the advice she sent him?

She took a deep breath of the damp sea-wind. Her older boys were already moving into Leudonus' world, but Medraut was still hers alone. *It is not advice I will give him, but commands,* she thought grimly, *when I come into my power. The princes of Britannia dream of bringing back the old days before they went under the yoke of Rome. I will bring back a time that is older still, the time of the queens!*

The rough-coated ponies made surprisingly swift progress

on the uneven ground. By the afternoon they had travelled a fair distance north and eastward along the shore. They passed a village of fishermen, their overturned coracles sprouting like mushrooms from the stony strand, and paused for a meal of barley cakes baked on the hearthstone and washed down with heather beer. When they mounted once more, they took a new trail that wound upward through the shelving cliffs to a band of woodland below the moor. One of the warriors was now carrying a bag before him, with something inside it that jerked and struggled as they began to climb.

Just as dusk was falling they passed through a tangle of ash and alder where a small burn trickled towards the sea. Beyond it, an area roughly the size of Leudonus' hall had been roughly cleared. In the last of the light she could see that it was bordered by a circle of stones, the largest no more than waist-high. They were too choked by undergrowth to count, but the grass around the three in the center, one upright and the others tumbled, had been cut so that they stood clear.

As the priestesses dismounted, some of the warriors bound torches to the poles that had been set into the ground, and the bag was laid beside a tree. Then the men saluted Tulach and led the ponies back down the hill.

"They know better than to be near when women work magic!" the Pictish woman laughed. From her bag she took two black mantles, one of which she handed to Morgause. "Take off your clothes and put this on. Then wait here until we call."

True, the wind was growing cold, but Morgause suspected it was the touch of the garment itself that had set her to shivering. To change one's semblance was to change the soul; as the black wool replaced the garments of the queen of the Votadini, she became someone else, someone she did not know.

The other women had already lit the torches and suspended a bronze kettle above a fire. The water inside it was beginning to steam. Morgause felt her lips twist in bitter amusement—it appeared that she was going to learn the mysteries of the cauldron after all.

Tulach moved sunwise around the inside of the circle, scattering herbs and chanting something in the old tongue. Morgause blinked, wondering if it were the gathering dusk that suddenly made it so hard to see.

Through the gloom she glimpsed Tulach coming towards her.

"Who are you, and why have you come here?"

"I am Morgause, daughter of Igierne," she heard herself answering, "and I come to offer my service to the old powers."

"That is well. Take up the offering—" she indicated the bag "—and enter."

What happened after that was hard to remember. There was more chanting in the strange language as the three old women cast herbs and mushrooms and other nameless things into the cauldron. The aromatic steam made Morgause dizzy, so that sometimes she thought she saw a host of shapes around them and at others it was only the three.

"We stand upon the graves of old ones," Tulach told her. "Do not be surprised if they are drawn to the ceremony."

Shortly thereafter the singing reached a climax. It was full dark now; in the circle the flickering torches chased shadows around the fire.

"Take up the bag," said Tulach, "and carefully bring out what you find there."

Morgause had already concluded it must be an animal, and was not surprised to find she had hold of a large hare. Everyone knew that the hare was a creature of great magic. A fisherman who saw one on his way to the boats would turn back and stay home that day. It was never hunted, never eaten except when it was offered to the Goddess. At first the beast struggled, but when she made it breathe the steam, it abruptly went still. Tulach grasped it by the ears and handed her a flint knife.

"Kill it—" she said, "and give the blood to the stones."

The stone knife was sharper than she had expected, but it was still a messy business. Then Morgause got the big vein open, and held the body so that blood spurted over the rock, pooling in the hollows and running down the sides. One of the other women took the victim and began to skin it, and in a few minutes the disjointed body was simmering in the cauldron with the herbs.

The head sat dripping on the largest stone, and Morgause blinked, for the rock was surrounded by a pale glow. She looked around her and saw that the other stones were glowing as well with a light that owed nothing to the fire. With every movement, Tulach and the three priestesses trailed a glimmering radiance. Morgause felt her head swim and knew that she was already deep in trance. The tiny spark within that could still think yammered frantically. Why should they stop with the hare, when they could sacrifice a Votadini queen?

The other women had stripped off their black robes. For a moment she thought that beneath they were wearing blue-embroidered garments. Then she realized that she was seeing skin, tattooed in intricate patterns with woad. She was too dazed to prevent them from removing her black mantle as well, but within the circle the air was warm.

Tulach began to speak, her voice blurred as if it came through water. "We will make no permanent mark upon your skin, but the sacred signs we paint upon your body will mark your spirit shape so that the powers can see . . ."

She dipped a small brush into a bowl in which hare's blood had been mixed with something else and began to draw upon Morgause's breast and belly the same spirals that marked her own. The brush tickled as it passed, and left a tingling behind it. By the time the priestesses had finished painting her front and back, upper arms and thighs, her entire body was throbbing with a pleasant, almost sexual pain.

The soft heartbeat of a drum brought Morgause to her feet again.

"Now you are ready . . . now we call *Her*. . . ."

The drum beat faster, and Morgause found herself dancing as she had not danced since before her first child. Sweat sheened her body, adding its own meanders to the painted designs; she could smell her own female musk mingling with the scent of the herbs. It was very late; the distorted husk of the waning moon hung in the eastern sky.

The priestesses were singing. Presently Morgause recognized goddess-names within the murmur of incantation. She began to listen more carefully, understanding without knowing whether she was hearing with the ears or the heart.

The goddesses they were calling were older and wilder than any face of the Lady she had heard of on the Isle, names that resonated in earth and fire, in the stone of the circle and the whisper of the distant sea.

"Call Her!" sang Tulach as she whirled by. "Call Her by the name of your deepest desire!"

For a moment Morgause faltered. Then the drumming drew from her belly a moan, a shout, a cry of rage she had not known she held within.

She spun in place, light and shadow whirling around her. And then it was not shadow, but ravens, a cloud of black birds whose hoarse cries echoed her own.

"Cathubodva! Cathubodva! Come!"

Was she still moving, or was it the birds who swept her up to the heart of the maelstrom, where it was suddenly, shockingly, still?

"You have called Me, and I have come . . . what do you need?"

"I want what my mother had, what my brother has! I have as much right as he does to rule—I want to be Tigernissa—I want to be queen!"

"The power of the Black Raven, not the White, is Mine. I am the Dark Face of the Moon . . ." came the answer. *"I madden the complacent and destroy that which is outworn. I drink red blood and feast upon the slain. . . ."*

"My mother clings to a power she can no longer wield! My brother fights for a dream that died with Rome! Let me be your priestess, Lady, and do your will!"

"What will you sacrifice?"

"I have a young son, who is also the son of the king! Help me, and I will raise him to be your champion!"

Abruptly sound returned in a cacophony that whirled her with it into a chaos of fire and shadow until she knew no more.

iii

FIRST BLOOD

A.D. 494

Bushes blurred by in a haze of green as Guendivar beat her heels against the white pony's sides. Then they burst out onto the sunny ridge, and the mare, seeing a clear trail before her, stretched out her neck and responded with a new burst of speed. Guendivar tightened her long legs around the blanket and whooped in delight. She was flying, lifting like a bird into the blue.

Then the road dipped, and the pony began to slow. Guendivar dug in her heels, but the mare snorted, shaking her head, and her canter became a jarring trot that compelled the girl to rein her in.

"Oh, very well—" she said crossly. "I suppose you deserve a rest. But you liked it too, didn't you, my swan? I wish you could really fly!"

Guendivar had gotten the pony for her seventh birthday. Now she was thirteen; too old, said her mother, to spend her days careering about the countryside. The dark shadow of adulthood was creeping towards her. Only on Cygnet's back could she be free.

A gull's cry brought her head up; she followed its flight, shading her eyes against the sunlight, as it wheeled above the ridge and away over the Vale. It had been a beautiful summer, especially after last year, when there was so much rain. Through the mist she glimpsed the distant glitter of the Sabrina estuary. Closer, golden haze lay across the lowlands, reminding her of the waters that in the winter turned it into an inland sea. A few hillocks poked through like islands, dominated by a pointed cone in the middle of the Vale. In this light, even the Tor seemed luminous; she wondered if that was why some folk called it the Isle of Glass.

The pony had halted and was tugging at the rein as she tried to reach the grass. Guendivar hauled the beast's head up and got her going again, frowning as she became aware of a dull ache across her lower back. In a canter, Cygnet was as graceful as the bird from which she took her name, but her trot was torture.

Suddenly the bag of apples and bread and cheese tied to her belt seemed very attractive. Guendivar gave the pony a kick and reined her down the hill towards the spring.

It was little more than a seep in the side of the hill, but the constant trickle of water had hollowed out a small pool, fringed with fern and stone-crop and shaded by a willow tree. On the sunny slopes, the grass was ripening, but near the spring the spreading moisture had kept it a vivid green. Cygnet tugged at the rein, eager to be at it, and laughing, Guendivar swung her right foot over the pony's neck and slid down.

"You are a goose, not a swan," she exclaimed, "and just as greedy. But while we eat we may as well be comfortable." She turned to uncinch the blanket and stilled, staring at the blood that had soaked into the cloth.

Frantically she unbuckled the cinch and pulled off the blanket, searching for the injury. But the pony's sweat-darkened hide was whole.

Guendivar's racing pulse thundered in her ears. She tethered the mare so that she could graze, and then, very reluctantly, she loosened her breeches, a pair that had been her older brother's when he was a boy, and pulling them down, saw on the inseam the betraying red stain.

Swearing softly, she pulled the breeches off. She could wash them, and no one would know. But even as she bent over the pool she felt warmth, and saw a new trickle of red snake down her inner thigh.

That was when panic changed to despair, and she curled up on the grass and let the hot tears flow.

Guendivar was still sniffling when she became aware that she was not alone. In that first moment, she could not have told what had changed. It was like hearing music, though there was no sound, or a scent, though there was no change in the air. As she sat up, her senses settled on vision as a mode of perception, and she saw a shimmer that she recognized as the spirit of the pool. Words formed in her awareness.

"You are different today . . ."

"I've got my moonblood," Guendivar said bitterly, "and now everything is going to change!"

"Everything is always changing. . . ."

"Some changes are worse than others. Now my mother will make me stay home and spin while she talks to me about ruling a house and a husband! After this, she'll never let me ride alone again! I don't want this blood! I don't want to change!"

"It was the blood that called me," came the reply.

"What?" She opened her eyes again. "I thought growing up would mean I couldn't see you."

"Not so. When you are in your blood it will be easier. . . ."

Guendivar felt the hairs lift on her arms. Around her the air was thickening with glimmering forms: the slender shape of the Willow girl bending over her; spirits of reed and flower; airy forms that drifted on the wind; squat shapes that emerged from the stones.

"Why are you here?" she whispered. "What does my woman blood mean to you?"

"It means life. It means you are part of the magic."

"I thought it just meant having babies. I don't want to be worn out like my mother, bearing child after child that dies." Petronilla had borne eight infants, but only the oldest boys and Guendivar survived.

"When man and maid lie down together in the fields they make magic. Before, you were only a bud on the branch. Now you are the flower."

Guendivar sat back, thinking about that. Abruptly she found herself hungry. She reached for the bag, and then, remembering, started to offer a portion to the pool.

"You have something better to give us—" came the voices around her. *"There is a special power in the first spurting of a boy's seed, and a girl's first flow. Wash yourself in the spring. . . . "*

Guendivar flushed with embarrassment, even though she knew that human conventions meant less than nothing to the faerie kind. But gradually her shame shifted to something else, a dawning awareness of power. She bent, and scooping up the cool water in her palm, poured it over her thighs until her blood swirled dark in the clear water. When she was clean, she washed out her breeches and the saddle cloth and laid them out in the sun to dry.

The faerie folk flitted around her in swirls of light.

"Sleep a little . . . " said the spirit of the pool, *"and we will send you dreams of power."*

Guendivar lay back and closed her eyes. Almost immediately images began to come: the running of the deer, mare and stallion, sow and boar, men and women circling the Beltain fire. All the great dance of life whirled before her, faster and faster, shaping itself at last into the figure of a laughing maiden formed out of flowers.

When she woke at last, the setting sun had turned all the vale into a blaze of gold. But the spirits had disappeared. Her clothing was dry, and for the moment, her flow of blood seemed to have ceased. Swiftly she dressed and cinched the saddle cloth back onto the mare. She was still not looking forward to telling her mother what had happened. But one thing had changed—the thought of growing up no longer made her afraid.

For all the years of Guendivar's childhood, the Tor had been a constant presence, felt, even when clouds kept it from being seen. But except for one visit made when she was too little to remember, she had never been there. As soon as she told her mother what had happened to her, Petronilla had decided to take her to the nuns who lived on the Isle of Glass for a blessing. The prospect filled her with mingled excitement and fear.

It is like growing up—she thought as they reached the base of the isle and the curve of the lower hill hid the Tor from view. *For so long it loomed on the horizon, and now I cannot see it because I am almost there. I will only be able to see my own womanhood reflected in others' eyes.*

The top of the round church that the holy Joseph had built showed above the trees. Around it clustered the smaller huts that were the monks' cells, and a little farther, a second group of buildings for the nuns. Nearby was the guesthouse where the visitors would stay. As they climbed the road, the deep sound of men's voices throbbed in the air. The monks were chanting the noon prayers, her mother said. Guendivar felt the hair lift on her arms with delight as the sweet sounds drifted through the trees. Then the shadowed orifice of the church door came into view and she shivered. The music was beautiful, but cooped up in the darkness like that, how could men sing?

She sighed with relief as they continued along the hillside toward the houses of the nuns. To one side she saw apple trees, ripening fruit already weighting their branches, and to the other, neat gardens. Beyond was a tall hedge, hiding the base of the hill that nestled next to the Tor. She wondered what was behind it. There was something in the air of this place that made her skin tingle as it did when the faerie folk were near. If she could escape her mother's watchful eye, this would be a good place to explore.

A tall woman came out of one of the houses, robed in a shapeless gown of natural wool with a wooden cross hanging from a thong around her neck, her hair hidden by a linen veil. But when she looked up, Guendivar saw a broad smile and twinkling eyes. For a moment that gaze rested on her in frank appraisal. Then she turned to Guendivar's mother.

"So, Petronilla, this is your maid-child—she has grown like a flower in good soil, tall and fair!"

"Nothing so rooted," answered her mother ruefully. "She is

a bird, or perhaps a wild pony, always off running about the hills. Guendivar, this is Mother Maruret. Show that you know how to give her a proper greeting!"

Still blushing, Guendivar slid down from her pony, took the woman's hand and bent to kiss it.

"You are welcome indeed, my child. My daughters will show you to your quarters. No doubt you will wish to wash before your meal."

Guendivar's belly growled in anicipation. Along with other changes, she was growing, and these days she was always hungry.

"You are not our only guests," said Mother Maruret as she led them towards the largest building. "The queen is here."

"Igierne?" asked Petronilla.

"Herself, with two of her women."

Petronilla lifted one eyebrow. "And you allow them to stay on the Isle?"

The nun smiled. "We have been in this place long enough to understand that the ways of the Creator of the World are many and mysterious. If the queen is deluded, how shall that trouble my own faith? But indeed, she has never been other than quiet and respectful when she was here . . ."

Guendivar listened, wide-eyed. She had heard many tales of Artor's mother, the most beautiful woman of her time. They said that King Uthir had fought a war to win her and killed her husband before her eyes, though others whispered that Merlin had murdered him with his magic. She lived now in the north, ran the tales, on a magic island. Of course by now Igierne must be quite old, but it would be exciting to meet her all the same.

But when they entered the guest-house, though the queen's two women were there, talking softly by the fire, Igierne was nowhere to be seen.

Just before dawn, Guendivar's mother awakened her. The girl rose quickly and dressed in the white gown they gave her— she had been fasting since noon the day before, and the sooner this was over the sooner she could get some food. Stumbling with sleepiness, she followed her mother and the two nuns, one of them young and one an old woman, who led the way with lanterns out of the guesthouse and up the hill.

Her interest quickened when she saw they were approaching the hazel hedge. There was a gate set amid the branches. The young woman lifted the iron latch and motioned for them to go in.

On the other side was a garden. Already a few birds were singing, though the sky was still dim and grey. She could hear the tinkle of falling water, and as the light grew, she saw that it was flowing down through a stone channel into a large pool.

"The spring is farther up the hill," the young nun said in a low voice. Her name, she remembered, was Julia. "Winter and summer the pure water flows from the holy well. Even in years of drought it has never failed."

Petronilla glanced at the sky, then turned to her daughter. "It is almost time. Take off the gown and step into the pool."

"I was baptized when I was a babe," muttered Guendivar as she obeyed. "Was not that not purification enough?"

"This is to cleanse you from childhood's sins. You will emerge, a woman, transformed by the blood of your body and the water of the spirit." Her mother took the gown and folded it across her arm.

Of the spirit, or the spirits? wondered Guendivar, remembering the spring on the hillside. It gave her the courage to set her foot on the steps that entered the dark water.

In that first shocked moment, she could not tell if the water was holy, only that it was freezingly cold. She stifled a yelp and stood shaking, the water lapping the joining of her thighs.

"In the name of the Blessed Virgin, may you be cleansed and purified of all sin and stain . . ." murmured Sister Julia, dipping up water in a wooden bowl and pouring it over Guendivar's shoulders.

"In the name of Maria Theotokos, may you be cleansed and purified—" Now it was her mother's turn.

"In the name of the Lady of Sorrows . . ." The old nun poured water over her head and stepped away.

In the name of all the gods, let me out of here before I freeze! thought Guendivar, edging back towards the steps. But her mother stopped her with a word. When Guendivar could escape her mother's eye, she ran free, but she had never yet dared to defy her directly. Shivering, the girl stood where she was.

The sky brightened to a luminous pink like the inside of a shell. Light lay like a mist above the water. Guendivar took a quick breath, and realized that her shivering had ceased and her skin was tingling.

"Spirit of the holy spring," her lips moved silently, "give me your blessing . . ." She scooped up water in her hand and drank, surprised at its iron tang. Then, before she could lose courage, she took a quick breath and submerged herself in the pool.

For a long moment she stayed there, her amber hair raying out across the surface, and each hair on her body lifted by its own bubble of air. The water she had swallowed sent a shock through every vein. The tingling of her skin intensified, as if the water were penetrating all the way to her bones. Then, just as it reached the edge of pain, it became light. The force of it brought Guendivar upright, arms uplifted, turning to face the rising sun.

She heard a sharp gasp of indrawn breath from one of the women. The sun was rising red above the slope of the hill. Rosy light glistened on her wet skin, glittered from the surface of the pool. For a moment she gazed, then the light brightened to gold and she could look no more.

"Receive the blessing of the Son of God—" her mother cried. But it was another voice that Guendivar heard.

"Be blessed by the shining sun, for while you walk in its light, no other power shall separate you from this bright and living world. . . ."

To that dawn ritual there was one other witness, who watched from the hillside as the women helped Guendivar from the pool and hid the radiance of her body in the shapeless robe of a penitent. When Igierne had first heard of the planned ritual, she had feared they meant to make the girl a nun; the actual intention was almost as hard to understand. What sins could a child of thirteen have committed? Before her marriage, Petronilla had spent some time as part of Igierne's court. She came from an old Roman family that had long been Christian. Igierne knew that it was not the stains of childhood that Guendivar's mother wanted to wash away, but her daughter's incipient sexuality.

If so, she had chosen the wrong place to do so. Igierne knew how to interpret the blaze of light she had seen in the pool, and she knew also that the colony of monks established here by Joseph of Arimathea had learned how to use the magic of the Tor, but had not changed it. The powers that dwelt here were ancient when the Druids first saw this hill. She should not be surprised that this girl, whose face she had first seen in vision, should be recognized by the spirits of the Tor.

But it did make it all the more imperative that she speak with Guendivar. It would be difficult, for Petronilla kept her daughter well guarded. When the women had left the pool Igierne made her own way down to it, and found tangled in the branches above the gateway a wisp of red-gold hair. She smiled, and pulling a few pale hairs from her own head, began to twine them together, whispering a spell.

The little community on the Tor retired early, the guests to sleep through the night, and the nuns to rest until they should be called to midnight prayer. At night, said the Christians, the Devil roamed the world, and only the incantations of the faithful kept him at bay. But to Igierne, the night was a friend.

When the sound of quiet breathing told her that the other women in the guesthouse were asleep, she rose, slipped her feet into sandals and took up a cloak, and went outside. If anyone had questioned her, she would have said she sought the privy, but in fact her goal was the orchard, where she found a seat, put on the ring of twined hair she had made that morning, and began to sing.

And presently, just as the moon was lifting above the trees, the door to the guest-house opened and a pale figure came through. Igierne told herself that it was only the effect of moonlight on a white gown that made Guendivar's figure seem luminous, but she could not help remembering the radiance of the morning and wondering.

Still, this opportunity must not be wasted. As Guendivar

started down the path, Igierne gathered up her cloak and came
out to meet her.

The girl started, eyes widening, but she stood her ground.

"Couldn't you sleep either?" Igierne asked softly. "Let us
walk. The gardens are beautiful in the light of the moon."

"You're human—" It was not quite a question.

"As human as you are," Igierne answered, although when
she remembered what she had seen that morning, she wondered.

"You are the queen—" Guendivar said then.

"The queen that was," Igierne replied, *as you are the queen
that will be. . . .* But it was not yet time to say so aloud.

They came out from beneath the moon-dappled shadows of
the orchard and continued along the path. The moon shone full
in a luminous sky, so bright that one could distinguish the red
of the roses that lined the path from the dim green of the hill.

"Where are we going?" Guendivar asked at last.

"To the White Spring. You bathed in the Red Spring this
morning, did you not? The Blood Well? Perhaps you did not
know there is another on the Tor."

"The Blood Well?" the girl echoed. "Then that is why . . . I
thought—" Her voice became a whisper. "I thought that my
flow had started again, that my blood had turned the water
red."

"They should have explained," Igierne said tartly. "There is
iron in the water, just as there is in our blood. Did they tell you
the water would wash away your sins? In the old days, maidens bathed here to establish their female cycle. Barren women
came also, that their wombs might become as bountiful as the
well."

"I felt a tingling . . . all through my body . . ." Guendivar
said then. "I suppose that now my mother will be trying to
marry me off. She is very ambitious. But I'm not ready."

"Indeed—" Igierne knew too well what it was to be married
young to an older man. But for the daughters of princes, a long
maidenhood was a luxury. And how long could Artor wait before his ministers compelled him to take a bride? "Do you
think you will be ready when you are fifteen?"

The girl shrugged. "That is the age at which my brother was allowed to ride to battle."

"It is the age at which my son became king . . ."

"That was a long time ago," said Guendivar.

Igierne's heart sank. What were the gods about, to make Artor wait so many years for his destined bride? Silent, she led the way down the path to the second gate, and the smaller enclosure where the White Spring welled up from the ground.

"What is this one for?" the girl asked.

"They say it brings hope and healing. You are in health, but sometimes the spirit needs healing as well. Let the water flow into this bowl, and then hold it up to catch the light of the moon."

Guendivar nodded. "There was sun-power in the Blood Well, but this feels different—" She lifted the bowl.

"I wish—" Igierne began, then paused. The girl looked at her expectantly. "Not many would have noticed that. If I thought there were any chance your mother would agree, I would take you for training on the Holy Isle . . ." *If only I could give Artor a queen who was an initiate of the ancient mysteries!*

"An island?" Guendivar shook her head. "I would feel prisoned if I could not gallop my pony beneath the sky. Why do you live there?"

"Long ago the Romans sought to destroy all Druids because they were the ones who preserved the soul of our people and reminded them of what it was to be free. Those who survived their attacks fled to Alba or Eriu, or secret places in Britannia where they could survive. The Lake is one such, hidden among high hills, and also it is very beautiful."

"I suppose—" the girl said dubiously. "But what do you find to do there all day?"

Igierne laughed. "Our life on the Isle of Maidens is not so different from the way the nuns live here, although we call ourselves maiden not because we are virgin but because we are bound to no man. We spin and weave and grow herbs as other women do, and beyond that, we pray. Do you think that sounds boring?" she answered Guendivar's grimace. "Our prayers are no abject plea to a distant god, but an act of magic.

We seek to put ourselves in harmony with the flow of energy through the world, and by understanding, to bend it—"

"To change things?" Guendivar asked.

"To help them to become what they should be, that all shall prosper."

For a few moments Guendivar considered this, her hair glistening in the light of the moon. Then, very softly, came another question. "Do you talk to the spirits, the faerie-folk?"

"Sometimes . . ." answered Igierne.

"I see them . . . they are my best friends. . . ."

The touch of faerie! That is the source of the strangeness I have seen in her, thought Igierne.

The girl shrugged ruefully. "Now you know more than I have ever told my mother. Do not tell her that we have spoken. She already looks at you as if she feared you might summon a chariot drawn by dragons to carry me away!" She stopped abruptly, and even in the gloom Igierne could tell that she was blushing.

"Does she think the Tigernissa of Britannia without honor? You are still a child, and in her ward. I will say only this, Guendivar—if in time to come you need help or counsel, write to me."

She could love this girl, she thought then, as her own daughter—more, she feared, than she had ever been able to love Morgause. But when the child was married to Artor she *would* be her daughter. Surely the goddess who had sent her that vision would not lie!

Guendivar nodded, set the bowl to her lips, and drank. After a moment she lifted her head, her eyes wide with wonder.

"The moon is in it—" With a ceremonial grace, she offered the bowl.

Moonlight flashed silver from trembling water as Igierne grasped the rim. The water was very cold, so pure it tasted sweet on the tongue. She closed her eyes, and let that sweetness spread through her. *Grant hope and healing . . .* she prayed, *to me and to Britannia. . . .*

Igierne held onto the wooden seat as her cart bumped up the street towards the Governor's Palace. She had forgotten how hot Londinium could get in the days between Midsummer and Harvest. Heat radiated from the stone walls of those buildings that remained, and the trees that had grown up among the ruins of others drooped with dusty leaves. Ceincair and Morut swayed in stoic silence beside her.

She ached in every joint from the jolting of the cart, her tunic was stuck to her back with perspiration, and her hair was full of dust despite the veil. For a moment of piercing regret, she wished she had never left the Lake. But there were baths at the palace—perhaps she would feel better when she was clean.

And then the cart pulled up at the gates. Guards straightened to attention, calling out her name. One or two were men she remembered from her days with Uthir. She smiled, giving orders, and for a little while, forgot that she was not still the queen.

By the time the three priestesses were settled it was evening, and Artor had returned to the palace. That was a relief. When Igierne had stopped in Isca on the way south she had heard he was in Londinium, but at any moment that could change. These days he seemed to conduct the business of Britannia from the back of a horse. She had sent a message to warn him of her coming, but she would not have been surprised to find him gone.

He was obviously not intending to stay long. The palace was understaffed, and the meal to which they sat down, though well-cooked, was little better than camp fare.

"I don't know why I should be surprised," said Igierne, taking another spoonful of lentil stew. "When I married him, your father was living on the same thing."

Artor gave her a wry smile. "A telling argument for any who still doubt my parentage. But in truth, I eat this way for the same reason he did. We are still at war. Icel is holding to the treaty I forced on him last summer, but the Irish in Demetia are making trouble again. I must ask you and your ladies to continue your prayers for us, for I will have to take my army westward soon."

Igierne sighed. Artor was taller, with a look that reminded her of her mother about the eyes, but his hair was the same nut brown, and his shoulders as broad as Uthir's had been. As Artor grew older, the resemblance sometimes took her breath away. Like Uthir, he was, in public, a Christian. But he knew very well that the priestesses of the Isle of Maidens did more than simply pray. That was not the issue now.

"No one who knew him would doubt that you are Uthir's son. Nor do I dispute that Britannia is still at war. But during all the years of our marriage it was the same. Nonetheless, your father and I managed to live like civilized people. There is no reason you cannot do so as well!"

"But I am not married . . ." he said softly, reaching for the wine.

Igierne stared unseeing at the faded frescoes on the wall behind him, thinking furiously. Every other time she had brought up the subject, he had turned the conversation. Why was he mentioning it now?

"Are you thinking of changing that?" she asked carefully.

Artor looked up, saw her face, and laughed. "Are you afraid I've fallen in love with someone unsuitable? When would I find the time?" He shook his head. "But even old Oesc has managed to find a woman—Prince Gorangonus' granddaughter, of all people. I've just returned from their wedding, where I gave the bride away. I always meant to marry once the country was secure, but at this rate, Oesc will have grandchildren by then." He took a deep breath. "I'm ready to consider it, mother, though I warn you, I have no time to go looking for a bride."

Igierne sipped wine, for a moment too astounded by this capitulation for words. "Perhaps you won't have to," she said slowly. "If my visions have not lied. There is a maiden, Prince Leodegranus' daughter, whom I believe the Goddess has chosen. But you will have to wait for her—she is only thirteen."

"She is a child!" he exclaimed.

"Any girl who is still unspoken for is going be young—" said Igierne. "Unless you choose a widow, but that is likely to cause complications." They both heard the unspoken, *As it did for me . . .*

"I won't force a maid into marriage with a man twice her age," Artor said grimly. "We must meet before things are settled."

"I will write to Leodegranus, and ask him not to betroth his daughter until you have seen her."

"She must be willing."

"Of course . . ." said Igierne, sighing. She herself had been willing to marry Gorlosius, and that had been a disaster. "Your sister had doubts about marrying Leudonus," she said aloud, "but she agreed to do it, and that pairing seems to have worked out well, even though he is much older than she."

She tried to interpret the play of expression on Artor's face at the mention of Morgause. She knew her daughter resented *him*, but Artor had hardly met his sister often enough to form an opinion.

"I have not seen her since we defeated Naiton Morbet and the Picts," he said finally. "She was . . . magnificent. Three of her boys are with me now, and they tell me that she is well."

Igierne nodded. "I last saw her five years ago, when she visited the Lake with her youngest child. She seemed troubled, but Leudonus was not the cause."

"What, then?" Artor straightened, and she knew he was thinking like a king once more.

"Since Medraut, there have been no more children, and Morgause is a woman who cherished her fertility. She wanted me to make her priestess of the Cauldron—I suspect she was looking for a new source of power."

"I knew you had kept the Sword of the Defender on the Isle of Maidens, but what is the Cauldron?" Artor asked.

"Perhaps, if there is ever a season of peace, you can visit the Lake and I will show you. It is a woman's mystery, but you are the High King, and there are some things you have a right to know." She paused, marshalling her memories. "It is silver . . . very ancient." She shook her head. "That is only what it looks like, not what it *is*. . . . The Cauldron . . . is the womb of the Goddess, the vessel from which comes the power to renew the world."

For a long moment, Artor simply stared. Then she saw a new light come into his eyes. ". . . To renew the world," he echoed. "Do you know how I have dreamed of it? I have been High King of Britannia since I was fifteen years old, and spent most of that time defending her. Do you understand what that means, Mother? All I have been able to do is react, to try and maintain the status quo. How I have longed to move forward, to make things better, to heal this land! If there is ever, as you say, a season of peace, I will beg you to invoke the Cauldron's power!"

Igierne reached out, and Artor took her hand. Her heartbeat was shaking her chest. For so long she had loved her son, yearned for him, and never known him at all. And now it seemed to her that she touched his soul through their clasped hands.

"I will be ready, my beloved. Together we will do it. This is what I too have been waiting for, all my life long!"

But even as her heart soared in triumph, Igierne wondered how Morgause was likely to react when she learned that Artor had been given yet one more thing that she herself had been denied.

Medraut was telling a story. Morgause heard his voice as she came around the side of the women's sun house, clear as a bard's, rising and falling as he spun out the tale.

"It was old Nessa's spirit I saw . . . hunched beside the fire just as when she lived. And anyone who takes that seat is her prey—first you'll feel a cold touch on your neck, and then—"

From the corner of his eye he saw his mother coming and fell silent. The younger children to whom he had been talking got to their feet, wide-eyed at the sight of the queen.

"Medraut, you will follow me—"

"As you wish, Mama," he answered politely. She had taught him not to talk back to her before he was three years old.

But as they neared the door she heard a stifled giggle from one of the children, and turning, surprised her son completing a swish of his hips that was obviously an imitation of her own walk. Her hand shot out and she gripped his ear and hauled him after her through the door.

"And what was *that?*" she asked, releasing him.

"Nothing—it was just to make them laugh," he added as she reached for him again, "so they'll like me."

Her fingers clenched in his hair, jerking it for emphasis. "You are a *prince,* Medraut. It is they who should be courting *you!* But if you *must* ridicule, attack those who are lower than yourself. It does not contribute to *your* standing to make them laugh at *me!* Do you understand?"

"I understand, Mama . . ." he whispered, and she let him go. His eyes glittered with tears, but weeping was another thing she had trained him out of long ago.

"You are a prince, my beloved," Morgause added, more gently. She set down the bag she was carrying, and bent, turning him to face her and gently stroking his hair. "Your blood is the highest in the land. And you are the brightest and best of my children. Remember that, Medraut. I will teach you things that none of the others could understand. You must not disappoint me, my little one. . . ." She took his face between her hands and kissed him on the brow.

As she straightened, she saw his gaze shift to the bag, which was twitching and bulging of its own accord.

"Is it alive?" he whispered.

"That is a surprise for you," she answered gaily, picking up the bag with one hand and offering the other to her son. As always, her heart lifted as his small fingers tightened on hers. *You are mine!* she thought, looking down at him, *the child of my heart and the son of my soul!*

"Are we going to do a ritual?" he asked as they turned down the path to the spring. "Is it something that you have been learning from Tulach and her friends?"

"Hush, child, we must not speak of that here," said Morgause. "What we will do is not one of their rites, though they have helped me to better understand it. You are seven years old. What I will show you today will set you on the road to power."

Medraut began to walk faster, and she smiled.

By the time they reached the spring, the sun was setting at the end of the gorge, and as it disappeared, the shadow of the cliff loomed dark across the grass. Sounds from the dun above them came to them faintly, as though from another world.

Morgause dropped the bag and hunkered down beside it, motioning to Medraut to do the same.

"This is the hour that lies between day and night. Now, we

are between times, between the worlds. It is a good time to speak with spirits, and those that dwell in the sacred springs and holy wells are among the most powerful."

He nodded, gazing into the dark pool with wondering eyes. What did he see? When Morgause was a child she had sometimes glimpsed the faerie-folk. These days, she was learning to do so again, with the aid of certain herbs and spells.

Carefully, she showed him how to cleanse head and hands, and made him drink a little from the spring.

"Make your prayer to the spirit that lives here . . ."

Obediently he shut his eyes, lips moving silently. She would rather have heard what he was saying, but that did not matter now. Presently he looked up at her once more.

In the distance Morgause could hear the lowing of cattle, but by the spring it was very still. But there was a weight to that silence, as if something was listening. She picked up the bag and smiled.

"The spirit of the spring is waiting. Now you must make your offering. Open the bag—"

With nimble fingers, Medraut untied the strings and pulled at the opening, dropping it with a squawk as something white and feathered burst free. It was a cockerel, and it was not happy at having been confined in the bag. But its feet had been tied, so for all its flapping, it could not go far.

"Blood is life," said Morgause. "Wring the bird's neck, and let its blood flow into the pool."

Medraut looked from the cockerel to his mother and shook his head, eyes dark with revulsion.

"What, are you afraid of a little blood? When you are a warrior, you will have to kill men! Do it, Medraut—do it now!"

The child shook his head again and started to edge away. Morgause fought to control her anger.

"I teach you secrets that grown men would pay to learn. You will not deny me. See—" she gentled her voice, "it is easy—"

With a swift pounce, she captured his hands and pressed them around the neck of the fowl. The boy fought to free himself, still shaking his head and weeping. Morgause could not afford pity. Tightening her grip, she twisted, ripped the cockerel's head off and tossed it aside. Medraut cried out as blood spurted, but still she held his hands on the body of the bird, and did not know if the tremors that pulsed through their clasped fingers were those of the dying cockerel or of her son.

iv

LADY OF THE EASTERN GATE

A.D. 495

 In the hour before dawn, the priestesses gathered in the largest of the roundhouses on the Isle of Maidens. Mist lay like a veil across the lake; glittered in golden haloes around the lamps. Silent and anxious, some still rubbing sleep from their eyes, they filed in and took their places around the hearth.

Igierne was waiting for them. From sunset of the night before, when her spirit, open in the evening meditation, had received Merlin's message to this moment, she had not been able to sleep at all. Since the beginning of this last and greatest Saxon rebellion, the priestesses had met three times daily to support with the strength of their spirits the Britons' campaign.

But this was the last battle, the final confrontation with the ancient enemy. Through Merlin's eyes she had seen the hill called Mons Badonicus where Artor's army stood at bay, the scattering of campfires on its summit surrounded by a multitude below. The men were tired, food was low, and their water was almost gone. With the dawning, they would stake all on one last throw and ride against the enemy.

The priestesses, huddled in their pale mantles against the chill, sat like a circle of stones, and like the stones, their strength was rooted in the earth of Britannia. With Igierne, they were nineteen—all the senior priestesses, and the most talented of the girls. She signaled to the drummer to begin her steady beat. Then she took a deep breath and let her own awareness sink down through the fluid layers around the island and deeper still into the bedrock that supported them. Slowly her pulsebeat steadied and her breathing slowed. Here, at the foundation of all things, there was neither hope nor fear. There was only pure Being, changeless and secure.

She could have remained in that safe and secret place forever, but though her anxiety had faded, the discipline of years brought her back to awareness of her need, fueled by her determination and deeper even than her fear for her country, to protect her child. Slowly she allowed her awareness to move upward, trailing a cord of connection to the earth below, until she reached the level where her body sat once more.

Igierne lifted her arms, and the drumming quickened. With the precision of long practice, the other priestesses stretched out their arms. One by one they connected, and as the circle was completed, a pulse of power flared from hand to hand. Now, with each breath, power was drawn up from the depths and through the body, out through the left palm to the hand it clasped and onward.

Around and around, with each circuit it grew, a vortex that spiraled above the hearth. Igierne kept it steady, resisting the temptation to release it all in one climactic explosion of energy. In her mind she held the image of Merlin, offering him the cone of power to support his own wizardry. As the link grew stronger, she sensed men and horses, confusion and blood-lust, exaltation and fear.

She held the circle even as she felt something flare towards him like a spear of light. But the shock as Merlin caught it shattered the link. For one terrified moment the spirits of the priestesses were tossed like leaves in a high wind. And then another power blossomed in the midst of them, rising from the hearth like a flame into which all other powers were subsumed.

Bright as fire, serene as pure water, strong as the earth below, Brigantia Herself arose from the midst of Her priestesses and directed their joined powers towards the goddess image on the boss of Artor's shield. Through Her eyes, Igierne saw the image blaze, saw an answering radiance in the faces of Britannia's warriors, and saw, as the Saxons felt the land itself turning against them, the enemy break and flee.

To Igierne, Aquae Sulis had always seemed an outpost of civility and culture in the midst of the wild hills. The warm stone of the temple of Sulis and the enclosure surrounding the baths in the center of the city glowed in the afternoon sunshine, and the tiled roofs of the Roman buildings around them had the mellow beauty of an earlier age. Even the Saxon war had not really touched it, though the land to the north had been trampled and torn by the two armies. Igierne had wept, passing the twin mounds where they had burned the bodies of the slain Britons and those of their foes. In life, she reflected, they had been enemies, but in death they all fed the same soil.

The Saxons had kicked down a few doors when they searched Aquae Sulis for foodstuffs, but by Artor's order, the town had been stripped of booty and abandoned before the armies arrived. If the place had not been full of wounded soldiers, she might never have guessed there had been a war.

Those fighters who were still fit to travel were already off to their homes, or harrying the retreating Saxons. Most of the warriors who had been badly wounded were dead. Those who remained in Aquae Sulis had wounds which were not severe enough to kill them outright but required a longer convalescence. The minerals in the water healed torn flesh as its warmth eased aching muscles, and each morning the altar of Sulis bore new offerings.

At dawn, before the day's complement of wounded came to seek the goddess, Igierne and her women visited the baths. Some of the hot and cold pools that had been added to the facilities in the previous century were no longer usable, but the rectangular great bath was still protected by its vaulted ceiling.

Seen through the steam that rose from the surface, the marble gods stationed around the pool seemed to nod and sway. Cradled in the warmth of the water, Igierne saluted them: Venus and Mercurius, Jupiter and Juno and Minerva, Ceres and Bacchus, Apollo and his sister Diana with her leaping deer.

Only Mars was missing from this place of healing. But on Mons Badonicus the Britons had made offerings enough to the god of war. Not only Oesc, but Ceretic, the leader of the West Saxons, had fallen there. Aelle, who had led the rebellion, was an old man. It would be a generation or more before the Saxons could hope to field such an army again.

Afterwards, relaxed and glowing, she joined Artor for breakfast in the house of the chief magistrate.

"You look well," he said as they sat down.

"I wish I could say the same for you," she answered. In the pitiless illumination of morning the lines that pain had drawn around his mouth and responsibility had graven on his brow showed even more clearly than they had by torchlight the night before. "You look as if you had lost the war."

"I lost a lot of good men," he said tonelessly. He had filled his bowl with porridge, but he was not eating it. "I lost Oesc."

"He was your enemy!"

Artor shook his head. "Never that. If I had not failed him, there would have been no war. I killed him," he said flatly.

"Not in hatred or anger . . ." she objected softly.

Her son sighed. "I was spared that, at least. It was by his request. His back was broken in the battle, and he wished the mercy stroke to come from my hand."

Igierne considered him, frowning. *You are wounded too, my son, as sorely as any of those men I saw outside the baths.*

"When Uthir died," she said slowly, "I saw no reason to go on. Morgause did not need me, and I did not know where you were. I was no longer a queen. It took time for me to understand that there was still a role for me to play, and things I was needed to do."

"Indeed . . ." Artor breathed, "I felt your presence on the battlefield. And then—" a memory of wonder flared briefly in his eyes "—the goddess came, Sulis Minerva, or Brigantia

Herself, filling our hearts with fire. Britannia owes a great debt to the women of the Holy Isle."

"And now you need me again—" she said, not quite questioning. He did not answer. His face was grim, and she realized that he was not seeing her at all. "Artor," she said sharply, "why did you summon me here?"

"I do need you." His face brightened with a rueful smile. "There remains one task that is too much for my courage. Only a woman—a priestess—can help me now."

Igierne set down her tea and looked at him expectantly.

"I swore to Oesc that I would bury his ashes beside Hengest's mound . . . and I promised to see his wife and infant son back to Cantium."

"Cataur will give her up to you?"

"Has already given—" Artor said grimly, "which is the only reason his head is still connected to his shoulders. Enough Saxon blood has been spilled to satisfy even the Dumnonians. Rigana and her child are safe now at Dun Tagell. I want you to go there and escort her home."

Igierne sat back in her chair, staring, her mind awhirl with memory. "I have not seen Dun Tagell since your father took me away to be married, after Gorlosius died. . . ."

After a moment she realized how much of that ancient grief and anger must have shown in her face by its reflection in Artor's eyes.

"Does it get any easier, Mother? Do the rage and the sorrow fade in time?" he asked then.

"They do . . ." she said slowly, "if you seek healing; if from the destruction you build something new."

He nodded, still holding her gaze. "Healing is what we all need now. After so many years of warfare, Britannia, bruised and battered as she is, knows peace at last. The Sword and the Spear must be put to rest. It is time to bring forth the Cauldron and use its power."

"And for that you need the Lady of the Lake," answered Igierne. "I understand. But you also need a queen."

"Still trying to marry me off, Mother?" The pain lines vanished in a brief grin. "Well, perhaps you are right. I will arrange to visit Leodegranus—after I have confirmed Oesc's son as lord of Cantium."

"So—did Artor send you because he was afraid to face me?" Rigana turned, skirts flaring as the sea breeze caught them, but then there was always wind at Dun Tagell.

"There are a great many demands on the High King's time," Igierne answered neutrally.

"Oh, indeed!" Rigana took a quick step away from the cliff's edge, brown curls blowing across her face and head cocked like an angry bird. "Too many for him to pay attention when that bastard Cataur abducted me, and far too many for him to take the time to rescue me! I would still have a husband, and you would not have had this war, if there had not been so many demands on your son's time!"

Igierne took a firm hold on her own temper. "The women of Demetia whom he saved from slavery in Eriu might not agree with you, but hindsight is a wonderful counselor." She had met Oesc a time or two when he was Artor's hostage, and thought him a pleasant, if rather dour, young man. How had he ended up married to this virago? "He sent me because I know what it is to lose a husband," she continued. "Artor will be waiting for us in Cantium."

"With Oesc's ashes." Rigana's narrow shoulders slumped. "At night I lie awake, remembering all our bitter words. And yet I loved the man, even though he was Saxon and the heir of my family's ancient enemy."

"Artor loved him too," said Igierne quietly.

Together, the two women started along the path that wound about the edge of the rock. The stone wall was low here, a protection for those inside rather than a defense, for no boat could live among the rocks at the base of the sheer cliff that faced the dancing glitter of the sea. They picked their way through the tumbled remains of beehive-shaped huts where monks had lived until Gorlosius turned Dun Tagell into a guardpost, following the curve of the rock back towards the hall.

"Oesc trusted him—" Rigana said bitterly. "He would not have turned against his own folk for my sake, but I think he might have done so, if Artor had called."

"He went to war with Artor for your sake," Igierne reminded her.

"Do you think I haven't blamed myself for that, too?"

"Blame Cataur—"

"Who goes unpunished!" Rigana exclaimed.

"Not entirely. I am told he will never sit a horse again."

"Artor should have killed him! He taunted me—called me a whore who had sold out to my country's enemy for the sake of a warm bed and a crimson gown!"

They had stopped once more. Below them the sea shone luminous as emerald in the slack water by the shore.

"He wanted to," answered Igierne, "but he needed Cataur's men. The greater good outweighed the desire for revenge—a lesson you will have to learn if you are to hold Cantium until your son is grown."

"Is *that* what Artor intends?" Rigana's eyes widened.

"Cantium is the Eastern Gate of Britannia. Artor trusted Oesc to hold it for him, and promised it to Oesc's son. You are of the old blood of the land. Until Eormenric comes of age, you will be Cantium's queen. You will have to choose a good man to lead the house-guard—" She stopped, for Rigana was not listening.

Overhead gulls darted and soared, squabbling. Rigana had turned towards the hall, and Igierne heard a fainter cry above the mewing of the birds.

"Eormenric—" Rigana crossed her arms above her breasts, where a dark stain was already spreading as her milk let down in response to the baby's cry, and hurried down the path.

Igierne followed more slowly, bracing herself against memories that surged like the waves of the sea. In her mind's eye, the bright afternoon gave way to moonlight, and once more she saw Uthir coming towards her. When a cloaked figure rose up before her, she was not surprised, and reached out eagerly.

"Lady . . . I greet you. . . ."

A woman's voice—Igierne recoiled, blinded by the light of day. Someone seized her hand and pulled her back to the path, and she stood shaking with reaction.

The woman who was holding her was a little bent, with grey

in her hair, wrapped in a grey shawl. It took a moment for Igierne to realize that the glimmer of light around the stranger was no failure of vision, but the aura of power. She took a deep breath, centered herself, and looked again.

"You are Hæthwæge, Oesc's wisewoman," she said then. "Merlin has told me about you."

Hæthwæge smiled, and suddenly she did not seem so old. "And all Britannia knows the Lady of the Lake." Her nod was the salutation of one priestess to another. "I am glad that you have come."

To Igierne's relief, she used the British speech, accented but clear. "Do *you* understand why Artor kept Rigana here?"

The wisewoman's gaze grew bleak. "To keep her safe until Oesc's Wyrd was accomplished. The runes told me what had to be. I loved him dearly, but I knew his life would not be long. Now he goes back to the land."

Igierne looked at her with sudden calculation. That the Saxon woman had power was clear—but what, besides the runes, did she know?

"A time of peace is coming in which our peoples must learn to live together," she said slowly. "And it seems to me that as the years pass, those of us who follow the old ways, both Saxon and Briton, will find we have more in common with each other than we do with the priests of the Christians. You would be welcome at the Lake, to teach our young priestesses, and learn our mysteries."

Hæthwæge stopped short, her gaze gone inward as if she were listening. Then she laughed. "I would like that well, but you must know that where I go, there also goes the god I serve. He has always been very willing to learn from women, and I may teach what I have learned from him. But my duty lies now with Oesc's young son. Until Eormenric is taken from the care of women, I must stay by him. If you are still willing, when that day arrives I will come to you."

"I understand," said Igierne, "and Rigana is fortunate to have you at her side. But we have a journey to make. While we bear each other company, let us share what wisdom we may. . . ."

* * *

The harvest was in and the first storm of autumn had swept the west country, cleansing the land and setting the first touch of vivid color in the leaves. But when it was past, the gods seemed to have regretted their threat of winter, for the skies cleared and the air grew warm once more. The Vale of Afallon lay in dreaming peace, and the hills that sheltered it basked beneath the sun.

Even at the villa, where the family of Prince Leodagranus had gone to escape the heat of Lindinis, the air was hot and still. Guendivar, clad in the sheerest linen tunica her mother would permit her, untied the waist cord to let the garment flow freely from the brooches that held it at the shoulders and still felt rivulets of perspiration twining across her skin. Even the wool she was spinning felt slick beneath her fingers. She detached them distastefully and tossed the spindle onto the bench that ran along the covered porch.

Sister Julia started at the clatter, then returned her attention to the even strand that was feeding from the cloud of wool wrapped around her distaff onto her own. She had been Guendivar's constant companion for almost a year, when Petronilla, dazzled by the prospects implied by Queen Igierne's letter, had sent to the Isle of Glass for a nun to guard her daughter's chastity. Mother Maruret had offered them Julia, an orphan of good family who had not yet taken her final vows. She was plain enough to convince Guendivar's mother of her virtue, and at eighteen, young enough so that Guendivar would tolerate her company.

"How can you bear to spin in this weather?" Guendivar exclaimed, resting her hands on the railing and gazing out across the stubble of the hay-meadow. "If they could, I daresay even the sheep would be shedding their fleeces now. But then—" she turned back to Julia "—you always look so cool."

Julia flushed a little, and Guendivar laughed. She had discovered very early that the young woman's fair skin showed every shift in emotion. She was clad, as always, in a gown of heavy undyed linen, and when Guendivar looked more closely, she saw a sheen of perspiration on Julia's brow.

"You *are* hot! Well, that settles it. We are going down to the stream to bathe!"

"But your mother—" Julia stopped her spinning.

"My mother will not be back from Lindinis until tonight, but why should she object? The war is over, and all the lust-crazed soldiers are on their way home!"

It was too bad, really—for all their fears, not one warrior, lusty or not, had come near. It would have brought a little excitement into what had been an anxious but boring summer. Guendivar sighed, knowing her mother would have told her to use the bathhouse attached to the villa, but she saw no reason to make more work for the slaves when what she really wanted was to get out into the woods once more.

Before Julia could protest further, Guendivar had dashed inside for her sandals and some towel cloths and a blanket, and was running down the path. In the next moment, she smiled as she heard the young nun hurrying after her. By now, she had found that within the limitations of her mother's rules, Julia was quite persuadable. Guendivar would even have been glad of her companionship if she could just, once in a while, have spent some time alone.

It had been months since she had had a glimpse of faerie radiance. Did growing up mean that one could no longer see them? But they had *promised* that she would stay the same! Guendivar clung to that knowledge in the lonely nights when she lay awake watching the moon pass her window and listening to Julia's quiet breathing from the other side of the room. Sometimes she thought about simply climbing out the window, but Julia was a light sleeper and would rouse the household to follow her.

But I will *do it!* she promised herself as she reached the woods and slowed. *No one, not even the High King himself, will keep me locked in for long!*

Julia gave her a reproachful glance as she caught up with her. She was breathing hard and sweating visibly. Guendivar suppressed an impulse of pity. It was Julia's own fault—she knew where Guendivar was going, after all.

But now she could hear the cheerful gurgle of the stream as it purled among the stones of the ford. Below the ford the ground had been cleared so the sheep and the cattle could come down to drink there, but above it, where a screen of alders shaded the water, her father had hollowed out a bathing pool.

Guendivar dropped her towel and stripped off her tunica in a single motion, and made a dash for the pool.

"Oh, it's delicious!" she cried as the coolness closed around her. She ducked beneath the surface and came up laughing, splashed Julia, who had folded her gown and was testing the water with one toe, and laughed again to see it sparkle in the sun. She leaned backward to let the water embrace her and floated, her bright hair raying out around her, her breasts bobbing like pale apples.

Carefully, Julia waded in. Standing, the water lapped her breasts, larger than Guendivar's, though the younger girl was taller, with rosy nipples, erect now in response to the water. Julia's face might be plain, reflected Guendivar, but her body was rounded and beautiful. It was a shame to hide that curving waist beneath a nun's shapeless robe.

She allowed herself to sink beneath the surface once more, turning, opening her legs so the cool water rushed between her thighs. She felt the pressure of the current against her side—or was it the spirit of the pool? Her spirit reached out in wordless longing, and she felt the current curl around her in an insubstantial embrace.

Too soon she had to come up for air, and the moment was gone. She could only be grateful that she was wet already, so Julia could not see her tears. She gathered up her hair and twisted it to wring out the water, then started for the shore.

"Do you want to go back now?" asked Julia. She was washing her hair, black now with moisture, like the delta of shadow between her thighs.

"I will rest awhile and let the air dry me." Guendivar spread out the blanket where the old leaves lay thick beneath the trees and lay down.

Presently Julia joined her, sighing with content as she stretched out at Guendivar's side.

"What is it?" the other girl asked presently. "You look so sad. Is it something I have said or done?"

Damn—thought Guendivar, wiping her eyes. "I used to range the hills like a wild pony! I hate being penned in the house like a mare being kept until the stallion comes. It's not your fault, Julia. You make it almost bearable!"

"Oh, my dear—" Julia reached out to touch her shoulder. "Don't you want to marry the king?"

"He doesn't even know me! Maybe it will come to nothing. Maybe this is all no more than my mother's dream. But if the High King doesn't want me, she will find someone else, and I will be in prison forevermore!"

"Guendivar, it's all right!" murmured Julia, drawing her close as she began to weep once more, holding her pillowed against her soft breast until she had cried herself out and was still.

It had been a long time, thought Guendivar in the peace that followed, since her mother had held her so. Julia's skin was as cool and smooth as her mother's silken gown. Dreamily, as if she were stroking her cat, she slid her fingers down that soft side. Again, and again, she stroked, exploring the contours of muscle and bone beneath the smooth skin, until her hand cupped the curve of the other woman's breast.

Julia gasped, and Guendivar, opening her eyes, saw the betraying flush, rosy as sunrise, beneath the fair skin. "Please—you should not—"

"Touch you? But why not?" asked Guendivar. "Your skin is lovely." She squeezed gently, fingers circling until they found the pink nipple and felt it harden.

"I think . . . it is a sin. . . ." Julia took a quick breath and started to pull away, but Guendivar held her.

"My mother says it is a sin if I let a man touch my body, but you are not a man." Guendivar smiled. "Look, our breasts are nestling together like doves. . . ." She moved closer, feeling a sweet fire begin to burn warm within her own body at the contact of skin on skin. She licked her lips, wondering if that skin would be as sweet to the taste as it was to touch. Julia made a small desperate sound and turned her head away.

"You like me, don't you?" Guendivar asked in sudden doubt. "It's not just because my mother makes you stay—"

"Oh Guendivar, my sweet child, I love you," Julia whispered brokenly, "Didn't you know?" The stiffness went out of her body and she reached up to stroke Guendivar's hair.

"I don't know about love, but I know that you like holding me—" She smiled again and kissed Julia's lips. There was a last moment of resistance, and then the other girl's arms tightened around her.

Together they sank back down on the blanket, and she learned just how much Julia liked her as, clumsy as colts and sensuous as kittens, they discovered the pleasure touch could bring. And presently, lost in sensation, Guendivar forgot the future that prisoned her, and was free.

At Midwinter, the High King came to Lindinis. He was travelling from Londinium to visit Cataur in Isca Dumnoniorum, his message told them, and Lindinis would be a good place to break his journey. He would be there, he said, in time for the festival.

"He has not said he is coming to see *me*," said Guendivar. Scrubbed and scented and swathed in Roman silks, she sat on the chest in her mother's bedchamber, kicking her heels against its carven side.

"He wrote to ask your father if you were spoken for," answered Petronilla, peering into her mirror of polished bronze as she hung discs of gold filigree and garnets in her ears. "God knows how he knew that Leodagranus even *has* a daughter, but if he is coming here, it is you he wants to see. Perhaps he fears that if he marries into Demetia or Dumnonia, the others will be jealous, whereas an alliance with Lindinis will not upset the balance of power. But you come of the blood of the Durotrige princes, and your ancestry is as royal as any in Britannia. So you will be on your best behavior, my girl—" she turned to fix her daughter with a repressive glare "—and show yourself worthy to be Artor's bride."

And why should I want to be a queen? Guendivar wondered mutinously. *From all I have heard, they have even less freedom than other wives*—but she did not say so aloud. Her mother had explained quite clearly the advantages to her family, and threatened to send her back to the Isle of Glass with Julia if she refused.

"At least," Petronilla continued as she settled the veil over her hair, "you are in blooming looks."

Guendivar felt a betraying flush heat her cheeks and hoped her mother would put it down to maidenly modesty. It was Julia's care for her and the joy they had together that had made these past months bearable.

Sounds from the street below brought both of them to their feet, listening. Petronilla moved swiftly to the porch that overlooked the atrium and glanced down.

"They've come—quickly now, we must be ready to greet them—" She reached for her daughter's hand and towed her out of the room.

Guendivar's first thought was that Artor was old. After a second glance, she decided that perhaps he was merely very tired. He was tall and well-muscled, though rather thin, and his brown hair showed only a few threads of grey. He might even be rather good looking, if he ever relaxed. She wondered if she were judging him so harshly because he had hardly looked at her? Once they were all seated in the triclinium and the slaves began to bring in the food, the king had directed all his remarks to her father and brother.

Artor's nephew Gualchmai, an enormous young man who reminded her of a mastiff puppy her brother had once brought home, was doing his best to compensate.

"Those two louts who are swilling at the end of yon table are my brothers Gwyhir and Aggarban—" he said, gesturing broadly, the goblet of pale green glass seeming impossibly fragile in his big hand. "And there's two more at Dun Eidyn still to come."

Guendivar lifted one eyebrow. Gwyhir, sitting beneath the garland of winter greenery that had been draped across the frescoed wall, was almost as tall as his brother, Aggarban shorter and more solid, but still a big man.

"And you go everywhere with the king?" she asked.

"We do, along with Betiver, that narrow dark lad yonder who is nephew to Riothamus in Gallia, and Cai, who was Artor's foster-brother."

"He has formidable protectors." She saw him blink as she smiled.

"Aye, well—we lost some good men at Mons Badonicus,

but seemingly we'll have less need of them from now on." Gualchmai looked as if he were trying to convince himself this was a good thing.

The slaves came in to clear the platters of venison and roast pork away and replace them with honeycakes and pies made from the apples of the vale. Soon the feast would be over. Would the men sit down to their drinking and send the women away? Guendivar no longer wished to avoid Artor; indeed, she had begun to think that if she did not arrange an encounter, she would have no chance to speak with him at all.

"I think my father is about to end the feasting—" she told Gualchmai. "You might tell your lord that even at midwinter I often walk in the atrium at night to breathe the fresh air. . . ."

"A good commander is always glad of information—" He grinned at her approvingly. "I will make certain that he knows."

Well, at least *he* seemed to like her, she thought as she followed her mother out of the room. If Artor did not want her, perhaps she could marry Gualchmai.

It was late, and even the hooded cloak was no longer quite sufficient to keep off the chill, when Guendivar heard a man's step upon the stones. Shivering, she stood up, and saw him stop short, then move slowly forward until he stood before her. She thought for a moment that it might be Gualchmai, come to tell her that Artor would not be there. But those senses with which she had learned to see the folk of faerie identified not the king's appearance but his unique aura of power.

"I am sorry—" he said finally. "I have kept you waiting, and you are cold." He shrugged off his crimson mantle and draped it around her shoulders. It still held the heat of his body and warmed her like a fire.

"But you will be cold—" she protested.

"I've campaigned in worse weather than this, in armor. *That* is cold!"

"I have never been cold without a way to get warm, never marched without food or panted from thirst, never done labor that I could not stop when I willed. Except for spinning, of course—" she added ruefully. He was surprisingly easy to talk to—perhaps it was because she could not see him. They were two spirits, speaking together in the dark.

"What *has* Gualchmai been telling you?" Artor said, on a breath of laughter. "I do not expect my queen to march with the army. I hope that in the next few years even *I* won't have to march with the army, at least not all the time."

"Would you then keep your wife like a jewel in a golden setting?" Guendivar's voice was very soft.

There was another charged silence, then Artor sighed. "Your brother tells me that you are a great rider, and can stay out all day, ranging the hills. I would not cage you, Guendivar, even in gold. If you wish it, I would be glad to have you riding at my side."

She straightened, trying to see his face. She was a tall girl, but still she had to look up at him. "From what Gualchmai says, you are never more than a moon in the same place. I think I will have to—"

"It is a bargain, then?" Relief made his voice unsteady as he set his hands on her shoulders.

"It is—" She had feared this marriage as a prison, but now she was beginning to think it might be an adventure. The pressure of his hands felt warm and secure.

"In the spring, then—" He stopped suddenly. "How old are you?"

"At the beginning of April I will be fifteen." She strove for dignity.

His hands dropped suddenly and he shook his head. "Sweet Goddess! And yet, if I was old enough to be king at that age, I suppose that you can be a queen."

Her assurance left her suddenly. "I will try—"

Artor eased back her hood. He took her face between his hands, gentle as if he were touching a butterfly, and kissed her on the brow.

V

THE FLOWER BRIDE

A.D. 496

 That year spring came early to Britannia, as if the land were adorning itself to celebrate the wedding of the High King. Every dell was scattered with creamy primroses; the woodland rides were flooded with bluebells; and in the hedges the starry white of hawthorn veiled each bough.

As the bridal procession left the Summer Country and made its slow way towards Londinium, folk thronged from tiled villas and thatched Celtic roundhouses, from shepherds' lonely huts and half-ruined towns to hail the bride whose marriage would set a seal of peace upon the land. Surely, they sang, the wars were truly ended, if the High King was at last giving them a queen. Where Guendivar passed, the road was strewn with flowers.

To Merlin, making his way southward from the Caledonian forest, the rumor of her progress was like a warm breath of wind from some fruitful southern land. He found himself hastening, moved by a hope he had not dared to feel for far too long. He had been born to serve the Defender of Britannia and set him on his throne, and he had succeeded in that task. None of them had dared to think about what might come afterward.

But now the land itself was providing the answer. After winter came the spring, after sorrow, this joy, after the death of the Britannia that had been ruled by Rome, a new nation in which all the gathered greatness of the peoples who had settled here could flower.

Igierne, riding south with Ceincair and Morut, could not help but contrast this wedding with her marriage to Uthir, that hurried, makeshift ceremony held in the dead of winter and the aftermath of a civil war to legitimize the child she was already carrying. Guendivar would come to her marriage a virgin, with neither memories of the past nor fears for the future to shadow the day. If the queen mother had not been so profoundly relieved at the prospect of passing on a part of the burden she had carried for so long, she would have envied her son's bride.

For Artor's sister, riding swiftly southward with her escort of Votadini tribesmen, each milestone on the old Roman road was a reminder of her own dilemma. For so long she had told herself that the freedom of a queen in Alba suited her far better than any title dying Britannia had to offer. Now she was about to find out if she really believed it. If Artor had never been born, her own descent from the House of Maximus might have given her husband a claim to torque and diadem. Yet the closer she got to Londinium, the more clearly Morgause understood that it was not Guendivar whom she envied, but Artor himself. She did not desire to be a consort, but the ruling queen.

Even in decline, the Romanized Britons for whom Boudicca was still a name with which to frighten children would never have accepted her. Artor's son would inherit his imperium. The only question was whether that son would be the child of her womb, or Guendivar's.

Artor himself, struggling with questions of personality and precedence, remembered the bright face of the girl he had met at midwinter and wondered if he had the right to plunge any woman into the political morass this wedding had become. Even the choice of a place to hold the ceremony had provoked a battle. Bishop Dubricius had offered his own church in Isca, but to marry there would have insulted the Dumnonians, already on the defensive because they were blamed for provoking the last Saxon war.

Artor could have been married in the bride's home, but Lindinis was only a secondary tribal civitas, and had no edifice large enough to hold all those who would want to come. Calleva or Sorviodunum were central, but too closely associated with the wars. At least Londinium had once been the country's undisputed capital, and in the basilica and the Palace of the Governors there would be room for all.

But as the first of May drew closer Artor would have been glad of an excuse to send some of them home again. Planning battles was much easier. He was beginning to think that the ancient custom of marriage by capture had a lot to recommend it. Guendivar had said she liked to ride—perhaps she would prefer being carried off. But when the king tried this theory out on his companions, they only laughed. Gualchmai, who had more experience with women than any three of the rest of them, assured him that women *liked* ceremonies with flowers and candles and uncomfortable new clothes.

As for Guendivar herself, she rode through the blossoming landscape in a haze of delight, accepting the gifts men brought her and the homage they paid her beauty; exulting in the movement of the horse beneath her, the brightness of the sunlight and the sweetness of the flowers. Focused on the excitement of each moment, she scarcely thought about the wedding towards which this journey was leading her.

"Old Oesc used to say these walls were like the work of etins—titans . . ." said Betiver, gesturing at the ruins of the gatehouse that had once guarded the Calleva Road. The rubble had been cleared away, but the gate had never been repaired.

Guendivar gazed around her with interest as they passed. "It looks old, and sad. Will Artor rebuild it?"

"Why should he trouble himself," asked Gualchmai, laughing, "when the walls are as full of holes as a cloak when the moths have been making free? Walls!" He made a rude gesture. "No good are they without brave men and sharp spears behind them!"

"Oh, indeed," said his brother Gwyhir, who rode just behind him, "and you yourself are as good as an army!"

Guendivar laughed. After three weeks on the road, she had taken their measure. Artor had sent the youngest and liveliest of his Companions to be her escort, and they had preened and pranced for her from Lindinis to Londinium. They reminded her of puppies showing off, even Betiver, who was said to have a permanent mistress in the town and a nine-year-old son.

"The high roof you see belongs to the basilica," he told her. "That is where the wedding feast will be—I think it is the only building in Britannia large enough to hold all the people Cai has invited. The church is nearer the river."

"And the palace?"

"Beyond the basilica, on the other side of the square. Of course only the main wing is still usable, but with luck, we'll be able to find enough sound roofs in Londinium to keep everyone dry!" He sent a suspicious glance skyward, but the overcast did not look as if it were going to deepen into rain.

Guendivar sighed. She had looked forward to staying in a palace, but this vast city, its old buildings leprous with decay, held little of the splendour of her dreams. Ghosts might dwell here, but not the folk of faerie. She thought wistfully of the fields through which they had passed to come here, adorned more richly than any work of the Romans with spring flowers.

But she must not let her escort sense her unease. "Is Artor here already?" she asked brightly. "Will he come to greet me?"

The Votadini brothers turned to Betiver, who replied with a wry smile, "I am sure that so soon as he knows you have arrived he will come to you—but as for where he is now—well, you will learn soon enough that Artor is not one for sitting still."

But the High King was not working. Igierne had arrived the previous day and, finding her son in the old office of the procurator, surrounded by scraps of paper, had carried him off to the river. As a boy he had learned the difficult art of paddling a coracle; she pressed him into service now as her boatman and ordered him to take her upstream.

High clouds had spread a silver veil partway across the

heavens. Each stroke of the paddle set reflections rippling like pearl. From time to time some other craft, coming downstream, would pass them. Igierne lifted a hand to answer their hails, but Artor had not the breath to reply.

She watched him with a critical eye, noting the flex and stretch of muscle in his arms and back as he drove the round skin-covered craft against the current. Sometimes an eddy would spin them, and Artor needed all of his strength as well as skill to get them back on course. He was sweating freely by the time she told him to stop.

The coracle spun round once more, then began to drift gently back towards the city whose smoke hazed the river below them like a shadow of the clouds. Artor rested the paddle on his knees, still breathing hard.

"Do you feel better?" she asked.

For a moment he stared; then his exasperation gave way to wonder.

"In fact, I do . . ."

"There is nothing like vigorous action to relieve strain, and you have been under a great deal, my child." He spent much time outdoors and his color was good, but she noticed more than one thread of silver in the brown hair, and there were new shadows around his eyes.

"I have never been required to plan a campaign of peace before," he said apologetically. "In war it is easy. If a man has a sword at your throat, he is an enemy. Here, I have only allies, who think they know what is needed better than I. I might believe them—if they could only all agree!"

Igierne laughed. "It is not so different among my priestesses on the Isle of Maidens." For a few moments they were silent, watching the ducks dive into the reedbeds as they passed. Then she spoke once more. "Tell me, is it easier to move the boat upstream or down?"

"Down, of course," he answered, one brow lifting in enquiry.

"Just so. Think—is not everything easier when you move with the current instead of fighting it?"

He nodded. "Like charging downhill."

"Like this wedding—" she said then. "Guendivar is the woman whom the fates have ordained for you. To make her your wife you don't have to fight the world. Let it be. Relax and allow her to come to you." She stopped suddenly. "Or are you afraid?"

He knew how to govern his face, but she saw his knuckles whiten as he gripped the oar.

"She is so young, Mother. She has never heard the ravens singing on a battlefield, or seen the life ebb from the face of a man you love. She has never known how fury can seize you and make you do terrible things, conscious of nothing until you come to yourself and see the blood on your hands. What can I say to her? What kind of a life can we have?"

"A life of peace," answered his mother, "though you will not have done with battles entirely while the Picts still ride south-ward and Eriu sends warriors across the sea. It is because she is innocent that you need this girl. You need say nothing—let her talk to you. . . . She will be Tigernissa, High Queen. Men fight for land, but the life of the land is in the waters that flow through it. The power of the waters belongs to the queen. It is for her to initiate you into its mysteries."

A gull swooped low, yammering, and when it saw they had no food, soared away. They could smell woodsmoke now, and on the shore the wharves of Londinium were beginning to come into view.

"The river has great power. See how swiftly we have re-turned? Beneath all the eddies, all the flotsam that rides its sur-face and the ruffling of the wind, the deep current of the river rolls. It is the same with the squabbles of humankind. Worship as you must for Britannia's peace, but never forget how strong these waters are as they move so steadily toward the sea. . . ."

The night before the wedding it rained. At dawn, clouds still covered the sky, but as they thinned, they admitted a little wa-tery sunshine. When Guendivar came out of the palace, the wet stones of the pavement were shining. She gazed around her, blinking at the brightness. At that moment, even this place of wood and stone was beautiful. Her escort was already formed up and waiting. When they saw her, they began to cheer, drowning out the clamor that marked the progress of the groom's procession, already two streets away.

Her mother twitched at the hawthorn wreath that held the bridal veil. Its fiery silk had been embroidered with golden flowers. More flowers were woven into the crimson damask of her dalmatic and worked into its golden borders in pearls. Jewels weighted the wide neckband and the strip of gold that ran from throat to hem. It was a magnificent garment, fit for an empress of the eastern lands from which it had come—everyone said so. But it was so heavy Guendivar could hardly move.

Her mother gripped her elbow, pulling her forward. For a moment Guendivar resisted, filled with a wild desire to strip down to her linen undergown and make a dash for the open fields. How could they praise her beauty when her body was encased in jewels like a relic and her face curtained by this veil? It was an image they shouted for, like the icon of the Virgin that was carried in procession at festivals.

But she had given her word to Artor.

"She comes! She comes—" cried the crowd "—the Flower Bride!"

Stiff as a jointed puppet, Guendivar mounted the cart, its railings wound with primroses and violets and its sides garlanded with eglantine. As it passed through the streets, people strewed the road with all the blooms of May. They brightened the way, but could not soften the rough stones. Guendivar gripped the rail, swaying as the cart jolted forward.

They turned a corner and came into the square before the church, a modest whitewashed structure dwarfed by what remained of the imperial buildings that still surrounded it. The hills of the Summer Country seemed very far away.

The groom's escort was already drawn up beside it, and the bishop waited before the church door, his white vestments as heavily ornamented as her gown. Even Artor was cased in cloth of gold that glittered in the pale sunlight. *We are all images,* she told herself, *existing only to play our roles in this ceremony.* But what force could manipulate kings for its pleasure? The people, perhaps? Or their gods?

The cart halted. Guendivar allowed them to help her descend, and her father, grinning as if she were his sole invention, led her to the church door. Marriages were blessed by the

Church, but they were not part of its liturgy. Still, the porch of the church seemed a strange place for a ceremony. Through the haze of silk she could see Artor, looking as stiff and uncomfortable as she. Bishop Dubricius cleared his throat, gathering the attention of the crowd.

"*In nomine Patris, et Filii, et Espiritu Sancti—*"

Guendivar felt her heart beat like that of a trapped hare as the sonorous Latin rolled on, a river of words that was sweeping her and Artor both away.

Only when the sound ceased did she rouse. Everyone was looking at her, waiting for her answer. Could she, even now, refuse? But as she gazed frantically around her the sun broke through the clouds, and suddenly all the world was a glitter of light. She shut her eyes against that brilliance, but behind her eyelids it still blazed.

"*Volo—*" she heard her own voice say.

There were more words, and then the deep murmur of Artor's reply. The priest bound their hands, turned them to show themselves to the people, whose joyous response smote the sky.

Then Artor led her into the darkness of the church for the nuptial mass.

The scent of flowers hung heavy in the hall, mingling unpleasantly with the odors of human sweat and spilled wine. From the high table on the dais at the end of the basilica, tables had been set end to end in front of the walls. Upon the benches of the king's side, all the princelings of Britannia, and on the queen's side, their wives and daughters, sat packed like pickles in a crock.

Morgause took another drink from her own cup, breathing deep to let the sharp fumes drive the other scents away. When the last of the Roman governors abandoned his post, the items he had left behind included some amphoras of good wine. It was a little past its prime—Artor had been right to use it now. She sighed, aware that the wine was making her melancholy. When she was a girl they had drunk wine like this in her father's hall, but in times to come they would have to swill like barbarians on mead and heather beer.

A clatter of steel on shield leather brought everyone upright as the sword dancers marched in. Some of the male guests leaped from their benches, reaching as if they expected to find their own weapons hanging behind them on the wall. Morgause grinned sourly. These were the champion dancers among her husband's tribesmen; it pleased her to see these fat southern lords, if only for a moment, feel afraid.

The dancers' tunics, though clean, were of rough wool, and the earthy hues woven into their mantles dull against the bright colors of the princes, but their swords flashed in the torchlight. Singing, they formed two squares. Shields lifted into position, and they began their deadly play.

The singers who had been performing earlier had almost been drowned out by the hum of conversation, but the sword dancers riveted everyone's attention. Even the little bride, who had been picking at the slice of roast boar which Artor had served her, put down her knife to stare.

"They are Votadini?" asked the woman beside Morgause. She was called Flavia, invited because she had been foster-mother to Artor.

She nodded. "They come from a clan on our border with Alta Cluta."

"They are most . . . energetic . . ." Flavia replied. "Your husband must be proud. But I do not see him. Is he well?"

"Well enough," answered Morgause tightly, "but his joints pain him too much to make such a journey."

"Ah, I understand—" Flavia grimaced in sympathy. "I came in a horselitter, and still it was two days before I could walk without wincing! It is the price of growing old. Of course *you* are still young—" she said after an uncomfortable moment had passed.

Morgause thought of her own aches and kept silence. On her other side the mothers of the bride and groom were deep in conversation. Morgause had stopped resenting having to sit below Guendivar's mother, when she realized that Petronilla, puffed with pride though she might be, would save her from having to talk to Igierne.

"And what do you think of our new queen?" asked Flavia.

Morgause bared her teeth in a smile. "She is pretty enough, but very young—"

Young enough to be Artor's daughter, if he had been married off at the age I was. Young enough to be a sister to Artor's son. . . . Medraut had begged to come with her to the wedding. He was quite self-possessed for a nine-year-old—she had trained him well, but instinct counselled her to wait. Medraut's time was yet to come.

"But you yourself were married at much the same age, were you not, and to a much older man?" Flavia commented, far too acutely.

And now I am tied to an ancient who is good for nothing but to sit by the fire, while I am still in my prime! Morgause thought then. It would serve Guendivar right if she found herself in the same situation with Artor. It could happen—Leudonus was proof that some warriors lived to be old.

"It is not her age but her intelligence that will make the difference," Morgause answered tartly. "A pretty face alone will not hold a man's interest for long."

"Then we must hope that she can do so, for my Arktos was always a conscientious lad, and I suspect he will remain faithful, whether she loves him or no."

Morgause regarded her thoughtfully. Igierne, for all her lofty sentiments, knew less of her son than this woman who had raised him. She leaned forward until she could see the middle of the table. The bride had given up all pretense of eating and was looking distinctly uncomfortable. Her face was flushed as if she had drunk more than she was used to. Morgause suppressed a smile.

Carefully she swung her legs over the bench and stood. "It is time I visited the privies," she said loudly. "Would anyone like to keep me company?"

Guendivar's eyes focused suddenly. "I would! If I drink any more I will burst!"

Petronilla looked pained, but she assisted the bride to disentangle her robes and rise. There was anxiety in Igierne's eyes as well, but what could be more natural than for a sister-in-law to escort the new queen?

Artor looked up, smiling with friendly concern. His companions had been seated at a lower table, but Gualchmai had left his place and was leaning with his arm draped across the top of the king's chair. He nodded politely to his mother, but his eyes were watchful. Morgause smiled blandly and took Guendivar's arm.

The old Roman lavatory facilities were still in use. Beyond them, a corridor opened out onto the colonnade. When they had finished and washed, Morgause paused.

"The air in the hall was so hot and warm; I still feel a little faint. Will you bear me company for a few moments in the fresh air?"

"Gladly—" answered Guendivar. "I had been hoping for a chance to speak with you," she added shyly. "You are still a reigning queen. I suspect there are things you can tell me that I will need to know."

Morgause peered at her through the darkness. Shouts of laughter echoed faintly from the hall. Could the child possibly be as ingenuous as she sounded?

"Do you love Artor?" she asked suddenly.

There was a constricted silence. "I agreed to marry him. I will do my best to make him happy."

Morgause considered. In these garments the girl looked like an overdressed doll, but she had good bones, and her hair, a reddish gold that curled to her waist, was beautiful. Did Artor want an ally or an adorer? If he had chosen Guendivar for her pretty face, she would not hold his interest for long.

Duty was an unexciting bedfellow, but a good companion. What would this girl find it hardest to give? It occurred to her that it would serve Medraut better if Artor did not find too much comfort in his queen.

"My brother is not a bad man," she said thoughtfully, "but he has been a king as long as you have been alive. He is accustomed to obedience. And he has been at war for many years. He will want diversion. Amuse him—be playful—feign passion, even if you do not feel it. And if he seems cold, well, you will be surrounded by virile young men. If you are discreet, you can use them for your pleasure. It has worked well for me."

And that was true enough. But Artor was not Leudonus,

who had known very well that his marriage was a political alliance, and never expected more. In Alba, the lustiness of the
queen was as important as that of the king. And Alba was not a
Christian land.

"You are young," said Morgause, "and know little of the
body's demands. But as you mature you will find that a woman
has needs too, and kings are very busy men. . . ."

A door opened and light and shadow barred the colonnade.

"They have missed us," Guendivar said quickly. "We had
better go in—"

"But of course," answered Morgause. "You are the queen,
and you command." But as she followed Guendivar back into
the hall, she was smiling.

A murmur of appreciation greeted Guendivar's entrance.
Morgause hung back a little, noting the gleam in men's eyes as
they watched her come. This one would not have to entice men
to her bed if she decided she wanted them—they would be lin-
ing up at her door. The remains of the feast lay about them like
a looted battlefield. Men had drunk enough now to want something else, and tonight, all their lust was projected upon the
king.

"Don't you think it time the little bride was bedded?" she
said to Gualchmai as she passed. "She is ready, and he should
not make her wait too long."

Some of the other men heard and began to bang their mugs
against the planks of the table. "To bed, to bed—let Artor
prove that he is king!"

Guendivar's face was nearly as scarlet as her gown, but even
the women were laughing.

"Very well," said Petronilla with what dignity she could
muster. "Come, ladies, let us escort the queen to the bridal
chamber and make her ready for her husband."

Shouting and singing, the women crowded around the new
queen and bore her away. But Morgause remained, waiting in
the shadow of a pillar as the masculine banter became ever
more explicit, until the king was blushing almost as hotly as
his bride.

Presently she saw the little nun who had been Guendivar's
chaperone returning to tell them she was ready.

The men, for a moment abashed by her grave gaze, grew quieter. Morgause stepped forward.

"And will you also, sister, wish me joy?" Artor asked. "I thought you would be with the women who are helping Guendivar—"

"Oh, I have given her my advice already—" answered Morgause.

"And have you any counsel for me? Your sons have been as frank as farmers with suggestions on how I should practice a husband's craft."

If he had not mentioned her sons, perhaps, even then, Morgause would have kept silent. But she smiled and slid her hand gently along his upper arm.

"But you already know how to deal with a woman, dear brother, *don't you remember?*" she said very softly. "And you have a son to prove it, begotten ten years since at the feast of Lugus. His name is Medraut." Still smiling, she took his face between her hands and kissed him.

His lips were cold, and as she released him, she saw, bleak as the morning after battle, the dawn of desolation in his eyes.

The bed linen smelled of lavender. Guendivar ran her hands across the cloth, smooth with many launderings, and sighed. The linen was old, like this chamber, whose stones seemed to whisper tales of those who had lain here in the years since the mud huts of the Trinovantes were replaced by the stone and plaster of Rome.

She sat up, wrapping her arms around her knees. *What am I doing here?* She belonged in the open land of wood and field, not in this box of stone. Even the silk nightrobe in which they had wrapped her seemed alien. Weather permitting, she preferred to sleep bare. She considered pulling the garment off, but her mother had impressed upon her the need to behave modestly—it would never do to shock her new husband, after all.

Guendivar found it hard to believe that a man who had been living in military camps for half his life would be disturbed by bare skin. Did Artor really believe that she was the simpering maiden her mother had counselled her to be? She tried to re-

member their single conversation—it had seemed to her then
that it was because she had red blood in her veins that he had
liked her.

As she started to untie the neckstrings she heard shouting
from the corridor and her fingers stilled. They were coming.
Suddenly the garment seemed not a constriction, but protection. She pulled up the bedclothes and sat staring as the door
swung open and torchlight, dimming the flicker of the lamps,
streamed into the room.

The doorway filled with faces, their laughter faltering as
they saw her sitting there. For a moment she saw herself with
their vision: eyes huge in her white face, mantled in shining
hair.

The crowd heaved as the men who were behind pushed forward, then moved aside to admit a figure that moved in a haze
of gold, from the band around his brows to the embroidery on
his mantle. But his face was in shadow, and though he was surrounded by a leaping, laughing crowd, his stillness matched
her own.

"The way is clear!" came Gualchmai's shout. "Get in with
you, man—I'll cover you!"

"Nay, it is Artor who will be covering his bride!" someone
replied, and the hall rang with masculine laughter. They
sounded like her brother and his friends when they had been
drinking.

"For shame, lads—give the man some privacy!" That came
from Betiver.

Morgause would have known how to command those boors
to leave them. Guendivar recalled the Votadini queen's words
to her and felt her skin grow hot with remembered embarrassment—perhaps Artor's sister would not have cared.

Then Artor turned to face his tormentors. Their laughter
faded, and she wondered what they were seeing in his eyes. He
swung round, and a long stride carried him over the threshold.
His arm swept out and the heavy door slammed behind him.

The noise outside fell suddenly to a murmur; she thought
they were singing and was glad she could not distinguish the
words. Inside, the dark shape by the door seemed to gather silence around him until it was a palpable weight in the air.

Guendivar drew the bedclothes closer, shivering. She had not expected her new husband to leap upon her, but why was he still standing there? Could he possibly be afraid?

When the silence had become more disturbing than anything she could imagine him doing, she cleared her throat.

"I do not know the etiquette of these things, but the priests assure me that you have a right to be here. Are you waiting for an invitation to lie down with me?"

Some of the tension went out of him and he laughed. "Perhaps I am. I will confess to you, Guendivar, that I have more experience in 'these things' than you do, but not . . . much—" His voice cracked. "I have a son."

She lifted an eyebrow. "Before he was married my father got three, and for all I know, more afterward. Did you think I would be scandalized?"

And yet it was strange that the High King could have a child that no one had heard of. Bastards begotten before marriage were not unusual, and for a man, no shame. If Morgause was to be believed, in Alba they were not shameful for a woman either, but this was hardly the moment to say so. For a moment she longed for the comfort of Julia's warm arms, even though she knew that for every hour they had lain together the other girl had spent three on her knees. It had always seemed strange to Guendivar to do penance for something that gave the same simple pleasure as a cat arching to the stroke of a caress, but at least she understood what Julia wanted when she was in her arms.

This male creature that radiated tension from the doorway was totally strange, but clearly, if she did not do something, he might well stand there until dawn.

"I am told that you begin by taking off your clothes," she said wryly. "Do you need help? It took three women to get me out of mine."

Artor laughed again, as if she had surprised him, and shook his head. But he did unbuckle his belt and then the brooch that held his mantle at the shoulder. The rustle of heavy silk seemed loud in the quiet of the room.

"And what do you suggest I do next?" he asked when he was down to the twist of linen about his loins.

Surely, she thought with an unexpected lift of the heart, that had been amusement she heard in his tone. But why should he need to ask? Did he really believe that one bastard had made him unfit to approach her?

"Next, you get into the bed . . ."

He drew a quick breath, and she had a sudden insight into how he must look before battle. She hoped he did not see her as an enemy. She twitched the covers aside and the leather straps of the bedstead creaked as he lay down. In the flicker of lamplight she could see the curves and planes of his body quite clearly. Except for his face and forearms, his skin was almost as fair as her own, scrolled here and there by the subtle pink or silvery tracery of old battle scars. She stared curiously. She had seen men's bodies before, stripped for labor in the fields or exposed to piss against a tree, but never at such close quarters.

After a moment she realized that Artor's breathing was too controlled. What was wrong? He hadn't been so tense when they talked at midwinter. Even this morning there had been open friendliness in his smile. This was not how she had imagined her wedding night would be.

"You did not marry me for love but because you needed an heir," Guendivar said finally. "So far as I know, there is only one way to get one. You may have a son, but he cannot inherit from you, so let us be about it. It would be a pity to disappoint all those people I hear making noise to encourage us out there!"

Artor turned, raising himself on one elbow to look at her. "I have been misled—men always speak of women as if they were creatures of flight and fancy, but I see it is not so—" He took her hand, callused fingers tracing spirals across her palm.

Guendivar drew a quick breath, all her senses focusing on his touch, from which warmth had begun to radiate in little bursts of sparks across her skin. *The female animal desires the male . . .* she told herself, *so why should I be surprised?* If they did not have love, lust was no bad foundation for a marriage, so long as it came linked with laughter. For surely there was nothing here to match the ecstasy she had found in the company of the faerie-folk, but she had not expected it.

"If it were, how could you trust us to manage your homes

and raise your children?" she asked tartly, and then, while she still had the courage, lifted his hand and pressed it to her breast.

As his fingers tightened, the sparks became a flame that leaped from nipple to nipple and focused in a throbbing ache between her thighs. Her play with Julia had awakened her body, and since they began this wedding journey there had been no way for them to be alone. If Artor was surprised, his changed breathing told her that the fire had kindled him as well.

She slid her hands from his shoulders down the hard muscle of his sides. Were men's and women's bodies so different? Heart pounding, she brushed upward across his nipples and heard him gasp. Guendivar smiled then, and reached down to tug at his clout. Artor tensed, but at least he did not pull away, and when she eased back down on the bed he came with her, his movement pushing her gown above her thighs.

She could feel his male member hard against her and wished she could see it, but at last he was kissing her. Guendivar held him tightly, a part of her mind cataloguing the differences between his hard strength and Julia's yielding softness, while the remainder was being consumed by an expanding flame.

Artor pushed against her and she opened her thighs, trembling with mingled excitement and fear. This, certainly, was something she had not experienced with Julia! His hands tightened painfully on her shoulders and he thrust again. She felt a tearing pain, them the pressure abruptly eased. He continued to batter against her for a few moments longer, but it was with his body only—the part that had taken her maidenhead slid free, and she had not the art to arouse it again.

Presently he stilled and collapsed onto the bed beside her, breathing hard.

"Was it like this," she said softly when he was still, "when you begot your son?"

"I do not know . . . I do not remember . . ." he groaned, "but it cannot have been," he added bitterly, "or there would have been no child . . ."

Only then did she understand that the act had been incomplete for him as well.

"Dear God!" He turned onto his back and she saw that he was weeping. "What have I done? What did she do to me?"

Guendivar let out her breath in a long sigh. She would not, she gathered, come from this night with child. She sensed the pain in the man beside her without understanding it.

"It will be all right," she said presently, "we have time."

Gradually the rasp of his breathing slowed. "Time . . ." he groaned. "Ten years . . ."

Guendivar touched his shoulder, but he did not respond. After that, they were silent. Even the noise outside their door had ceased. The place between her thighs throbbed with a mingling of pleasure and pain. Presently she pulled the covers over her, and used her hand to release the tension Artor's touch had aroused.

Her husband lay very still beside her, and if he realized what she was doing, he made no sign.

That night, while Artor's Companions were finishing off the last of the Procurator's wine, the mother of his son lay in the arms of a lusty guardsman in a union which, however unblessed, was considerably more rewarding. Igierne slept alone in the room she had once shared with Uthir, plagued by troubled dreams. But Merlin watched out the night at the top of the ancient guard tower, striving to understand the portents he glimpsed in the stars, and in the church where Guendivar had been married, Julia lay stretched upon the cold stones, wrestling with her soul in prayer.

VI

The Sacred Round

A.D. 497

Camalot smelled of raw wood and rang with the sound of hammers. It seemed to have grown every time the king's household returned to it, the timber and stone ramparts raised higher, the framing of the great henge hall and the other buildings more solid against the spring sky. The hall had been part of Guendivar's dowry, and if the past year had seen little progress in the intimate side of their marriage, externally, Artor had accomplished a great deal.

From the timber guard tower above the southwest gate the queen saw small figures of men and horses climbing the road. That would be Matauc of Durnovaria—she recognized the standard. He was an old man now, and Artor had not been sure he would come. No doubt curiosity had brought him, as it had so many others—Britannia was full of tales about the new stronghold Artor was building in Leodagranus' land.

Most of the other princes were here already—the place was full of men and horses, and the clusters of hide tents and brushwood bothies that sheltered their escorts nestled close to the wall. According to Leodagranus, it had been a Durotrige fortress when the Romans came, destroyed in the years after Boudicca's war, and then it had been the site of a pagan shrine. But Merlin said the Durotriges were only the latest of the peoples who had sheltered on the hill, tribes now so long gone that no one even remembered their names.

Cai had laughed at him, for on first sight its tree-choked slopes seemed no different from any of the surrounding hills. But when they reached the summit, they found a roughly flattened oblong with a swell of earth around it, and three additional ramparts carved into the side of the hill. The trees they cut to clear the site had provided timber to brace the rubble wall and planks for the breastwork that topped it.

Guendivar climbed the ladder from the sentry walk to the gatehouse often. Here, she could lean on the wickerwork railing and watch the bustle without being overwhelmed by it, and there was usually a breeze. Gazing out across the tree-clad hills she could almost imagine herself free.

Below her, men were setting more stones into the rough facing of the rampart. Just because Artor had called a consilium did not mean work could cease. From here Camalot was a place of circles within circles: the ramparts that ringed the hill, and the huts within the wall, and in the space to the east of the more conventional rectangular building where Artor had his quarters, the great henge hall.

In truth, it was not so much a hall as a shelter, for sections of its wickerwork walling could be removed to let in light and air. Its design had also been one of Merlin's suggestions, neither a Roman basilica nor even a Celtic roundhouse, although it most resembled the latter. Merlin said it was another inspiration from ancient days. The thatched roof was supported on a triple henge of stout wooden pillars, its diameter so great that a hundred and fifty warriors could sit in a circle around the central fire. The old sorcerer still made Guendivar uneasy, but there was no denying his ideas were sometimes useful.

She turned and saw the gate guard lifting an earthenware jug to his lips.

"Is that wine?" she asked, feeling suddenly dry.

The man blushed—surely he should have been accustomed to her by now. "Oh no, lady—'tis water only. My lord king would have my ears did I drink while on guard. But you're welcome to share it—" he added, flushing again. He wiped the rim of the jug with the hem of his tunic and offered it to her.

She eyed it a little dubiously, for his tunic was not over-clean, but she could not insult him by refusing it now. And the water was good, kept cold by the clay. She savored it, rolling it on her tongue, before swallowing. When she had drunk, she handed back the jug and smiled, a thirst that no water could ease fed by the admiration with which he gazed back at her. Tomorrow at the council she would see her beauty reflected in the gleam of other men's eyes.

A hail from below brought her around. She leaned over the railing and waved at Betiver, who had been sent to escort Matauc to the hill. The first gate had opened, and Betiver, preceding the horselitter in which the old man had travelled, was passing beneath the tower. Matauc would need some time to recover and refresh himself, but then Artor would no doubt be wanting her to extend an official welcome. It was time for her to go do so.

Dark and light, shadowed and bright, the oblong of the doorway flickered as the princes of Britannia came into the new henge hall. The flare and glint of gold, abruptly extinguished, dazzled the eye, and Betiver, standing at his accustomed place at Artor's shoulder, had to look away. After a moment his vision adjusted, and he began counting once more.

Light coming in beneath the low eaves where the wicker screens had been removed lent the lower parts of the interior a diffuse illumination, and the fire in the center cast a warm glow; beneath the peak of the roof, all was shadow. Betiver suppressed a smile as he watched the princes and their followers attempting to figure out which were the most honorable benches when the seating was circular. That was exactly why Merlin had suggested that Artor build this round hall. In the end, the choice of seats became roughly geographical, as the little groups found places near their allies and neighbors.

Matauc of Durnovaria had taken a seat beside Leodagranus,

just down from Cataur of Dumnonia, who had brought his son Constantine. The Demetian contingent was dominated by Agricola, a war-leader from an old Roman family who made up in effectiveness for what he lacked in bloodlines. Being Roman, he did not call himself a prince, but Protector, though his powers were the same. He had also brought a son, called Vortipor. His northern neighbor was Catwallaun Longhand, still bearing the scars of his last campaign against the Irishmen of Laigin who had settled there under king Illan.

There were other, more familiar faces: old Eleutherius from Eboracum and his son Peretur; Eldaul, who ruled the area around Glevum; and Catraut, who kept a wary eye on the Saxons of the east from Verulamium. As his gaze moved around the circle it was the younger men who drew Betiver's attention. They were the ones upon whose strength Artor would build Britannia, whose focus was on the future.

But the silver hairs of age and experience were still much in evidence. Ridarchus had come down from Dun Breatann. He was as old as Leudonus, though he looked stronger. Men said he was married to a sister of Merlin. Betiver found it hard to imagine. Next to him was his half-brother Dumnoval, a grandson of the great Germanianus, who now held the Votadini lands south of the Tava under Leudonus, who had been too ill to come.

Instead, young Cunobelinus was there to speak for the Votadini of Dun Eidyn. There had some discussion about that earlier, for Gualchmai was Leudonus' named heir. But Gualchmai was sitting on Artor's right hand, as Cai held the place on his left, and no one had dared to ask whether that meant the northerner had renounced his birthright to serve the High King, or was claiming a greater one, as Artor's heir.

It seemed unlikely, for although in a year of marriage the queen had not kindled, she was young and healthy, and surely one day she would bear a child. As if the thought had been a summons, Betiver noted a change in the faces of the men across the circle and turned to see Guendivar herself, standing in a nimbus of light in the doorway.

Old or young, men fell silent as the High Queen made her way around the circle, carrying the great silver krater by the handles at each side. This, thought Betiver, was not the laughing girl who had become his friend, but the High Queen, remote and perfect as an icon in a dalmatic of creamy damask set with pearls, the finest of linen veiling her hair beneath the diadem. As she came to each man, she offered the krater. As the wine flowed over the bright silver, it caught the light with a garnet-colored glow.

"The blood of the grape is the blood of the land," she said softly. "And you are its strong arms. Drink in peace, drink in unity, and be welcome in this hall . . ."

"Lady, you lend us grace—" murmured Vortipor, and then flushed as he realized he had spoken aloud. But no one else seemed to notice—he was saying no more than what they all felt, after all.

Guendivar completed the circle and brought the krater to Artor. "The blood of the grape is the blood of the land, and you, Pendragon, are its head—"

Artor's hands closed over hers on the krater, drawing her closer as he lifted it to his lips. His face bore an expression Betiver had never seen there before—he could not tell if it were joy or pain. Then he let go, looking up at her.

"As you are its heart, my queen . . ." he murmured. For a moment his eyes closed. When he opened them again his features had regained their usual calm. Now it was Guendivar in whose eyes Betiver saw pain. For a moment the queen bowed her head, then she lifted the krater once more and with the same gliding gait bore it out of the hall.

Slowly the murmur of conversation resumed, but the mood had changed. It reminded Betiver of something—abruptly he remembered rapt faces in the church of his boyhood when the icon of the Virgin had been carried around. His breath caught—was the thought sacrilege? A churchman might say so, but his heart told him that a power that was in its way as holy as anything blessed by the church had rested upon the queen as she moved through the hall.

But Artor was speaking—

"In my own name, also, I bid you welcome. We have much to discuss, and more to think on. The Saxons are beaten and for a time their oaths will hold them. We must plan how to use that time to keep them divided in heart and in territory, so that they do not combine against us again. We must plan also a new campaign against the men of Eriu who have seized land in Demetia, and bring it once more under British rule. But these tasks, however pressing, are only a beginning. For too long, force has been our only governor—if we wish to restore the security we knew under the Romans, we must return to the rule of law."

Betiver shifted his weight as Artor's opening speech continued. If he had stayed at home in Gallia, he thought, he might have been addressing such a meeting in his own father's hall. But like Gualchmai, he had chosen to remain in Britannia and serve Artor.

In the afternoon Artor released the members of the council to rest, to think on the matters he had set before them, and to seek exercise. Betiver offered to guide some of the younger men around the countryside, and when he met them at the horse pens, he found that Guendivar, dressed for riding, was waiting too. Her presence might inhibit some of their speech, but she would not impede their exercise. He knew already that she could ride as well as any man. And if the princes were dubious—he smiled quietly—they were in for a surprise.

Certainly the girl who leaped unassisted to the back of the white mare Artor had given her was a very different creature from the image of sovereignty who had brought them wine in the hall. For riding, Guendivar wore breeches and a short tunic. Only the linen cloth that bound her hair showed her to be a woman, and the embroidered blue mantle pinned at the shoulder, a queen.

When they were mounted, it was she who led the way. Indeed, thought Betiver as he brought up the rear, she could have guided the visitors with no help from him. But as he watched her laugh at some word of Peretur's, or smile at young Vortipor, he realized that it was not her safety, but her reputation, he would be guarding today.

At the bottom of the steep hill, Guendivar reined in. They had departed through the gate on the northeast side of the hill, past the well. From its base, the road ran straight towards the little village that had grown up in the days when the only structure on the hill was the shrine. The queen's mare snorted and shook its head and she laughed.

"Swanwhite wants to stretch her legs!" She gestured towards the village. "Do you think you can catch her if we run?"

By the time they arrived at the village, both horses and riders were quite willing to keep to a more leisurely pace. Guendivar's head wrap had come off and her hair tumbled down her back in a tangle of spilled gold. Her cheeks were flushed, her eyes bright. She looked, thought Betiver, twice as alive as the woman who had stood beside Artor in the council hall, and he felt an odd pang in the region of his heart.

They ambled through the spring green of the countryside, talking. In the warmth of her presence, Vortipor and the other princes lost all their shyness. The air rumbled with their deep laughter. *She is charming them,* thought Betiver. *Artor should be pleased.*

Vortipor told them a long story about hunting stag in the mountains of Demetia, and Peretur countered with a tale of a bear hunt in the dales west of Eboracum. Everyone, it seemed, had some tale of manly prowess—vying with words, the young men strutted and pranced like stallions before a mare. It was Ebicatos, the Irishman who commanded the garrison at Calleva, who protested that the queen must be becoming bored by all these stories of blood and battle, though Betiver had seen no sign of it in her face. But when the Irishman praised her white mare for winning the race to the village, and began the tale of the Children of Lir, who had been transformed by a jealous stepmother into swans, Guendivar listened with parted lips and shining eyes.

Their ride brought them around in a wide half-circle to the southwest. When the hill loomed before them once more, they slowed. The young men gazed at it in amazement. It did not seem possible they had come all this way so quickly, but the sun, which had reached its zenith when they set out, was well along in its downward slide.

The evening session of the council would be beginning. Merlin had returned from his most recent wanderings, and tonight he would report on what he had seen. That should be more interesting than the endless debates they had been listening to, though it would no doubt lead to more.

"Ah, lady," cried Vortipor, "I wish we did not have to return. I wish we could ride westward without stopping until we reached the sea, and then our horses would all become swans, to carry us to the Isles of the Hesperides!"

"The Isles of the Blessed, the Isle of Fair Women, and the Isle of Birds—" murmured Ebicatos.

"There is no need, surely, when the fairest of all women is here with us on this hallowed isle," said Peretur. He caught her outstretched hand and kissed it fervently.

Betiver's breath caught as Guendivar's beauty took on an intensity that was almost painful. Then she shook her head and bitterness muted her radiance like a cloud hiding the sun.

"And here I must stay—" A sudden dig of the heels sent her mare curvetting forward. Startled to silence, the others followed.

What is this that I am feeling? Betiver asked himself as they began to climb the hill. *My sweet Roud is a good woman, and I love her and my son . . .*

The red-headed Alban girl whom he had tumbled in the inebriation of the Feast of Lugus eleven years before had been an unexpected mate, but a good one. It was a soldier's marriage, unblessed by the Church, but recorded by the clerks of Artor's army. But the contentment Roud brought him had nothing in common with the painful way his heart leaped when he looked at Guendivar. A glance at the other men told him that they felt the same. They would serve her—they would die for her— with no hope of any reward beyond a word or a smile.

She is Venus—the remnants of a Classical education prompted him—*and we are her worshippers. And that is only fitting, for she is the queen.* But as they clattered beneath the gatehouse he wondered why, with such a woman in his bed, did the king seem to have so little joy?

Artor is not happy. . . . Merlin glanced at the king from beneath his bushy brows and frowned. Seated on the king's right hand, he could not look at him directly, but the evidence of his eyes only confirmed what other senses had been telling him.

Artor was paler than he had been, and thickening around the middle—those changes were a natural result of sitting so much in council chambers and eating well. But there was something haunted about his eyes.

It was not the council, which was going as well as such things ever did. It had become clear that Roman order would never return to Britannia until Roman law ruled once more. The princes must learn to think of themselves as *rectors,* and their war-leaders as *duces,* the generals of the country. Those who had ruled as chieftains had to become judges and magistrates, deriving their power from rector and emperor once more. Thus, and in this way only, could they separate their civilization from the ways of the barbarians.

To Merlin, longing for his northern wilderness, they were both equally constricting, but he had been born to serve the Defender of Britannia, and with him, its Law. Artor's attempts to restore the old ways even looked as if they might be successful. He should have been, if not triumphant, at least well pleased. Something was wrong, and Merlin supposed it was his duty to try and set it right. The thought made him tired, and he yearned to be back in the forest and the undemanding society of the wild folk who lived there. One day, he thought then, he would seek those green mysteries and not return.

The tone of the voices around him changed and he brought his awareness back to the present. The discussion of titles and duties was coming to a close.

"That is well, then, and we can move to the next topic," said Artor. "The Saxons. Merlin has been going among them—they seem to respect him as a holy man—and I believe we can benefit from his observations."

Merlin's lips twitched. He had wandered through the territory of the enemy in times past in safety, protected by their respect for those they thought old or mad. Their response to him now was different, and he knew why.

As if the thought had awakened it, he felt a throb of force from the rune-carved Spear that leaned against his chair, and the familiar pressure in his mind, as if Someone were listening. The head of the Spear was shrouded in silk, and a wrapping of leather thongs hid the runes carved into the shaft, but it still carried the power of the god Woden, and when Merlin came to a Saxon farmstead, holding that staff and with his long beard flying and an old hat drawn down over his eyes, he knew whom they believed him to be.

Merlin got to his feet and moved to the central hearth, leaning on the Spear. Artor straightened, eyes narrowing, as if something within him scented its power. Or perhaps it was the Sword at his side that had recognized another Hallow. Once, the god of the Spear had fought the one that lived in the Sword, but now they seemed to be in alliance. He must explain to Artor what had happened, one day.

But for now, he had to tell these British leaders what he had seen in the Saxon lands.

"In Cantium, the lady Rigana has gathered a council of thanes to advise her. The child, Oesc's son, is healthy, and the men seem very willing to support an extended regency. Many of their young warriors died at Mons Badonicus. They have sufficient men to defend the coasts against small groups of raiders, but I do not believe they will be a danger to us until at least another generation is grown."

"That is all very well," said Catraut, "but what about the Saxons of the south and west?"

"Aelle is an old man—" said Merlin. *My age, but Mons Badonicus broke him. . . .* "He will not ride to war again. And Ceretic's son is little more than a boy. Even if he should seek vengeance, it is clear that his father's thanes will not support him."

"And the Anglians?" asked Peretur.

"There also, for different reasons, I see no danger," said Merlin, and began to lay out his analysis of Icel's position as sacred king, and the reasons why the oath he had given Artor would continue to bind him.

"Separate, these tribes do not present a danger. It is my counsel that you choose brave men to settle the lands that lie between their holdings. So long as the Saxons perceive their portions as tribal territories, they will find it hard to combine. They may hold half Britannia, but they will not see it that way, and so long as you, my lords, remain united, you will be the stronger."

Even Cataur of Dumnonia could see that this was good counsel. Merlin resumed his seat as the princes of Britannia began to debate which borderlands should be resettled, and where they would find the men.

That night, after everyone had eaten, Merlin walked along the sentryway built into the wall, troubled in his mind. While they feasted, he had watched Artor, seated at the central table with his lady beside him. The king should have been smiling, for the council had gone well that day. With a wife like Guendivar, he should have been eager to retire. But though Artor's body showed his awareness of her every movement, they did not touch, and his smiles did not reach his eyes. And when the queen made her farewells and departed into the royal chamber that was partitioned off from the main part of the hall, the king remained talking with Eldaul and Agricola by the fire.

A full moon was rising, its cool light glittering from the open water of pond and stream, and glowing softly in the mist that rose off the fields. The distant hills seemed ghostly; in that glimmering illumination, he could not tell if it was with the eyes of the flesh or of the spirit that he saw, away to the northwest, the pointed shape of the Tor.

Merlin had been standing there for some time, drinking in peace as a thirsty man gulps water, when he sensed that he was no longer alone. A pale shape moved along the walkway, too graceful to be any of the men. The White Phantom, that was one meaning of her name . . . Guendivar. . . .

He drew his spirit entirely into his body once more and took a step towards her. She whirled, the indrawn gasp of her breath loud in the stillness, and pressed her back against the wall.

"It is true, you *can* make yourself invisible!"

"Not invisible, only very still. . . . I came to enjoy the peace of the night," he answered, extending his awareness to encompass her, smiling a little as the tension left her body and she took a step towards him.

"So did I . . ." she said in a low voice.

"I thought you would have been in bed by now, with your husband—"

She jerked, staring. "What do you mean? What do you know?"

"I know that all is not well between you. I know that you have no child . . ." he said softly.

She straightened, drawing dignity around her, and he felt her barriers strengthening.

"You have no right—" Her voice shook.

"I am one of the guardians of Britannia, and you are the High Queen. What is wrong, Guendivar?"

"Why do you assume the fault is mine? Ask Artor!"

He shook his head. "The power passes from male to female, and from female to male. You are the Lady of Britannia. If the difficulty is his, still, the healing must come from you."

"And I suppose the knowledge of how to do that will come from *you*? You flatter yourself, old man!" She turned, watching him over her shoulder.

Her hair was silver-gilt in the light of the moon. Even he, who had admitted desire for only one mortal woman in his lifetime, felt a stirring of the senses. But he shook his head.

"The body serves the spirit," he said steadily. "It is in the spirit that I would teach you."

"Tell the woman who wounded Artor to help him! Let him seek healing from the mother of his son! Then, perhaps, he can come to me!"

In the instant that shock held him still she flowed into motion. For a few moments he heard the patter of her retreating footsteps, and then she was gone. Even then, a word of power could have held her, but to such work as he would bid her, the spirit could not be constrained.

Igierne had foreseen this. But she had not seen the mother, only the child. The child would bring war to Britannia, but its mother had already struck a heavy blow. Who was she? In one thing, Guendivar had the right of it, he thought then. He must speak to Artor.

The fortress had been closed up for the night, but the guard on duty at the north gate was a very young man, and half in love with his queen, so he let her through. *They are all in love with me!* Guendivar thought bitterly. *All except the only one I am allowed to love.*

Stumbling in her haste, she made her way down the trail to the well. A pale shape swooped across the path and she started and nearly fell. For a moment she stared, heart pounding, then relaxed as she saw that it was only a white owl. On such a night, when the sky was clear and the full moon sailed in triumph through the skies, she felt stifled indoors. Even Julia's warm arms were a prison, where she stifled beneath the weight of the other woman's need.

Guendivar had thought a walk on the walls would allow her spirit to soar as freely as the bird, but Merlin was before her. What had she said to him? Surely he, who knew everything, must have known about Artor. The old sorcerer had offered her help—for a moment she wondered if she had been a fool to flee.

But how could a change in *her* do any good? The sin was Artor's, if sin it was—certainly he seemed to think so. He had attempted to be a husband to her two times after that first disastrous encounter, with even less success than on their wedding night. After that, they had not tried again. He was kind to her, and in public gave her all honor, but in the bed that should have been the heart and wellspring of their marriage, they slept without touching, proximity only making them more alone.

Guendivar knew this path well, but she had never been here in the night. In the uncertain light, the familiar shapes of the lower ramparts swelled like serpent coils. Beneath the melancholy calling of the owl she could hear the sweet music of running water. Everywhere else, the trees had been cut to clear a field of fire from the the walls of the fortress, but halfway down the hill, birch trees still clustered protectively around the spring.

Guendivar had never visited the hill until Artor began to build his fortress there, but the people of her father's lands had many tales of the days when it had been a place of pilgrimage. When the lords of Lindinis became Christian they had ceased to support the shrine, and after its last priestess died, the square building with its deep porch had fallen into decay. Now its tumbled stones were part of Artor's walls.

But the sacred spring from which the priestesses had drawn water to use in their spells of healing remained, bubbling up from the depths beneath the hill to form a quiet pool. The stone coping that edged it was worn, but the spout that channeled the overflow had remained clear. From there, it fell in a musical trickle down the hillside in a little stream. Moonlight, filtering through the birch trees, shrouded pool and stone alike in dappled shade.

Guendivar blinked, uncertain, in that glamoured illumination, of her way. The old powers had been banished from the hilltop, but here she could still feel them. She stretched out her arms, calling as she had called when she ranged the hills at home. Gown and mantle weighted her limbs; she stripped them off and unpinned the heavy coils of her hair. She stretched, exulting in the free play of muscle and limb. A little breeze lifted the fine strands and caressed her naked body, set the birch leaves shivering until the shifting dappling of moonlight glittered on the troubled waters of the pool.

Light swirled above it like a mist off the waters, shaping the form of a woman, clad, like Guendivar, only in her shining hair.

"Who are you?" Guendivar whispered. She was accustomed to the folk of faerie, but this was a being of nobler kind than any she had met before.

"*I am Cama, the curve of the hill and the winding water. I am the sacred round. It has been long . . . very long . . . since any mortal called to Me. . . . What is your need?*"

Guendivar felt her skin pebble with holy fear. The new faith had not yet succeeded in banishing the old wisdom so completely that she could not recognize the ancient goddess of this part of the land. But her cry had been wordless. She struggled for an answer.

"The water flows—the wind blows—but I am bound! I want to be free!"

"*Free . . .* " The goddess tested the sound as if she did not quite understand. "*The waters flow downhill to the sea . . . heat and cold drive the currents of the wind. They are free to follow their natures. Is that what you desire?*"

"And what is my nature? I am wed, but no wife!"

"*You are the Queen . . .* "

"I am a gilded image. I have no power—"

"*You* are *the power . . .* "

Guendivar, her mouth still opening in protest, halted, almost understanding. Then the owl called, and the insight was gone. She saw the figure of the Lady dislimning into a column of glimmering light.

"Help me!" she cried. She heard no answer, but the figure opened its arms.

Shivering, Guendivar climbed over the coping and stepped into the pool. Soft mud gave beneath her feet and she slid into the cold depths too swiftly for a scream. Water closed over her head, darkness enclosed her. *This is death,* she thought, but there was no time for fear. And then she was rushing upwards into the light. Power swirled around her, but she was the center of the circle—*being* and *doing,* the motion and her stillness, one and the same.

In this place there was no time, but time must have passed, for presently, with no sense of transition, Guendivar found herself experiencing the world with her normal senses once more. The moon had moved a quarter of the way across the sky, and its light no longer fell full on the pool. She was standing, streaming with water, but the bottom of the pool was solid beneath her feet.

She felt empty, and realized that what had departed from her was her despair. Perhaps this serenity would not last, but she did not think she would ever entirely forget what she had seen.

VII

THE WOUNDED KING

A.D. 498

 Guendivar huddled next to the hearth of the house the king's household had commandeered, listening to the hiss of the fire and the dull thud of rain on the thatching. If she sat any closer, she thought unhappily, she would catch fire herself, but her back still felt damp even when her front was steaming.

None of the other dwellings in this village were any better. She pitied the men of Artor's army, shivering in the dubious shelter of tents made of oiled hide as they cursed the Irish. The euphoria of their great victory at Urbs Legionis—the city of legions that was also called Deva—had worn away. Illan, king of the men of Laigin who had settled in northern Guenet a generation ago, was on the run, but he was going to make the British fight for every measure of ground between Deva and the Irish Sea.

She laid another stick on the fire, wondering why she had been so eager to accompany Artor on this campaign. For most of the past week it had been raining, grey veils of cloud dissolving into the silver sea. With each day's march, the stony hills that edged the green pasturelands had grown nearer. Now they rose in a grim wall on the left, broken by an occasional steep glen from which shrieking bands of Irishmen might at any moment emerge to harry the army that was pushing steadily westward along the narrowing band of flat land between the mountains and the sea.

Artor was up ahead somewhere with the scouts. It had been foolish to think that their relationship might improve if she accompanied him. The king spent his days in the saddle, returning tired, wet, and hungry when night fell, usually escorting wounded men. Artor had not wanted to bring her, but during their brief courtship he had said she could ride with the army, and she had sworn she would neither complain nor slow them down.

There was no risk of the latter, Guendivar thought bitterly, since she travelled with the rearguard. As for complaining, so far she had held her tongue, but she knew that if she had to stay cooped up in this hut for much longer she was going to scream.

With that thought, she found that she was on her feet and turning towards the door. She pushed past the cowhide that covered it and stood beneath the overhang of the roof, breathing deeply of the clean air. It was damp, heavy with mingled scents of wet grass and seaweed. Mist still clung to the hilltops, but a fresh wind was blowing, and here and there a stray gleam of sunlight spangled the sea.

It might only be temporary, but the skies were clearing. Guendivar gazed longingly at the slopes whose green grew brighter with every moment. Surely, she told herself, they could not be entirely different from the gentle hills of her home. Some of the same herbs would grow there, plants that her old nurse had taught her to use in healing. . . .

The young soldier who had been assigned to her personal escort straightened as she came out into the open. His name was Cau, one of the men who had come down from the Votadini lands with Marianus. There was some tension between the followers of Marianus and Catwallaun, both grandsons of the great Cuneta, though Catwallaun's branch of the family had been settled in Guenet a generation before. Many of the newcomers resented being set to guard the rear of the army, but Cau had attached himself to Guendivar's service with a dedication reminiscent of those monks who served the Virgin Mary. He had left a wife back in Deva with their infant son, Gildas, but he still flushed crimson whenever Guendivar smiled.

"Look—it has stopped raining." She stretched out a hand, palm upward, and laughed. "We should take advantage of the change in weather. I would ride a little way into those hills to gather herbs for healing."

Cau was already shaking his head. "My lord king ordered me to keep you safe here—"

"The king has also ordered that his wounded be cared for. Surely he would not object if I go out in search of medicines to help them. Please, Cau—" she gave him a tremulous smile "— I think I will go mad if I do not get some exercise. Surely all the enemy are far ahead of us by now!"

Cau still looked uncertain, but he and his men were as frustrated by their inaction as she was. She suppressed a smile, knowing even before he spoke that he was going to agree.

After the stink and smoke of the hut, to be out in the fresh air was heaven. When the grasslands began to slope upward, they dismounted, and Guendivar wandered over the meadow searching for useful herbs while Cau followed with a basket and the other men sat their horses, grinning in their beards.

Guendivar made sure she found enough herbs among the grasses to justify the expedition. She picked the five-lobed leaves of Lady's Mantle and Self-heal with its clustered purple trumpets, both good for cleansing wounds. As they wandered farther, she glimpsed the creamy flowers and tooth-shaped leaves of Traveller's Joy, whose bark made an effective infusion for reducing fever, and Centaury, also good for fever, and for soothing the stomach and toning the system as well. Purging Flax went into the basket, and wild Marjoram to bathe sore muscles and reduce bruises.

It was a hard land, whipped by the sea winds, and nowhere did the useful plants grow in abundance, but by midafternoon they had nearly filled the basket. Her men had earned a rest, and Guendivar led them towards the musical trickle of water that came from a small ravine. The stream itself was hidden by a fringe of hazel and thorn, with a few straggling birch trees, but after all the running about she had been doing, its moist breath was welcome.

She had opened her mouth to tell Cau to bring the bread and cheese from her saddlebags when a wild shriek and a crashing in the bushes brought her whirling around. From out of the brush men came leaping, brandishing spears. There must have been fifty of them, against the dozen men of the queen's guard. Her escort spurred their mounts forward to meet them, but the ground was steep and broken; two horses went down and the others plunged as men ran towards them.

"Selenn! Run! Get help—" cried Cau. The last of the riders pulled up as the attackers surrounded the others, stabbing with their spears. In another moment he had hauled his mount's head around and was galloping down the slope.

Cau grabbed Guendivar's arm and thrust her down, standing over her with drawn sword. One enemy got too close and a sweeping swordstroke felled him, but a word from the leader directed the others towards the rest of her escort, and in minutes they were dead or captive, and the queen and her protector surrounded by leveled spears. Guendivar got to her feet, chin held up defiantly.

"You will be putting down your blade now, and none will harm you—" said the leader. An Irish accent, of course—but she had guessed that from the jackets and breeches of padded leather they wore.

"Artor will kill me . . ." muttered Cau, lowering his sword.

Guendivar shook her head. "It was my will, my responsibility—"

The enemy leader made a swift step forward, took the weapon and handed it to one of his men. He drew two lengths of thong from his belt and tied first Cau's and then Guendivar's hands.

"Come now, for we have far to go."

"You are mad," said the queen. "Release us, and perhaps Artor will not hunt you down."

"Lady, would you be refusing our hospitality?" He eyed her

appreciatively. "I'm thinking that your king will pay well to have you back again."

One of the spears swung purposefully towards Cau's back. The warrior's grin told her he would not hesitate to spear his captive, and Guendivar started forward, knowing that Cau must follow her.

"It is myself, Melguas son of Ciaran, that has the honor to be your captor," he said over his shoulder, teeth flashing in his russet beard. His hair was more blond than red, confined in many small braids bound and ornamented with bits of silver and gold. He led the way at a swift trot and it took all Guendivar's breath to keep up with him.

"It is Guendivar daughter of Leodagranus who has the misfortune to be your captive, and lord Cau, who commands my guards," she said when they paused for a moment at the top of the slope. The ravine deepened here, and in the shelter of the trees ponies were waiting, surefooted native beasts that could go swiftly on the rough terrain.

"And do you think we did not know it? For many and many a day we have been watching you." Melguas tipped back his head, laughing, and she saw the torque of silver that gleamed beneath the beard.

"A damned cheerful villain," murmured Cau, but Guendivar closed her eyes in pain. This had been no evil chance, but the enemy's careful plan, waiting only on her foolishness. She thought of the three men of her escort whom the Irish had left dead on the field and knew their blood was on her hands.

Darkness had fallen by the time they stopped at last, and they had covered many miles. Sick at heart and aching from the pony's jolting, Guendivar allowed Melguas to pull her off the horse and thrust her into a brush hut without protest. They left Cau to lie beside the fire, still bound, with a blanket thrown over him. It did no good to tell herself that Artor would be as wounded by the loss of any of his companions as by her capture—none of *them* could have been taken so easily.

That night she huddled in the odorous blankets in silent misery. How long, she wondered, before Selenn reached the rearguard and told his tale? How long for another messenger to get to Artor? By the time he could send men to her rescue, the rain she heard pattering on the brush would have wiped out their trail. *Perhaps he will think himself well rid of me. . . .* She contemplated the prospect of an endless captivity with sour satisfaction. She was glad now that Julia had been left behind in Camalot, so that she was not weighted by the burden of the sister's grief as well.

In the morning she was given a bowl of gruel and made to mount the pony once more. For most of the day they moved steadily, following the hidden paths through the hills. Here in the high country, the wind blew cold and pure, as if it had never passed through mortal lungs; an eagle, hanging in the air halfway between the earth and the sun, was the only living thing they saw. When Guendivar expressed surprise that the Irish should know these paths, Melguas laughed.

"My father is a prince in the land of Laigin, but 'tis here I was born and I am on speaking terms with every peak and valley."

As I am in the Summer Country, Guendivar thought then, wishing she were there now. "Are you taking me to King Illan?" she asked aloud.

"Surely—better than a wall of stone to protect us is the lovely body of Artor's queen."

"Do not be so certain," Guendivar said grimly.

"How not?" Melguas looked at her in surprise. "Are you not the White Lady, with the fertility of the land between your round thighs and its sovereignty shining from your brow?"

Not for Artor, thought Guendivar, but she would not betray him by saying so. These Irish seemed so confident of her value— what magic did queens have, there in Eriu, that these exiled sons should hold them in such reverence? Melguas had forced her obedience, but neither he nor his men had dared to offer her either insult or familiarity. *This is what Merlin was trying to tell me,* she thought then, *but I must be a fraud as well as a failure, for there is something missing within me that prevents me from becoming truly Artor's queen!*

That night they slept wrapped in cloaks beneath rude brush shelters. In the middle of the night, Guendivar felt the need to relieve herself and crawled out from the shelter, shivering as the chill touched her skin. The privy trench had been dug a little down the slope. When she was finished, she stood, gazing at the black shapes of the mountains humped against the stars. If this had been her own country, she would have tried to slip away in the darkness, but she did not know this land, and besides, Melguas was a careful commander, and though she could not see them, there would be guards.

She turned, and as if the thought had summoned him, saw a dark man-shape rising out of the rocks.

"Ah, lady, you are cold—let me make you warm—"

It was Melguas, but something within her had already known it. With a sense of inevitability, she felt his hands close on her shoulders, the scent of male sweat as he pulled her against him and kissed her mouth.

"I am a queen—" she whispered when he released her at last. "Is this how you respect me?" But her heart was thumping in her breast, and she had not wanted him to let her go.

"It is—as I would serve the land herself, had she a body I could worship . . ." The soft Irish voice was trembling, but his grip was firm.

I must stop this, Guendivar told herself as he pulled her close once more, his hands reverent on her skin. But if she cried out, no one would help her—there would only be more witnesses to her shame. His hand moved to her breast, and she swayed, all her frustrated sensuality asserting its claim. He laughed then, sensing her body yielding, and bore her to the shelter of a stony outcrop and on the soft grass laid her down.

Pressed against the earth by the weight of Melguas' body, the queen had no power of resistance. And at the moment of fulfillment, it seemed to her as if she *was* the earth, opening ecstatically to receive his love.

Guendivar woke, shamed and aching, to a soft drizzle that continued throughout the day. She drew her shawl over her head, peering at the faces of the warriors. But there were no sly looks or secret smiles, and if Melguas looked triumphant, her capture was excuse enough. Perhaps her secret was secure. She wondered if Cau suspected. Their captors had left him bound all night, and he must be feeling even worse than she was. He sat his pony without complaining, but he no longer smiled.

The cloud cover was beginning to darken when Melguas drew rein.

"Illan's camp lies yonder—" He gestured towards the next fold in the hills, and it seemed to Guendivar, accustomed after two days to the cold silences of the heights, that she could hear a distant murmur like a river in flood. "If you wish it, we will be stopping for a moment so that you may dress your hair and brush your garments and appear before my lord as a queen." There was a familiar warmth in his gaze.

Guendivar stared at him. Riding with Artor's men, she had packed away her royal ornaments so that they would think of her as a sister and comrade. After two days in the saddle, she must look like one of the women who followed the army, her face grimed and bits of brush tangled in her hair. *If all my jewels cannot make me a real queen, how will it serve if I tidy my hair?*

Melguas was waiting. Guendivar's mother had been constantly carping at her to at least *pretend* she was a lady. Why should this be any different? For three years now she had been pretending to be a queen. What had happened to her last night should have destroyed even the pretense of legitimacy, but her captor's belief compelled her. She took the comb the Irishman held out to her and began to untangle her braids.

Through the veil of her hair she could see the light in Melguas' eyes become a flame of adoration. As the red-gold strands blew out upon the wind the other men stared; even Cau had straightened in the saddle, watching with some of his old worship in his eyes. Their faces were mirrors in which she saw the reflection of a queen. She slowed, drawing out each stroke of the comb with intention, drawing from the men who watched her the power to become what they needed her to be.

And in that moment, when the attention of her captors was focused on her beauty, riders burst suddenly over the rim of the hill and the warcry of the Pendragon echoed against the sky.

Gualchmai was in the lead, as big and barbaric as any of the

Irishmen. Melguas made a grab for Guendivar's rein, but she recovered from the first shock of recognition in time to boot her pony into motion. She dropped the comb and grabbed for the pony's mane as the beast leaped into a jolting canter, managing to collect the reins herself in time to stop the animal before it ran away with her.

By this time Melguas and Gualchmai were trading blows, the clangor of steel assaulting the trembling air. She glimpsed Betiver and Cai and Gualchmai's brothers—Christ! Artor had sent all his Companions! And then she realized that he had not sent but led them, that the big man in silver mail and the spangenhelm that hid his features was Artor himself, charging into battle like the Great Bear.

She had never before seen Artor in combat. Gualchmai fought with more gleeful ferocity, Betiver with more precision, but Artor faced his foes with a grim intensity she had not observed in any other man, the Chalybe blade falling like the stroke of doom on any fighter who dared to face him.

Is this for me, wondered Guendivar, *or for his honor? Or for the sake of that imaginary being, the High Queen?*

Just as the Irishmen had overmatched her escort, they were overwhelmed by Artor's Companions, even though they outnumbered them. In a few moments, it seemed, her captors were dead or fleeing, except for Melguas himself, who was still holding off Betiver and Aggarban, laughing. But they fell back when Artor finished off his last opponent and strode towards them, his bloody sword poised.

"Not worthy of her—" Melguas said breathlessly, "but I see . . . you are an honorable man!"

Silently, Artor settled into a fighter's crouch, every line in his body expressing deadly purpose. Melguas' eyes narrowed, as if he had only now begun to appreciate the caliber of his enemy, and he braced his feet, lifting his sword. For a long moment, neither man stirred. Then, as if at some unspoken signal, both fighters blurred into action. The swords moved too swiftly for her eye to follow, but when the two figures separated, Artor was still upright, and Melguas was falling, a red gash opening like a flower across his belly and breast.

Guendivar let out a breath she had not known she was holding in a long sigh. Melguas lay where he had fallen, chest heaving in loud gasps as blood spread over his leather armor and began to drip onto the ground. She took a step forward, and then another, staring in appalled fascination at the wreck of the man who had made her captive.

"End it—" whispered Melguas. "You . . . have the best of me. . . ."

"My lord," Betiver started forward, dagger already drawn, "there is no need for you to soil your hands—"

Artor shook his head. "A good hunter always finishes off his kill." He took the dagger from Betiver and knelt beside his foe, laying his sword beside him on the ground.

Melguas twisted, his body contorting as if momentarily overcome by pain. Only Guendivar, coming closer, saw his fingers close on the hilt of the dagger strapped to his thigh. In the moment it took her mind to comprehend what her eyes had seen, Melguas jerked the weapon free and slashed upward beneath the hanging skirt of Artor's mail.

The king jerked away with a muffled oath.

"No good to her—" Melguas began, but Artor, his face suffused with fury, reeled forward, supporting himself on his left hand, and with his right plunged the dagger into his enemy's throat above the silver torque and tore sideways so that the Irishman's head flopped suddenly to the side, his eyes still widening in surprise.

Artor stared down at him, grimacing, then slowly collapsed to his side, blood spreading down the cloth of his breeches.

"Artor!" "My lord!" Gualchmai and Betiver cried out together as they reached his side. Carefully they stretched him out, dragging the mail aside. The dagger had torn the flesh of Artor's inner thigh and all the way up into the groin. The king made no sound, but his skin was paling, and his body quivered with the pain.

"He didn't get the artery—" murmured Betiver, peeling the cloth back from the wound. Blood was flowing steadily, but not in the red tide that no surgery could stop.

"Nor yet your manhood!" added Gualchmai, gripping Artor's shoulder. "Let it bleed for the moment—it will clean the wound. Do you lie now on your right side, and we'll get you out of this mail."

Guendivar's fists were clenched in her skirts, but these men knew more of wounds and armor than she. There was nothing she could do until they had got off sword belt and mail shirt and cut away his breeches and were looking for cloth with which to stanch the wound.

After three days in the saddle, her own clothes were none too clean, but she had more, and softer, fabric about her than anything the Companions had to offer. She hauled up her skirts and cut half the front of her shift away, folding it into a pad which she bound across the wound with her veil.

"You will have to make a litter," she told the men. "He cannot ride this way."

"Aye, and swiftly," agreed Gualchmai, "before the bastards that got away are bringing Illan down on us to finish the job."

"Betiver . . . you will lead the army—" whispered Artor as the men began to hack at a young oak tree that clung to the side of the hill. "Take most of the men and head straight for the coast. Pursuit should . . . follow you."

"And what of you, my lord?" Betiver kept his voice steady, but his face was nearly as pale as Artor's own.

"Gualchmai will take . . . me to the Lake . . . to Igierne."

"I will go with you," Guendivar said firmly. Artor, who had not met her gaze since she bandaged his wound, said nothing, and as she stared down the others, she realized that at least for this moment, she was queen in truth as well as name.

When her women came to tell her that a messenger had arrived, Morgause was not surprised—galloping hooves had haunted her dreams. The rider was the man she had sent to be her eyes and ears in Artor's army. As she recognized him, she felt something twist painfully in her belly, and that did surprise her.

"What is it?" she asked, controlling her voice. "Has something happened to the king?"

"He is not dead, my lady," the man said quickly. "But he is wounded, too badly to continue the campaign. He has left Betiver in command."

"Not Gualchmai?" Morgause frowned.

"Your son is with Artor. They are progressing by slow stages northward—no one would say where or why."

"To the Lake—" Morgause said thoughtfully, "that has to be their destination. His wound must be serious indeed, if he goes to my mother for healing."

To Igierne, and to the Cauldron, she added silently, fists clenching in the skirts of her gown. Was the injury so severe, or had Artor seized the excuse to gain access to the Cauldron's mysteries?

"What is the nature of the wound?" she asked then.

"I do not know for certain," said the spy. "He is not able to ride. They say—" he added in some embarrassment "—that the king is wounded in the thighs . . ."

Morgause stifled a triumphant smile. The queen had borne Artor no child. Whether that was because the words she gave to each of them at their wedding had cursed their bed, or it was the will of the gods, she did not know. But if the king was injured in his manhood, it might be long before he could try again to beget an heir. Gualchmai was known to everyone as Artor's sister-son, the bravest of his Companions. Britannia would find it easy to accept him as the king's heir. And if he refused the honor, she still had Medraut. . . .

"You did well to bring me this news." Morgause paused, considering the messenger. He was called Doli, a man of the ancient race of the hills. In feature he was fine-boned and dark, devoted to her service by rites of the old magic. Some years earlier she had arranged for his sister to enter the community of priestesses on the Isle of Maidens.

"Now I have another task for you," she said then. "I wish you to ride to the Lake and pay a visit to your sister. If, as you say, the king's party is moving slowly, you may be there and gone before ever he arrives."

"And when I am come?" Doli lifted one dark eyebrow inquiringly.

"You will give her the flask I shall send with you, and a message. But this, I dare not commit to writing. I shall record it in your memory, and only when your sister Ia speaks the words, 'by star and stone' shall the message be set free.

"It is well—" Doli bowed his head in submission, then settled himself cross-legged on the floor, eyes closed and chest rising and falling in the ancient rhythm of trance.

When she sensed that his energy had sunk and steadied, Morgause called his spirit to attention by uttering his secret name. Then she began to chant the message that he must carry.

"Thus, the words of the Lady of Dun Eidyn who is called the Vor-Tigerna, the Great Queen, to Ia daughter of Malcuin. The priestesses will work the rite of healing for King Artor. Add the contents of the flask your brother shall give you to the water in the pool. When you do this, these are the words you must say: 'Thou art a stagnant pool in a poisoned land, a barren field and a fruitless tree. Thy seed shall fail, and thy sovereignty pass away. By the will of the Great Queen, so shall it be!' "

Morgause waited a moment, then spoke the ritual words to rouse Doli from his trance. Then she sent him off to be fed, and went herself to the hut where she prepared her herbs and brewed her medicines to distill a potion strong enough to counter the power of the Cauldron and all her mother's magic as well.

Asleep, Artor was so like Uthir that Igierne felt the pain of it in her breast each time she looked at him. Perhaps it was because he was ill, and the image of how her husband had appeared in his last years was still vivid in Igierne's memory. But Artor was only thirty-four, and she would not let him die. Even asleep his face showed the lines that responsibility had graven around his mouth and between his brows, and there were more strands of silver in the brown hair.

They had put the king to bed in the guest chamber of the Isle of Maidens, where a fresh breeze off the lake could blow through the window, bearing with it the scent the sun released from the pines. From time to time Artor twitched, as if even in sleep his wound pained him. The Irishman's blade had sliced through the muscles of the inner thigh and up into the groin, but it had not, quite, penetrated the belly. Nor had it cut into his scrotum, although the slash came perilously close. The great danger now was wound fever, for the rough field dressing had done little more than stop the bleeding, and during the jolting journey north the wound had become inflamed.

She leaned forward to stroke the damp hair off of his brow and felt the heat of fever, though it seemed to her that the strong infusion of willow-bark tea she had given Artor when he arrived had begun to bring the burning down. When he was a little rested, they would have to cleanse the wound and pack it with a poultice of spear-leek to combat the infection. As if in anticipation of the pain, Artor twisted restlessly, muttering, and she bent closer to hear.

"Guendivar . . . so beautiful. . . ." That he should call his wife's name was to be expected, but why was there such anguish in his tone? "Did he touch her? Did he . . . I have no right! It was my sin. . . ."

Frowning, Igierne dipped the cloth into the basin of cool water and laid it once more on his brow. She knew that Artor had been wounded by the Irishman who abducted the queen, but Guendivar swore she had not been harmed. Why was he babbling about sin?

"Be easy, my child . . ." she murmured. "It is all over now and you are safe here. . . ."

He shook his head, groaning, as if even in his delirium his mother's words had reached him. "She told me . . . I have a son. . . ."

Igierne sat back, eyes widening. "Who, Artor?" her voice hardened. "Whose son?"

"Morgause . . ." came the answer. "Why should she hate me? I didn't know. . . ."

"It is all right . . . the sin was not yours . . ." Igierne replied, but her mind was racing, remembering a sullen, red-headed boy sorting pebbles on a garden path. She had assumed the family resemblance came all from Morgause—but what if Medraut had a double heritage?

It was no wonder that Artor was fevered, if this knowledge was festering in his memory. It would not be enough to deal with the wound to his body—somehow, she would have to heal his soul.

The Lake was very beautiful, thought Guendivar, especially now, when the first turning leaves of autumn set glimmering reflections of gold and russet dancing in the water, and the tawny hills lifted bare shoulders against a sky that shone pure clear blue after the past days of rain. But after a week cooped up on the island with the priestesses, she felt as confined as she had with the army, and Gualchmai, who was camped with the other men in the meadow by the landing across from the island, had said he would be happy to escort her on a walk along the shore.

"If we are attacked," she said bitterly, "let them take me. I am not worth the lives of any more good men." Throughout that long ride northward, no one had accused her, no one suspected that she had lain in Melguas' arms. In the stress of the journey she had almost been able to forget it herself. But now, with nothing to do, the memory tormented her.

"Lady! You must not say it. You are the queen!" Gualchmai's voice held real pain.

She shook her head. "Igierne is the queen. On the way north Artor needed me, but I have neither the knowledge nor the magic to help him now."

"Nor do I, Guendivar—I would give my heart's blood if it would heal him, but I have no skill to fight the enemy he battles." Gualchmai's broad shoulders slumped.

Hearing the anguish in his voice, the queen found her own a little eased. She breathed in the spicy scent of fallen leaves and exhaled again in a long sigh, feeling tension go out of her. Leaves rustled with each footstep, and squirrels chittered to each other from the trees.

"But you fight his other foes," she said presently. "You are the bulwark of his throne."

"That is all I desire. I am happier on the field of battle than in the council hall. To deal with the bickering of the princes would drive me to blows within a year and plunge the land into civil war."

His tone had brightened, and Guendivar laughed.

"Surely the Lady of the Lake will make the king well again, and I will be spared the temptation," he said then. "She is a wise woman. And she has agreed to take my daughter as one of her maidens here."

"Your daughter! I did not know you had a child," exclaimed Guendivar.

"Until last year, I did not know it either," Gualchmai answered ruefully. "I got her on a woman of the little dark folk of the hills, one time I was out hunting and my pony went lame when I was yet far from home. She is as wild as a doe, but her hair is the same color as my own, and her mother died this past winter, so I must find her a home."

"What is she called?" asked the queen, finding it as hard to imagine Gualchmai a father as he did himself.

"Ninive—"

So Morgause is a grandmother! Does she know? wondered Guendivar, but she did not voice that thought aloud.

"Igierne will understand how to tame her," said Gualchmai. He stooped to pick up a spray of chestnuts brought down by the wind, and stripped off the prickly rind and the leathery shell before offering one to the queen. The nut inside was moist and sweet. "And she will make Artor well."

"She will," Guendivar echoed his affirmation. "His fever has been down for two days now, and they tell me that the wound is beginning to heal."

No man had ever entered the cave of the Cauldron, but in the dell below it, a basin had been hollowed out of the stone foundations of the island which could be filled with water for baths of purification or healing, and here, when there was great need, a man could come. It was large enough for several women to sit together or for a grown man to lie. Here, at dusk when the new moon was first visible in the evening sky, they brought Artor to complete his healing.

The Lady of the Lake sat on a bench at the head of the pool. It was set into the niche where the image of the Goddess had stood since the first priestesses came to the island. Or perhaps before—the image was fashioned from lead, bare-breasted above a bell-shaped skirt, in a style that had been ancient when the Romans came. A terra-cotta lamp cast a wavering light on the image. To Igierne, it seemed that She was smiling.

It would take many weeks before the king was entirely whole, but the wound had closed. For health to return, the balance of his body must be restored, and his bruised spirit persuaded to add its blessing. More lamps flickered around the pool, and the breeze from the lake brought with it the scent of woodsmoke from the fire where they were heating the water. Sometimes she longed for the natural hot springs of Aquae Sulis, and yet there was a more focused magic in the building of a fire and the brewing of the herbs that infused the water.

As the season turned towards autumn the nights were growing cold, but now, while the memory of the sun still glowed in the western sky, the air held the warmth of the afternoon. In the purple dusk the maiden moon hung like a rind of pearl. The air had the hush that comes with the end of day, but as Igierne listened, she began to perceive another sound. Her priestesses were singing as they escorted Artor along the path.

> *"Water of life, water of love—*
> *We come from the Mother and to*
> *Her we return . . ."*

Igierne got to her feet. As she raised her arms in welcome, the black folds of her sleeves fell back from her white arms. The silver-and-moonstone diadem of the high priestess was a familiar weight upon her brow.

> *"Water of healing flows from above,*
> *We come from the Mother. . . ."*

Two by two, the white-clad priestesses passed between the twin oak trees that guarded the pool, each carrying a vessel of water that steamed gently in the cooling air. The pairs separated to either side, kneeling to pour the contents of the basins into the bath, then rising and turning away to either side to return for more.

"Water of passage, water of birth . . ." the priestesses sang.

As the level of liquid grew, the scents of the herbs that had been steeped in it grew heavy in the air—various mints and camomile, rosemary and lavender, salvia and sweet woodruff and substances such as sea salt and powdered white willow that had little fragrance but great power.

Some of them they grew on the island, and some they gathered in the wild lands, and some were brought from afar. The fragrance was almost dizzying in its intensity. And yet, as Igierne breathed in, something seemed different from before, a hint of something spoiled. She took another breath, testing the air, but it was no scent she recognized. She wondered if it were physical at all, or if she was sensing some spiritual corruption. At the thought, her hands moved instinctively in the gesture used to ward and banish, and her awareness of the wrongness began to pass away.

"Water of blessing flows from the earth . . ."

She shook her head—perhaps it had been her imagination. She knew that with age her senses had become less dependable.

Now the bath was three-quarters full. Nest and Ceincair were coming through the gateway with Artor, wrapped in a green robe between them. He moved slowly, depending on the priestesses for support, but he was on his feet, though the beads of sweat stood out on his brow.

"We come from the Mother and to Her we return . . ." the women sang, and then were still.

The king and his escorts stopped at the edge of the pool.

"Child of the Goddess, why have you come here?" asked Igierne.

"I seek to be healed in body and in soul—" came Artor's answer. She held his gaze, hoping that it was true, for she had not been able to get from him, waking, an explanation of the words he had muttered in his fevered dream.

"Return, then, to the womb of the Mother, and be made whole."

The priestesses untied the cord and eased the robe from his shoulders. Face and arms were sallow where illness had faded his tan, but the rest of Artor's body was pale, growing rosy now as he realized he stood naked before nine women. But their gaze was impersonal, half tranced already by the ritual, and after a moment he regained his composure and allowed Nest and Ceincair to steady him as he descended the steps into the pool.

He halted again at the first level, as if surprised by the heat, then, biting his lip, continued downward until he stood in water halfway up his thighs, the mark of his injury livid against the pale skin. At the end of the bath there was a stone headrest.

When the priestesses had helped him all the way down, the headrest enabled him to lie half-floating, his body completely submerged.

The priestesses had settled themselves cross-legged around the pool, singing softly to invoke the healing powers of the herbs. From time to time one of them would fetch more water to maintain the heat of the bath. Gradually the tension faded from Artor's body. He lay with eyes closed, perspiration streaming from his face.

The singing continued as the night grew darker, gradually increasing in intensity. Igierne, who had been watching the gateway, saw first the pale figure appear within it, and then, as if some change in the air had aroused him, a sudden tension in the slack body of the king. He opened his eyes, and they widened as a light that transcended the blaze of the torches glowed around the shining robes of the priestess and the silver Cauldron in her arms.

The wonder remained as the maiden came fully into the light and he saw her dark hair, but the hope that had been there also was gone. Igierne understood. She had tried to persuade Guendivar to bear the Cauldron, and could not understand why the queen would not agree. Neither her son nor her daughter-in-law would share their secrets, but she understood now that Artor loved his queen. For a moment sorrow shook Igierne's concentration. Then the momentum of the ritual swept all other awareness away.

"Be reborn from the water of life!" her voice rang against the stones. "Be healed by the water of love!"

The priestess lifted the cauldron, and the hallowed water it held poured in a stream of light into the pool.

VIII

THE GREAT QUEEN

A.D. 500

 The skirling of bagpipes throbbed like an old wound in the chill spring air, so constant that one forgot it until a touch, or a memory, brought the pain of loss to consciousness once more. King Leudonus was dead, and the Votadini were gathering to mourn him. The great dun on the rock of Eidyn was filled with chieftains, and the gorge below crammed with the skin tents and brushwood bothies of their followers. Morgause, marshalling provisions and cooks for the funeral feast, settling quarrels over precedence and ordering the rituals, was too busy to question whether what she felt was grief, or relief that he was gone.

These past ten years she had been a nurse to him, not a wife, watching his strength fade until he lay like a ruined fortress, never leaving his bed. And as the rule of the Votadini had passed into her hands, Morgause had become not only the symbol of sovereignty, but its reality. In his day, Leudonus had been a mighty warrior, but in the end death had taken him from ambush, with no struggle at all. She had drawn aside the curtain that screened his bed place one morning and found him stiff and cold.

It was just as well, thought Morgause as Dumnoval and the southern Votadini chieftains came marching in, that grief did not overwhelm her, for upon the strength she showed now, her future here would depend. She had sent word to her sons who were with Artor, but she had little hope they would come. The spring campaign against those Irish who still clung to the coasts of Guenet and Demetia had just begun, and the king's nephews were among his most valued commanders.

Perhaps it was as well, for the fighting provided a credible excuse for Gualchmai's absence. As it was, she could pretend that only a greater duty kept him away, though it had long been clear to her just how little he cared for the lordship of his father's land. Nonetheless, just as her marriage to Leudonus had legitimated her authority, her status as mother to the heir might continue to do so, even when everyone knew his rule to be a fiction.

It was not, she thought as she offered the meadhorn to Dumnoval in welcome, as if she had not prepared for this day. There was scarcely a family in the land that had not cause to be grateful for food in a hard year, the loan of a bride-price to win a family alliance, gifts of weapons or cattle or honors. And so, as Dumnoval slid down off his pony, she greeted him as the Great Queen of Alba, receiving one of her men.

That evening she dressed in silk, its crimson folds glowing blood-red in the torchlight. Ornaments of amber and jet gleamed from her neck and wrists, amber drops swung from her ears. For some years now she had used henna to hide the silver in her hair, and kohl to emphasize her eyes. In the firelight, the marks that time and power had graven in her face were hidden. She was forever young, and beautiful. She passed among the benches, smiling, flattering, reminding them of her ties with the Picts and the benefits that a united Alba could bring, persuading them that they still needed her to be their queen.

The next morning, veiled, she walked behind Leudonus' bier, her son Goriat, who at seventeen towered like a young tree, on one side, and the thirteen-year-old Medraut, with his shining bronze hair and secret smile, on the other. Up from the Rock of Eidyn to the Watch Hill above it wound the procession, and then around the slope to the little lake on whose shores they had prepared the pyre. The ashes would be buried by the tribal kingstone below the ancient Votadini fortress, a day's journey to the southeast. It was here where the king had ruled that the Druids chanted their prayers and spells; and here, while the pipes wailed and the drums pounded heavy as heartbeats, that the holy fire released Leudonus' spirit to the winds.

That night the men drank to their dead king's memory while the bards chanted his deeds. The queen remained in the women's quarters, as was fitting. Morgause was grateful for the custom, for her woman's courses, which for several moons had been absent, had returned in a flood. She was lying in her bed, listening to the distant sounds of revelry and wondering whether she could sleep if she drank more mead, when she heard from the direction of the gate the sounds of a new arrival.

"My lady—" Dugech spoke from the door. "Are you still awake, Morgause?"

"Someone has come. I heard. Tell him to join the other drunkards in the hall—" she answered, lying back on her pillows again.

"But lady, it is your mother who is here!"

Morgause sat up, calculating swiftly the time it would have taken for a messenger to reach the Lake, and for Igierne to make the journey to Dun Eidyn. Did her mother have a spy here, as she herself did on the Isle of Maidens, or was it Ia, receiving the word from her brother, who had willingly or unwillingly let the high priestess know?

She swung her feet over the edge of the bed and reached for a shawl. Whatever the truth might be, she must suppress any reaction until she could find out why her mother was here.

Even the warmth of the firelight could not disguise the pallor of Igierne's skin, and Morgause was aware of an unexpected and surprisingly painful pang of fear. At times she had longed for the day when her mother would be gone and she should inherit her place on the Isle of Maidens. But not now, when she was battling to retain her hold on the Votadini. The idea that she might still long for her mother's love was a thought she could not allow.

"Bring us some chamomile tea, and show my mother's women where they will be sleeping," she told Dugech. Igierne had brought two priestesses whom Morgause did not know, an older woman and a dark-eyed girl with corn-colored hair, who were bringing in baskets and bundles.

"The burning was this morning. You missed it—" she said then. "Did you think I needed a shoulder to weep on? I am doing well. You did not have to make such a journey for my sake."

"Gracious as ever . . ." murmured Igierne, drinking from the cup of tea Dugech set before her. A little color began to return to her cheeks. "Perhaps I came to honor Leudonus."

"Since your son could not be bothered," said Morgause. "Or was Artor unable to come? I hear he has never quite recovered from his wounding two years ago, despite your attempts to heal him."

"He can ride—" Igierne answered, frowning. "Yet even if he could leave his army, the king would not have been here in time for the funeral. But I remember Leudonus in his youth, and even if you do not, I will mourn him. It was long since I had seen him, but he was one of the last men of Uthir's generation. The world is poorer for having lost him."

Morgause snorted and lifted a hand as men do to acknowledge a hit when they practice with swords. "Very well. But you cannot wonder that I am surprised to see you. We have not been close these past years."

"I will not quarrel with you regarding whose fault that is. I am too tired." Igierne set down her tea. "I had hoped that now you are a grandmother yourself, you might be able to put aside your resentment of me. . . ."

Morgause felt the color flood up into her face and then recede again. "What do you mean?"

"Gualchmai has a girl-child, did not you know? She is the daughter of some woman he met in the hills. She is twelve now. He sent her to me last year." At the words, the younger of her companions looked up, her eyes wide and dark as those of a startled doe. "Come, Ninive, and greet your grandmother—"

Seen close to, Ninive was obviously a child, gazing around her as if any sudden sound would send her bounding away. *A wild one, but I could tame her,* thought Morgause as the girl bent to kiss her hand. *Why did Gualchmai not give her to me?*

But at a deeper level, she knew. Her brother had stolen her two elder sons already, and now her mother was claiming the girl, the granddaughter that she could have trained as a priestess in a tradition older than anything in Igierne's mysteries. Igierne had been foolish to bring her here, or foolishly sure of her own power.

"You are very certain of her—" she said when Ninive had been sent off for more tea. "It is not an easy life, there on the island. What if the child wants a man in her bed and children at her knee? She ought to have the chance to choose—"

"Why do you think I brought her here?" Igierne replied, with that lift of the eyebrow that had always exasperated her daughter, so eloquent in its assumption of authority.

For a moment, Morgause could only stare. "How generous! Well, I will speak with Ninive after the assembly, and then we will see if she takes after you, or me.... But I can see why Gualchmai did not wish to bring a girl-child to Artor's court," she added reflectively.

"What do you mean?"

"My brother does not write to me, but others do," Morgause replied, "and there are many who say that the queen's bed is not empty, though Artor does not lie there."

"It is not so—" said Igierne, but Morgause suppressed a smile, seeing the uncertainty in her mother's eyes.

"Is it not? Well, I have no objection if Guendivar follows northern ways. If the king is not potent, it is up to the queen to empower the land."

"By taking lovers, as you have? Who fathered your sons, Morgause?"

Morgause laughed, having goaded her mother to a direct attack at last. "What man would dare to boast of having fathered a child on the queen, especially when it was not she with whom he lay, but the Goddess, wearing her form, and he himself possessed by the God? My children are more than royal, Mother, they are gifts of the gods!"

In the next moment she realized that this stroke had missed its mark. Igierne sat back and took another sip of tea.

"Ah—so that is how it came to pass. Beware, daughter, lest the gods call you to account for what you have made of their gifts to you."

Morgause frowned, aware of having revealed more than she meant to. But even if Igierne knew Medraut's parentage, what could she do? This child, at least, was her own, body and soul.

"You have had a long journey, Mother, and you must be weary," she said then. "And I must be fresh for tomorrow's assembly of the clans. Dugech will show you where you are to sleep." Morgause rose, summoning the woman who waited by the door. But despite her words, she herself tossed restlessly until the dawn.

Still, the gods had not abandoned her, for by the end of the council, the clans, while recognizing the claim of Dumnoval to lead the southern Votadini, and choosing Cunobelinus as warleader for the northern clans, had agreed that Morgause should continue to rule in Dun Eidyn as regent for Gualchmai. But Ninive chose to return to the Isle of Maidens with Igierne.

"They tell me that you are shaping well as a warrior." Morgause looked up at her fourth son as they stood on the guard path built into the rampart of Dun Eidyn. Goriat over-topped her by more than a head, and she was a big woman. Indeed, he towered over most men. She was not entirely certain who had fathered him, but as he grew it seemed likely that it was a man of Lochlann, who had come bringing furs and timber from the Northlands that lay eastward across the sea. She remembered the beauty of the trader's long-fingered hands.

"Men say that Gualchmai is the greatest warrior in Britannia. If I cannot surpass him, I have sworn to be the second." Goriat grinned.

"But are you the best fighter in Alba?" she asked then.

"I can take any man of the tribes—"

"South of the Bodotria," she corrected, "but you have not yet measured yourself against the men of the Pretani." Morgause gestured northward, where the lands of the Picts were blossoming in tender green beneath the sun.

Goriat shrugged. "If Artor fights them, I suppose I shall find out."

She looked up, startled by his tone. It was natural that he should think of following his brothers into his uncle's service, but she had not realized he considered it a certainty.

"Perhaps Artor will not have to fight them," she said carefully. "If one of his kindred is their warleader. . . . The Pretani have a princess of the highest lineage who is ripe for marriage. You know they seek outlanders to husband their royal women to avoid competition within the clans. They have sent a messenger, asking me for one of my sons. Marry the girl, and you will lead their armies and father kings."

"The Pretani!" Goriat exclaimed in revulsion.

"Alba!" Morgause replied. "If the Votadini and the Pretani make alliance, the north will be united at last!"

"And then may the gods pity Britannia!" He turned to face her, his long fingers curling into fists. "But it will not happen. If you think I will lend myself to this plot, Mother, you have gone mad. Play your games with Medraut, if you will, but I will stand on the other side of the board."

"You are an idiot without understanding," she hissed. "With one of my sons on the high seat of Britannia and my grandson on the sacred stone of the Pretani, we will rule this entire Hallowed Isle! You will go north, Goriat, or you will go nowhere! You think yourself a man and a warrior, but I am the Great Queen!"

Morgause turned and stalked away along the parapet, leaving him there. He was young and rebellious, but she held the purse-strings. His brothers had gone outfitted with arms and horses and servants as befitted their station, but her fourth son should have nothing until he agreed to do her will.

But the next morning, when she called for him, Goriat had disappeared.

For three days, Morgause raged. Then she began to think once more. For a time she considered sending Medraut to the Picts instead, but he was not yet a warrior, although in other areas he was precocious enough to give her concern. Yet even if he had been of an age to marry, Medraut had a different destiny. At heart, Morgause, like Goriat, held Britannia to be the greater prize, and of all her sons, Medraut was the one with the greatest right to it.

At Midsummer, the tribes of the north celebrated the sun's triumph by clan and district, making the offerings and feasting and blessing their cattle and their fields. Each year, it had been the custom of the queen to keep the festival with a different clan, but the summer after the death of Leudonus, she gave out that this year she would observe the holiday in seclusion, and her youngest son with her, in honor of her lord.

A few days before the solstice they set out east along the shore of the firth, towards a headland with a house to which Morgause had often retired when she needed to recuperate from the demands made on a queen. Her folk were accustomed to this, and there was no surprise when she dismissed all attendants except Dugech and Leuku. But none knew that the following evening a boat was beached on the shore below, whose crew spoke with Pretani tongues, or that it pushed off once more before the sun was in the sky, bearing the queen of the Votadini, her maid Dugech, and her son.

"Why does Leuku not come with us?" asked Medraut as the land grew dim behind them.

"She will keep a fire going in the house so that any who pass will believe we are all still there."

For a few moments he was silent. "Does that mean we will be gone for some time?"

"For a space of several days. It is time you saw how folk who have not abandoned the most ancient ways of our people keep the festival."

Medraut's eyes brightened as he realized that she was at last going to share with him the secret of her mysterious journeys.

At thirteen, he had reached an uneasy balance between boy and man. He would never, she thought, have the height and sheer muscular power of his brothers. But the size of his hands and feet promised growth, and even now, at a boy's most awkward age, he had an agility that should develop into uncommon speed and grace. Gualchmai and Gwyhir and Goriat possessed physical splendor, while Aggarban, when last she saw him, had been cultivating a dark truculence that was impressive in its own way. Her youngest son would have an elegance that verged on beauty. Already, when he chose to do so, Medraut knew how to charm.

And sexual maturity was coming early as well. She had seen him bathing with the other boys, and though the fuzz on his cheeks was not yet worth shaving, his man's parts were full sized, surrounded by a bush of red hair. Medraut had an eye for women already, and only the most dire of threats to her maidservants had preserved his virginity thus far. Morgause would have preferred that he hold on to that power, but since chastity was probably unattainable, she meant to channel the magic of Medraut's sexual initiation through ritual.

"And in what way, Mother, are the rites of the Pretani different from Votadini ways?"

From his expression, Morgause could tell that there was something strange about her answering smile. "There is more blood in them," she said softly, "and more power."

The current had been with them, and the northern shore was already near. On the beach, horsemen were waiting. Morgause felt her pulse begin to beat more strongly. She took a deep breath, scenting woodsmoke and roasted flesh on the wind.

They came to Fodreu in the evening when the sun, still clinging to his season of triumph, turned the smoke from a multitude of cookfires to a golden haze. Coming over the rim of the hill they could see the gleam of water where the Tava curved abruptly eastward. Just above the bend was a ferry, with rafts to take them across the swift-running stream, and then they were following the road along the far bank towards the royal dun. Drest Gurthinmoch had emerged victorious from the turmoil following the death of Nectain Morbet and married the queen. He reigned now over the Pretani of both north and south from a stout dun near the sacred grove that held the coronation stone.

But that was another mystery. Today, their way led to the wide meadow where a women's enclosure had been prepared for the honored guests of the Pretani queen. Here, Morgause parted from Medraut, with certain words of warning to the warrior assigned to escort him. Then she passed through the gateway where Tulach was waiting to escort her to the queen.

The inner enclosure had been hung with woolen cloths embroidered with sacred symbols. Behind the queen's high seat the hanging stirred in the draft, so that the red mare pictured upon it seemed to move. Above it were images of the comb and mirror, symbols of the Goddess who ruled both in this world and the next. The queen herself wore red garments, also heavily embroidered, and was eating dried apples from a woven platter held by one of her maidens.

Uorepona—the Great Mare—was for her both a name and a title, always borne by the ruling queen. She was older than her husband, having been queen to Nectain Morbet before him, a little woman with grey hair, her body sagging with age.

Morgause made her obeisance, wondering nervously if Uorepona had loved her first husband, and if so, whether she might seek vengeance on the sister of the man who had killed him.

"The Great Mare of the Pretani bids you welcome," said Tulach in the British tongue.

"The Great Queen of the Votadini gives thanks, and offers her these gifts in token of her friendship," answered Dugech, motioning one of the slaves to bring forward the casket. Courtesy was all very well, but too much humility would be taken as weakness.

The atmosphere warmed perceptibly as Uorepona examined the ivory comb, the ornaments of golden filigree, and the vessels of Roman glass. A length of crimson silk was unfolded and immediately put to service as a mantle. The queen's woman offered Morgause apples from the platter, and she began to relax, understanding that as an accepted guest, she would be safe from now on.

"I have brought with me my son to be initiated into manhood—" she said later that evening as they sat around the women's fire. "He is the son of a king and comes of a line of warriors, and has never lain with a woman. I will give you the first offering of his seed if you have among your servants a clean maiden to receive it."

Uorepona spoke to her women in the Pictish dialect and laughed, by which Morgause concluded that though she did not speak British well, she understood it. When she had finished, one of the women replied.

"He is the bronze-haired lad that came with you, is it not so? My lady says that if she were younger she would take his seed herself, but as she is old, she will set her ornaments upon one of her servants to stand in her stead. The lady Tulach shall help you to choose . . ."

The Great Mare was served entirely by women. Even the slaves were of good blood, captives taken in war. Almost immediately, one of the girls caught Morgause's eye, a slim child scarcely older than Medraut, though her breasts were grown. But what had attracted the queen's attention was the bright red-gold of her hair and her amber eyes. She was very like Guendivar. . . .

"That one—" she gestured. "Where is she from?"

Tulach shrugged. "She is British, taken as a child in Nectain Morbet's war, but her lineage is not known."

Morgause nodded. "She will do very well."

The longest day continued endlessly beneath the northern sky. Earlier, the men had competed in contests of strength and skill, and the cattle had been driven through the smoke of the herb-laden fires. Now the sun was sinking, although it would be close to midnight before the last light was gone from the sky. The scent of cooking meat drifted through the encampment as the carcasses of sacrificed cattle roasted over many fires, but the smell of blood still hung in the air.

Tonight, the gods of the Pretani must be rejoicing, thought Morgause. Even the Votadini festivals were not so lavish, and as Christianity strengthened in the south, Artor's feasts had become bloodless travesties. A distant drum beat was taken up by others; her blood pulsed in time to the rhythm that throbbed in the air. Soon, the Goddess would receive another kind of offering.

Morgause had been given a place of honor with the women. On the other side of the circle she could see Medraut, sitting with the other boys. He had a gift for languages, and his agile tongue had clearly mastered the speech of the Pretani well enough to make them laugh. But from time to time his gaze would flicker towards her, questioning.

Trust me—She sent reassurance back with her smile. *This is for your good. You will see. . . .*

The slaves brought platters of meat still steaming from the spit, and skins of mead and heather beer. Some of the men were already becoming drunken, but what was given to the boys had been diluted. The ritual required that they be merry, but not incapable. Chieftains rose in place to boast of their achievements and praise the king. Young warriors marched into the center of the circle and danced with swords. And presently, after Drest's bard had completed a song in his honor, the drumbeat quickened, and the boys, with the awkward grace of colts just beginning their training, danced into the circle in a wavering line.

Morgause had spared no pains in her son's education. At this age, all boys were somewhat ungainly, but Medraut had not yet begun the growth spurt that would make his body for a time a stranger's, and in addition to her more private teaching, he had been rigorously schooled in running and leaping, in riding and in swordplay, and in the stylized movements of the warrior's dance.

It was a tradition the Votadini shared with their northern neighbors. Medraut's thin body took on grace as he recognized the quickening rhythm, spine straightening, shoulders braced, and the belted kilt that was all he wore swinging as his feet stamped in time. This was a tradition of unarmed combat. The beat shifted and the boys paired off, leaping and feinting with clenched fists or open hands, proud as young cocks of their energy and skill.

Skinny torsos shone with perspiration; differences in conditioning became apparent as some of the boys began to slow. Medraut, who had learned a few movements not included in the formal sequence, leaned close to his partner as they switched positions, feet flickering, and in the next moment the other boy fell. Face flaming with shame, he pulled himself upright and shambled off to the sidelines to join those whose endurance had given out.

Again a shift in the drumbeat signaled a change, and the pairs became a line once more. Faster and faster the rhythm drove them, and the dancers circled and spun. Another boy fell, with no help from Medraut, and rolled away. The drumming crescendoed and fell silent. The boys stopped dancing, one or two of them sinking to their knees, chests heaving, as the power of the music let go. Medraut stood with his head up, perspiration running in glittering rivulets down his chest and sides. The hair that clung damply to his neck was the color of old blood, but he had the air of a young stallion that has won his maiden race and vindicated his breeding.

Now a shimmer of tinkling metal brought heads up, eyes widening. A line of young women was filing in, their garments sewn with bits of silver and bronze. Singing and clapping hands, they circled the boys, and then drew back, leaving the girl Morgause had chosen standing alone.

She moved along the line of boys, as if considering them. Her movements were stiff and her smile anxious, as if she were not quite certain she would be able to follow her instructions. Her bright hair, combed in a shining cape across her shoulders, stirred gently as she moved. The boys twitched and licked their lips as she passed them, and halted at last before Medraut, as she had been told to do.

Medraut's eyes widened, and his mother smiled. The ornaments the girl was wearing belonged to the Great Mare, but the gown was one he would recognize as her own, with her perfume still clinging to every fold. *When you take her in your arms you will see Guendivar's face, but it is my scent you will smell, and my magic that will bind you. . . .*

She had borne five strong sons in pain and suffering, and except for the last, she might as well have been a barren tree. One by one, Artor had seduced them away. Her granddaughter had been taken by Igierne. Medraut was all that remained to her, and she meant to use all her magic to make sure that the link between them stayed as strong as if the cord still connected him to her womb.

The maiden twirled before her chosen champion. From around the circle came a soft murmur of appreciation as she unpinned the brooch that held her garment at the shoulder and let it fall. The girls sang louder and she swayed, cupping her naked breasts in her two hands. They were small, but perfect, pale nipples uptilted beneath the necklet of amber and gold. Medraut's kilt stood out in a little tent before his thighs, and Morgause knew that the girl was arousing him.

The boy had been told what the reward would be if he did well in the dancing, just as the maiden had been told what to do. Did he understand how the act was accomplished? Surely no lad brought up in the dun could be ignorant—he had seen animals coupling, and humans as well, when the revelry became too drunken in the hall.

Seeing the admiration in Medraut's eyes, the girl smiled and held out her hand. He sent a quick glance of appeal towards his mother, who nodded. Then he allowed the maiden to lead him away to the bower that had been prepared for them. The other girls followed, singing, and the rest of the boys, relieved or resentful, went back to their place in the circle and began to tease the serving girls to give them more beer.

To the queens, they offered mead. Now that her son had met his challenge, Morgause could afford to relax. She accepted a beaker and drank deeply, tasting the fire beneath the sweetness and sighing as the familiar faint buzz began to detach her from the world.

The royal circle began to break up as they prepared to light the great bonfire that had been built in the center of the field where they had held the competitions earlier that day. The sun had set some time ago, and the half-light was fading, soft as memory, into a purple glow. In the east, the waning moon, late rising as an old woman, was just beginning to climb the sky.

Morgause got to her feet, taking a deep breath as the world spun dizzily around her. Her heartbeat pounded in her ears, or was it the Pictish drums she was hearing? Uorepona was retiring with her women, but Morgause felt desire rising within her. Since those few days during Leudonus' funeral, her courses had not come. Surely, if she worshipped the Goddess at the Midsummer fires, she would become fertile once more!

The drumming deepened. From the other end of the encampment a procession was coming; the light of torches danced and flickered across the grass. Morgause joined the throng that was forming a circle around the pyramid of logs. Tinder of all kinds had been stuffed within it, and the whole doused with oil. In times of danger, that frame of tinder would have held a man.

It will burn, she thought, taking her place in the circle, *and so will I. . . .*

Shouting, the torchbearers danced around the waiting pyre, rushing inward and then retreating once more. Again and again they surged, in and back and in again, while the first stars began to prick through the silken curtain of the sky. Each thrust was echoed by a cry from the crowd. The shouting got louder, the dance more frenzied, and Morgause swayed, feeling warmth kindle between her thighs. And then, as if the need of the gathered clans had driven them to climax, the dancers leaped forward and plunged their torches into the pyre.

The tinder caught; flame began to spark along the logs. Morgause felt a blast of warmth against her cheeks as fire billowed skyward. The drumming picked up and suddenly everyone was dancing. She laughed, whirling in place, and then began to move sunwise around the bonfire, hips swaying, arms outstretched.

One of the men caught her eye and began to dance with her, but she did not like his looks, and whirled away. Soon enough a bright-haired warrior found favor, mirroring her movements as they danced together, burning with the same flame. The dance brought them closer and closer, until her bobbing breasts brushed his chest. He seized her then, kissing her hungrily, and staggering like drunkards they wove among the other dancers until they reached the edge of the circle and collapsed together, bodies straining, on the grass.

Her warrior served her well, but when he had left her, Morgause still felt hunger. *Take me!* her heart cried as she began to dance once more, *fill me with your seed, and I will live forever!*

And soon another man came to her, and when she had exhausted him, a third. By this time, her clothing had gone, and she danced clad only in her own sweat and her necklaces of amber and jet. After that, she ceased counting. At one point she lay with two men together, and then, just as the early dawn was lightening the eastern sky, she enticed one of the drummers, for there were not many dancers left upright, though coupling figures still writhed upon the grass.

Morgause drew him down, pulling at his clothing with hasty caresses until he grunted and entered her. He was tired, and took his time at it, but a satiated exhaustion was finally overcoming her as well. She lay spread-eagled on the earth, quivering to his thrusts, until above his harsh breathing another sound caught her attention. She looked up, and gazing past the man's muscled shoulder saw Medraut, his hair glinting in the first light, disgust in his eyes.

"You are a man now—" Morgause said harshly. "This is what men do. Did you think you were so different?" Her partner groaned then and convulsed against her, and she laughed.

It was nearly noon when Morgause woke, her head throbbing from too much mead and her body aching from rutting in the grass. After she had bathed, she began to feel better and returned to the women's enclosure. Medraut was nowhere to be seen, but she recognized his maiden, working with the other slave girls to clear the detritus of the night's carousing away. She was wearing a bracelet that Morgause had last seen on her son's arm.

She ducked beneath the shade of the striped awning to pay her respects to the queen.

"Your son performed well last night," Uorepona said through her interpreter.

"He did. But now the girl may bear his child. Will you sell her to me?"

"If that is so, she would be all the more valuable," came the answer.

"I will be frank with you," said Morgause. "The children of princes must be begotten at the proper time and season. It is not my desire that there should be a child, nor that the vessel that received this holy sacrifice should be tainted by the use of one less worthy. But I cannot dispose of your property."

Uorepona bent to whisper into Tulach's ear.

"Ah—now I begin to understand you. But she is a pretty thing, and has been useful. If I had known your intention, I would have offered you a slave of less value."

"She was the best choice for my purpose," answered Morgause. "I will pay well."

Tulach nodded, and they began the delicate process of haggling.

For the two nights that remained of the festival, Medraut slept with the slave girl and hardly spoke to his mother at all. The girl herself had not been informed of the change of ownership, and when the time came for Medraut to depart, clung to him, weeping. The boy had already tried to persuade Morgause to bring the slave south with them and been refused. When at last they took the road towards the firth, there were tears in his eyes as well.

"Will we come back here? Will they be kind to her?" he asked as the grey waters of the Bodotria came into view.

"She will be well taken care of," answered Morgause, knowing that by now the slave collar would have been replaced by the mark of the strangler's cord. In time, she would tell Medraut that the girl was dead, and he would forget her.

"Why did you bring me here?" muttered the boy. "Every time something good happens to me, you take the joy away. . . ."

"You are a prince. You must learn to master your desires."

"As you did at the festival?" he snapped back, then flushed and looked away.

Morgause took a deep breath, striving to control her temper. This was the child of her heart, and she must not drive him off. "I had a reason," she said finally. "What is important is not *what* you do so much as why."

"And you won't tell me. . . . Will you answer any of my questions? You have taught me things you never showed my brothers, and they are princes too!"

Morgause took a deep breath. Was now the moment she had been awaiting? Now, when he was beginning to understand what it meant to be a man?

"Your brothers are only princes of the Votadini. You are by birth the heir to all Britannia."

Medraut reined in sharply, all color draining from his face, staring at her.

"Your father and I lay together unknowing, god with goddess, in the sacred rite of the feast of Lugus. But the seed that was planted in my belly was that of Artor," Morgause said calmly. "In the old days, you would have been proclaimed before all the people, but Britannia is ruled now by Christians, who would count what we did a sin. Nonetheless, you are Artor's only child."

From pale, Medraut's face had flushed red. Slowly his complexion returned to normal, but his eyes were shining.

Oh my brother, thought Morgause, *you fathered this child, but I possess his soul. . . .*

IX

A Vessel of Light

 In the second year of the new century, sickness stalked the land. It came with vomiting and fever, and when it killed, took by preference the young and strong. The first cases appeared in Londinium, where a few trading vessels still put in at the wharves, and the illness spread along the roads to such other centers of population as remained. Then it began to strike in the countryside. If not so deadly as the great plague that had devastated the empire some forty years before, it was fearful enough to make people flee the towns that were beginning to rise from the ashes of the Saxon wars.

That year, the rains of winter persisted into the summer months, blighting the grain. Those who were still healthy shivered along with the sick and cursed whichever gods commanded their loyalty. And some, especially those who held to the old ways, began to speak against the king.

Artor had never entirely recovered from the wound he got in the Irish wars. He could walk and fight and ride, but not for long. He had moved to Deva to direct the conclusion of the campaigning, but he had delegated its execution to Agricola in Demetia, and Catwallaun Longhand in the north of Guenet. And the British efforts had been rewarded with victory. Even the holy isle of Mona was now free. The only Irishmen remaining in Britannia were those who had given oath to defend it for Artor—Brocagnus in Cicutio, and others farther inland. To Cunorix, who had once been his hostage, he gave the defense of Viroconium, and the Irish mercenary Ebicatos was installed in Calleva.

But to the common folk of Britannia, coughing beneath their leaky thatching and watching the rain batter down the young grain, these great victories were distant and irrelevant. Any warrior could kill enemies, but the power that kept health in man and beast and brought good harvests came from the king.

And the king, or so ran the rumor, was not a whole man. For six years he had been married, and yet his young queen bore no child. Merchants who braved the dangers of the road to come to Camalot bore tales as well as cloth and knife blades and spices. By his life or by his death, it was the duty of the High King to heal the land.

Guendivar took a handful of coins from her pouch and pushed them past the packets of herbs and spices to the peddler. There were more than the pepper and nutmeg, the hyssop and saffron and sandalwood warranted, but she would not haggle. From the smile with which the old man took them, he understood that she was paying for the information as well.

If only, she thought as she gathered up her purchases in the corner of her mantle and set off for the kitchen, she could have acquired so easily some specific for the problems he had described to her. She had gone to Cama's sacred spring to pray, and learned only that she herself would be protected. And last Beltain, she had gone, veiled, to the sacred fires where the country folk still lit them in the hills, and allowed a fair young man to draw her into the woods during the dancing, but she had not kindled from his lovemaking. This year, it was likely to be too wet to even light the fire.

There was some lack in her, she thought sadly, as well as in the king. For her to bear a child would have stilled wagging tongues, no matter who the father might be. But she was a barren field. Since Melguas had seduced her when she was his captive, Guendivar had lain with several men, but despite their caresses, she, whose body throbbed with pleasure at the warmth of the sun on her back or the feel of a cat's soft fur, had responded to none of them. Only with the folk of faerie did she feel fully alive, and her responsibilities often prevented her from seeking them. If Merlin had been with them, she would have begged him to teach her the mysteries she had once refused. But his absences had grown longer in recent years.

She regretted now that shame had kept her from touching the Cauldron. If she had had the courage, it might have healed her, and through her, the king. Artor had spoken sometimes of the Cauldron's power to renew the land. But in the condition he was now he could never spare the time it would take to travel back to the Lake.

She stopped short, still standing on the muddy path between the royal hall and the cookhouse, heedless of the fine rain that was scattering beads of crystal across her mantle and her hair. Artor could not go to the Cauldron, but could the Cauldron come here?

She did not believe that the king could be brought to appeal to his mother, even—or perhaps especially—if it concerned his own safety. But perhaps the Lady of the Lake would respond to a message from the High Queen.

A change in the wind brought her the scent of cooking, and Guendivar began to walk once more. If she wished to appeal to Igierne, she must find a messenger—not one of Artor's warriors, who would insist on getting confirmation from his commander, but someone with the strength and wit to make the journey swiftly, who would carry the message simply because it was the queen's desire.

Folk looked up, smiling, as she pulled open the door. Guendivar had never thought to be glad of her mother's training, but she did understand how to talk to the men and women who served her, and the cooks were always glad to see her, knowing she would make no demands without reason, and do her best to see that they had the resources they needed to do their job. As for the queen, she had noticed that males were more likely to be reasonable when they were well fed, and in this, Artor's champions were no different from any other men.

"A peddler has come, and I have bought out his store of spices—" She spilled the contents of her mantle out onto the scrubbed wooden table.

The chief of the cooks, a big, red-faced man called Lollius, set down his cleaver to look at them. The others clustered around him, chattering as the packets were identified, except for one lad, a strongly built fellow who was so tall he had to stoop to get through the door. He had looked up briefly when she came in, coloring to the roots of his fair hair, and then returned his attention to the bulbs of spear-leek that he was peeling. The sharp scent hung in the air.

That one—thought Guendivar. *He is in love with me.*

That, of course, was not unusual—half of Artor's men dreamed of her, or some fantasy that they gave her name. But this lad, who despite his northern burr spoke better than fit his station, seemed to look at *her*. She moved around the tables as the cook held forth upon the virtues and uses of the spices, examining a vegetable, or sniffing the contents of a bowl, until she stood beside him.

"Will the spear-leek go into the stew?" she asked softly.

"Lollius says it will fight sickness," he answered. "Surely it is strong enough!" He ventured a shy smile.

"You are very deft. What do they call you?"

"Manus—" He flushed again. "*Manus Formosus*," he added, "because of my hands."

"Indeed, they are very well-shaped and beautiful," Guendivar agreed. "But that is not the name your mother gave you, and you did not gain those shoulder muscles using a paring knife, but swinging a sword. Who are you, lad?"

At that, his clever fingers, which had continued to strip the papery rind from the bulbs, fell still.

"I have sworn not to say . . ." Manus answered finally, "until I have been in the king's service for a year and a day."

"That time is almost over," said the queen. She remembered his arrival now, though he had been much thinner then, as if he had been long on the road and lived hard. "When it is done, you will ask my lord for the boon he promised. But until then, your service belongs to me."

"Always . . ." he muttered, though he would not meet her eyes.

"I wish you to carry a message to the Lady of the Lake. But none must know where you go or why. Will you do that for me?" There was a short silence. One of the other servants began to hack vigorously at a peeled turnip, and she drew Manus after her to the end of the table, wondering if the young man had heard.

"My lady, I will go," Manus answered at last.

"I am too old to go racketing about the countryside this way . . ." said Igierne, twisting uncomfortably. The other priestesses she had brought with her from the Isle of Maidens moved around the room, unpacking clothing and hanging cloaks and mantles up to dry, for they had reached Camalot on the wings of an oncoming storm. But the chest at the foot of her bed they left strictly alone.

"Is the bed too hard?" Guendivar patted the pillows into shape as Igierne lay back again. The queen's bright hair was hidden by a veil, and there were smudges of fatigue beneath her eyes. What business did *she* have looking so tired, wondered Igierne? She had not travelled for two weeks in the rain.

"The bed is well enough, but every heartbeat jolts me as if I were still in that damned horse-litter," she snapped in reply. "I thought to find Artor on his deathbed at the very least, but aside from an indoor pallor and some weight around his middle that's due to lack of exercise, he seems well enough. So why did you summon me?"

"You know in what state he was when he left the Isle of Maidens." Guendivar frowned. "He may be no worse, but he is certainly no better. But that is not why I wrote to you. It is the land that is sick, and the people who are dying, and if you do not understand that, then why did you come?"

Igierne sighed, letting go of her anger. "Not entirely because of your message, so you need feel neither guilt nor pride. For the past moon I have had evil dreams. . . ."

"Dreams of water rushing in a great wave, overwhelming the land?" asked Guendivar in a shaking voice.

Igierne raised herself on one elbow, remembering the potential she had once seen in this child—but no, Guendivar was twenty-one, a woman now. Was she at last beginning to grow into her power?

"Just so," she said softly. "I think it is one of the gifts of the queens to have such dreams. But the last of those dreams was different. With the water came a great light, and a voice that sang."

"I heard it too," whispered Guendivar, "though I could not understand the words. But the light came from the Cauldron."

Igierne nodded, her gaze moving involuntarily to the chest. In externals, it seemed no different than any of the others, though it was heavier because of the sheets of lead with which it was lined. Even so, she could feel the presence of the cauldron it held like a buzz along her nerves—perhaps it was that, and not the travel, that had made her so tired. Now she understood why it had always been kept within the shielding earth and stone of the shrine.

"What will you do with it?" the queen asked then.

"I do not know. The Goddess has not told me. We can only wait for her to show us Her will. . . ."

Throughout that night it rained steadily, and yet this was only the harbinger of a storm such as the West Country had rarely known, driven straight from the Hibernian Sea. In the levels below the Isle of Glass the sea-swell would be backing up the rivers and making islands of the high ground. Guendivar could imagine how the marsh-folk must be taking refuge on the Tor while the monks and the nuns chanted desperate prayers to their god.

In the sheltered lowlands, the waters were rising, but on the heights, one felt the full force of the wind. Artor's walls were small protection. The storm swept over the ramparts of Camalot to pluck at the thatching of the buildings within. Of them all, only the great round henge hall that Merlin had designed was entirely undamaged, though drafts swept through its wicker partitions and it flexed and shuddered with each onslaught of the storm. Father Kebi, the Christian priest who had spoken darkly of sorcery when the hall was being built, came meekly enough to take refuge with the others, though he crossed himself when he passed through the door. It was not council season, and many of Artor's chieftains were home on their own lands. With his Companions and his servants and the priestesses from the Isle of Maidens inside, there was just room for them all.

All that afternoon, Guendivar worked with her maidservants to bring food and drink and bedding, and then there was nothing she could do but take her place beside Artor, and force herself to keep smiling as she watched the torch flames flicker in the draft, and wait for the dawn.

Igierne shivered, wondering if the touch she had felt on her cheek had really been a drop of water. With her mind, she knew the hall would not fail them—she could sense Merlin's magic, binding post to pillar and thatching to beam—but her gut was not so certain. Ceincair helped her to settle her mantle more securely around her shoulders, and she thanked her, searching the crowd for her other priestesses as she turned.

"Where is Ninive?"

"She went to the side door, to relieve herself, she said, though I think she really wanted to see the storm," said Ceincair.

Igierne shook her head with a sigh. Bringing the child here had been a risk—in three years Ninive had learned a great deal, but she was still a woodscolt at heart, and if at times she found the serene society of the Isle of Maidens too confining, she must be suffering in this crowded hall. She was young and would take no harm from a wetting, but her absence was not the true cause of the priestess' unease.

It was the Cauldron.

Igierne had believed that the Goddess wanted her to bring it south, but what if her own concern for Artor had deceived her? In Eriu they had a tale of a woman who insulted a sacred spring and caused a flood that drowned the land. Was this a natural storm, or by taking the Cauldron from its spell-shielded sanctuary had she so unbalanced the elements that they would destroy Britannia? If it were required, she would take up the Cauldron with her own two hands and carry it to the sea, but she did not know what she ought to do. If the stakes had not been so high, Igierne would have accepted her panic as a necessary lesson in humility, but as it was, all she could do was close her eyes and pray.

"Lord have mercy upon us, Christ have mercy upon us," muttered the little priest as the storm raged. Betiver, who had hardly said a prayer since his childhood, found himself murmuring an echo, and so did many another of those who had been raised in Roman ways. A flare of lightning outlined the great door, and in another moment thunder clapped and rattled above them. Behind him, he heard men calling on Jupiter and Taranis and even Thunor of the Saxons.

He stiffened, veins singing with the same mingled fear and fury he felt before battle, and instinctively his gaze sought the royal high seat and his king. Artor, every nerve strained at attention as he waited for the next bolt to fall, nonetheless looked far better than the lethargic figure of yesterday. This was the valiant commander Betiver remembered from a hundred campaigns. Guendivar said something, and Artor leaned close to answer her, smiling and reaching out to grasp her hand.

It was almost the first time Betiver could remember seeing the king touch her, but before he could wonder, the lightning and thunder crashed around them once again.

Guendivar felt the warm strength of Artor's grip and squeezed back convulsively as the thunder shook the hall.

Lady, help us! For the sake of the king, for all this land! I will do whatever you ask, but I pray you, shelter us now!

She had never been afraid of thunderstorms, but this one had an unexpected and elemental power. Each flare of lightning showed clearly the unimportance of her own fears and frustrations. There was a life in the storm that had nothing to do with the problems of the queen of Britannia. Oddly enough, that relieved her. She sat, a still point in the midst of fury, rooted to the earth by the steady grip of her husband's hand, and waited for the next convulsion of the skies.

This time, the lightning's flare and the thunder were almost simultaneous. The hall trembled, the great doors sprang wide. Wind howled and every torch was extinguished, but in the same moment a blue iridescence burst through the opening and whirled about, edging post and beam and benches alike with livid light.

"It is Pentecost!" cried Father Kebi, "and the Holy Spirit has come to us in wind and fire!"

But the lightning passed, and the raging of the heavens was replaced by a sudden singing silence. They were in the eye of the storm. They sat, staring, while the blood beat in their ears, and the lightning focused to a single sphere of radiance that floated slowly around the interior of the hall. So bright it was that no man could say who bore it, or if indeed it moved by any human agency at all.

Guendivar stared at that brightness and knew that she was weeping, though she made no sound. From one person to another it passed, pausing for a few moments and then moving on, awarding as much time to a chieftain as to a serving lad, and to the woman who fed the pigs as to the priestesses who had come with Igierne. She saw it surrounding Julia, who crossed herself and then reached out, her cheeks shining with tears.

What are you? Who are you? the queen's heart cried as the light drew closer. Now it seemed to her that forms moved within that radiance; a procession of bright beings was passing through the hall. *What do you want from me?*

And then it was before her, swallowing up all other sensation except the pressure of her husband's hand.

An answer came. "*I am as full of wonders as Faerie, and as common as day. I am what you most desire. Now I stand before you, but only when I stand behind you will you understand Me truly, and be fulfilled.*"

And then it seemed to her that the light shimmered, and she glimpsed within it a woman's form. The radiance surrounded her, and she tasted sweetness beyond the capacity of mortal food, though she never afterward was able to say if it had been truly taste instead of sight or sound.

* * *

Betiver heard singing, as he had heard it in the great church of Saint Martin as a child. With it came the sweetness of frankincense, filling the hall in great smoking clouds of light. The brightness drew closer, surrounded by a shifting glimmer like the movement of mighty wings. For a moment then he glimpsed a Chalice, through whose pure curve a rose-red radiance glowed.

"*I am thy true Lord and thy Commander. Follow Me!*"came a soundless Voice, and Betiver's spirit responded in an ecstasy of self-offering—

"I am Thy man until my life's end. How shall I serve Thee?"

"*Serve Britannia . . . serve the King. . . .* " came the answer, and he bowed his head in homage.

"Always . . ." he murmured, "always, wherever the road may lead. . . ."

To Igierne, alone among all that company, the visitation had a tangible form. She saw the glowing silver and knew it for the Cauldron, but as it approached, the image of the Goddess grew out of the low relief of its central panel to a full figure that expanded until it filled the hall.

"Brigantia, Exalted One, power upwelling—" she whispered, "watch over Your children."

"*When have I failed to do so? It is you who turn away from Me . . .* "

"Did I do wrong to bring the Cauldron to the king?"

"*You did well, though a time will come soon when you will question that choosing. But for now, be comforted, for in the flesh your son has his healing, though he will not be whole in spirit until he sees Me in another guise.*"

The radiance intensified, growing until she could no longer bear its brilliance, carrying her to a realm where the spirit and the senses were one, and she knew no more.

To each soul in that circle the Cauldron came, after the fashion in which he or she could see it most clearly, and each one received the nourishment, in body and in spirit, that was most desired.

And presently folk began to blink and stir, gazing around

them as if the painted pillars and the woven hangings, their own hands and each other's faces were equally strange and wonderful. It was no supernal radiance that showed them these things—that Light had disappeared. But the great door to the hall still stood open, and beyond it glowed a clear, rose-tinted sky, and the first golden rays of the rising sun.

Betiver looked exalted, as a warrior who has seen his victory. It was an expression that illuminated the faces of many of Artor's Companions, though they gazed around them now in confusion and loss.

"I had it—" whispered someone, "I almost understood— where has it gone?"

Igierne lay still, with her priestesses around her, but her breast rose and fell, and Guendivar knew that in time she would wake, restored. Father Kebi was murmuring prayers, on his face an unaccustomed peace. The cooks and the kitchen slaves gazed about them in amazement. But Manus' eyes shone like two stars.

Guendivar turned to her husband, understanding that she had seen the thing that was behind the faerie-folk who had once so enchanted her, and the source of their magic, though the images were fading so swiftly that she could no longer say just what it had been.

"What did you see, Artor?" she whispered. "What did you see?"

But he only shook his head, his eyes still wide, half-blinded by looking on too much light. She reached out, and he drew her to him and held her close against his heart, and for that moment, both of them were free.

Morgause gazed at the glory of the new day and cursed the gods. A night of elemental fury, followed by a dawning that might have belonged to the morning of the world, could only mean that Igierne had unveiled the Cauldron. The mysteries Morgause had studied during these past years had taught her how to sense the cycles of the land as once she had charted her own moontides, and she knew that this had been no natural storm. Such lore as she had been able to glean in the years she spent on the Isle of Maidens suggested that the precautions with which the Cauldron had always been surrounded were not only intended to control access to it—they were needed to control its power.

On the night just past they had surely seen the result of letting that power flow free. The ground was littered with leaves, and the woodlands were striped with pale slashes where entire branches had been torn from the trees. As the horses picked their way along the muddy trackway towards Camalot, she saw that the homes of men had fared even worse. Huts stood like half-plucked chickens, the bracing of their roofs bared where the thatching had been torn away. At that, the Celtic roundhouses, whose frames flexed with the storm, had fared better than the square-built Roman dwellings, which tended to crumble when the wind ripped off their terra-cotta tiles.

For anyone caught in the open, as she and her escort had been, the hours of darkness had been a nightmare. The cloak Morgause wore still steamed with moisture. Only the yew wood in which they had found shelter had saved them from an even worse battering by the storm.

And then, in the most secret hours before the dawning, the wind had dropped. For a few moments Morgause had wondered if the fury of the storm had transcended her powers of hearing. Then the air grew warmer, and she knew that the stillness betokened a Presence and no mere lack of sound.

Until then, she had hoped her suspicions might be mistaken. Her spy in Artor's kitchens knew only that Guendivar had summoned the Lady of the Lake. But in her dreams Morgause had seen the Cauldron rising like a great moon above the land. And so she had come south—but not swiftly enough to prevent her mother from bringing the Cauldron—the Hallow that was Morgause's birthright—to Artor.

This smiling morning only confirmed her in her conclusion. She felt orphaned; she felt furious. She had learned much from the witches of the Pretani, and yet she was a foreigner among them, always conscious that they kept secrets she could never learn. With the Cauldron, she could face them as an equal. During the past few years her desire for it had grown from an irritation to an obsession. It had to be hers!

There was no point in following her mother to Camalot and confronting her—the damage was done. Still, Igierne must leave eventually. Better, Morgause thought now, to keep her presence in the area a secret. Just ahead, the road had been washed out by the storm. Any party attempting to return to the Lake from the south must detour through the woodland. The damaged forest could hardly have been better arranged for setting an ambush. Limbs of alder and oak littered the ground, while sallow and willow had bowed to the blast. The marsh grasses were half submerged and the higher ground muddy. At her feet a marigold nodded in the light breeze. Morgause wondered how it had escaped the fury of the storm.

"We will stop here," she told her men. "Uinist, set a watch and send scouts around the woods to watch the southern road. Doli, it will be your task to position the men where they can attack successfully. And when we have finished, we will flee westward. If there is suspicion, they will be searching the main road that leads north from Lindinis. No one will expect us to skirt the higher ground and push towards the sea."

They had three days to wait before her men reported a large party coming up the road from the direction of Camalot. The horselitter, Morgause knew, must be carrying her mother. But even without the scouts she would have known who, and what, was coming—she could *feel* the presence of the Cauldron, as if its recent exercise had increased its power. She could feel it, and she wanted it, as a thirsty man desires the well.

Morgause ordered her men to do no harm to the Lady of the Lake. Far better, she thought vengefully, to let her mother live with the knowledge of what she had lost, as she herself had had to live without her birthright. The others they might kill, so long as they carried off all of the baggage and gear.

And so she waited while her men disappeared into the woodland, and just past the hour of noon, she heard women screaming and northern warcries, and smiled.

"Mother, it was not your fault!" Artor grasped Igierne's hands, chafing them. "Were it not for my weakness, the Cauldron would never have left the Isle of Maidens."

"It was my message that brought you—" echoed Guendivar.

"—but my decision to respond . . ." Igierne forced out the words.

She was still shivering, as she had ever since the attack. The men of her escort had been killed, but Ninive had caught one of the horses and galloped back to Camalot for help. That had been at midmorning, and now it was nearly eventide. The Cauldron was gone, and since Uthir's death, she had known no greater disaster. Ceincair wrapped blankets around her and spoke of shock, but Igierne knew it was fear.

"But who *were* they?" asked Aggarban.

"Men, with spears and bucklers and shirts of hardened leather," answered Nest. "The only words I heard were in British as we speak it in the north, but not the Pictish tongue. They could have been reivers, or masterless men."

"I thought all such had been hunted down by the king's soldiers," said Guendivar.

Artor's eyes flickered dangerously. "So did I . . ."

"It does not matter who they are—we must be after them!" exclaimed Gualchmai. "If that was indeed the Cauldron that by the power of the gods came shining through the hall, I would give my heart's blood to see it again!"

"And I!" said Vortipor. Other voices echoed his vow.

When the priestesses returned to the House of Women after that night of storm and glory, they had found the Cauldron safe in its chest, and no one could be brought to admit having touched or moved it. But what else could it have been? Now it was gone, and Igierne shuddered to think of the disaster it might bring in hostile hands.

She coughed and tugged at Ceincair's sleeve. "Did you note, among the riders, any women?"

"I did not," answered the priestess. "Do you think that Morgause—" She fell silent, seeing Gualchmai's stricken gaze.

"Do you think it is not as hard for me to say it, grandson, as for you to hear?" asked Igierne. "But your mother has always desired the Cauldron. In your searching do not forget the northern roads." *And if she has taken it, the fault is mine*—her thought continued. *Morgause begged me to teach her its mysteries, and I refused.*

"We will search *all* the roads, Mother," said Artor. She heard him giving orders as she sank back into the shelter of her blankets.

"And we will take care of you here," added Guendivar, "where you can hear the reports as the searchers come in."

Igierne shook her head. "The quest must take place in the mortal realm, and it is the High Queen, the Tigernissa, who is for your warriors the image of the Goddess in the world. I will go back to the Lake . . . I should never have left it, for I am Branuen, the Hidden Queen, and the quest of the spirit must be directed from there. Perhaps the Cauldron will hear our prayers and make its own way home."

X

†HE QUEST

Of those who had ridden out from Camalot in search of the Cauldron, the first to return was Betiver. When he came in, Guendivar was in the herb hut, stripping the tender leaves from mints she had gathered in the woods. The sharp, sweet fragrance filled the air.

"Where is the king?" he asked when he had saluted her.

"He rode over to Lindinis. He should be back for the evening meal."

"The king is riding?" he asked, astonishment sharpening his tone.

"He is much better," Guendivar said softly, "and the weather has been fine as well. If anyone doubts that what we saw was holy, surely its works speak for it."

"*I* do not doubt it, though I believe that vision is all that I shall ever see—" He sank down upon a bench, the glow which his eyes always held when he looked at her intensifying. "Perhaps that is why I do not feel compelled to continue trying to see it again."

"What do you mean?" she asked, watching him closely.

"When the Light came to me, what I saw within it was the Chalice of our Lord, and I was fed, and made whole. We have no assurance that the wonder that moved through the hall was the Cauldron. Igierne's priestesses say they did not take it from its chest, so how could it account for such a miracle?"

Guendivar frowned thoughtfully. Igierne had told her that she saw the figure of a goddess emerge from the Cauldron, while Julia's vision, like that of Betiver, had been of the chalice of the Christian mass. She herself had seen only luminous forms in a haze of light, and no vessel at all.

"The others who have gone said that the vision left them with an aching desire to see it again . . ." she said then.

"That is so, but when I had gone away, I found that all I truly longed for was here."

For a moment Betiver's gaze held hers, and she flinched, seeing his unvoiced love for her naked in his eyes. She had become accustomed to recognizing lust or longing when men looked at her. One or two had threatened to seek death in battle when she would not return their passion. Only Betiver seemed able to love her without being unfaithful either to his concubine in Londinium or to his king. She had not realized what a comfort that steady, undemanding devotion was until she noted her own happiness at seeing him back again.

His tone flattened as he went on, "But the theft of the Cauldron must not go unpunished, whatever its nature may be. I have sent word to all our garrisons, and set a watch upon the ports, and having done so, see no purpose in continuing to wander the countryside when I could better serve Britannia by helping Artor."

"The king will be grateful," Guendivar said carefully, "and so will I. It has been very quiet here, and lonely, with all of you gone."

The power of the Cauldron grew with the waxing of the moon. As Morgause and her men worked their way cross-country along the edges of the sodden lowlands, travelling by night and lying up during the day, she found herself constantly aware of its presence, as even with eyes closed, one can sense the direction of a fire. But this was a white flame, cool as water, seductive as the hidden current in a stream. She could feel her moods change as they had done before her moon cycles came to an end. At some times the smallest frustration could drive her to fury or tears, and at others, and these were ever more frequent as the moon grew from a silver sickle towards its first quarter, she was uplififted on a tide of joy.

Slowly, for the paths were rough and they often had to backtrack and find a new path, they travelled westward. Presently the folded hills with their meadows and patches of woodland gave way to a high heathland where a constant wind carried the sharp breath of the sea. In the days of the empire, these hills had been well populated, for Rome needed the lead from Britannia's mines. But most of the shafts had been worked out or abandoned when the trade routes were interrupted, and grass grew on the piled earth and rock where they had been.

Morgause and her party moved more openly now, taking the old road to the mouth of the Uxela where the lead ships used to come in. Only once did they pass a huddle of huts beside a working mine shaft, and no one greeted them. At the river-mouth they saw the remains of the port, which now was home only to a few fishermen whose boats were drawn up on shore. Saltmarsh and mudflat stretched along the coast to either side of the narrow channel; at low tide the atmosphere was redolent with their rank perfume. But when it changed, the waters surged up the estuary of the Sabrina, bringing with them fresh sea air and seabirds crying on the wind.

And there, as if the gods themselves had conspired to help her, a boat was waiting.

"Go to the captain and ask where he comes from and what he carries," she told Uinist. "If he is loading lead to take to Gallia say no more, but if he is sailing northward, ask if he will accept a few passengers."

Morgause had meant to follow the estuary and strike across country from there, but as her awareness of the Cauldron grew, it had come to her that perhaps Igierne would be able to trace the movement of power. If the Cauldron were at sea, surely its identity would be masked by that of the element to which it belonged.

And so it was that Morgause took ship with three of her men while the others turned back with the horses, travelling in groups of two and three to divert any pursuers who might have traced them.

Aggarban returned to Camalot on a stretcher. Hearing the commotion, Guendivar came running from the hall. For a moment she thought they had brought her a corpse to bury, then she saw his chest rise and fall.

"We heard there were strange riders in the hills to the west," said Edrit, the half-Saxon lad whom Aggarban had taken into his service. "We caught up with them just as night was falling, and when they would not stop, we fought. In the confusion, my lord and I were separated. It took me too long to kill my man, and by the time I found my way back it was full dark. There was a dead man in the clearing, but I had to wait until morning to track my master. He was lying in his blood with the body of his opponent beside him. I bound up his wounds as best I could, and then I had to find a farm with a cart to bear him. I am sorry, my lady—" He gazed at her with sorrowful eyes. "I did the best I could. . . ."

"I am sure you did," she said reassuringly, one eye on the old woman, of all their folk the most skilled in treating injuries, who was examining Aggarban.

"He was unconscious when I found him," Edrit babbled on, "and by the time I came back with the cart, he was burning with fever. But now that we are here he will better. You will heal him, lady, I know!"

"If God wills it—" she answered cautiously, but he was looking at her as if she were the Goddess, or perhaps only the Tigernissa. Only now was Guendivar beginning to understand that for some, that was almost the same thing.

The healer had finished her examination

"Will he recover?" she asked.

"I believe so, with time and careful nursing," the woman answered her. "He can make back the blood he has lost, and his wounds are not too severe. But I don't like that fever."

No more did Guendivar, but she had promised Edrit that she would try to save his master. For three nights she took turns with the other women to sit by the wounded man, sponging his brow and listening to his mutterings, until the crisis came.

It was past midnight, and the queen herself was half asleep in her chair, when a groan woke her.

"Hold!" Aggarban spoke quite clearly but his eyes were closed. "Don't trouble to deny it—I know ye for a northern man. Is my mother tangled in this business?" There was a silence, as if someone invisible were answering, and then, once more, that terrible groan. When he spoke again, his voice was softer, edged by pain.

"Ah, my mother, you were in the Light that came through the hall—and then you abandoned us. Do you not care for your sons? But you never did, save for that red-haired brat. Festival-bastard, king's-get—oh, I have heard the tales. Can you name *any* of our fathers?" The accusations faded into anguished mutterings.

"Aggarban—" The queen wrung water from the cloth and laid it on his brow. "It's all right now, it's over . . . you must sleep and get well."

His eyes opened suddenly, and it seemed that he knew her. "Queen Guendivar . . . you shine like the moon . . . and are you faithless too?"

She recoiled as if he had struck her, but his eyes had closed. He stopped speaking, and after a few moments she took a deep breath and laying her hand on his brow, found it cool. Guendivar rose then and called the healer to examine him; and after, she went to her own bed, and wept until sleep came.

It was sunset, and the moon, now in its first quarter, hovered halfway up the sky. To Morgause, sitting on a coil of rope beside the stern rail, it looked like a cauldron into which all the light was trickling as the sky dimmed from rose to mauve and then a soft violet blue. When her gaze returned to the sea, she saw the undulating landscape before her, opalescent with color, its billows refracting blue and purple as they caught the light and subsiding into dusk grey when they fell.

The ship flexed and dipped, angling across the waves towards her evening anchorage. She was called the *Siren*, and in a week of travel Morgause had come to know her routine. Unless the weather was exceptionally fine and the wind steady, they put in each night at some sheltered cove, trading for fresh food and water and exchanging news. In these remote places there had been no rumor of the search for the Cauldron, but even here folk had felt the storm and rejoiced in the peace that came after. Those who had not died of the great sickness were on the mend, and hope had returned to the land.

At first, such interrupted progress had frustrated Morgause to the edge of rage. If the first few villages had been able to sell them horses, she would have left the ship and gone overland— to struggle with the hazards of the mountains would have matched her mood. But as day succeeded day, ever changing and always the same, she found her anger dissolving away. Even the presence of the Cauldron did not disturb her, for at sea, she was in its element and there was no separation between them.

Moving across the surface of the waters, suspended between earth and heaven, she found herself suspended also between the time before she took the Cauldron and whatever the future might hold. Her desire for the Cauldron was unchanging, but she wondered now why she had fought so hard to rule the north. Beside its reality, even her ambitions for Medraut paled. She was beginning to understand that whatever happened now, the woman who returned to the north would not be the same as the one who had ridden away a moon ago.

Vortipor rode in to Camalot with ravens wheeling around him. When those who came out to welcome him realized that the round objects dangling from his saddlebow were severed heads, they understood why.

The man who had taken them was brown and healthy and grinning triumphantly. The heads were rather less so, and even Vortipor did not protest too much when Artor tactfully suggested that Father Kebi might be willing to give them Christian burial.

"Though I doubt very much that they deserve it. I was outnumbered, and could not afford them time to confess their sins." He did not sound sorry.

"I trust that they deserved the death you gave them—" Artor observed, but the steel in his tone did little to dim the young man's smile.

"Oh, yes. The cave where they held me was littered with the remains of *their* victims. We'll have to send a party to give them a grave as least as good as that of their murderers."

"They were robbers, then," said Guendivar.

"Most certainly, but they bit off more than they could chew when they captured me! I am sorry, my lady, that I have no news of the Cauldron, but when the Light passed through the hall, what I saw was a Warrior Angel, and I can only serve the truth I see. . . ."

"None of us can say more than that," answered the king, and led him into the hall.

Even on dry land the ground seemed to be heaving. Morgause stumbled and halted, laughing. The *Siren* had put them ashore on the north bank of the Belisama, for her master would sail no farther. A half-day's journey would set them on the Bremetennacum road. It was far enough—no one would think to look for the fugitives here. Indeed, the fear of pursuit had ceased to trouble her, as had any ambivalence regarding her theft of the Cauldron.

It was *hers*, as the gods had always intended, and the time to claim her inheritance had arrived. When Doli began to ask her about the next stage of their journey, she waved him away.

"We can take thought for that tomorrow. Tonight is the full of the moon. Carry the chest up the beach—there, beyond the trees—and let no one disturb me." He was a Pict, and she knew he would not question his queen.

The sun was already sinking into the western sea, and as they reached the spot Morgause had chosen, a rim of silver edged the distant hill.

Swiftly she stripped off her clothes and stood, arms lifted in adoration, as the silver wheel of the moon rolled up the eastern sky. It had been long since she had saluted the moon with the priestesses, but she still remembered the beginning of their hymn.

"*Lady of the Silver Wheel, Lady of the Three-fold Way . . .* " For a moment she hummed, trying to recall how the next lines ran, then words came to her—"*Thy deepest mysteries reveal, hear me, Goddess, as I pray!*" She repeated the phrase, sinking deeper into the chant, finding new verses to continue the song.

Words of power she sang, to confirm her mastery, but gradually it seemed to her that she was hearing other voices and singing the old words after all, and she did not know if they came from memory, or whether the familiar melody had somehow linked her in spirit to the priestesses who even now would be drawing down the moon on the Holy Isle.

"*Holiness is your abode . . . Help and healing there abound. . . .*" But Morgause had not wanted healing, only power.

"*Ever-changing, you abide . . . Grant us motion, give us rest. . . .*" As she sang the words, her strength left her and she sank down onto her scattered clothing, her breath coming in stifled sobs. It took a long time before she could find a stillness to match that of the night around her.

And all that while, the moon had continued to rise. Morgause sat watching it, and draped her mantle over her naked shoulders against the night chill. She realized gradually that the quiet was a breathing stillness, compounded of the chirring of frogs, the gentle lap of the waves against the sand, and the whisper of wind in the grass. And now, as she watched, she saw the first spark of light on the water, and the moon, lifting ever higher, began to lay down a path of light across the sea.

Ripple by ripple the moonpath lengthened. Moving with dreamlike slowness, Morgause rose, undid the hasps that had secured the chest, and raised the lid. White silk swathed the Cauldron. Gently she folded it back, and drew in her breath at the glimmer of silver inside. It was as bright as if newly polished. The priestesses on the Isle of Maidens used to whisper that it never grew tarnished or needed to be cleaned.

For a moment longer awe kept her from moving, then she lifted the Cauldron and carried it to the water's edge. The tide was fully in, and she had not far to go. The moon was high, serene in a sky of indigo, so bright that the sea showed deep blue as well, but moving across the river came a dancing glitter of light. Still holding the Cauldron, Morgause waded into the water, and when it lapped the tops of her thighs, she lowered the vessel and let it fill.

Here, where the outflow of the river met the tide, the water was both sweet and salt. *It is all the waters of the world,* thought Morgause, bearing the Cauldron back to the shore.

She set it down at the water's edge and knelt behind it. A last wave ran up the sand and splashed her, and then the tide began to turn, but the moonpath continued to lengthen, glistening on the wet sand, until the light struck first the rim of the Cauldron and then the water within, and began to glow.

It was the power she had glimpsed in her mother's ritual, increased a thousandfold. It was all she had ever hoped for, or desired. Heart pounding, Morgause gripped the rim of the Cauldron and looked in.

In the first moment, she saw only the moon reflected in the surface of the water. In the next, light flared around her. She did not know if the water had fountained or she were falling in. Glowing shapes moved around her; she blinked, and recognized the goddesses whose outer images had been embossed upon the Cauldron's skin. The Lady of the Silver Wheel and the Lady of Ravens, the Flower Bride and the Great Mother, the Lady of Healing and the Death Crone, all of them passed before her—but now she perceived them without the veils of form that human minds had imposed to shield eyes unready to gaze on glory.

Morgause floated in the center of their circle, trembling as one by one they turned to look at her. She tried to hide her face, but she had no hands, and no feet with which to run even if there had been anywhere to go. A naked soul, she cowered beneath that pitiless contemplation that beheld and judged every angry thought and selfish deed and bitter word. In that brilliance all her justifications and excuses dissolved and disappeared.

And with them, the separate images dislimned and flowed together until there was only one Goddess, who wore her mother's face, and gazed at her with all the love that Morgause had ever longed for in Her eyes, and then that image also gave way to a radiance beyond all forms and gender, and she knew no more.

Half a hundred of Artor's Companions had ridden out to search for the Cauldron. As the infant moon grew to maturity and then began to dwindle, more and more of them returned. Some, like Aggarban, came back wounded. Sullen and taciturn once his fever left him, Aggarban was recovering well, but there were others who reached Camalot only to die, or who never returned at all, and Guendivar could not help but wonder whether Morgause had managed to curse the Cauldron.

And yet there were others who came back with a new light in their eyes, having found, if not the Cauldron, the thing that gave it meaning. It had taken her some days to realize that Manus, who had accompanied Igierne back down from the north, had gone out to search with the other men. He had not returned either, but she could not explain why she was worried about a kitchen lad.

The days passed, and Cai came in. He seemed more peaceful than he had been, though he refused to say much of his journey.

"I never even found a trace of the theives," he told them. "But I do feel better—perhaps I just needed to get away. . . ."

Peretur had a strange tale of a girl he met by a sacred spring that made Guendivar wonder if he too had encountered the folk of faerie. Gwyhir returned triumphant, having surpassed Vortipor's tally of slain outlaws. Young Amminius did not come back, but sent word that he was leaving the world to join a hermit he had found in the forest.

By the dark of the moon, of the most notable warriors all had been accounted for save Gualchmai. At first, Artor refused to worry. His nephew was widely recognized as the best fighter in an army that was the best in Britannia. Surely he could deal with any foe who might challenge him. But as time went on with no word, men began to remember that even the greatest fighter could be taken down from ambush or overwhelmed by numbers. And yet, even outnumbered, Gualchmai must have given an account of himself that would make the heavens ring.

And then, as the first sliver of new moon glimmered in the afternoon sky, the gate guard sent word that a single rider was coming up the road, a big man with a shock of wheat-colored hair. That hair, and the red-and-white shield, were famous all over Britannia. By the time Gualchmai rode through the gate, the entire population of Camalot was turned out to meet him.

"What is it?" he asked, looking around him. "Is there a festival?"

Whatever he had been doing, it was not fighting, for there was not a mark upon him. In fact he looked younger. The tunic he was wearing was new, made from green linen with embroidery around the neck and hems.

"To look at you, there must be!" exclaimed Gwyhir. "Where have you been, man? We've been worried about you!"

"Oh . . ." A becoming flush reddened Gualchmai's skin. "I didn't realize." There was another pause. "I got married . . ." he said then.

He could hardly have caused a greater uproar, thought Guendivar, if he had announced a new invasion of Saxons. In time of war, Gualchmai was a great fighter. In peace he had gained an equal reputation as a lover of women. One could believe almost any feat in the bedchamber or the battlefield. But not marriage.

He told them about it later, when they were all gathered in the hall. He had taken the northern road, and after a day found the tracks of a large party of men. Gualchmai followed them onto a path that led through a patch of woodland, catching up just in time to break up an attack on an ancient Roman two-wheeled carriage with two women and an old man inside.

"Her name is Gracilia, and she was a widow, living in an old villa and struggling to keep the farm going with three slaves."

"She must be very beautiful . . ." said Vortipor, but Guendivar wondered. It had always seemed to her that Gualchmai was so successful with women just because he found *all* of them beautiful.

"She . . ." Gualchmai gestured helplessly, seeking for words. "She is what I need."

She is his Vessel of Light—thought Guendivar as the conversation continued.

"I thought I had made Britannia safe because there were no more enemies attacking from outside her borders," said Artor at last, "but you are not the only one to have encountered worse evil within. My own injuries kept me confined to Camalot for too long. In the future it will be different, I swear."

For three days, after the full of the moon, Morgause lay half conscious and drained of energy. When Doli, concerned because she had not called him in the morning, had gone to her, he had found the Cauldron back in its chest and his mistress lying unconscious beside it. Morgause had no memory of having put it there, but for some time, her memories of the entire night remained fragmented, like something remembered from a dream.

But certain facts remained with her, and as the days passed, they became clearer.

The Cauldron's power was far greater than she had imagined, and far less amenable to human control, and the Isle of Maidens was the only place where it might be safely kept in this world.

The Goddess for whom it was the physical gateway was also greater than Morgause had allowed herself to believe, and the aspects that she had for the past ten years worshipped were no more adequate to represent the whole than the pallid version she had scorned the priestesses of the Isle of Maidens for honoring.

Her mother loved her, and the hostility between them was as much her own fault as it was Igierne's.

When a week had passed and Morgause could stand up without her legs turning to water, she ordered her men to break camp and took the road north towards Luguvalium. They traveled slowly while her strength was returning, and so the moon had grown dark and was beginning to wax once more when they came to the fortress of Voreda.

That night they sheltered in the barracks, abandoned for nearly a century. In the morning, Morgause led the way to the track that wound westward through the hills.

Once, she had known this way well. Now, she took in the prospect revealed by each turn of the road with new eyes.

Never before had she been so conscious that this was a place outside ordinary reality, a realm of mountains sculptured by giants, rising like guardians behind the familiar hills. They hid a secret country that she, always so preoccupied by her own concerns, had never really known.

In body Morgause grew steadily stronger. Her past was forgotten, the future unknown. She greeted each dawn with increasing eagerness, wondering what the new day would bring, until they crested the last rise and saw through the black fringe of pine trees a glint of blue.

Where the trail curved round towards the trees stood an ancient boulder. When she had lived here as a child, the maidens used to call it the throne.

Someone was sitting there.

Even before Morgause could see the figure clearly, she sensed who it must be. *Just as my mother knew that I would be coming,* she thought then. *I always believed that we fought because we were too different, but perhaps it was because we are too much the same. . . .*

With a few words she halted Uinuist and Doli. She dismounted, then and took the rein of the pony to whose back the chest had been bound, and started towards the stone.

As she drew closer, Morgause realized that she was not the only one who had changed. She had never believed that her mother could look so fragile. The sunlight that dappled the ground beneath the pine needles seemed to shine through her.

There was another thing. Igierne was a trained priestess, and Morgause had seen her often in the willed and disciplined stillness of ritual. But there had always been a tension, a sense of leashed power in reserve, like a warhorse on a tight rein. Now, her mother simply sat still.

"I have brought the gift of the Goddess back to its place . . ." said Morgause, letting the lead rope fall.

"You do not say that you have brought it back to *me*," observed Igierne.

"It is not yours," said Morgause. "Nor is it mine . . . that is what I have learned."

"If you know that, you have learned a great deal."

"I have indeed . . ." Morgause gave a rather shaky sigh and

dropped down to sit cross-legged in the dust at her mother's feet. Through the trees she could see sunlight dancing on the blue water, and knew the Lake for another vessel of power.

Manus was nearly the last of the seekers to come back to Camalot, and when he returned, he rode clad as a warrior, escorting a young priestess who had been sent by Igierne.

"I am glad to see you!" said Guendivar when the babble of welcome had died down. "But what is all this?" she indicated his armor. "You have changed!"

He blushed as everyone turned to look at him once more, but all could see that he wore the gear as one accustomed, not like a kitchen boy who had stripped some armor from a body he found by the road.

"Why did the Lady send *you* to guard her messenger?" wondered someone.

Aggarban pointed the stick upon which he had been leaning at the kitchen boy.

"And why are ye wearing a Votadini plaid?"

"Because it is mine!" snapped Manus, reddening once more. "And you are a blind oaf, brother, that never stooped to *look* at the folk who serve ye, or ye would have recognized me before!"

There was a moment of stunned silence, and then Gualchmai guffawed with laughter. "Oh indeed, he has ye there, Aggarban. And in truth he does have the look of Goriat, does he not, Gwyhir?"

"Oh, he does, he does—" agreed the second brother, his gaze travelling upward, "but much, much larger. . . ." And then everyone, even Artor, who had finished his conversation with the priestess, began to laugh.

"And he has outdone you all," said the king, "for Goriat has found the Cauldron, or at least brought word of it. That is the message my mother has sent to me. The sacred vessel is safe in its shrine, and the Lady of the Votadini is there as well."

"*Mother?*" exclaimed the three older brothers, amazement stamping their faces with a momentary identity.

"Was it Morgause who stole it, then?" exclaimed Cai amidst a rising babble of speculation.

"The message does not say, and whatever lies between my sister and my mother is their own affair," Artor said repressively.

"If the Cauldron has been found, then all our wandering warriors can come home," Guendivar said then.

"It will not matter," observed Betiver. "Pagan though it was, I think the Cauldron was what the priests mean by a sacrament—an earthly symbol that points the way to something beyond. That was what we saw that night, and that is what they are looking for."

"Perhaps we have been too successful," Cai said ruefully. "When we were constantly in danger from the Saxons or the Irish, men had no time to worry about much beyond their own skins."

"And now they worry about their sins. . . ." Artor sighed.

"Take comfort, my lord. So long as human beings must live in the world, they will need good government, and heaven does not hold the only beauty of which men dream."

For a moment, Betiver's glance touched Guendivar. Then he looked away. But others had followed the motion, and now she stood at the center of all men's gaze. She heard their thought clearly, though it was not with her physical ears.

"For some, the Vessel of Light is here . . ."

Igierne made her way along the edge of the Lake. Beyond the farther shore, the humped shapes of the mountains rose up against the luminous blue of the night sky like a black wall, shutting out the world. Beyond the lapping of the water and the crunch of her footsteps on stone and gravel, the night was still. The surface was uneven and she moved carefully, using her staff for support, for her stiff joints would not be able to save her if she should fall. It was one of the disadvantages of growing older, and at this moment, she felt both old and tired.

But for the first time in many moons, she was at peace. Her daughter had come home as Igierne's own mother had foretold. Morgause had much to unlearn as well as to learn before the rage and hatred in which she had lived for so many years were entirely replaced by wisdom and love. Igierne did not suppose that their relationship would always be peaceful, but at least they now *had* one, instead of a state of war. And the Lady of the Lake had no desire to break her daughter's will—to rule the Isle of Maidens, Morgause would need to be strong, as she had been strong. But Igierne could foresee, now, a time when she herself would be able to let go.

The Lake slept beneath the stars, reflecting only an occasional flicker of light, and on the island, the priestesses slept likewise. Only the Lady of the Lake was still wakeful. On the eastern point a bench had been set for those who wished to salute the sun or watch the moonrise. With a sigh Igierne settled herself upon it and laid down the staff. Her priestesses came here often when the moon was new or full. But the waning moon was an old woman who rose late and ruled the silent hours between midnight and dawn, and she had few worshippers.

She is like me . . . Igierne smiled to herself. Let Morgause learn to wield the full moon's power. Her coming had freed her mother to study the secrets of the waning moon and the dark, to truly become the raven whose wings shine white in the Otherworld—Branuen, the Hidden Queen.

As if the thought had been a summons, Igierne glimpsed behind the mountain a pallid glow. In another moment, the Crone's silver sickle appeared in the sky.

"Lady of Wisdom, be welcome," whispered Igierne. "Cut away that which I need no longer, and purify my spirit, until it is time for me to return to your dark Cauldron and be reborn. . . ."

PEOPLE and PLACES

A note on pronunciation:

British names are given in fifth-century spelling, which does not yet reflect pronunciation changes. Initial letters should be pronounced as they are in English. Medial letters are as follows.

<u>SPELLED</u>   <u>PRONOUNCED</u>

p . . . . .b
t . . . . .d
k/c . . . . . .(soft) g
b . . . . .v (approximately)
d . . . . .soft "th" (modern Welsh "dd")
g . . . ."yuh"
m v

†
PEOPLE IN THE STORY:
CAPITALS—major character
* = historical personage
( ) = dead before story begins
[ ]–ame as given in later literature
Italics = deity or mythological personage

*Aelle, king of the South Saxons

Aggarban [Agravaine]—third son of Morgause

(*Ambrosius Aurelianus—emperor of Britannia and Vitalinus' rival)

(Amlodius, Artor's grandfather)

Amminius—one of Artor's men

ARTOR [Arthur]—son of Uthir and Igierne, High King of Britannia

(Artoria Argantel—Artor's grandmother)

BETIVER [Bedivere]—nephew to Riothamus, one of Artor's Companions

Bleitisbluth—a Pictish chieftain

Brigantia/Brigid—British goddess of healing, inspiration, and the land

CAI—son of Caius Turpilius, Artor's foster-brother and Companion

CATAUR [Cador]—prince of Dumnonia

Cathubodva—Lady of Ravens, a British war goddess

*Catraut, prince of Verulamium

*Ceawlin—son of Ceretic

Ceincair—a priestess on the Isle of Maidens

(*Ceretic [Cerdic]—king of the West Saxons)

*Chlodovechus [Clovis]—king of the Franks in Gallia

*Constantine—son of Cataur

*Cunobelinus—warleader of the northern Votadini

Cunorix—an Irish warleader, formerly Artor's hostage

*Cymen—Aelle's eldest son

Doli—a Pictish warrior in the service of Morgause

*Drest Gurthinmoch—High King of the Picts

Dugech—one of Morgause's women

*Dubricius—bishop of Isca and head of the Church in Britannia

*Dumnoval [Dyfnwal]—lord of the S. Votadini

Ebrdila—an old priestess on the Isle of Maidens

Edrit—a young warrior in the service of Aggarban

Eldaul the younger [Eldol]—prince of Glevum

*Eormenric—son of Oesc, child king of Cantuware

Ganeda [Ganiedda]—Merlin's half-sister, wife of Ridarchus

(Gorlosius [Gorlois]—first husband of Igierne, father of Morgause)

Goriat [Gareth]—fourth son of Morgause

Gracilia—wife of Gualchmai

GUALCHMAI [Gawain]—first son of Morgause

GUENDIVAR [Gwenivere]—Artor's queen

Gwyhir [Gaheris]—second son of Morgause

Hæthwæge—a wisewoman in the service of Eormenric

(*Hengest—king of Cantuware, leader of Saxon revolt)

Ia—a priestess on the Isle of Maidens, in service of Morgause

*Icel—king of the Anglians in Britannia

IGIERNE [Igraine]—Artor's mother, Lady of the Lake

*Illan—King of Leinster, who for a time holds part of North Wales

Julia—a nun from the Isle of Glass, Guendivar's companion

Father Kedi—an Irish priest at the court of Artor

Leodagranus [Leoderance]—prince of Lindinis, Guendivar's father

Leudonus [Lot]—king of the Votadini

Leuku—one of Morgause's women

Mother Maduret—abbess of the nuns at the Isle of Glass

Matauc [Madoc]—king of the Durotriges

MEDRAUT [Mordred]—fifth son of Morgause, by Artor

Melguas [Meleagrance]—an Irishman born in Guenet, abductor of Guendivar

MERLIN—druid and wizard, Artor's advisor

MORGAUSE—daughter of Igierne and Gorlosius, queen of the Votadini

Morut—a priestess on the Isle of Maidens

(*Naitan Morbet—king of all the provinces of the Picts)

Nest—a priestess on the Isle of Maidens

Ninive—daughter of Gualchmai by a woman of the hills

(*Oesc—grandson of Hengest and king of Cantuware, Eormenric's father)

Peretur [Peredur]—son of Eleutherius, lord of Eboracum

Petronilla—wife of Leodegranus, Guendivar's mother

*Ridarchus—king at Alta Cluta and protector of Luguvalium

Rigana—widow of Oesc, Eormenric's mother

*Riothamus—ruler of Armorica

Tulach—a Pictish priestess, wife of Blietisbluth

Uinist—a Votadini warrior who serves Morgause

Uorepona—"the Great Mare," High Queen of the Picts

(Uthir [Uther Pendragon]—Artor's father)

(*Vitalinus, the Vor-Tigernus—ruler of Britannia who brought in the Saxons)

†
PLACES

Afallon [Avalon]—Isle of Apples, Glastonbury

Alba—Scotland

Alta Cluta—Kingdom of the Clyde

Anglia—Lindsey and Lincolnshire

Aquae Sulis—Bath

Belisama Fluvius—River Ribble, Lancashire
Bodotria Aestuarius—Firth of Forth
Britannia—Great Britain
Caledonian forest—southern Scotland
Calleva—Silchester
Camalot [Camelot]—Cadbury Castle, Somerset
Cantium, Cantuware—Kent
Cantuwareburh—Canterbury
Cicutio—Brecon, Wales
Demetia—Pembroke and Carmanthenshire
Durnovaria—Dorchester, Dorset
Fodreu—Fortriu, Fife
Gallia—France
Glevum—Gloucester
Guenet [Gwynedd]—Denbigh and Caernarvonshire
Isle of Glass [Inis Witrin]—Glastonbury
Isle of Maidens, the Lake—Derwentwater, Cumbria
Isca (Silurum)—Caerwent
Lindinis—Ilchester, Somerset
Lindum—Lincoln
Londinium—London
Mona—Anglesey
Sabrina Fluvia—the Severn River and estuary
Segontium—Caernarvon, Wales
Sorviodunum—Old Sarum, Salisbury
Summer Country—Somerset
Urbs Legionis [Deva]—Chester
Uxela Fluvius—River Axe, Severn estuary
Venta Belgarum—Winchester
Venta Siluricum—Caerwent, Wales
Viroconium—Wroxeter
Voreda—Old Penrith, Cumberland

THE BOOK
OF THE
STONE

ACKNOWLEDGMENTS

To do justice to my sources for *Hallowed Isle* would require a bibliography the size of a chapter. These are only some of the materials that have been most useful.

First and foremost, *The Age of Arthur* by John Morris, recently reprinted by Barnes and Noble. This is the best historical overview of the Arthurian period, and with a few exceptions, I have adopted his dates for events.

For names and places, *Roman Britain*, by Plantagenet Somerset Fry, also published by Barnes and Noble; and the British Ordnance Survey maps of Roman Britain and Britain in the Dark Ages.

For fauna and flora, the Country Life book of *The Natural History of the British Isles*.

The History of the Kings of Britain, by Geoffrey of Monmouth, with an occasional glance at Malory's *Morte D'Arthur*.

For the history of the North, *Scotland Before History*, by Stuart Piggott, and W. A. Cummings' *The Age of the Picts*.

For the Anglo-Saxons, the fine series of booklets published by Anglo-Saxon Books, 25 Malpas Dr., Pinner, Middlesex, England.

For insight and inspiration, *Ladies of the Lake*, by John and Caitlin Matthews, and *Merlin through the Ages*, edited by R. J. Stewart and John Matthews.

And a great many maps, local guidebooks, and booklets on regional folklore.

My special thanks to Heather Rose Jones, for her Welsh name lists and instruction on the mysteries of fifth-century British spelling, and to Winifred Hodge for checking my Old English.

Through the fields of European literature, the Matter of Britain flows as a broad and noble stream. I offer this tributary with thanks and recognition to all those who have gone before.

Feast of Brigid, 1999

PROLOGUE

Earth is the mother of us all, and the bones of of the earth are made of stone. Stone is the foundation of the world.

Born from fire, stone heaves skyward, taking a thousand forms. Cooling and coalescing, it endures the wearing of water, the rasp of the wind, becomes soil from which living things can grow. The earth convulses, burying the soil, and pressure compresses it into rock once more. As age follows age, the cycle repeats, preserving the bones of plant and animal in eternal stone. The lives of her creatures are but instants in the ages of the earth, but the stone preserves their memories.

Stone is the historian of humanity. The first primates to know themselves as men make from stone the tools that carry their identity. Time passes and the ice comes and goes again. Humans cut wood with tools of stone and build houses, till the soil and form communities. Laboring together, they drag great

*stones across the land, raise menhirs and barrows, great
henges to chart the movements of the stars, and grave them
with the spiral patterns of power.*

*With boundary stones the tribes mark off their territories,
but in the center of each land lies the* omphalos, *the navel
stone, the sacred center of their world. When the destined king
sets foot upon it, the stone sings in triumphant vindication for
those who have ears to hear.*

*But kings die, and one tribe gives way to another on the
land. The makers of the henges pass away, and only their
stones remember them. Wise Druids incorporate them into
their own mysteries. The men of the Eagles net the land with
straight tracks of stone, and around the king stones the grass
grows high. But the earth turns, and in time the Romans, too,
are gone.*

But stone endures.

*The bones of the earth uphold the world. In the stones of the
earth, all that has been lives still in memory.*

i

†HE SEED OᴨCE SOWᴨ

A.D. 502

The bones of the earth were close to the surface here.

Artor let the horse he was leading halt and gazed around him at grey stone scoured bare by the storms, furred here and there by a thin pelt of grass where seeds had rooted themselves in pockets of soil. Harsh though they were, the mountains where once the Silure tribesmen had roamed had their own uncompromising beauty, but they had little mercy for those footed creatures that dared to search out their mysteries. Shepherds followed their sheep across these hills, but even they rarely climbed so high.

The black horse, finding the grass too short and thin to be worth grazing, butted Artor gently and the high king took a step forward. In the clear light Raven's coat gleamed like the wing of the bird that had given him his name. The stallion had gone lame a little past mid-morning. The stag they were trailing was long gone, and the rest of the hunters after it. The track that Artor was following now, though it crested the ridge before descending into the valley, was the shortest way home.

A stone turned beneath his foot and he tensed against remembered pain. But his muscles, warmed by the exercise, flexed and held without a twinge. Indeed, at forty-two, he was as hale and strong as he had ever been. And Britannia was at peace after untold years of war.

It still seemed strange to him to contemplate a year without a campaign. He would have to think of something—public works, perhaps—on which his chieftains could spend their energy so they did not begin fighting one another. He had even begun to hope that he might find it in him to be a true husband to Guendivar.

Artor was still not quite accustomed to being able to move freely—for three years the wound that Melguas' spear had torn through his groin had pained him. The night when the Cauldron, borne through the hall of Camalot by invisible hands, had healed them all was scarcely three months ago.

And a good thing, too—half lamed, he could never have made this climb under his own power. But, now, gazing out across a landscape of blue distances ribbed by ridge and valley, the king blessed the mischance that had brought him here. On the Sunday past, Father Paternus had preached about the temptation of Christ, whom the Devil had carried off to a high place to show him all the kingdoms of the world and their glory. Looking around him, Artor thought that the writer of the gospel must have gotten it wrong somehow, for he himself was high king of all he could see, and the sight of it did not fill him with pride and power, but with wonder.

And, he thought as the next moment brought new awareness, with humility. How could any man look upon this mighty expanse of plain and mountain and say he ruled it all?

Below him the land fell away in long green slopes towards the estuary of the Sabrina, touched here and there with the gold of turning leaves. A smudge of smoke dimmed the tiled roofs of Castra Legionis; beyond them he could just make out the blue gleam of the Sabrina itself. Closer still he glimpsed the villa from which the hunting party had set out that morning. To the south across the water stretched the dim blur of the Dumnonian lands. Eastward lay the midlands, and beyond them Londinium and the Saxon territories. Looking north he could imagine the whole length of the island, all the way to the Alban tribes beyond the Wall. The sky to the north was curdled with clouds. A storm was coming, but he had a little time before it was here.

From this mountaintop, the works of humankind were no more than smudges upon the hallowed isle of Britannia, set like a jewel in the shining silver of the sea.

But it does not belong to me— Artor thought then. *Better to say that I belong to the land.*

A nudge from Raven brought him back from his reverie and he grinned, turning to rub the horse behind his swiveling ears, where the black hide sweated beneath the bridle. Men were not made to live on such heights, and at this time of year darkness would be gathering before he reached shelter. He patted the black's neck, took up the reins, and started down the hill.

For years, thought Medraut, these hills had haunted his dreams. But he had not visited the Isle of Maidens since his childhood, and he had convinced himself that the dark and looming shapes he remembered were no more than a child's imaginings. He was accustomed to mountains—the high, wild hills of the Pictish country, and the tangled hills of the Votadini lands. Why should these be so different? But with every hour he rode, the humped shapes grew closer, and more terrible.

They are my mother's hills . . . he thought grimly. *They are like her.* As he dreaded these hills, he dreaded the thought of confronting her. But he was fifteen, and a man. Neither fear could stop him now.

At Voreda he found a shepherd who agreed to guide him in exchange for a few pieces of gold. For three days they followed the narrow trail that led through the high meadows and down among the trees. Like many men who have lived much alone, the shepherd was inclined to chatter when in company, and gabbled cheerfully until a glare from Medraut stopped him. After that, they rode in a gloomy silence that preyed upon the young man's nerves until he was almost ready to order the shepherd to start talking again.

But by then they had reached the pass below the circle of

stones, and Medraut could see the Lake, and the round island, and the thatched roofs of buildings gleaming through its trees. He paid the shepherd then and sent him away, saying that from here he could follow the trail to the coast without a guide. He did not particularly care if the old man believed him, as long as he went away. The remainder of this journey must be accomplished alone.

To be alone was frightening, but it carried with it the heady taste of freedom. Throughout the years of his growing, his mother had always been present even when she was not physically there, as if the belly cord still connected them. And then, three months ago, when the full moon hung in the sky, the link had disappeared.

For weeks he had been half paralyzed with terror, expecting every messenger to tell them that Morgause was dead. It was Cunobelinus, riding through the great gates with his men behind him, who informed Medraut that his mother was at the Lake with the priestesses of the Isle of Maidens, and that from now on Cunobelinus himself would serve as regent as well as warleader for the northern Votadini, and rule from Dun Eidyn.

The new regent was civil, and his people treated Medraut as a royal prince when they had time to notice him at all. It was not loss of status that had sent him southward. It was the thing he had learned while he still feared Morgause dead that burned in his belly and had driven him here to confront her. It was hard to admit anger when one was torn by the grief of loss. But his mother was still alive.

Medraut was free to hate her now.

"What are you doing here?"

Medraut spun around, for a moment too astonished not to have sensed that his mother had entered the small, white-washed chamber where the priestesses had placed him to answer her. Tuned since birth to her presence, he should have vibrated like a harpstring when its octave is plucked. But the link between them was broken; if he had doubted, he felt the truth of that now.

"Without a word, you abandoned me. Is it so surprising I should come to see how you fared?"

Morgause eyed him uncertainly. Clearly she too felt the difference in the energy between them, all the more, he reflected angrily, because she had not been expecting it. Obviously she had not known their bond was broken. Since she went away she had not thought about him at all.

"As you see," she said finally, "I am well."

His eyes narrowed. "You are changed." And indeed it was so, though at first glance it was hard to describe what had altered. Where before she had always worn black and crimson, now she was dressed in the dark blue of a senior priestess on the Isle. But that was only external. Perhaps it was the fact that her high color had faded that made her seem different, or the new silver in her hair. Or perhaps it was the aura of power, almost of violence, that had always surrounded her, that was gone.

Medraut probed with his inner senses, as she had taught him, and recoiled, blinking. The power was still there, but leashed and contained. It occurred to him that her inner stillness might, if anything, make her stronger. A frightening thought, but it would make no difference, he reminded himself. After today nothing she did could hurt him anymore.

His mother's shoulders twitched in a shrug—a subtle, complex movement that simultaneously suggested apology, pride, and oddly, laughter. She looked at him directly then, and he shivered.

"So are you." Her voice was without expression. She asked again, "Why did you come?"

"To accuse you—" The words came out in a whisper, and Medraut cleared his throat angrily. "You killed her. Without a word to me. You had Kea murdered! Why?!"

He had expected disdain or anger, but not the flat incomprehension with which Morgause gazed back at him.

"The slave girl!" he said desperately. "The one I slept with at Fodreu!" How inadequate those words were for what Kea had done for him, making of her forced choice a gift that transformed him, as if by receiving his first seed, she had given birth to him as a man.

For a moment her eyes flashed in the way he remembered, then she sighed. "Did you love her? I am sorry."

He cleared his throat. "Sorry that I loved her, or that you had her put down like a sick dog?"

"At the time . . . it seemed best to ensure that there should be no child," Morgause answered at last.

"Do you truly believe that? Surely your wisewomen could have made sure any child she might conceive was not born!" He shook his head, temples beginning to pound with the sick headache that came from suppressing rage. "If death was a fit remedy for inappropriate conception, you should have hanged yourself on the nearest tree when you found yourself pregnant with me!

"You did not kill her because of my child, *Mother* . . . " all the bitterness Medraut had carried so long poured out at last, "but because of *yours.* I think you ordered Kea's death because you feared I might love her more than you!"

Morgause's hands fluttered outward in a little helpless gesture that snapped the last of his control.

"Well, you failed! I hate you, Queen-bitch, royal whore!" He flew at her and discovered that even without stirring she still had the power to stop him, shaking, where he stood.

"You are a prince! Show some control!"

"I am an abomination! I am what you have made me!"

"You will be free of me . . ." Morgause said tiredly. "I will not be returning to Dun Eidyn."

"Do you think that will make a difference, when every room holds your scent, and every stone the impress of your power? I am going south. Perhaps my *father* will teach me what it means to be a man. He could hardly do a worse job of it than you!"

The long hours in the saddle had given him the time to think it through. His mother had raised him to believe himself meant for a special destiny, and for two years now, he had thought himself true heir to Britannia. But in discovering her treachery, he had begun to question everything, and it had come to him that Artor's high seat was not hers to bestow. Neither would the inheritance come to him through Christian law. It was Artor himself he must persuade if he wanted his heritage.

"You will do nothing of the kind!" For the first time, Morgause looked alarmed. "You will stay in Alba and inherit the

Votadini lands. Artor has all of your brothers. He does not need you."

"Do you still hate him, Mother?" Medraut asked maliciously. "Or has this conversion to holiness taken even that away?"

"Artor . . ." she said stiffly, "is no longer my concern."

"Nor am I, mother dear, nor am I . . ." Medraut's fury was fading, to be replaced by a cold detachment, as if the rage had burned all his humanity away. He liked the feeling—it took away the pain. "I am the age Artor was when he became king, no longer subject to a woman's rule. Will you lock me up to keep me from going where I choose?"

"If I have to—" Morgause said shortly.

Medraut laughed as she left him. But when he opened the door to follow, he found it guarded by two sturdy young women who looked as if they knew how to use the short spears gripped in their hands. In some things his mother's lessons still served him well. His first outraged response was suppressed so swiftly they scarcely noted it.

"Have you come to protect me? I am afraid my mother still considers me a child." He eyed them appreciatively and his smile became a complicit grin. They were young and, living among women, must be curious about beings of a gender they saw only at festivals. In another moment one of the girls began to smile back, and he knew that she, at least, was not seeing him as a child at all.

"Do not say that it serves me right, after all the trouble I gave you, to find an enemy in my son!" exclaimed Morgause, whirling to glare at Igierne, who sat still in her great carven chair. So still—even in the throes of her confusion, Morgause felt a pang. With each day Igierne seemed to grow more fragile, as if her substance was evaporating like the morning dew.

But her voice, when she replied, was strong. "Have I said so? But if he is rebelling, surely you, of all mothers, ought to understand."

"That is not what has upset me. Medraut has grown as I shaped him, and now that I no longer desire to do so, I am afraid to loose him upon the world."

"You shaped him," observed the third woman, who had been sitting with Igierne when Morgause slammed through the door into the room. "But the wisefolk of my land teach that the Norns are three. You bear responsibility for what has been, maybe, but now your son is becoming a new person, and he must choose what shall be."

"What do you know of it, outlander?" Morgause spat back. Igierne lifted a hand in protest, and Morgause bit back her next words. She had grown unaccustomed to self-control.

Hæthwæge gazed back at her, unfazed, and Morgause glared. She had been raised to think of the Saxon kind as enemy, and found Hæthwæge's name and race alike disturbing, but Igierne had welcomed her, and in truth, the old woman who had helped to raise the child-king of Cantuware had knowledge they could use.

"I was not happy when the time came for me to give up Eormenric to the care of men—it still seems to me that seven is too young," Hæthwæge said then. "But it is true that a child needs the teaching of both male and female to grow. Let Medraut's father take him if he needs a stronger hand."

There was a short, charged silence.

"His father is the high king. . . ." Through clenched teeth Morgause got out the words.

"Ah—and he is your brother. . . ." Hæthwæge nodded. "I know that the Christians are not understanding about such things."

For a moment longer Morgause stared at her. Then she began, rather helplessly, to laugh. Weathered and bent like an old elder tree, Hæthwæge played the role of a simple village wisewoman very well, but Morgause could see past the mask. If the *wicce* had made light of the danger, it was on purpose, to comfort her.

She was trying to think of a polite rejoinder when there was a knock at the door. In the next moment it swung open and they saw Verica, one of the young priestesses who had been set to guard Medraut.

"He's gone!"

Morgause felt suddenly cold.

"Did he harm Cunovinda?" asked Igierne.

"Oh, Vinda is just fine—unless you call a broken heart a wound," Verica said bitterly. "I left her guarding a locked door, and when I returned it was open and she was crying her eyes out because he had persuaded her to open it and then left her!"

It could have been worse, thought Morgause numbly. He could have taken the girl with him, and then killed or abandoned her. Who knew what Medraut might do?

"He is beyond your reach, daughter," Igierne said then, and Hæthwæge added, "He will make his own wyrd now. . . ."

"That is so, but this child's wyrd could shake a kingdom," said Igierne.

Morgause nodded. What that fate might be she dared not imagine, but she knew where he was going, and for the first time in her life, felt pity for Artor.

The high king of Britannia sat in his chair of state to receive the ambassadors. The basilica at Calleva would have been more impressive, or the one in Londinium, but the long chamber that had once been the pride of the commander of the fort at Isca had been restored when he rebuilt the town's defenses. The walls bore no frescoes, but they had been newly whitewashed, with a bright band of geometric designs painted along the top and bottom, and there were touches of gilding on the columns that ran down the nave. The cloaks of the chieftains and princes who had crowded inside, chequered and banded or bright with embroidery, made a vivid spectacle. Artor had been in Castra Legionis for a little over a month, long enough for everyone in the area who had a petition or a grievance to travel here.

But for this audience Artor had chosen to wear the full panoply of an emperor, and the length of time it had been since the previous occasion was marked by the difficulty they had in finding a jewel-sewn mantle in a shade that would match the deep green tunic, with its orphreys and apparels of gold woven brocade. That had been when they made peace with King Icel, said Betiver when Artor tried to remember. Then, thought the king as he tried to shift position without dislodging the stiff folds of the mantle, he had wanted to impress barbarians. Today his purpose was to appear as an heir of Rome's imperium before other heirs of Rome.

Artor felt Betiver stir nervously in his place behind the chair and turned his head to smile reassuringly.

"I should have been the one to welcome him," muttered the younger man. "But I didn't know what to say. Christ! It's been more than twenty years!"

Twenty years ago, Betiver had been an awestruck boy and Artor himself just learning to wield the power of a king, and now the child who had been left with him to seal an alliance was one of the supports of his kingdom.

"He is your father," Artor said aloud. "He will forgive. It is I who should earn his wrath for keeping you here—"

Then the great double doors at the end of the hall swung open, and men moved aside to clear an aisle as the embassy from Gallia marched in.

Johannes Rutilius seemed smaller than Artor remembered, worn by the years. For the men of Gallia, as for Britannia, those years had been filled by fighting. Rutilius walked with a limp now, and there was abundant silver in his hair. But he still stood erect, and the only change in his expression came when he realized who the warrior standing behind Artor must be.

But the formal Latin greetings did not falter, nor did Artor's welcome.

"Is your lord in good health?" he asked. "He must be ripe in years."

Rutilius sighed as he sank into the chair they brought for him. "He is old indeed, and not much time is left to him. Hence this embassy. When I came before, we offered you alliance. Now I come to ask for the help you swore to give. Riothamus is dying, my lord, but Chlodovechus of the Franks is in the flower of his age, seeking to extend the Frankish lands in the north, while Alaric II leads the Visigoths of Tolosa against us in the south.

"The only son of Riothamus, Daniel Dremrud, was killed some years ago, fighting in the German lands. My lord's grandsons intrigue against each other—" He cast a tired glance at a dark young man who stood glowering among the warriors who had escorted him into the hall.

"Budic, there, is one of them. Five years ago, he and his brother Maxentius attacked Civitas Aquilonia in the south of

Armorica, to which they had a claim from their mother's father. Now Budic's brother has expelled him in turn. He hopes you will give him an army with which to take it back again."

"Then Riothamus is not asking my support for Budic as his heir?" asked Artor.

"We are Romans," Rutilius said simply: "And the Empire has always prospered when we sought heirs not of the body but of the spirit. Well, I know that it is so—does not my own son cleave to you before his own kin?"

He looked past Artor to Betiver, who flushed painfully, but he was smiling. He gestured towards Artor's mantle. "And I see that you, my lord, also hold to the spirit of Rome—so you will understand."

"What?" Artor said into the silence. "What does he wish of me?"

"You will make up your own mind whether to give aid to Budic in Aquilonia—but Riothamus judges neither of his grandsons of the stature to defend Gallia. The Emperor of the East is far away, and an Ostrogoth rules in Rome. The last strength of the West lies here, lord, in Britannia, where you have driven out the wild Irish and set the Saxon beneath your heel. What will your soldiers do now?"

There was a little stir among the watching warriors as Rutilius looked around.

"Bring them to Gallia, *princeps*, and Riothamus will make you his heir. Your fame is great in Armorica, and the grandsons of the men who followed Maximian will flock to your standard. Come to our aid, my lord Artor, and we will make you Emperor!"

The old dream reborn! Struggling to keep his face impassive, Artor sat back in his chair, the ghosts of Magnentius and Maximian, who had led the legions of Britannia to fight for the Empire, whispering in his ear. Constantine himself had been acclaimed in Eboracum before marching south to his destiny. Aegidius and his son Syagrius had tried to restore the Western Empire in Gallia, but without the resources of Britannia they could not endure. His foster-father Caius Turpilius had brought him up on these tales.

But with the power of Britannia and the blessing of Riothamus behind him, Artor might well succeed where no other man could. He had already succeeded in uniting Britannia, which neither Vitalinus nor Ambrosius nor Uthir had been able to do. Was it for this that he had been healed of his injury? He blinked, dazzled at the prospect. Oh, what a noble dream!

"My lord?" said a voice close by, and Artor forced his attention to the present once more.

"This is . . . an unexpected . . . offer," he managed to say. "It will require careful thought and discussion."

"Of course," answered Rutilius.

"You are my guest, and have scarcely tasted our hospitality," the king said in a more normal tone. "Let Betiver be my deputy, and do his duty to both of us in arranging for your lodging. Budic shall be our guest as well. Whatever the future may hold, I am still king in Britannia, and there are men waiting whose petitions I must hear."

Medraut ran his hand up the kitchen girl's leg beneath her skirts and pulled her back to the bed. "One more kiss—don't waste it. Once we reach the court you may never see me again."

"Let me go, you silly boy—I'll be late—" she protested, but she was laughing, and when he held her down and kissed her, she sighed and melted against him.

It was his turn to laugh, then, as a single smooth movement brought him off the bed and upright. He crossed to the basin he had made her bring to the room, and began to wash. It was little more than a cubbyhole, with a single pallet that would hold two people only if they were very friendly. But if Medraut had not had a knack for gaining what the Irish liked to call the "friendship of the thighs," he would not have been here.

He remembered, with momentary regret, the young priestess who had helped him to escape from the Isle of Maidens. Her kisses had been shy but sweet; it was too bad he had not had the time to take her maidenhead. To seduce one of the girls whose virginity his mother—the hypocrite—was guarding would have been a satisfactory first step to his revenge.

"You are mad," said the kitchen girl, who still lay on the bed with her skirts rucked up about her thighs. "The high king does not hand out places at his court to every nameless wanderer. Even the lord Goriat served for two seasons in the kitchen."

"Oh, I have a name," answered Medraut, "though I have not shared it with you." In truth, he had already forgotten hers. "But Goriat will no doubt remember you. Bring me to him, and you will have done all I require."

"Oh, you *are* a proud one!" she exclaimed, lifting her chin with a mocking sniff. "I will bring you to my lord, and see how far you fly when he throws you out the door!"

Ignoring her, Medraut went to his pack and pulled out the garments he had carried all the way from Dun Eidyn. At the flare of crimson silk, the girl fell silent, her eyes widening as he pulled on breeches of finely woven brown wool and shoes of tooled calfskin whose laces criss-crossed up his calves. The silk unrolled into a tunic, ornamented at shoulders and hem with bands embroidered with silver thread. From the folds of his chequered mantle he pulled a silver torc, and twisting, slid it around his neck, pulled a comb through his dark auburn hair and picked up the mantle.

"Who *are* you?" breathed the girl.

"Take me to Goriat, and you may learn—" Medraut gave her a sardonic smile. "If you remember what I told you to say. . . ."

During the time it took for her to lead him from the cubbyhole in the old barracks through the narrow lanes of the fortress to the wide porch before the audience hall he refused to say another word.

He had learned that Gualchmai was newly wedded, and away on his wife's lands in the south, and Aggarban still on sick leave. That did not matter. It was Goriat who would be most likely to recognize him, and who must stand, however reluctantly, his ally. He had no difficulty recognizing him, standing with Gwyhir in the midst of laughing warriors, for his brothers overtopped most of the other men by a head.

Only the court and its servants could enter. He had to depend on the girl to make her way through the men to Goriat. He saw his brother turn, frowning. Medraut grinned. He had told the girl to say a message had come for "Dandelion," Goriat's baby-name, but he gave it in the dialect of the north. In another moment both of his brothers were pushing through the crowd.

"It's the brat!" exclaimed Goriat, staring at Medraut. Then he looked anxiously around him. "Where's Mother?"

"With the holy bitches at the Lake, rump aimed at the moon and nose in the dust, muttering sorceries. . . ."

"Oh . . . my . . . mother's baby boy has fled the nest indeed!" breathed Gwyhir. "I thought that you at least would stay with her in Dun Eidyn!"

"I thought she would have married you off to a Pictish princess by now," said Goriat. "That's what she tried to do to me!"

He blinked at the venom in Medraut's answering glare, but it was quickly quenched. There was no way, he thought, that Goriat could know about Kea.

"I do hope that Gualchmai was not expecting to stand on the Votadini coronation stone—" he said aloud. "Cunobelinus rules there now, and even for Leudonus' son I do not think he will give it up again."

"And Mother did not fight it? She simply walked away?" repeated Gwyhir in amazement. "Has she gone mad?"

Medraut shrugged. When, he wondered, had Morgause ever been sane?

"I have come south to seek my fortune with the rest of you," he said then. "They say that our mother's brother is throned on high in yonder hall. Will not one of you escort me there and make the introductions?"

The messenger from Dun Breatann had been speaking for some time. Artor focused his attention with an effort as a change in the man's voice heralded a conclusion. "And so, it is the request of my master Ridarchus that the high king journey to confer with him on this matter—"

What matter? Artor had been thinking of Gallia and had scarcely heard. The Irish—that was it—the king of the Dal Riadans had offered alliance. He cleared his throat and straightened.

"I will consider Ridarchus' request, but it is my judgment that the men of Eriu will lie quiet at least until next spring. I will come, but I must consider the needs of the rest of Britannia before I decide on when."

That was a tactful answer that would not bind him, but it was true. Even if he decided to accept Riothamus' offer, he must spend some time settling things here before he could leave. Perhaps Betiver could lead a token force to Gallia. . . .

The man from Dun Breatann bowed and backed away. The crowd stirred, and he saw the fair heads of Goriat and Gwyhir moving above the others like swans on a stream.

"My lord uncle!" called Gwyhir. "We have brought a new recruit to your service!"

Another man was with them—no, a boy just beginning his growth spurt, with dark red hair. Artor caught the gleam of a silver torc, but the features were a blur. His heart pounded suddenly, as if he had come upon an enemy unaware.

"The last of my mother's sons has come south to join us," added Goriat heartily. "Here is Medraut, lord king. Will you welcome him?"

Artor stared down at the boy's bent head. He had recognized him already, without yet understanding. But how had the time passed so quickly? This boy was almost grown! Medraut did not resemble his brothers, though there was the promise of height in those long bones. But as he began to get up, the king suppressed an instinctive recoil, for in that fine-boned face he saw Morgause. He wondered if his sister had told her son the truth about his parentage.

"Is it your wish to serve me, boy?" His voice sounded harsh in his own ears.

"You shall be as a father to me . . ." answered Medraut, and smiled.

ii

A CIRCLE OF KINGS

A.D. 503

The plain stretched away to a grey line of hills, a new layer of green grass poking through last year's trampled straw. Medraut's mare jerked at the rein, reaching for a bite, and he hauled up her head. Since joining Artor's court the previous autumn he had gotten a lot more practice in riding. Even in winter the high king moved often, and his household went with him. Medraut found these southern lands fair and fat, with their thick woods and fertile fields, but to one accustomed to the harsh vistas of the north, their very luxuriance felt confining.

From Castra Legionis they had travelled south to Dumnonia, and then to Camalot for the Midwinter holy days. He wished they could have stayed there, for Artor's queen had been kind to him. Guendivar's golden beauty reminded him of his lost Kea. But perhaps it was just as well they did not stay long, he thought then. She might not have been so friendly if someone had told her he was Artor's son.

If so, he had only himself to blame, he thought ruefully. Or perhaps his brothers—when they persisted in treating him as if he were still a child there had been a stupid argument, and he had retorted that of them all, only he and Gualchmai could truly say who their fathers had been. They had only agreed to keep silent on the matter after tempers had cooled, but someone must have overheard. He could tell by the way people looked at him, afterward.

He would not make that mistake again, he told himself, shifting in the saddle. And yet perhaps it was just as well, if Artor was going to acknowledge him, that the news did not come as a complete surprise.

They had finished the winter in Londinium, and now they were on their way north once more. But the straightest way to Alba would have been to follow the old Roman road to Lindum, through the Anglian lands. Instead, the royal party had turned west through Calleva to Sorviodunum before taking the track that led north to this plain, the largest expanse of open land in Britannia.

Medraut shivered. It was cold here, with nothing to break the wind. Even at high summer, he suspected, that wind would blow. Now, a week after the Feast of the Resurrection, the wind probed the weave of his cloak with chill fingers and whispered like a restless soul.

Ahead he could see the first of the barrows that marched across the plain. Perhaps that was why the thought had come to him. He grimaced. His mother would have welcomed the ghosts, avid and smiling. His . . . father . . . riding near the head of the line, sat his big black horse easily, his watchful gaze revealing no emotion at all.

Medraut squeezed the red mare's sides and moved forward. There was plenty of room to go abreast, and the warrior who had been riding nearest reined aside to let him bring his mare up next to the king. Artor's grey gaze flickered towards him and away.

Do I make you uneasy, my father-uncle? The king had made him welcome with the greatest courtesy, but there was always a tension between them. Was it guilt that made Artor so wary, wondered Medraut, or had his mother warped him into something that no one could love?

"This is not the way to Glevum—" he said aloud.

"Not the most direct, it is true," Artor replied.

"Then why have we come here? No doubt it is very interesting, but is your kingdom so peaceful that you can waste time sightseeing? I thought you were eager to see the land settled so that you could go to Gallia—"

"When Maximian set out to claim the Imperium, the wild tribes of the north attacked like wolves when the shepherd has left the fold. Until I am satisfied regarding our defenses, I will not leave these shores. Betiver and the men he has taken yonder will bolster Riothamus until I come."

"Betiver is the old man's sister-son—" Medraut observed with a sidelong smile. "Are you not afraid that Riothamus will make him his heir?"

"It would be very natural," Artor said softly, his gaze still on the land ahead. "If that should come to pass I would rejoice for Betiver and swear alliance gladly, though I would miss his presence at my side."

Medraut's heart raced in his breast. *He means to make me his heir! I am sure of it, or why would he be talking to me this way?*

"There—" said Artor as they reached the top of the rise. "That is why we have come here."

Medraut straightened, shading his eyes with his hand. To their right, the line of barrows stretched away across the plain. The nearest was larger than the others, its sides still rough beneath the furring of grass, as if it had not yet had time to settle completely into the land.

"These are the graves of ancient kings, gone back to the earth of the land they loved."

Medraut shivered as he heard the echo of his thoughts in Artor's words.

"The mound at the end holds the bones of the British princes whom Hengest killed by treachery on the Night of the Long Knives. My uncle Ambrosius is buried there, and Uthir, my father, as well."

My grandfather . . . thought Medraut. This was a heritage his mother did not share, and he looked at the mound curiously, trying to remember what he had heard about those long ago days when the Saxons had overrun the land in blood and fire.

"Well, you have avenged them," he said then. "The Saxon wolf is tamed."

"For now," Artor agreed. "While we stay strong. But in Gallia, the Franks and Burgunds and Visigoths that were settled on the land to defend it rule the Romans now. They may pretend to adopt our ways, but even Oesc—" He broke off, shaking his head. Then he gestured towards the mounds. "It will take time to make us all one people. When the bones of Saxon and Briton are mingled together with the dust of this land perhaps we may trust them. But it will take time."

Medraut looked at him skeptically. Old men, he had heard, tended to live in the past. The high king looked strong, but there was silver in his beard. Was he getting old?

The wind blew more strongly. From overhead he heard the harsh cry of a raven and looked upward. The bird circled the riders once and then flapped away to the westward. Medraut, turning to track its flight, stilled, staring at the circle of stones that seemed to have risen out of the ground. He had seen Roman buildings that were larger, but never such mighty pieces of stone. Standing proud as kings come to council, their stark simplicity chilled his soul.

Something in his silence must have alerted the king, for Artor followed his gaze and smiled.

"It is the Giant's Dance. Merlin brought me here when I was a boy."

Medraut twitched involuntarily at the sound of that name. The Druid had arrived at Castra Legionis not long after he himself had come there. There was no reason to think it had anything to do with him. Men said that Merlin had always come and gone at his own will—not even the high king could command him. But there was something in the dark stare beneath those bushy brows that made Medraut feel naked. He had been surprised at the depth of his own relief when the old man went away once more.

"Why?" he asked baldly.

Artor looked at him, one eyebrow lifting. "Come and see—"

With a word to Cai, he reined his horse towards the stone circle, and after a moment's astonished hesitation, Medraut followed.

As he neared the circle, he looked over his shoulder. The rest of the column was continuing its march across the plain. The boy looked around him nervously. Had the king decided he posed too great a danger and found this opportunity to get rid of him? Reason told him it was unlikely. Artor could have gotten away with such a deed far more easily in Londinium than in this empty land where everyone would know.

"Don't be afraid," said Artor, interpreting his hesitation correctly even if, one hoped, he did not divine its cause. He pulled up before a stone that stood in front of the others like a sentinel, slid off of his mount and motioned to Medraut to do the same. "At this time of day and at this season, the circle is not dangerous."

Medraut started forward. As he passed through the outer circle of uprights he flinched. A buzz, more felt than heard, vibrated through his bones.

"Don't you feel it?" he asked as Artor turned inquiringly. "This place is warded."

"Not precisely—Merlin says that a current of power flows between the stones. I have learned to sense such things, but when I was your age I could not feel it. Is this a natural talent, Medraut, or *her* teaching?"

The boy felt himself flushing. No need to ask whom he meant. What had his mother done to Artor to make *him* fear her? He took another step towards the middle trilithon. Everything beyond the circle appeared to waver, as if he were looking at it through glass.

"Wait—" Artor set his hand on Medraut's shoulder. He twitched, but the touch steadied him, and he did not pull away. Together, they moved between the huge capped uprights of the inner circle into the level space within. As they neared the altar stone Medraut sensed a subliminal hum, as if he were standing next to a hive of bees.

Artor's gaze had gone inward. "Power flows beneath the soil as water flows through riverbeds, from circle to circle, and from stone to stone. Here, two great currents cross. It is a place of mighty magic."

"Have you brought my brothers here?" Medraut asked softly after a time, still anchored by the king's hand.

Artor shook his head.

"You know, don't you . . ." Medraut said then, "about me. . . ."

For the first time, he allowed himself to stare at the man who had fathered him. The high king, if not quite so tall as Medraut's older brothers, was still bigger than most men, his torso heavy with muscle. His features were too rugged for beauty, weathered by years of responsibility into a mask of power. But there were laughter lines around the grey eyes that watched him from beneath level brows. Except, perhaps, in those eyes, he could see nothing of himself in this man at all.

The king let go of his shoulder, looking away. "She did not tell me you existed until you were ten years old."

"Why didn't you take me away from her?"

"I had no proof . . ." Artor whispered.

At ten, Medraut had still believed that his mother was good, and that he himself would grow up to be a hero one day. If the king had taken him then, his son might have been able to love him.

"You were newly married and expected to get a legitimate child," he said flatly. "But you have none. Will you make me your heir?"

"You have a son's claim on me, Medraut. But I am more a Roman than a Briton when it comes to the Imperium. They did not make me king because I was my father's son, or not wholly, but because of the Sword."

Artor's hand settled over the pommel of the blade at his side, and Medraut shivered as a new note pierced the circle's hum, so high and clear that it hurt to hear. He knew about the Sword, of course, but it was always the Cauldron that his mother had coveted. This was man's magic, and this too, he thought with a tremor of excitement, was his heritage.

The sound faded as the high king's hand moved once more to his side, and he sighed. "When the time comes, if there is a man fit to hold it, he will become the Defender of Britannia. I will do what I can for you, but I can make no promises."

Medraut frowned. *If you had raised me, Father, I might believe that. But in the North we know that bloodright binds the king to his land. Britannia belongs to me. . . .* But he did not voice those thoughts aloud.

The road from Mamucium to Bremetennacum led through low hills. The king and his escort had spent the night in the abandoned fort above the river. The timber barracks buildings had long ago collapsed, but the gatehouse and parts of the praetorium, where once the commander of the garrison had ruled, still provided some shelter. But it was a cheerless camp, for the town outside the walls had fallen into ruin a generation before.

It was fear that had killed the town, thought Artor, not the Saxons, for there was no sign of burning. The people who had once inhabited those mute, overgrown heaps of rubble had simply moved away. *But they will return . . .* he told himself. *The site on the river is a good one. From these ruins some day a mighty city will rise.*

Something moved in the tangle of hazels that flanked the road. By the time he identified the whistle of arrows Artor was already turning, flattening himself against the stallion's neck as he grabbed for his shield. A horse squealed, rearing. Behind him a man slid from his mount, a black-feathered arrow jutting from his chest. Artor straightened, peering back down the line from the shelter of his shield. He sighed with unexpected relief as he saw that Medraut, who had been riding with Goriat, had his shield up as well.

An arrow thunked into his own, and he realized that the enemy were concentrating their fire on the forward part of the line. Masterless men who lived by banditry, he thought. This time they had chosen the wrong prey.

"Vanguard, dismount!" he cried. "Goriat, take your riders and hit them from the rear!"

He slid from the saddle. A swat sent Raven trotting down the road. Afoot, Artor and his men were smaller targets.

Though he had no recollection of drawing it, his sword was in his hand. It flared in the sunlight as he ran towards the trees.

Branches thrashed, scratching his shield. Artor crashed through them, glimpsed a man's shape and thrust. The blade bit and someone yelled. The king jerked the sword free and pushed onward. From ahead came more yelling. He cut down two more enemies before he reached the clearing where the horsemen had caught the fleeing men.

Several bodies lay crumpled on the grass. The fifteen or so outlaws who remained glared at the horsemen whose circle held them, lances pointing at their breasts. The king straightened, shield still up, waiting for his pulse to slow. It was more than a year since he had drawn his sword in anger; the fading rush of battle fury warred with the ache of stressed muscles and the smart where a branch had whipped across his brow.

That felt too good— he thought wryly, *like the first beaker of beer at the end of a long, hot day.* Automatically, he was making a headcount of friend and foe. He noted Medraut's auburn head and once more, tension he had not been aware of suddenly eased. Why? There were others—Betiver or Gualchmai—whom he loved better than he did this sullen boy, but he had never sagged with relief after a fight to find them still alive.

Medraut's face was pale with excitement, his eyes burning like coals. A bloodstained scarf was tied around his arm. Artor swallowed as he saw it. He would have to get the boy some armor. The others were his friends, but this boy was his future. *I have a hostage to fortune now.*

He shook himself and strode forward. "Cai, get rope to bind them."

The prisoners were a sorry lot, stinking and unshaven, clad in tattered wool and badly cured leather. One man was missing an ear. But the weapons they had thrown down looked well-used.

"We're poor men, lord—" whined one of the prisoners, "refugees from the Saxon wars."

"Indeed? It seems to me that you speak like a man of Glevum—"

"My father was from Camulodunum," the complainer said quickly. "He was a sandalmaker there. But the towns are dying, and where shall I practice the trade he taught me now? Surely you'll not be too harsh with folk who are only trying to survive!"

"Work then!" Artor said harshly. "Britannia is full of abandoned farms. Learn to get food by the sweat of your own brows, rather than taking it from better men! You complain that there are no towns!" He shook his head in disgust. "When you make the roads unsafe for honest travelers, how in the Lady's name do you expect towns to survive?"

"Shall we hang them here, lord?" called one of the horsemen, and the robber's face showed his fear.

Artor shook his head. "There is still a magistrate at Bremetennacum. These wretches shall be judged by the people on whom they have preyed."

There was blood on his blade, but it seemed to him he could feel a hum of satisfaction from the sword. Carefully he wiped it and slid it into the sheath once more. When he looked up, he met Medraut's considering gaze.

He says he will not make me his heir, thought Medraut, watching the high king as he took his place on the bench the monks had set out for him, *but why has he brought me along on this journey if not to show me what it is to be a king?*

Gaining Artor's throne was not going to be easy. The gash where the arrow had nicked his arm throbbed dully and he adjusted the sling to support it, remembering the first shock of pain, and the next even more disturbing awareness that the arrow had come from behind. He had said nothing to Artor, for he could prove nothing. But the psychic defenses honed by years with Morgause had snapped back into place like a king's houseguard. It was only when he felt that familiar wary tension return that he realized that traveling with his father, he had begun to let them down.

The fort at Bremetennacum had fallen into ruin, but the townsfolk here had managed to maintain their ditch and palisade. Perhaps the reason was the rich bottomlands of the valley and the river with its easy access to the sea. The land was good here, and so was the trade, but that only made the place a more attractive target for raids. The magistrates who had been seated on their own benches beside him gazed sourly around them, torn between gratitude to the king for capturing the robbers and resentment of the pace at which they were required to deal with them.

They had sentenced the leaders to hang, but the remainder they enslaved, arguing that it was justice that those who had stolen the fruit of others' labors should be denied the use of their own. As the last of the prisoners was marched off to death or servitude, the townsmen straightened, anticipating the feast that had been prepared to honor their visitor.

But Artor was not yet done with them.

"We've cleared out one nest of vermin, and you and your goods will have safe passage to Mamucium and Deva—for a time. But what happens when some other ruffian decides to settle in? I cannot be everywhere, and who will protect you then?"

"We are merchants and farmers, lord, not fighting men—" one of the magistrates said sullenly. He gestured in the direction in which the prisoners had gone. "If we were, do you think we would have suffered that lot for so long?"

"If you cannot defend yourselves, then I will have to appoint you a protector . . ." the king said slowly. "Is that what you desire?"

"Oh, my lord—" Another man looked up eagerly. "Indeed it is! He and his men can stay at the old fort, and—"

Artor's features creased in a sardonic smile, as if he had heard this before. "And who will rebuild it? And what will they eat? An ill-fed man cannot swing a sword—"

"But you— We supposed—" The magistrates wilted beneath his glare.

"I will give you Paulinus Clutorix, a veteran of the Saxon wars, and three experienced men."

"But that's not enough—"

"Very true," Artor continued briskly. "He will take on more, enough to mount a regular patrol, and he will drill every man of fighting age in this valley in the use of arms so that when the time comes to go after a band of outlaws, or you see yon river bobbing with Irish coracles, you'll have a force sufficient to deal with them."

The town fathers were frowning. Their reluctance seemed strange to Medraut, who had grown up among a warrior people who had never been forbidden by the Romans to bear arms. But he could see that some of the younger men were grinning. He had seen his father fight the day before. Now, he was seeing how Artor ruled.

"And there will be a levy, in goods or coin, upon each household for their keep." The townsmen began to protest while Artor's warriors tried to hide their grins. The king held up one hand. "Did you assume I would send gold? How do you think I feed my men if not by taking tithes and levying taxes? At least this way you will know where your tax money goes. And the burden must be shared by everyone—" He gazed sternly around him. "Even the monks who own these rich fields. . . ."

Now it was the churchmen who were protesting. The defending force would have their prayers, of course, but their produce belonged to God. In Artor's face there was no yielding. Medraut suppressed an anticipatory grin.

"Good father, if prayer had protected you from outlaw spears or Irish swords I might agree," said the king. "But I have seen too many burnt monasteries. Pay your share, holy brethren, if you expect my men to come to your call!" He sat back, eyes glinting, a grim smile twitching the brown beard.

Morgause had always said that Artor let the priests rule him, but Medraut saw now that it was not so. He sat hunched on his bench, resting his chin on his fist as he watched. In how many other ways had she been wrong? The priests would call his birth ungodly, but he was *glad* now to be Artor's son. And if he worked hard, he thought, perhaps the wary courtesy with which the high king treated him would change to true affection, and Medraut could prove himself a worthy heir. . . .

"It looks . . . defensible . . ." said Gwyhir, whose turn it was to ride beside the king.

Artor laughed. The firth of the Clutha lay before them, its waters a shifting sheet of silver beneath the high clouds. Low hills ran along the peninsula behind it, featureless as if carved from shadow. The great rock of Altaclutha rose from those opalescent waters like an island, its sheer sides carved by the gods into a fortress that needed little help from man to be secure. From this distance, he could scarcely distinguish the stone walls and slate roofs from the native stone, and the causeway that connected it to the land was hidden from view.

"Dun Breatann is the fortress of the Britons indeed. Since my father's time the Rock has guarded the west of Alba. But Ridarchus is old now, and I do not know his heir."

"It is Morcant Bulc, is it not?" Gwyhir answered him. "Ridarchus' grandson. They came once to Dun Eidyn when I was a child."

Artor nodded. He did not want to think about inheritance, but he supposed it was his duty. Unbidden, the face of Medraut came to mind. He had hoped to learn more of the boy on this long journey up from the south, and to some extent he had done so. But Medraut's smooth surface repelled intimacy. How he could have come from the same nest as his brothers was cause for amazement. Gualchmai could not conceal a thought if he tried. Aggarban's sullen silences were easily read, and the eyes of Gwyhir and Goriat were deep pools into which one had only to gaze to see their souls.

Medraut was clearly doing his best to please, thought the king. He was observant, and did not make the same mistake twice, but he reminded the king of a man struggling to learn a new language, learning by rote the turns of phrase for which he had no natural ear. It was not because he had been brought up in Alba—his brothers had been accepted by Artor's household immediately. But their actions, even their mistakes, came from the heart. One sensed that Medraut's were the result of calculation.

In the next moment Artor shook his head, blaming his distrust on his own fears. Most likely the boy was simply shy.

The high king glanced back along the line. Men who had been slumped in the saddle reined in straying mounts and straightened to military alertness when they felt his eye upon them. Artor turned back, gesturing to Gwyhir to blow his horn. The sound echoed across the pewter waters, and in a few moments he heard an answer from the dun, faint and sweet with distance, like an echo of faerie horns.

The night after their arrival a storm rolled in from the sea, dense clouds wrapping close about the Rock, blanketing the ever-changing tides. For five days they huddled beneath the slate roofs of the fortress, the only thing solid in a dissolving world. But the ale-vats of Dun Breatann were deep, and if it was wet outside, the drink flowed just as freely within.

"I gather that your journey here was not altogether peaceful—" said Ridarchus, indicating the bits of bandage that still adorned some of Artor's men.

Unlike his brother-in-law, Merlin, who still towered like a tree, Ridarchus had shrunk with the years, flesh and bone fined down to a twisted, sinewy frame. Only his nose still jutted fiercely. Sitting there with his black mantle and glinting dark eyes he reminded Artor of a raven. And like the bird, Ridarchus had grown wise with years.

"It's true, and makes your hospitality all the more welcome. But you will find the roads to the south safer, for awhile."

"You should have found them safe already, once you entered my lands," rasped Ridarchus. "I must thank you for ridding me of young Cuil and his band. But his death has won you few friends here, I warn you. He was popular with the common folk, with whom he used to share his booty."

"Do they not understand that without safe roads there will be no trade, and no long-term prosperity?"

"In their children's time, perhaps," said the prince, "but Cuil gave them gifts they could hold in their hands."

"I suppose so, and I am sorry he was killed in the fighting," said Artor, "for he was the brother of a man who captained the queen's guard when we campaigned in Demetia, and after I had drawn his teeth I would have spared him." He blinked as a change in the wind outside rippled through the hangings that were supposed to keep out drafts and sent smoke billowing sideways from the central fire.

"Maybe now news will reach us as well," said Ridarchus. "We hear little of what is happening in the world outside this isle."

Artor shook his head. "The Empire of the West is besieged on every side. Theoderic rules in Italia, and has just married his daughter Amalafrida to Thraseric of the Vandals in the north of Africa. In Gallia, Chlodovechus is expanding his borders in all directions. Three years ago he captured Burdigala. They say that the Romans in the Gothic lands fought for Alaric, their Gothic ruler, but the Franks were still too strong for them. Alaric made peace and paid Chlodovechus tribute last year."

"Will the Visigoths become a subject kingdom then?"

Artor shrugged. "They have a foothold in Iberia already—they have moved so many times, perhaps they will all pass over the Pyrenaei montes and abandon the south of Gallia to the Franks entirely."

The men who sat around the fire were singing, first the warriors from the dun, and then, as they caught the chorus, Artor's men as well. The king did not see Medraut among them and wondered where he had gone.

"I perceive that this matters to you," Ridarchus said after a moment had passed. "But we have our own troubles here in Britannia. Why do you care what happens across the sea?"

"No doubt Cassivellaunus might have said the same, before Caesar came," Artor observed dryly. "The Franks have proved themselves a warlike people. If they are not controlled now, your son's sons may see them at your gates. And there are men of our blood in Gallia who will certainly be overrun."

"I have heard a rumor that you mean to cross the sea yourself." Ridarchus cocked his head, bright eyes fixing the king.

"Riothamus has appealed to me. But before I go I must make Britannia secure."

"Hence this journey—" Ridarchus said slowly.

The high king nodded. "Until the Saxons came, the wild tribes of the North were always the greatest danger, and after them, the men of Eriu. When I have done what I can for you, I will move on to Dun Eidyn and seek a treaty with the Pictish king."

Ridarchus signaled to one of the serving girls to bring them more ale. He drank, then set his beaker down with an appreciative sigh.

"You can make a treaty for me, too, if you will—" he said then. "You know that for many years there have been men of Eriu on the peninsula of Cendtire, the old Epidii lands. Far from increasing the danger from their kinfolk across the water, I think they have protected us. They have been good neighbors, and we have fought side by side when the Picts got too strong. But perhaps too many of them have left Dal Riada, for in Eriu, Feragussos their king can no longer hold against the Ui Niall.

"Do you see those two men in the saffron tunics, there by the door?" He paused to drink once more and Artor followed the direction of his gaze. "They arrived a little before you did. They are men of Cendtire, ambassadors. Feragussos wishes to move himself and his court and the rest of his clan here from Dal Riada, and offers friendship. I could tolerate their presence unofficially, but I would not enter into such an alliance without your good will."

Particularly, thought Artor, *when I am sitting in your hall.* But he smiled. "I agree. I shall prepare a letter of invitation to Feragussos and welcome him as an ally."

Medraut moved away from the shelter of the inner wall, leaning against the wind. For the moment it had ceased to rain, but there was still enough moisture in the air to sting. He picked his way across the uneven rock to the breast-high wall that edged the clifftop and clung to it, gulping deep breaths of the brisk wind.

To the south and west stretched the silver dimpled waters of the Clutha. Beneath banks of low cloud he could just make out the darker masses of the far shore. He looked up as a gull screamed overhead, flung across the sky by the wind.

Free— he thought, *what would it feel like to be that free?* Even through the thick folds of his woolen mantle he was beginning to feel the chill, but after the odorous warmth of the hall it was welcome. He turned, his gaze moving from the watchtower on the highest point of the Rock to the great hall set into the niche halfway down one side.

He wondered why he felt so constricted—he could find no fault with Ridarchus' hospitality . . . and then, as the gull called again, he remembered the seabirds wheeling above the

Bodotria, and realized it was the scent of northern fires, and the sound of northern voices, that had disturbed him. They reminded him of Dun Eidyn.

I can't go back there, he thought, and still less did he desire to revisit Pictland, where he would remember Kea every time he turned around. But where could he run to? Certainly not to his mother. He had proved that he could manage on his own, but then he had been traveling with a goal, a place at the court of the high king. It was no part of his life-plan to become a nameless wanderer upon the roads. He wondered if Gualchmai and his new wife would take him in.

The sky was darkening. He felt one cold drop strike his hand and then a spattering of others as the heavens began to open once more. He sucked in a last breath of the cold, salt-tanged air and started back towards the inner wall. The squall was coming quickly now; he pulled his mantle over his head and hunched against the rain.

After the wall, one gained the next level by a steep flight of steps cut into the rock. Fighting the buffeting of the wind, Medraut had nearly gained the top when he sensed something dark rise up before him, recoiled, and slipped on the rain-slick stone. He flailed wildly, but there was nothing to hold onto. His falling body hit one outcrop and then another, and slid to the base of the wall.

When he came to himself, it was full dark. He hurt all over, and he was *cold.* Head throbbing, he tried to remember what had happened. If someone had pushed him, why had they not taken advantage of his unconsciousness to toss him into the sea? And if not, why was he still lying here? But if no one had seen him fall, surely someone should be wondering where he had gone. . . .

At least he could feel all his limbs. Very carefully, he tried to move. Everything ached, but it was only in his right leg that he felt real pain. Still, it was only going to get colder. He had to get up somehow.

Medraut had made it to the steps when he heard voices from above. Torches flared wildly as the wind caught them. Someone was calling his name.

"Look, there at the foot of the stair," someone cried.

"Here—" He let his dark mantle fall back so that the paler tunic could be seen. "I'm here. . . ."

He tensed as someone hurried towards him, torch held too high for features to be seen. Then the man was kneeling, and Medraut looked up into the anxious eyes of Artor the king.

The storm had passed, but the high king of Britannia remained at Dun Breatann. The boy, Medraut, had broken his leg, and was not yet fit to ride. That Artor should stay for the sake of a nephew was a matter of wonder, but presently men began to speak of a greater wonder, that the nephew was also a son. Artor knew they said it, though he did not know from whom the rumor first had come. It was inevitable, he thought, that the truth would eventually be known. That did not disturb him so much as the whisper he had heard as he lifted his son in his arms.

"Still living? A pity—if the bastard broke his neck it would be better for the king and for us all!"

Artor had not recognized the voice, and the situation could only be made worse by questioning, but in the dark hours of the night he lay wakeful, remembering the moment of thought, instantly suppressed, in which he had hoped it might be true.

He was still there a week later, when horns proclaimed the arrival of another party and the Saxon lords rode in. When Artor had spoken with them he went to the terrace where Medraut, his leg splinted and bound, sat looking out at the sea.

"Who has come?" asked the boy, looking up at him.

Artor continued to gaze at the bright glitter of sun on water. "The brother of Cynric, who rules the south Saxons now," he said without turning. "I had sent to them before we left Londinium, requesting his son as hostage, to guarantee the peace while I am in Gallia."

"And he has refused?"

Artor shook his head, turning to face his son. "They have brought me the boy. Ceawlin is his name."

"Then why are you troubled? And why are you telling this to me?" Medraut swung his splinted leg down from the bench and sat up, the sunlight sparking on his hair in glints of fire.

Artor stared at him, striving to see past the coloring and the fine bones that reminded him so painfully of Morgause. *Who are you really, boy? What is going on behind those eyes?*

"He desires me to send a man of my own kindred in exchange—'*to increase understanding between our peoples.* . . .'"

"And Goriat doesn't want to go, so you are thinking of sending me?" Medraut asked mockingly, and Artor felt his face grow red.

"Were you pushed down those stairs?" He held the boy's gaze and saw a glimmer of some emotion, swiftly shut away.

Artor had been king since he was the same age as this boy and he thought he knew how to judge men, but Medraut's personality offered no point of attachment on which to build a relationship.

Is that really true? he asked himself suddenly. *Or is it that you have been afraid to try?* He had kept the boy with him for almost a year, but how much time together had they really had?

After a moment, Medraut looked down.

"It was dark and raining . . . I thought there was someone, but I could not really see. I will tell you this, though. The arrow that wounded me in the south came from behind."

"You did not tell me!" Artor took a step forward, frowning, but Medraut's eyes were limpid as the sea.

"I had no proof, my lord, nor do I now. . . ."

Artor stood over him, fists clenching. *What are you hiding?* he thought, and then, *What am I?* He felt a vast weariness as his anger drained away.

"I will send you to the Saxons. Here, I cannot guarantee your safety, but Cynric will guard you like a she-wolf her last cub." *Against his own people, and mine,* his thought went on, *and perhaps against me. . . .*

"If you wish it, I will obey," answered Medraut, looking away.

Artor eyed at him narrowly, hearing in the boy's voice something almost like satisfaction, and wondered why.

iii

In the Place of Stones

A.D. 503

To travel across the neck of Alba in high summer, neither pursued nor pursuing, was pure pleasure. The Roman forts that had once defended the Antonine Wall were now no more than dimpled mounds, but the road that connected them was still passable. To the north rose the outriders of the highlands, blue with distance, the nearer slopes cloaked like an emperor in heather. Alba was all purple and gold beneath a pale northern sky, and the air had the same sweet tang as the peat-brown waters that rippled down from the hills.

Artor breathed deeply and sat straighter, as cares he had not known he carried fell away. Even the weather held fair, as if to welcome him.

"It won't last," said Goriat. "A week, or two, and we'll see fog and rain so thick you'd think it was winter in the southern lands."

"All the more reason to enjoy it now!" Artor grinned back at him, and Raven, sensing his rider's mood, pranced and pulled at the rein. "By the time the weather changes, we'll be safe at Fodreu."

Cai, who was riding on his other side, made a sound halfway between a grunt and a growl. "If we can trust them—I still say you're a fool to put yourself in their power!"

Goriat opened his eyes at the language, but Artor only smiled. There were times when Cai forgot the king was not still the little foster-brother who had followed him about when they were young. But the blood Cai had shed in his service since then, thought Artor, entitled him to a few blunt words. He was only four years older than the king, but he looked ten, the dark hair grizzled, and his face weathered and lined.

"Maybe so," Artor answered mildly, "but if they can't be trusted, better to find out now than have them break the border while I'm in Gallia!"

"Hmph!" Cai replied. "Or else you just enjoy the risk. I remember how it was when we were boys . . ."

Goriat kicked his horse in the ribs and drew level, brows quirked enquiringly.

"Whenever things got too quiet, Artor would find some fool thing to do. . . ." Cai exchanged rueful smiles with the king.

"Was I that bad?" asked Artor.

"Remember the miller's donkey?"

Artor's grin grew broader.

"What did he do?" asked Goriat in an awed voice.

"Tied the donkey to a threshing flail—"

"It could have worked," protested the king. "We use oxen to grind the corn, after all."

"What happened?" Goriat persisted, obviously delighted to be let in on this secret history.

"The donkey ate the grain and both Artor and I got a beating. They said I should have stopped him, but I knew even then the futility of trying to change Artor's mind when he gets that look in his eye," Cai answered resignedly.

"I learned something, though . . ." Artor continued after a moment had passed. "Beasts, or men, must be led in the direction their nature compels them. It is my judgment that the Picts are ready for peace. I would hate to think that I have grown so accustomed to fighting that I crave it as a drunkard his wine! Still, just in case, Cai has the right of it: there is one whom I have no right to lead into danger—" He glanced back down the line, seeking the gleam of Ceawlin's ruddy hair.

"Goriat, go back down the line and bring Cynric's cub up here to ride with me."

"And that's another risk . . ." mumured Cai as the younger man rode off.

"The child is nine years old! Do you fear he will attack me?" exclaimed Artor.

"He is a fox kit. I am afraid you will love him, and be hurt when he goes back to his wild kin. . . ."

Artor shut his lips, remembering the incident Cai referred to. He was grateful that his foster-brother had not mentioned Oesc, whom he had also made his hostage, and loved, and at Mons Badonicus been forced to kill. *His* little son must be almost eight by now.

He shook off the memory as Goriat returned, the frowning child kicking his pony to keep up with him. Despite his Saxon name, Ceawlin had the look of the Belgic royal house from whom his grandfather Ceretic had come.

Our blood is already mingling, thought Artor. *How long before we will be one in spirit?* He thought once more of the other little boy, Oesc's son, whose mother was Britannic and royal as well.

"Are you enjoying the journey?"

The grey glance flickered swiftly upward, then Ceawlin fixed his gaze on the road once more.

"You will have seen more of Britannia by now than any of the boys at home." Artor saw the frown began to ease and hid a smile. "But perhaps you miss the southern lands. It is in my mind to send you to stay at Camalot, under the care of my queen."

"Does she have a little boy?"

Artor twitched, momentarily astonished that the question should bring such pain. But Ceawlin could have no idea he had even struck a blow, much less how near to the bone. Would Guendivar learn to love this fox kit he was sending her? Or would she weep in secret because her husband had not been able to give her a child?

Goriat was telling the boy about Camalot, where the children of the folk who cooked and kept the livestock and stood guard ran laughing along the walls. The princes and chieftains brought their sons when they came visiting, but they were all British. At least Oesc had had Cunorix and Betiver as companions.

"Perhaps we will send for Eormenric of Cantuware to keep you company—" he said then. "Would you like that?"

Ceawlin nodded. "His father was my grandfather's ally."

Cai raised an eyebrow. This kit was not going to be easy to tame.

Eormenric had been raised by his mother to be Artor's friend. Still, he would need friends among the Saxons as well, and perhaps Ceawlin would be more willing to listen to another boy. They could guard each other's backs against the British child-pack, and Guendivar would win them over as she did everyone.

Artor closed his eyes for a moment, seeing against his eyelids the gleam of her amber hair. When he was at home, the knowledge of how he had failed her was sometimes so painful he longed to be away. But when he was far from her, Guendivar haunted his dreams.

"That is settled, then," he said briskly. "Goriat, I will give you an escort to take the boy south, and letters to the queen." Then, as the young man looked mutinous, "Do not fear for my safety—Cai here will be suspicious enough for two. Besides, was there not some story that the Picts wanted you to husband one of their princesses? I fear to let them set eyes on you!"

At the blush that suffused Goriat's cheeks everyone began to laugh, and Artor knew that his nephew would not dare to protest again.

Two more days of travel brought them a glimpse of bright water to the east, where the estuary of the Bodotria cut deeply into the land. Here their ways parted, Goriat and his men to continue on to Dun Eidyn and then south with the boy, and Artor and his party north to seek the headwaters of the Tava and the Pictish clanholds of Fodreu.

"Goriat was right! The fair weather didn't last," grumbled Cai. "Damn this Devil's murk—how are we to see our road?"

Artor wiped rain from his eyes and peered ahead. The weather had closed in as predicted, and all day they had travelled through a drizzling rain. If they had not come so far already, he might have been tempted to turn around, but at this point he judged them close to Fodreu. If they could find it, he thought gloomily. But they were as likely to get lost going back as keeping on. He could only hope that the Picts kept a good watch on their hunting runs, and would guide them in.

The track they followed wound between rolling hills. From time to time he glimpsed above them the shadows of higher mountains, as if they had been conjured from the mists for a moment, only to vanish away. *Merlin could conjure them back again*, he thought wistfully. *I wish Merlin were here.*

The black horse stumbled on the rocky path and instinctively he tightened the rein, sending reassurance with knees and hands. Raven collected himself and began, more carefully, to move once more. Artor shifted position on the saddle, whose hard frame was beginning to chafe through the damp leather breeches. The superb steel of his sword, kept oiled and clean, would be all right, but it seemed to him that the lesser metal of his mail shirt, inherited from some barbarian auxiliary, was beginning to rust already.

Another few steps and the black horse checked again, head up and nostrils flaring.

"It's all right, old boy—" The king leaned forward to pat the damp neck, and stilled as the humped shapes of shrub and boulder on the hillside ahead of them began to move. Dim figures of men on shaggy ponies seemed to emerge from the hill.

Someone shouted a warning, and Cai kicked his mount forward to cover the king, sword hissing from its sheath. He was swearing softly. Artor himself straightened, reaching for the hilt of his own blade. Then he paused. Why weren't they yelling? And why had there been no preliminary flight of arrows to cut the Britons down?

Behind him his own men were frantically struggling to string their bows. Artor lifted one hand. "Wait!"

Quivering with tension, the Britons stared as the Pictish riders emerged from the mist. They rode swathed in lengths of heavy cloth striped and chequered in the natural colors of the wool, to which the moisture beaded and clung. As they came closer, Artor noted that they smelled like sheep too.

The first riders were small men, wild haired and heavily bearded, but they drew aside for another, tall as a Briton, with the gold torque of a chieftain glinting from beneath his plaid. He halted his pony without appearing to signal and surveyed the strangers from beneath bent brows.

"Who is leader of the southern men?" His accent was odd, but his speech clear enough.

The king moved out from behind Cai, hand still lifted in the sign of peace. "It is I, Artor of Britannia. We seek the dun of Drest Gurthinmoch, King of all the Picts. Can you take us there?"

The Pictish chieftain nodded. "He sent us to find you. Fire and food are waiting, and" his lips twitched beneath the russet mustache—"dry clothes."

That night, as he sat drinking heather ale at the Pict-king's fire, Artor reflected that Drest Gurthinmoch's hospitality was certainly preferable to his hostility. Artor's stiffening muscles made movement painful, but a good fire and a full belly more than compensated. And above all, he was glad, as the Pictish chieftain had promised, to be dry.

Overhead the peak of the thatched roof rose to unknown distances behind the smoke that veiled it, but at the level of the fire the air was clear. Artor had seen roundhouses in the western parts of Britannia, but never one of such size. In Roman lands, princes preferred the elegant villas, plastered and painted, of the conqueror. The roundhouse that formed the center of King Drest's dun was nearly as wide as the basilica in Calleva, its concentric uprights carved and painted with zigzags, crescents and circles and the abstract renderings of boar and salmon, bull and horse and bird that he took to be the totems of the Pictish clans.

My ancestors lived like this before the Romans came . . .
Artor thought then. He felt as if he had gone into a faerie hill
where time ran backwards, returning him to the past.

King Drest was speaking. Artor turned, cupping one ear as if
it was the noise, and not his own abstraction, that had made
him miss the Pict-king's words.

"It is good my men found you," said Drest in his gutteral accent. The speech of the Pict-lords was as old-fashioned as their
hall, a Brythonic dialect mixed with other words from a language he did not know.

"Truly—" Artor replied. "It was ill weather to be out on the
moors."

"Ach—'tis of another danger I'd be warning you," the Pict
replied. "There are worse things than weather, or even the wild
beasts that haunt the hills."

His voice had lowered to a conspiratorial whisper and Artor
leaned back, brows lifting, sensing a story.

"You'd not be likely to meet Bloody Comb, now, riding in a
large and well-armed company. But he's a fearsome sight to a
lone traveler, with his red eyes and his talon nails."

"And a bloody head?"

Drest grimaced. "It is the head of the traveler that grows
bloody, when the creature has pelted him with heavy stones,
and carries off the blood in his cap to feed."

"Bloody Comb is fearsome," said one of his chieftains, grinning, "but the Hidden People are more dangerous, they that
live under the hills."

"It is because they look like men," a big man with fair hair
put in. "But old age does not touch them. They steal our
women, and change their sickly babes for our own."

"Do they have treasure?" asked Artor, remembering some of
the tales he had heard. These stories were known everywhere,
though the fair folk seemed to dwindle in the Roman lands.

"Surely, for they have been here since the first mothers of
our folk came into this land. They are creatures of night and
shadow, but they grow weak and ugly if you catch them in the
full light of day. You can kill them then with ease."

"And they would liefer die than reveal where their treasure
is hid," said the chieftain. "Like the female we caught two

moons past. She screamed, but would say nothing until she died."

Artor looked away, trying not to imagine the treatment that had made the woman, whatever she was, scream. Suddenly the barbaric splendor of Drest Gurthinmoch's dun seemed less attractive. And yet he had to admit that many Romans, if they had believed in the treasure at all, might have done the same.

"I see that I have had a narrow escape," he said in a neutral tone, "and bless the fate that led me to Drest Gurthinmoch's dun. If I had known your hospitality was so generous, I would have come before. . . ."

Without a sword in your hand? The echo of his words showed clearly in the sardonic gleam of the Pict-king's eyes.

"If there has been less than friendship between your people and mine, it was not by my will—" Artor said quietly.

"Nor by mine—" his host agreed. "But we will speak more of that in the morning. For now, let you drink with me, and we shall see if the Britons can match the Pretani as well at the alevats as they do on the battlefield!" He began to laugh.

Artor awoke with a throbbing head. When he staggered out to the horse trough he saw that it was well past dawn. His memories of the preceding evening were chaotic, culminating in a tide of boozy good fellowship that had borne him to his bed. *I hope I may not have sworn away half Britannia . . . what do they put in their beer?*

By the time he had doused his head in the chill water, he was feeling less like a victim of Bloody Comb, and could greet Drest Gurthinmoch, stout, ruddy, and apparently unaffected by the night's carouse, without wincing as his own words echoed against his skull.

"Come," said the Pict, "we will walk, and complete your cure in the sweet air."

Artor grimaced. His condition must be more obvious than he had thought. Still it was a good suggestion, and as movement worked the stiffness out of his muscles, he began to feel more like a man, if not yet entirely like a king.

The royal dun lay on the shore of the Tava, which here ran deep and smoothly between two lines of hills. Beyond the great feasting hall lay the house of the queen, its thatching dyed in patterns of dull red and green and blue. The gate to the palisade was open, and in the meadow horses and cattle were grazing. At first Artor thought he had been brought out here to admire them, but the Pict-king led him along a path that led towards the trees. Seeing the noble stand of oaks that rose before him, Artor understood that he was being taken to the *nemeton* of the tribe.

The meadow had been full of sounds—the whicker of a pony and the stamp of hooves, bee song, and the twitter of birds—but the *nemeton* was very still. The whisper of wind in the upper leaves seemed to intensify the silence below. As they came to the edge of the clearing, Artor felt a change in pressure and stopped short.

Drest Gurthinmoch turned back, smiling. "Ah, you feel it? That is well, but the guardians will allow you to enter, since you are with me." He reached out, and after a moment Artor grasped his hand.

For a moment the shift dizzied him; then he was in, surrounded by trees that seemed to watch him like the standing stones at the Giant's Dance. And in the center of this circle there also lay a stone.

"The king stone . . ." said the Pict. "When I stood upon it at my king-making, it cried out, for those who know how to hear. Do you not have the custom in your land?"

Artor considered the chunk of sandstone, a rough rectangle of a height for a man to sit on, with an indentation that might have been a footprint on its upper side. In the north, he knew, every tribe had its navel stone, the focus of gatherings. There were sacred stones in Britannia as well, but where the Romans ruled, their use had been forgotten.

"No longer—" he whispered.

"I come here when I need to think like a king. . . ." Drest motioned him to sit beside him on the fallen log that lay at the edge of the clearing. "Why do you want to cross the narrow sea?"

The sudden question took Artor by surprise. No point in asking the old wolf how he knew it—no doubt he had an in-

formant in Artor's household just as there were men in Pictland who carried news to the British king.

"To fight the Franks," he said at last.

"Why? They do not raid your shores."

"Not yet. But they are hungry. One day, like the Romans,
they will cross the sea. Better to stop them now than wait until
they are in our hunting runs—or yours."

Drest looked thoughtful. "So this war that you go to will defend us as well?"

"That is what I believe." Artor was thinking, he realized,
like a Roman, who had protected their borders by conquering
what lay beyond them. But the Romans had not known when
to stop. He would be wiser.

The Pict-king grunted. "Then I will guard your back."

Artor sat up, skin flushing with the release from tension he
had not known he carried until now.

"Blood seals an alliance better than breath," Drest said then.
"It is a pity that you have no child."

I have a son. . . . Medraut's face sprang suddenly to mind,
but Artor kept silent.

"One of your sister's sons will be your heir, as is right, but
she bore several. It would be well if one of them could be sent
here to wed one of our royal women." He looked at Artor slyly.
"One day your blood might rule the Pretani after all . . ."

Artor licked dry lips. "They are grown men. I . . . cannot
choose for them. But I will ask."

"Or a man of your Companions, though my people will not
see that as so binding. Still, they would value for his own sake
any man trained in your war-band."

Artor's lips twitched at the compliment. "I will ask."

The Britons took care to delay their departure until the sun
returned, but Artor was fast learning that the weather this far
north could never be relied on. By the time they reached the
firth, a chill wind was gusting in from the sea, driving dark
clouds that trailed veils of rain. He only hoped that the Picts
were more trustworthy than the sky.

Across the firth he could see in silhouette the Rock of Dun

Eidyn, stark against the clouds. But the water between frothed with foam. Clearly no boat would ply those seas until the wind died down. The king halted his black horse at the edge of the sand, gazing across the heaving waves with a longing that surprised him. He wanted to be back in his own country!

Cai was saying something about a wood in whose shelter they could wait out the storm, but Artor shook his head.

"I've never liked boats anyway," he said crossly. "We'll ride east, go around."

Cai shook his head gloomily, but he turned away and began to give the necessary orders all the same. The king felt a moment's compunction—he knew that the knee his foster-brother had injured at Mons Badonicus gave him trouble in wet weather, but no doubt it would ache as much sitting still in a damp forest as on the trail.

Yet for a time it seemed that Artor's decision had been a good one. Away from the sea the storm's strength lessened, and the rain diminished to a drizzle as night drew near. Their campsite was damp, but even when wet, the lengths of tightly woven natural wool that King Drest had given them to use as riding cloaks stayed warm.

In the morning the air seemed warmer, and the rain had almost ceased, but before they had been an hour on the trail they wished it back again, for the rain-soaked earth was giving up its moisture in the form of fog. Heavy and clinging, it weighted the lungs and penetrated to the bone. A trackway seemed to lead away to the right; they turned their mounts uphill, hoping to get above the fog and find shelter. The Picts who had escorted them knew the lay of the land, but none had the intimate local knowledge of each rock and tree that could have guided them now.

The mist deadened sound. They had dismounted, and Artor could hear the clop and scrape behind him as Raven picked his way over mud and stone. The sounds of the other horses came faintly, and as darkness fell, their shapes faded to shadows more sensed than seen. Something loomed ahead and the black horse threw up his head, snorting in alarm. Artor pulled him down, stroking the sweated neck to soothe him. It was only a big boulder, though in the half-dark it humped like a crouching beast. He led Raven around it, and pulled him gently after the receding shape of the horse ahead of him.

Or at least that was what he thought he was doing. He had walked for perhaps as long as it takes to boil an egg before he realized that the figure he thought he was following was another boulder. He paused, listening. The heavy whuff of Raven's breathing was the only sound.

For a moment the king stood and swore. Then he fumbled for the strap that held his horn. He set it to his lips and blew, the sound dull in the heavy air. From somewhere above him came an answer. Artor loosened the rein and the horse started forward.

Three more times after that he blew the horn, and each time the reply came more faintly, until he could hear nothing at all. It was full dark now, and if he wandered further, he risked damaging the horse's legs in some unseen hole. The ground was rising. He stubbed his toe on a large stone and stepped aside, finding more even ground beyond it. His mount stopped short, trembling, and Artor yanked on the rein. Even in the thick air he noticed the shift in pressure that told him the rock he had just passed had been no ordinary boulder, but by now he scarcely cared. If the place made the horse nervous, perhaps wild creatures would avoid it. In any case, he could go no further now.

He hobbled the horse by feel and removed the bridle, ungirthed the saddle pad and laid it on the ground next to an upended slab of stone. Another slab lay half over it, and he pulled the pad beneath it, grateful for whatever protection it might afford. Then, wrapping the Pictish plaid around him, he lay down.

It was warmer than he had expected in the shelter of the stones. He felt pieces of something like broken pottery beneath the blanket and swept them aside. Fragments of warning tugged at his memory, but exhaustion was already overwhelming him. He was asleep before he could decide whether he ought to be afraid.

"Artor . . . Defender of Britannia . . . arise. . . ."
Blinking, the king sat up. He was glad to wake from the old

nightmare about Mons Badonicus, but as he stared around him he wondered if he had passed into another dream. It was still night, but there was no mist within the circle, and the stones glowed. In their eerie light he saw that his shelter consisted of a slab of rock balanced on two others like a small table, but instead of the bare earth he expected beneath it, he saw a lighted tunnel that led down into the hill.

"Artor, come to Me. . . ."

The king glanced swiftly around him. His horse stood hip-slung, head low in sleep. The call was coming from the depths. A whisper from his waking mind warned him not to answer, but the voice was sweet as his mother's croon, golden as Guendivar's laughter. No mortal could have resisted that call.

He knelt, peering into the opening. And it seemed to him that the space grew larger, or perhaps it was he who was becoming small, for what he saw now was a tunnel through which he could walk easily.

The light flared before him. When he could see once more, he found himself in a round chamber carved out of the rock. He could not see the passage through which he had entered, and there were people all around him. With a start of of pure terror, he understood that the Hidden People had him in their power.

Artor took a deep breath and looked around him. They did not seem hostile. Men and women stared back at him. They had the look of some of the men he had seen among the Picts, sturdy of body with grey eyes and thick-springing earth-brown hair, but they were not dressed like anyone he had ever seen. Warriors went bare-chested, their loins wrapped in woolen kilts held by belts ornamented with plaques of gold. Their skin was blue with tattooed designs, and at their sides hung leaf-shaped bronze swords. Other men wore the skins of beasts, clasped on one shoulder. There were women in gathered skirts and shawls, their hair coiled in netted caps, while others wore a single garment held at the shoulders with brooches of bronze or gold.

They had wealth enough, whoever they were—gold at wrist and ear, and crescent necklets of beaten gold. As he wondered, the crowd parted and a man robed in white wool appeared. He had a look of Merlin, but he was smaller, his breast and shoulders sheathed in gold. An imperious gesture summoned Artor, and the people drew back, pointing at his mail shirt and his sword.

At the back of the cave a woman sat throned on an outcropping of stone. There were carvings on it; he realized that the entire cavern was carved in spirals so that its contours blurred. But he had no attention to spare for them now. Those same spirals twined across the ivory flesh of the woman's bare torso—no, not merely a woman, he thought as he noted the diadem of gold that gleamed from the cloud of dark hair—a queen. She was very like Drest Gurthinmoch's woman whom the Picts called the Great Mare. A skirt of painted linen fell in stiff folds beneath her belly; for mantle she had the thick furs of forest cats, the wicked heads drawn over her shoulders. Cairngorms glinted from their slanted eyes.

"Defender. . . ."

Unbidden, Artor fell to his knees. Her eyes, too, were like those of the Pictish queen.

"What do you want of me?" His voice was harsh in his own ears.

"Defend this land—"

"I have done so since I was fifteen winters old."

"Defend your people," the queen said then. "All of them—the children of the earth-folk as well as the children of the sun."

Artor set his hand on the pommel of his sword. "I am pledged to deal justly with all those who dwell in this hallowed isle."

"Men need not justice only, but hope, and a dream." Her voice was harsh honey.

Artor shook his head. "How can I give them that, Lady? I am only a man. . . ."

"You are the child of the Bear, you are the Raven of Britannia," she continued implacably. "Are you willing to become her eternal king?"

Artor remembered the oaths he had sworn at his anointing. But this was something different, a bright shadow on the soul. As he hesitated, she spoke again.

"There is a price to be paid."

"What do you want?"

"Touch the Stone, and you will understand."

For a long moment he stared at her. "Where shall I find it?" he whispered at last.

Her eyes held his, and his head began to swim. "It is here . . ." The stone on which she was sitting began to glow. As Artor reached towards it her words were echoed from all around him: "Here . . . *here* . . . *HERE*!"

The blaze became blinding and he fell into light.

Artor awakened to a sharp and localized pain just above his breastbone. His eyes opened, and he became very still. Beneath his nose he glimpsed the dull gleam of a flint spearhead. His gaze followed the shaft to the man who held it. For a moment he thought he was still dreaming, for the spearman was stocky, with a brown bush of hair like the warriors he had seen in the cavern. Then he realized that this man was weathered, his hide cape tattered with wear. He was not alone.

"Who are you?" one of the other men asked in guttural Brythonic. He was a little better dressed than the others, but Artor recognized his captors as the people of the hills against whom the Pict-lords had warned him. But he knew them now for the first inhabitants of this land. One of the strangers held Raven by the bridle. The black horse stamped and shook his head, but did not try to get away.

Moving very slowly, the king edged away from under the spear and sat up, brushing more potsherds away as he set down his hand. Someone gasped and made a sign of warding.

"I am the Defender of Britannia . . ." he answered, his mind still filled with echoes of his dream.

"You are here all night?"

Artor nodded. The sky was still grey, but the mist no longer hugged the hills. A light wind gave hope that it might clear later in the day.

"I was lost in the mist." He looked around him, only now appreciating the strangeness of his refuge. "This place seemed . . . warm."

"You sleep with the Old Ones. . . ." The speaker showed broken teeth in a grim smile. "This is their tomb."

Artor looked around him at the kerb of stones and the megaliths in whose shelter he had lain, understanding now the nervousness with which they eyed him.

"I am a living man."

The speaker reached out and gripped his shoulder. "He is solid," he confirmed.

"I feel hollow—" Artor added with a smile. "I have not eaten since yestermorn."

"We kill strangers who come into our hunting runs—do the children of the Great Mare not tell you so?" the first man said bitterly.

Artor drew up his knees and rested his arms upon them, knowing it would be fatal to show himself afraid. "If your ancestors did not take my soul, it is not for you to do so."

The speaker muttered to the others then turned back again. "I know you. You are the one they call the Bear, the lord of the sun-people beyond the Wall."

"I am he." Artor nodded, wondering if admitting it was wise. But he found himself compelled to speak truth here.

"Come—it is not well to stay in a place of the old ones, even by day. We give you food and lead you to your men. We watch them since sunset past, but they do not see us there." The grim smile flickered again. "But there is a price."

"There is always a price—" said Artor, remembering his vision of the night. "Name it."

"Speak for us to the children of the Great Mare. They drive us from the best lands already. Let them leave us alone, not hunt us like deer."

Artor looked at them, noting bad teeth and thinning hair, legs bowed with malnutrition. Saxon and Roman, Briton and Pict alike were newcomers next to these, the original inhabitants of Britannia. Slowly he got to his feet and set his hand on the pommel of the Chalybe sword.

"Will you take me as your king?"

The speaker looked him up and down, then grinned. "By star and stone we swear it."

"Then by star and stone I will swear also to protect you."

iv

THE ORCHARD

A.D. 504

Artor walked with his mother by the Lake, where the apple orchard came down to the shore. Igierne used a cane now, and paused often to catch her breath. It was clear that movement was painful, but she had refused to stop, nor did she complain. When they came to the long rock that had been shaped roughly into a seat she eased down with a sigh.

He stood behind her, one hand resting lightly on her thin shoulder. Trees circled the lake and clung to the lower slopes of the hills, dark masses of evergreen mingled with bare branches just showing the first haze of spring green. On the apple trees, buds were swelling, and branches were framing the shining silver water and the shaded masses of surrounding hills that held the lake like a cup in their strong hands.

Here the bones of the earth showed strong and clear. In the mountains Artor found an enduring beauty for which the changing displays of leaf and flower were only an adornment—like his mother, he thought, whose fine bone structure retained its beauty despite the softly wrinkled skin.

"It is beautiful," Igierne said softly. "It is worth the labor of getting here for the refreshment of spirit it brings."

"I might say the same," answered the king. He had spent much of the winter with Cunobelinus at Trimontium, and seen him sworn king over the Votadini on the stone at the base of its hill, and at the moment the chieftain's foot touched the stone, Artor had heard the earth's exultant cry.

From there he had travelled down the eastern coast. He was glad now that he had decided to follow the old Roman Wall west again to the Isle of Maidens. Since the last time he had seen her, his mother had grown visibly more frail.

"Look—" She pointed towards the eastern hills. "There is the path that leads up to the circle of stones."

"I stopped there on my way," said Artor, remembering the ring of stones. Some had fallen, and the tallest were no more than breast high, as if the earth were slowly reclaiming a broken crown. "How many are there? I counted three times and the answer was never the same."

"Ah, that secret belongs to our Mysteries—"

Artor shook his head, laughing. "Is that why those stones are so—*alive*? Most of the circles I have seen are somnolent as an old dog in the sun. But the ones on the hill hummed with energy."

"And how would you know that?" Igierne turned to look up at him.

Artor kept his gaze on the hills. "Because I have met the folk who built them. Or their spirits. I wish I had thought to ask them *why*!"

"Tell me—" Igierne's voice changed, and Artor knew that she was speaking as Lady of the Lake. Easing down beside her, he began to describe the night he had spent beneath the ancient stones.

"And now," he ended, "it is as if I were growing new senses. I can tell, before I even touch it, if a stone has weathered naturally or was shaped by the Old Ones of this land. Who was the Lady I saw, and what did her question mean?"

"I would guess . . . she was a great queen of the elder days, so bound to the land that after her death she would not pass onward to the Blessed Isles, but became one with the spirits of the earth. To some . . ." she spoke ever more slowly, "that choice is given. They become part of the Otherworld that lies like a veil above our own. In some places the fabric is folded, and there, the two worlds touch."

"That grave was one of them . . ." he said slowly. "As are all the places where the old ones worked the stones. . . ."

"In their proper times and seasons, it is so."

Artor realized that he was gripping the rock on which he sat. Beneath his palm its chill surface was warming; he felt a vibration as if some great beast purred beneath his hand, and let go quickly.

"What is the price? And where is the Stone? The Votadini king stone belongs to that land and that people only. Where is the Stone that will hail me as king and emperor?"

Igierne shook her head. "That is *your* mystery." She looked at him again. "Why do you want to be emperor? Is it the old dream of glory that draws you—the need to avenge Maximian?"

"Perhaps it was . . . at first," he replied. "I admit that Riothamus' offer was flattering. But I have been thinking about it as I travelled around this land. The Lady commanded me to defend all the races who dwell in Britannia, from the earth-folk to the Saxons. At its best, the justice of Rome did that, but the Pax Romana has failed."

"Will you impose a Pax Britannica upon the world?"

"Perhaps, to keep this Island safe, that is what I will have to do. . . ."

Igierne sighed. "You have seen the tumbled stones of the second wall that the Romans built to defend the first one that Hadrianus made. Each conquest only gave them a new land that had to be protected. But in the end they could not hold all they had taken. To be accepted by all of Britannia is more than any other prince of our people has achieved—do you truly believe that you can be a king for Gallia as well?"

"Mother, I do not know. But to bring peace to the world

and justice to its peoples, we need a dream. I think I have to try. . . ."

Morgause was in the weaving shed, supervising the younger priestesses as they checked the bags of raw fleece, when she realized that someone was standing in the doorway. She looked up, eyes narrowed against the glare. For a moment he was only a shape outlined in light; then she recognized the broad shoulders and height of the king. Slowly she straightened. For the three days of Artor's visit she had managed to avoid him, but there was no evading a confrontation now.

"Verica, I must go—make sure that any bags that have gotten moths in them over the winter are taken to the other shed. If we wash the fleeces thoroughly, we may be able to save some of the wool."

The younger priestess nodded, and Morgause made her way past the women to the door.

"Ah—" Artor essayed a smile. "I am glad you came out to me. I would rather charge a Saxon army than intrude on all those chattering girls."

"Truly? I thought there was nothing you would not dare—" Morgause fought to keep her tone even.

Artor shook his head. "Will you walk with me? We need to speak about Medraut." Together, they moved down the path.

"What has he done?"

"Why should you ask that? Was he so difficult a child to raise?" Artor asked quickly.

Not at all. Not until the last. . . . Morgause pulled her shawl more tightly around her, for clouds were gathering, pushed by a chilly wind. "Your tone suggested he was in trouble . . ." she said aloud.

"On the way north there were . . . accidents. I sent Medraut to the Saxons—to Cynric at Venta Belgarum, who for the sake of his own cub's life will guard him as the apple of his eye. It would seem that the secret of Medraut's parentage has become known, and perhaps there are some who think they would be doing me a favor to get rid of him."

"Perhaps they are right," Morgause answered bitterly. "Why

should you trust him, when he is what I made him? You have good reason to distrust *me.*"

"For the Lady's sake, Morgause! It may be that he should never have been born, but he is here, and he deserves a chance. I have not come here to blame you, but you know him better than anyone else. Like it or not, he is my son. I need to understand. . . ."

Morgause stared up at the brother she had hated so long and so intimately betrayed. He was still strong, but there was silver in the brown hair, and his face was carved by lines of responsibility and power. He seemed so sure of himself, as if he had never doubted his own integrity, that she almost began to hate him once more.

Should I tell him that Medraut is brilliant and seductive and dangerous? How much am I willing to admit? How much do I dare? Looking back, the woman who had manipulated and schemed seemed like a stranger, but the reverberations of that woman's past actions still troubled the present, like the ripples from a cast stone.

"Medraut is very intelligent," she said slowly, shame moderating her words. "But his brothers were too much older—he has been very much alone. He does not have much experience of friendship." She paused. "I raised him to think he had a right to your throne."

"That is the one thing I cannot give him," Artor replied, his gaze troubled. "Even if his birth were acceptable, what I have to leave will go to the man best fitted to hold it. To the man, if there is one, who is chosen by the spirit of this Sword. I told him that. I do not know if he believed me—" he said then, gripping the hilt of the weapon that hung at his side.

"Then you must somehow teach him to be worthy of it," said Morgause, "for that is what he will desire."

Perhaps, she thought, *in rejecting me, Medraut will reject what I taught him.* But she found that hard to believe.

Artor was staring out across the lake, his gaze as grey as the troubled surface of the water.

"One thing I would ask of you—" she said aloud. "To take Gualchmai's daughter with you when you go. She is a wild creature of the moors, not suited by nature for the quiet life we have here. Perhaps Guendivar will be able to tame her."

"Very well. What is her name?"

"She is called Ninive."

At the feast of Christ's Resurrection, the queen and her household journeyed from Camalot to the Isle of Afallon to hear mass at the round church there. Sister Julia was here, having finally taken full vows as a nun, but to Guendivar, it was as if she walked with the ghost of the girl she had once been. Here, Queen Igierne had set her on the path to her destiny. And now she was woman and queen, but not a mother.

Men were beginning to whisper that that strange boy, Medraut, was Artor's son. It seemed to Guendivar that they looked on her less kindly now, holding her a barren stock and no true queen. *But even the most fertile field will not bear without sowing*, she thought bitterly. If she was at fault, it was not because she could not conceive, but because she had not been able to awaken the manhood of the king.

When the service was over, Guendivar walked out of its scented darkness and stood blinking in the sunshine. On this day, the Church forgot its mysteries of blood and sorrow and rejoiced in life reborn, and the world seemed to echo that joy. Above the smooth peak of the Tor, the clouds from last night's storm hung white and fluffy in a blue sky.

The wind was chilly enough for her cloak to be welcome, but there was a promise of warming weather in the heat of the sun. She could not waste such a day cooped up with a flock of chattering women—but she glimpsed two small heads, one red, one fair, by the horse trough, and began to smile.

"Ceawlin! Eormenric! Come walk with me!" she called.

"Oh my lady, wait—" Netta, the woman who tended the boys, came bustling over. "The wretched children have soaked each other with their splashing and must have dry things!"

Eormenric shook himself like a puppy and Ceawlin looked mutinous as Guendivar bent to touch the cloth.

"They are a little damp, truly, but the day is growing warmer. They will dry off soon enough if they run about in the sun!" She turned to the boys. "Will you escort me, my warriors? I would walk in the orchard for awhile."

Yipping gleefully, they dashed ahead, then circled back around her. Fox-red Ceawlin had the features of his Belgic forebears, but in thought and speech he was all Saxon. It was Eormenric, in appearance a lanky, blond reincarnation of Oesc, his father, who was most fluent in the British tongue and easy with their ways. That was the doing of Rigana, who had been born a princess of Cantium and now was Cantuware's queen. Artor had been wise to ask her to send her son to Camalot. The boys had become fast friends.

The apple trees were leafing out, with only a few flowered branches remaining to bear witness to their former snowy glory. Guendivar had pulled one down to smell the scent when she heard a cry behind her.

Ceawlin lay sprawled on the grass, like a doll dropped by some child in play. Eormenric bent over him, then straightened, gazing at Guendivar in mute appeal.

"He fell out of the tree—"

Guendivar knelt. She could feel her own heart thumping alarm as she felt at his throat for the pulse that beat in answer to her own.

"Did he fall on his head?" she asked, sitting back on her heels.

"I think so—" answered Eormenric. "Is he going to die?"

"Not today," she said, hoping it was true. "But he will have a sore head when he wakes up." Carefully she felt his limbs.

Ceawlin stirred, whimpering. "*Modor. . . .*"

It needed no knowledge of Saxon to interpret that. Guendivar settled herself with her back to the tree trunk and gathered the boy against her breast. For a moment she remembered how the priest had wept over the image of Christ's mother with her dead son in her arms. But this boy would not die—she would not allow it! She tightened her grip on Ceawlin, and as naturally as a puppy, Eormenric snuggled beneath her other arm.

"It will be all right," she murmured. "All will be well. . . ."

The tree at her back was a steady support, the scent of crushed grass intoxicating. Guendivar leaned into its strength, and suddenly it seemed to her as if she had become the tree, rooting herself in the awakening earth and drawing up strength through her spine. Power welled through her from the depths of the earth to the child in her arms.

Ceawlin stirred again, and this time when his eyes opened there was recognition in his gaze. She waited for him to tense and pull away, but he only sighed and burrowed more comfortably against her.

She steadied her breathing, willing the shift in vision that would show her the spirits of the apple trees. The world began to change around her, but the shift was going too fast. Held in this moment, she went deeper than ever before. She *was* the solid earth and the warmth of the sunlight, the wind that stirred her hair and the pliant strength of the tree, a woman's body and the children in her arms, all part of a single whole. Life was reborn from the womb of earth with the springtime as the Christian god came forth from his earthen tomb. And in that moment, Guendivar understood that she was not barren at all.

She did not count the passing of time, but surely the sun had not moved far across the sky when she became aware that someone was speaking. For a time she simply listened to the musical rise and fall of the language, for it was a tongue she did not know. The sound seemed to come from all around her, as if the wind were speaking in the leaves.

> *"Come to the holy temple of the virgins*
> *Where the pleasant grove of apple trees*
> *Circles an altar smoking with frankincense."*

The words became more distinct, and she realized that now she was hearing the British tongue.

> *"The roses leave shadow on the ground*
> *And cool springs murmur through apple*
>   *branches*
> *Where shuddering leaves pour down*
>   *profound sleep."*

It must be true, thought Guendivar, for Ceawlin, eyes closed and breathing even, had passed into a healing slumber, and even Eormenric lay quiet against her breast. But her expanded soul was returning to the confines of her body. She heard with her mortal senses; therefore the words she was hearing must have some tangible source.

> *"In that meadow where horses have*
>   *grown glossy,*
> *And all spring flowers grow wild,*
> *The anise shoots fill the air with aroma."*

She straightened a little, turning her head, and saw a man, his limbs as gnarled and brown as the branches, sitting in one of the apple trees. In that first moment, the sight seemed quite normal, as if he had grown there. And so she was not startled when returning awareness resolved the abstract pattern of bearded face and skin-clad body into the figure of Merlin.

Seeing her gaze upon him, the Druid slid down from the tree and took up the staff that had been leaning against it.

> *"And there our queen Aphrodite pours*
> *Celestial nectar in the gold cups,*
> *Which she fills gracefully with sudden joy."*

"Heathen words . . ." Guendivar said softly, "for such a holy day."

"Holy words, first sung for the Goddess by a lovely lady in the Grecian isles. In those days it was the death of Her lover Attis that the women mourned in the spring. The gods die and are reborn, but the Goddess, like the earth, is eternal. You know this to be true—I see the understanding in your eyes." Merlin came closer and squatted on his haunches, the staff leaning against his shoulder.

"Perhaps . . . but I am no goddess, to be hailed with such words."

"Are you not?" He laughed softly. "At least you are Her image, sitting there with your sons in your arms."

Guendivar looked at him in alarm, remembering the sense of union she had experienced only a few moments ago. How could the old man know what she was feeling? The last time he had tried to talk to her she had run from him, but she could not disturb the sleeping boys.

"And you are Her image to your husband's warriors, their Lady and Queen."

"But not to my husband," Guendivar said bitterly.

"All things change, even he, even you. Is it not so?"

"Even you?" she asked then.

He laughed softly, long fingers stroking lightly over the staff that lay against his arm. Its head was swathed in yellowed linen, but she could see now that strange symbols were carved up and down the shaft.

"I have been a salmon in the stream and a stag upon the hill. I have been an acorn in the forest, and the falcon floating in the wind. I was an old man once, but now I am as young as the cub just born this spring. . . ."

It was true, she thought. He had not moved like an old man, though the hair that covered his body was grizzled as a wolf's pelt, and streaks of pure silver glinted in his hair and beard.

"I think sometimes that I will be old without ever having seen my prime, passing directly from virginity to senility . . ." Guendivar said then.

"Do you believe that to bear in the body is the only fertility? I was a father to Artor, though another man begot him. It is not what you receive, but what you give, that will grant you fulfillment. You must become a conduit for power."

Ceawlin stirred, and she soothed him with a gentle touch. "How?" she asked when the boy had settled once more.

"You have done it already, when you brought the earth power through the tree. Build up an image of the Lady of Life standing behind you, and you will become a doorway through which Her force can flow."

Did she dare to believe it might be so? She would have questioned him further, but Eormenric opened his eyes and seeing Merlin, sat up, staring. Ceawlin, disturbed by his motion, began to wake as well.

"What's *he* doing here?" whispered Eormenric.

"He is wise in all the ancient magics," Guendivar answered. "He will make sure that your friend is well. . . ."

And Merlin, taking his cue, rose in a single smooth motion

and came to her, passing his hands above the boy's body and resting them on his brow. Ceawlin, who lay with eyes rolling like those of a frightened horse, whispered something in the Saxon tongue.

"What did he say?" Guendivar asked Eormenric.

"He called the old man by the name of Woden and asked if he had come to take him to his hall . . ."

Merlin grunted and got to his feet. "Nay, child, I am a prophet sometimes, but no god." He stood looking down at the boy, his face growing grim. "I foresee for you a long life, and many victories."

His dark gaze lifted to meet hers, and Guendivar recoiled, wondering what it was he had seen. But without another word he turned and strode off and in a few moments had disappeared among the trees.

Guendivar stared after him. If he was not a god, she thought then, still, Merlin was something more than a man.

On a day of mingled sunlight and shadow towards the end of May, the high king of Britannia returned to Camalot. Another year's storms had weathered the timbers, and the thatching had been bleached by another year's suns to a paler gold. Artor remembered it half finished, all raw wood and pale stone, but now buildings and fortifications alike seemed to have grown out of the hill.

As always, he approached Camalot with mixed emotions. This was his home, the heart of his power, and here, in perpetual reminder of his greatest failure, was Guendivar. If he had been able to give her children, would she by now have grown fat and frowsy? But he had not, and so she remained in essence virgin, forever young, beautiful, and not to be possessed by any man.

Then they were passing beneath the gate, and the entire population of the fortress surged around him, obliterating thought in an ecstasy of welcome.

It was late that night before Artor and his queen were alone. He found himself grateful that the day had left him physically exhausted. Without the distracting demands of the body, it would be easier to remember the things he had to say.

Guendivar sat in her sleeping shift on the chest at the foot of their bed, combing out her hair. Long habit had taught him not to think of her with desire, but there were times when her beauty broke through his defenses.

She is a woman, he thought, his gaze lingering on the firm curves of breast and thigh, *no longer the green girl I took from her father's hall. A woman,* the thought went on, *who deserves better than I have been able to give. . . .*

He paused in his pacing and turned. "My lady, we need to talk—"

She picked up the comb again, features still half-veiled by the golden fall of her hair, but he sensed her attention. Her movement made the lamp flame flicker, sending a flurry of shadows across the woven hangings on the wall.

He cleared his throat. "I told you once that I had a son, but not by whom. I begot him on my sister, when I lay with her, all unknowing, at the rites of Lughnasa."

There was a charged silence, then the comb began to move once more.

"If you did not know, there was no sin—" Guendivar said slowly, then paused, thinking. "It is that boy Medraut, isn't it? The youngest son of Morgause who came to you last winter."

Artor nodded. "I hoped to keep his birth hidden, but the word has gotten around. It may be that he himself told someone the secret. Medraut can be . . . strange."

"Do you wish to make him your heir?" she asked, frowning.

"Were he as good a man as Gualchmai, still the priests would never stand for it. Medraut cannot inherit, but men are saying . . . that his existence proves my fertility. Some of the chieftains came to me, suggesting that I should take another queen."

"Do you wish to divorce me?" Guendivar set down the comb and faced him, her eyes huge in a face drained of color.

"Guendivar—" Despite his will he could hear his voice shaking. "You know better than anyone that the fault lies in me. But it has come to me that by holding you to a barren bed I have wronged you. I thought things might have changed—in the North, I tried to take a girl, but I could do nothing. Morgause has repented, but she cannot alter the past. If you wish it,

I will release you from the marriage, free you to find a man who can be a husband to you in fact as well as name."

She turned away and began once more, very slowly, to pull the ivory comb through her hair. "And if I do, and my new husband gets me with child, and men begin to say that the king has lost his manhood?"

"Be damned to them, so long as you are happy!" What was she thinking? He wished he could see her eyes!

"Then be damned to those who say that I am sterile. I wish no other husband than you."

Artor had not known he was holding his breath until it rushed out of him in a long sigh. Guendivar set down the comb and began to braid the golden silk of her hair. Her gaze was on the long strands, but he could see the smooth curve of cheek and brow, and her beauty smote him like a sword. The leather straps that supported the mattress creaked as he sat down.

"And I . . . no other queen. . . ." He forced the words past a thickened throat.

Guendivar tied off her braid, blew out the lamp on her side of the bed, and climbed in.

"You have guarded my honor," he said then. "Now I ask you to guard Britannia. Except for Cataur, I have spoken with all of the princes. I will go to Dumnonia to gather ships, and my army will make the journey to Gallia. When I cross the sea, I want you to rule. I think my treaties will hold, but if they do not, I will leave you Gualchmai to lead the warriors, and Cai to handle the administration. Someone must make our proud princes work together. You have power over men, my queen. The authority will be yours."

Guendivar raised herself on one elbow. The light of the remaining lamp seemed to dance in her eyes. "You have given me those two Saxon cubs to raise already, and now you will give me a kingdom to rule?"

"I know of none other to whom I would entrust it," he said slowly, shrugging off his chamber robe and tossing it to the foot of the bed.

"Then I will be the mother of many," she said softly, "and watch over the land until you return. But while you are still here, come to bed." She paused, and for a moment he thought

she would say something more, but her gaze slid away from
his, and she lay back down.

At the beginning of summer the Isca flowed calmly past the
old capital of the Dumnonii. In the riverside meadow where
the feasting tables had been arranged, a fresh wind was blowing up off the water, and though Artor could not see it, he
thought he could smell the sea. He leaned back in the carved
chair that once had graced the home of a Roman magistrate
and took a deep breath, seeking the current of fresh air above
the heavy scents of roasting meat and ale.

This campaign had been too long in the planning, but this
summer, surely, he would see Gallia. On the plain above Portus Adurni his army was gathering even now. He had made all
secure behind him. Only Dumnonia remained to settle, and the
king was beginning to think that Cataur's country would be
more trouble than the rest of Britannia combined.

"Do not be telling me that this campaign has nothing to do
with you!" exclaimed Betiver, who had come back from Gallia
to help with the final preparations. "In the North they provided
men and horses, as I have heard, and they have far less reason
to fear the Frankish power. I have been in Armorica, my
friends, and I know well that half the country is ruled by
princes from Dumnonia and Kernow. It is your own lands and
kin we will be fighting for! The king expects you be to generous with ships and men."

Artor eyed Cataur, who sat at the other end of the long
table, with a grim smile. The northerners might well think it
worth the price to be out from under the king's eye for
awhile, whereas the Dumnonians were unwilling to give up
the independence they enjoyed across the sea. But that freedom from royal control was a luxury that they could no
longer afford.

Cataur was shaking his head, complaining about bad harvests and hard times.

"The seasons have been no worse here than elsewhere," Artor put in suddenly, "and you never suffered from the Saxons.
Even here in Isca you have found folk from Demetia to repo-
ulate the town. You have the ships, and men who sail to Ar-

morica every moon to steer them. And you shall have them back again once they have made a few voyages for me."

"Very well, that is fair enough." Abruptly Cataur capitulated, grinning through teeth gone bad with age. He had never really recovered from the wound he took in the last Saxon revolt, and his sons led his armies now.

"I will not ask you for more than a company of men," the king went on, "and your son Constantine to lead them. Together, we will raise more troops among your cousins in Armorica."

Cataur scowled at that, but Constantine was smiling. Not quite old enough to fight at Mons Badonicus, he had grown up on tales of the heroes of the Saxon wars. Artor suspected he regretted never having had a chance to win his own glory. Long ago Cataur had been a contender for the kingship, and Constantine, who came of the same blood as Uthir, was a potential heir. Let him come and show what he was made of in this war.

"And from the Church," Artor went on, "I will ask only a tithe of grain—"

The abbot of Saint Germanus, who was also bishop for Dumnonia, sat up suddenly.

"It is for men to tithe to the Church, not the Church to men!"

Cups and platters jumped as Artor's fist struck the table, impatience getting the better of him at last, and everyone sat up and paid attention.

"Do you wish your brethren in Gallia to pay in blood instead? The Frankish king may call himself a Christian, but his warriors have little respect for churchmen. The murdered monks win a martyr's crown, but that does little good to the souls for whom they cared!"

In the silence that followed he sensed movement under the table. He had drawn back his foot to kick, thinking it a dog, when he heard a giggle. Frowning, he pushed back his chair, reached down, and hauled up by the neck of his tunic the small, dark-haired boy who had been hiding there.

"And whose pup are you?" Artor tried to gentle his tone as he set the boy on his knee.

The color that had left the child's face flooded back again. "Marc'h . . . son of Constantine. . . ."

The king shook his head, smiling. "I think you are Cunomorus, a great hunting dog who is waiting to steal the bones! Here's one for you, with the meat still on—" He took a pork rib from his platter, put it in the boy's grubby hand, and set him down. "Run off now and gnaw it!"

Flushing again at the men's laughter, the child scampered away.

"My lord, I am sorry—" Constantine's face was nearly as red as his son's.

"He's a fine lad, and does you credit," answered Artor, with a momentary twinge of regret because he had not known his own son's childhood. "Enjoy him while you can." Perhaps, when his army was assembling at Portus Adurni, he would have the time to visit Medraut in Venta and say farewell.

He looked down the table, his expression sobering, and the Dumnonians sighed and prepared to take up the argument once more. If they fought in battle as hard as they were fighting in council, Artor thought ruefully, this campaign was certain to go well.

Medraut walked with his father along the bank of the Icene, where some forgotten Roman had planted apple trees. Long untended, they had grown tall and twisted; the ground between them littered with branches brought down by storms. But the trees had survived, and on their branches the green apples were beginning to swell.

I am like those apples, thought Medraut. *Wild and untended, still I grow, and no power can keep me from fulfilling my destiny.*

Just over the hill, three thousand men were camped in tents of hide; the meadows behind them were full of horses, but here in the old orchard they might have been in a land deserted since the last legion sailed over the sea. To Medraut, Britannia still held a world of wonders. Why did the king want to go away?

Artor was gazing across the marshes, his eyes clouded by memory.

"I fought a battle here, when I was a little younger than you . . ." said the king. "The man I loved best in the world was killed, and I took Oesc, who became my friend, as a hostage."

"And now I am hostage to Ceretic's son—" observed Medraut. "How history repeats itself!"

Artor gave him a quick look, and Medraut realized he had not entirely kept the bitterness out of his tone. Since they had last met he had gotten taller, and he no longer had to look up to meet his father's eyes.

"They are not treating you well?" There was an edge to the king's reply that made Medraut smile.

For a moment he considered telling Artor that Cynric had been harsh to him just to see what his father would do. But whether or not Artor believed him, the consequences would not serve his purpose. He shook his head, scooped up a little green apple that had fallen untimely, and began to toss it from hand to hand.

"Oh they have been kind enough. Indeed, they remind me of my own tribesmen in the North. No doubt I fit better here than I would among the cultured magnates of Demetia. That, if anything, is my complaint. I left my mother's dun because I wanted to learn about my father's world."

"Would you rather I sent you to Londinium?" Artor asked, frowning. "I suppose I could arrange for you to be tutored there. Or perhaps one of the monasteries . . ."

"Father!" Medraut did not try to keep the mockery from his laugh. "You cannot imagine that the good monks would welcome *me*! Nor do I wish a tutor! If you want me to learn the ways of the Romans, take me with you to Gallia! You have just told me—at my age, you were fighting battles. Do you want the Saxons to be your son's instructors in the arts of war?"

He watched as anger flushed and faded in the king's face, or was it shame? *He grows uncomfortable when I remind him,* Medraut noted, *but he is too honest to deny it.* It had occurred to him, some months into his exile, that Artor could easily deny their relationship and brand him a deluded child. He realized now that it would be against the king's nature to do that—it was a useful thing to know.

"I wish they did not teach their own!" came the muttered reply. "But you must learn from them what you can. You are getting your growth, but if you were with me there would still be danger. In Gallia the priests have great influence. I will have a hard enough time getting them to accept *me*. . . ."

And your incestuous bastard would be a burden you do not want to bear! It would have been different if his father had loved him. But why should he? Medraut knew well that his begetting had been an accident, and his birth a revenge. He should count himself lucky that the king felt any responsibility towards him at all.

It did not occur to him to wonder why he should want Artor's love. There was only the pain of realization, and an anger he did not even try to understand.

"So you will not take me with you?"

"I cannot—" Artor spread his hands, then let them fall to his sides. He turned and began to walk once more. "I am leaving the government of Britannia in the hands of my queen. If there is trouble here, you must go to Guendivar."

Medraut nodded, then, realizing his father could not see him, mumbled something the king could take as agreement. His eyes were stinging, and he told himself it was the wind. But as anguish welled up within him, he threw the apple in his hand with all his strength. It arched up and out, then fell into the river with a splash. Together he and Artor watched as the current caught and carried it towards the sea.

V

The High Queen

A.D. 507–512

 At Camalot someone was always coming or going, and one got used to the noise, especially now, when a series of hot days in early June had opened every window and door. But the voices outside the small building where the queen did her accounts were getting louder. Guendivar set down the tallies of taxes paid in beef or grain as Ninive came in, her fair hair curling wildly in the damp heat.

"My lady—there's a rider, with messages from Gallia—"

The queen's heart drummed in her breast, but she had learned to show no sign. Suddenly she could feel the fine linen of her tunica clinging to back and breast, and perspiration beading on her brow. But she waited with tightly folded hands as the messenger, his tunic still stained with salt from the journey oversea, came in.

"The king is well—" he said quickly, and she realized that her face had betrayed her after all, but that did not matter now. She recognized Artor's seal on the rawhide case in which he sent his dispatches, and held out her hand. The swift, angular writing that she had come to know so well blurred, then resolved into words.

"... *and so I am settled once more at Civitas Aquilonia. The rains have been heavy here, and there is some sickness among the men, but we hope for better weather soon.*"

She would have been happy to share the sunshine they were having here. But if the weather on both sides of the narrow sea was the same, Armorica would be drying out by now. Artor had not been used to write to her when he travelled in Britannia. But now the queen seemed to be his link to home. Deciphering his handwriting was only one of the many skills she had acquired since the king left her to rule in his name.

"*The news from the south of Gallia continues bad, at least for the kingdom of Tolosa. Chlodovechus is moving against the Goths at last, and this time I do not think Alaric will be able to hold. For us, it means peace for as long as it takes for the Franks to digest their new conquest. But in another year or two, they will look about them and notice that this last Roman stronghold is still defying them.*

"*I judge that I have that long to forge alliances among the British chieftains of Armorica that will withstand the storm. Dare I hope to restore the Empire of the West? I no longer know—but where once I saw Gallia as territory to be regained, now I see men who have put their trust in me, and whom I must not betray. . . .*"

There was a break in the writing. The remainder of the letter was written in a different shade of ink, the writing more angular still.

"*Tolosa has fallen. The Visigoths are in full retreat, and the Franks boast that they will keep them on the run all the way to the Pyrenaei montes and beyond. They are probably correct. Alaric must want very much to put a range of mountains between him and his foes. He will be safe in Iberia, for a time. But I predict that one day a Frankish king will follow, dreaming of Empire. Unless, that is, we can break their pride. Already we are seeing refugees from Tolosa, both Romans and Goths. If they wish to join the fight here they will be welcome. Some, I may send to you in Britannia.*

"Watch well over my own kingdom, my queen. You hold my heart in your hands. . . ."

How, she wondered, was she to take that? Surely, Artor was referring to the land, but for a moment she wondered what it would be like to claim not only his duty, but his love. She had almost understood it, listening to Merlin's poetry. But even unclothed, Artor kept his spirit armored, and the moment of possibility had passed. It would require some power even greater than Merlin's, she thought sadly, to bring him to her arms. . . .

She tried to tell herself that her husband's absence had at last made her a queen. Was she still fair? She did not know—men had learned that she was better pleased by praises for her wisdom. She had grown into the authority Artor had laid upon her, and discovered that she had a talent for rule. She might have failed him as a wife, but not as Britannia's queen.

But each letter revealed more of the man hidden within the king, the human soul who had guarded himself so carefully when they were alone. Artor had been back to Britannia only three times since beginning the Gallian campaign, brief visits spent settling disputes between the princes or persuading them to send him more men. Guendivar had scarcely seen him.

And she missed him, this husband whom she was only now coming to know. If it was her beauty that had unmanned him, she hoped that she had lost it. She reached for a piece of vellum, and after a moment began to set down words.

"To my lord and husband, greetings. The weather here has turned hot and fair and we have hope for a good harvest. I can send you some of last year's grain store now, and the taxes from Dumnonia. Gualchmai has brought his wife to Camalot. She is an intelligent woman, well read in the Latin poets, not at all the sort one would have expected Gualchmai to choose. But he is happy with her—the wild boy grown up at last. The news from the North is not so good. Morgause writes that your lady mother is ailing. If we hear more, I will send you word. . . ."

Guendivar paused, remembering the lake that lay like a jewel in the lap of the mountains, and the hush that one feared to break with any but sacred sounds. She had been there only once, but the memory was vivid. And yet she had no desire to return. She was a child of the southern lands, and her heart's home was the Vale of Afallon.

Merlin moved through the forest as a stag moves, scarcely stirring a leaf as he passed. But when he reached the river he was an otter, breasting the surface with undulant ease. When night came, the senses of a wolf carried him onward. But when he noticed at last that he was weary, he sank down between the roots of an ancient oak and became a tree.

Waking with the first light of morning, he thought for a moment that he was a bird. The pain of limbs that had stiffened with inaction brought him back to awareness of his body. He stretched out one forelimb, blinking at the sinewy length of a human arm, furred though it was with wiry, silver-brindled hair. Splayed twigs became fingers that reached out to the smooth, rune-carved wood of the Spear, which he had continued to carry through all his transformations.

With that touch, full consciousness returned to him, and he remembered his humanity. To stay a bird would have been easier, he thought grimly. A bird had no thought beyond the next insect, the next song. The long thoughts of trees, slowly stretching towards the skies, would be better still. A man could remember the message that had started him on this journey; a man could weep, trying to imagine a world without Igierne.

He gazed at the wooded heights above him and knew that the instinct that guided him had led him deep into the Lakeland hills, where once the Brigantes had ruled. A few hours more would bring him to the Isle of Maidens. Animal senses tugged at his awareness—he scented wild onion on the hillside, and grubs beneath a fallen log. Food he must have, and water, but it was necessary that he complete this journey as a man.

When Merlin came to the Lake it was nearing noon. The water lay flat and silver beneath the blue bowl of the sky; even the trees stood sentinel with no leaf stirring. Human reason told him that such calms often preceded storms, but a deeper instinct gibbered that the world was holding its breath, waiting for the Lady of the Lake to give up her own. When he climbed into the coracle drawn up on the shore, he pushed off carefully, as if even the ripples of his passage might be enough to upset that fragile equilibrium.

The priestesses had set Igierne's bed in the garden, beneath a wickerwork shade. Merlin would have thought her dead already if he had not seen the linen cloth that covered her stir. Nine priestesses stood around her, chanting softly. As he approached, the woman who sat at the head of the bed straightened, and he saw that it was Morgause. The clear light that filtered through the wicker showed clearly the lines that had been carved into her face by passion and by pride, but it revealed also the enduring strength of bone. Distracted by the surface differences in coloring and the deeper differences in spirit, he had never realized how much she looked like her mother.

Igierne's eyes were closed; her breathing labored and slow. Her silver hair rayed out upon the pillow, combed by loving hands, but he could see the skull beneath the skin.

"How long—"

"Has she lain thus?" asked Morgause. "She weakened suddenly two days since."

"Have you called on the power of the Cauldron?"

Morgause shook her head, frowning. "She forbade it."

Merlin sighed. He should have expected that, for the power of the Cauldron was to fulfill the way of nature, not to deny it. Morgause spoke again.

"Yesterday she would still take broth, but since last night she has not stirred. She is going away from us, and there is nothing I can do."

"Have *you* slept?" When she shook her head, he touched her hand. "Go, rest, and let me watch awhile. I will call you if there is any change."

It was good advice, though Merlin did not know if he had given it for her sake, or his own. Her anger and her need battered against his hard-won composure.

When she had gone he leaned the Spear against the post, sat down in her place, and took Igierne's hand. It was cool and dry; only when he pressed could he feel the pulse within. He closed his eyes, letting his own breathing deepen, matching his life-force to hers.

"Igierne . . . my lady . . . Igierne. . . ." Awareness extended; he felt himself moving out of the body, reaching for that place where her spirit hovered, tethered to her body by a silver cord that thinned with every beat of her heart.

"Merlin, my old friend—" He sensed Igierne as a bright presence, turning towards him. *"Do not tell me I must come back with you, for I will not go!"* The radiance that surrounded them quivered with her laughter.

"Then let me come with you!"

"Your flesh is still bound to the earth. It is not your time. . . ."

"The years pass, yet my body only grows stronger. The only thing that held my spirit to the human world was my love for you!"

"When you wandered, I watched over you from the Lake . . ." came her reply. *"Now I will love you from the Hidden Realm. It is not so far away—"*

He could sense that this was true, for beyond the flicker of her spirit, a bright doorway was growing. He was aware that Morgause had returned, but her grief could not touch him now. From a great distance, it seemed, his mortal senses told him that Igierne's breath came harshly, rattling in her chest. The chanting of the priestesses faltered as someone began to weep, then resumed.

"Your children still need you—" he thought hopelessly.

"My children are grown! Surely they know I love them. Merlin, you would not condemn me to live on in a body that is outworn! Help me, my dear one. Let me go!"

He was not so sure of that, but it was his own need, not that of Morgause, that reached out and drew the spirit of the younger woman into the link as well.

"There you are, my daughter—you see—" Igierne moved closer to the light. *"This is what I tried to tell you. There is only this last bit, that is a little . . . difficult, and then all will be well. This, too, is part of your training. Help me. . . ."*

He could sense when the turmoil in Morgause's spirit began to give way to wonder.

"You see the doorway opening before you—" The words that the younger woman whispered came from ritual, but they carried conviction now, and resonated in both worlds. "The bright spirits of those you love await you, ready to welcome you home. . . ."

And as she spoke, Merlin realized that it was so. He glimpsed those radiant beings drawing nearer, and recognized, with a certainty beyond the senses, Uthir, and behind him Igierne's parents, Amlodius and Argantel.

"Go through the gate. Let our love support you through your own self-judgment. Over you the dark shall have no power. Farewell—we release you into the Lady's waiting arms. . . ."

Somewhere far away, the failing body struggled for breath, sighed, and was still. But that hardly mattered. For a moment, Merlin's inner vision embraced the brightness and he saw Igierne clearly, growing ever younger as she moved away from them until she was the gold-crowned maiden whom he had loved. And then she passed through the portal. The Light intensified beyond mortal comprehension, and Merlin was blown back into the pallid illumination of an earthly day.

The surface of the lake wrinkled as wind brushed the water. A vanguard of cloud was just rising beyond the western hills. Morgause shivered, though the temperature had barely begun to drop; the cold she felt came from the soul. Merlin, beside her, moved as she had seen men move coming half-stunned from the battlefield.

"It was a good death—" she said aloud. "Why am I so angry?" Behind them the ritual wailing of the priestesses swelled and faded like the rising wind, but Morgause felt her throat hard, the muscles tight, and her eyes were dry.

"Because your mother has abandoned you," came the deep rumble of his reply. "Even a death less triumphant than this one is a release for the one who passes. We grieve for ourselves, because she has left us alone."

Morgause stared. For most of her life she had hated this man, the architect of her father's death and her mother's first treachery. Of all people in the world, she had not expected him to understand.

"I remember when my grandmother was dying," she said then. "My mother wept, while I played, uncomprehending, on the shore. Argantel foretold that I would be the Lady of the Lake one day. For so many years I fought my mother, fearing she would deny me my destiny. And now that fate is come upon me, and I am afraid."

"So was she . . ." answered Merlin. "Like you, she had been long away from the Lake. But you have had your mother's teaching. Much of the old wisdom has been lost—it is for you to preserve what you can. I do not know your mysteries . . ." he said with some difficulty, "but you have the Cauldron. Call upon your Goddess—surely She will comfort you."

"And you—" she answered him.

Merlin shook his head. "My goddess has gone out of the world. . . ."

Morgause looked at him in amazement, understanding only now that this man, like her father, had been denied Igierne's love. The wind blew again, more strongly, hissing in the trees. Merlin had turned to gaze across the lake to the heights where, even in those few moments, the clouds had doubled their size.

"I must go—" he said then. "Your mother is High Queen now in the Otherworld, and in this world, the Tigernissa is Guendivar. But you are Lady of the Lake, Morgause—the Hidden Queen, the White Raven of Britannia. Guard it well!"

He held her gaze, and she saw a woman crowned with splendor reflected in his eyes.

"I am the Lady of the Lake . . ." she affirmed, accepting his vision of her at last. "And who are you?"

The certainty in Merlin's eyes flickered out, to be replaced by desolation. "I am a leaf blown by the wind . . . I am a sea-smoothed rock . . . I am a sun-bleached bone . . . I do not know what I am, save that my body lives still in a world that my spirit finds strange. Up there"—he gestured towards the hills—"perhaps I may learn. . . ."

Above the trees, one entered the kingdom of the wind. Merlin struggled upward, reeling as a new gust swept across the slope and the purple bells of the heather rang with soundless urgency. A wren was tossed skyward, crying, caught by the blast. Clouds boiled above him, flinging splatters of rain. Merlin stumbled, jabbed the Spear into the earth to keep his balance, and pulled himself upright once more.

"Blow! Blow! Cry out in rage!" he shouted, shaking his fist at the sky. This violence of nature might be harsh to the body, but it matched the anguish in his soul. "World, weep, let my grief gust forth with every blast of wind!"

He took a step forward, realized he could climb no higher, and sank to his knees. "Why—" he gasped, "am I still alive?"

There were words in the blast that whipped at hair and beard. Merlin grasped the shaft of the Spear, feeling it thrum beneath his hands like a tree in the wind, and abruptly their meaning became clear.

"Unless you will it, you shall not leave this world. . . . "

"Am I less than human, then?"

"Perhaps you are more. . . ."

Merlin shivered. The Voice was all around him, in the wail of the wind, the vibration of the spearshaft, the rasp of air in his throat. He shook his head.

"Who are you?"

The air rippled with laughter. *"I am every breath you take, every thought you think; I am ecstasy."* The laughter rolled once more. *"You carry My Spear. . . ."*

Merlin recoiled. "The god of the Saxons!"

"You may call me that, or Lugos, if it makes you feel easier, or Mercurius. I have walked in many lands, and been called by many names. When men use wit and will and words, I am there. And you have borne my Spear for a dozen winters. Why are you so surprised?"

"Why did you allow it? What do you want with me?"

"O, man of Wisdom! Even now, do you not understand?"

Abruptly the wind failed. The storm was passing. Merlin stared as the light of sunset, blazing suddenly beneath the clouds, filled the world with gold. His grief for Igierne might never leave him, but now his mind buzzed with phrases, riddles, insights and imaginings, and a great curiosity. Holding onto the Spear, he levered himself upright once more. Then he plucked it from the earth and started down the mountain.

* * *

Dust rose in golden clouds, stirred by the feet of the harvesters. The cart they drew was piled with sheaves of corn and garlanded with summer flowers. Singing rose in descant to the rhythmic creak of wheels as they pushed it towards the meadow below the villa where the harvest feast had been laid. Guendivar, sitting with Cai and Gualchmai in the place of honor, drew her veil half over her face. But the precaution was needless, for as evening drew nearer, a light breeze had come up to blow the dust away.

She had been glad of Cai's invitation to keep the festival in the place where Artor had been a boy. It was Cai's home now, though the king's service had allowed him to spend little time here. His health had not been good, and she had come partly in hopes of getting him to take some rest. He did seem to be better here. She had smiled at his stories, trying to imagine the great king of Britannia as an eager boy. Her only regret was that Artor was not here with them. Five years he had spent campaigning in Gallia, with little result that she could see. He had not even returned when his mother died the year before.

The procession rounded the last curve, and she heard the chorus more clearly:

> *"Oh where is he hidden, and where*
> *has he gone?*
> *The corn is all cut, and the harvest is done!"*

The workers who had cut and bound the last sheaf, that they called "the neck," or sometimes, "the old man," held it high. They had already been soaked with water from the river to bring luck, but in this weather they did not seem to mind. Guendivar remembered with longing the secret pool where she used to bathe when she was a girl, and how she and Julia had discovered the pleasure their bodies could bring. These days, most of the time she felt as virgin as the Mother of God, but as she watched the reapers pursuing the women who had followed to bind the sheaves, she had to suppress a spurt of envy for the fulfillment she had been denied.

> *"In the first flush of springtime, the young*
>   *king is born*
> *The ploughed fields rejoice in the growth of*
>   *the corn—*
> *Oh where is he hidden, and where—"*

Guendivar felt unexpected tears prick in her eyes. Men called her the Flower Bride and swore that her beauty was unchanged. But it was not the way of nature for spring to last forever. . . .

The cart was drawn up before the tables and the men who had hitched themselves to it threw off the traces. The woman who had been carrying the last sheaf handed it over to laughing girls, who bore it to the central upright of the drying shed and tied it there, wreathed with flowers. The light of the setting sun, slanting through the trees, turned stalk and seed to gold.

> *"The sun rises high and the fields they grow*
>   *green.*
> *Our king now is bearded, so fair to be*
>   *seen—"*

Cai held out his beaker to be refilled as the serving girl came by and sat back with a sigh. "It seems strange to sit here drinking cider, after so many years of war."

"And Artor not here to enjoy it," Gualchmai replied. "It is not right for the king to be so long from his own land. If he had the army with which we won at Mons Badonicus, by now he would be emperor!"

Still singing, men and women joined hands and began to dance around the post.

> *"The sun rises high and the fields turn to*
>   *gold,*
> *The king hangs his head, now that he has*
>   *grown old—"*

"Too many died on the quest for the Cauldron, and some of us are getting older . . ." Cai eyed Gualchmai wryly, rubbing his left arm as if it pained him. "Except, of course, for you."

Gualchmai frowned, uncomprehending. Years of war had battered his face like bronze, the sandy hair was receding from his high brow, but his arms were still oak-hard.

"It is too peaceful," he said truculently, and Guendivar laughed. "My lord set me here to guard you, but all our enemies are still frightened of his name." He sighed, and then turned to look at her, his eyes pleading. "Let me go to him, lady. Those Frankish lords would not dare to laugh if I were with him. Artor needs me. I am of use to no one here!"

> *"The reaper swings high and the binder*
> *bends low,*
> *The king is cut down and to earth he must*
> *go."*

Guendivar shivered, touched by a fear she thought she had forgotten. For so long, Artor had been a bodiless intelligence that spoke to her through the written word; she had nearly forgotten that he wore mortal flesh that was vulnerable to cold, hunger, and enemy swords.

"Ninive, bring me my shawl—" she said, but the girl was not there. It should not have surprised her; the child made no secret of her discomfort in large gatherings. No doubt she was wandering in the woods on the hill, and would return when darkness fell. And in truth, the chill the queen felt was an internal one, that neither shawl nor mantle could ease.

"Very well—" Both men turned to look at her. "It comforts me to have you here, and your wife will not thank me for letting you go, but I agree that Artor needs you more."

The harvesters rushed inward towards the last sheaf, arms upraised.

> *"And we shall make merry with bread and*
> *with beer,*
> *Until he returns with the spring of the*
> *year. . . ."*

Then the circle dissolved into laughter as they descended on the vats of harvest ale.

Grinning, Gualchmai downed his own in a single swallow and held out his cup for more.

"But be sure that you make good on your boast, my champion," Guendivar said then. "Beat the breeches off the Franks and bring my lord swiftly home."

> *"Oh where is he hidden, and where has he
>   gone?
> The corn is all cut, and the harvest is done!"*

Merlin walked in the oakwood above the villa in the golden light of a harvest moon. He had to remind himself that Turpilius and Flavia were both dead these twenty years and the farm belonged to Cai, for seen from the hillside, nothing seemed to have changed. Even from here the sound of celebration came clearly. Around the threshing sheds torches glittered; the revellers moving among them in a flickering dance of light and shadow. Stubbled fields gleamed faintly beyond them, waiting to rest through the fallow moons of wintertide.

He had intended to join the celebration, but the rites of the seeded earth were not his mysteries. Long experience had taught him that his presence would cast a chill on the festival, like a breath of wind from the wilderness beyond their fenced fields. It was far too beautiful a night to sleep, and these days he needed little rest, and had no need for the shelter of walls.

And so he walked, hair stirred lightly by the breathing darkness, feeding on the rich, organic scents of leaf mold and drying hay. On such a night it was easy to forget the dutiful impulse that had sent him south to offer his counsel to Artor's queen. He belonged in the wilderness, with only his daimon for companion and the god of the Spear for guide.

These days, the god was always with him. But the bright spirit that he called his daimon, the companion of his childhood, he had not seen for many years. Now that he was ancient he found himself remembering her bright eyes and shining hair ever more vividly. It was the fate of the old, he had heard, to become childlike.

Thinking so, he laughed softly, and out of the night, like a shiver of bells, came an answer.

Merlin stood still, senses questing outward. It was beyond belief that a man could have been present without his knowledge on this hill. What he found at last was a glimmering whiteness perched in an oak tree, the human mind so tuned to the rhythms of the night he had thought it a perturbation of the wind.

"The hour grows late—" came a silvery voice from the branches. "Why does the greatest Druid in Britannia wander the hills?"

Merlin shaped his sight to an owl's vision and saw a fine-boned face haloed by fair hair. For a moment he could not breathe. It was the face of his daimon, and yet she was no part of his imagining—even as a child, he had always understood the difference between the images that came from outside and those that lived within. And now he could sense the warmth of a human body and hear the faint whisper of breath. She stirred, and he glimpsed the glint of embroidery on her gown.

"Why is a maiden of the court sitting in a tree?"

"You do not know me, and yet we are kin." She laughed again. "I am Gualchmai's daughter by a woman of the hills, and if I cannot be roaming there, in this oak I can at least pretend to be free."

"That is so. I have myself lived for a time in a tree. Would it displease you to have an old man's company?" To his sight, a radiance seemed to flow from her slim form, more lovely than the light of the moon.

She cocked her head like a bird. "I have never before met anyone who felt like a part of the forest. You know all its secrets, is it not so? Stay then, and talk to me. . . ."

Merlin swayed, as if something were melting within him that had been frozen since Igierne died. He put out his hand to the oak tree, and carefully eased himself to the solid ground.

"Gladly . . ." he said softly. "Gladly will I stay with you."

Merlin's return was a wonder that had men buzzing for a season. When they saw how often he walked with the girl Ninive, they laughed, thinking they knew the reason. But Guendivar, having promised Gualchmai that she would watch over his child, understood that there was nothing sexual in the attraction between the old man and the maiden. And she had other, more pressing, concerns.

Gualchmai's departure had not loosed all Britannia's old enemies upon them, as some had feared. The Picts were holding to Artor's treaty, and there was only an occasional raider from Eriu. It was the princes of Britannia who were beginning to grow restive, like horses kept too long in pasture who forget the governance of bit and rein. Merlin told her that after Uthir died it had been the same. The counsel of the Druid was valuable; with his guidance Guendivar grew into her queenship like a tree in fertile soil. But he could not show an iron fist to the princes. She wrote to Artor, but another year passed, and he did not return.

Gualchmai had been gone for two years when new trouble between the men of Dumnonia and the West Saxons impelled her to appeal to Artor again. She had summoned Constantine and Cynric to meet with her at Durnovaria. The spring had been a fine one, and they had no excuse for not traveling. But if she could not reconcile them with her wisdom, she and they both knew that she had no teeth with which to compel obedience.

Through her window came the rich, organic scent of the river that Durnovaria guarded, mixed with the sharper tang of the sea. Few men lived permanently in the town—even the prince preferred to spend most of his time at his villa in the hills. But folk still gathered here for the weekly market, and the clamor of mixed tongues made a deeper background to the crying of gulls. Guendivar set down the vellum on which she had been working and took up the most recent letter that Artor had sent to her.

"Pompeius Regalis paid me a visit last month; he is building a stronghold near Brioc's monastery in the west of the coastal plain and has realized he needs allies. There are so many Dumnonians there now the place is called by their name. His son Fracanus was with him. He has invented a new sport that he persuaded some of my men to try. Instead of racing their horses with chariots, they measure out a course and put up the lightest boys into the saddle. Of course it is dangerous if the lad is thrown, but the horses do go faster. . . ."

Guendivar shook her head. In conversation, Artor had never been one for humor, but in these letters he seemed anxious to amuse as well as to inform her. Indeed, she had learned more of his mind since he went over the sea than when they lived together.

"Summer is almost upon us. I believe that I can get Regalis and Conan of Venetorum to agree to an alliance, and with them, Guenomarcus of Plebs Legionorum. With them behind me, I will count Armorica as secured. The sons of Chlodovech-us, having settled matters in Tolosa, are gazing northward, and the Britons who took up land in Lugdunensis have asked our aid."

That meant that Artor would be fighting soon, might be in battle even now. Guendivar realized that her grip had creased the vellum, and gently let it fall. The king had spent his life in warfare and rarely taken any harm. And now he had Gualchmai. Why should the prospect concern her now? Was it because he was not fighting for Britannia?

From the direction of the city gate came a blare of cowhorns; the babble in the marketplace crested to a roar. Cynric had arrived at last. Guendivar closed her eyes, massaging the skin above her brows. Then she rolled and tied Artor's letter, stood and called for her maidens to attire her in the stiff ceremonial garments of the high queen.

Robed in a Druid's snowy white and leaning on Woden's Spear, Merlin waited behind the high queen's throne. In almost three years, he had become accustomed to wearing civilized garments once more. Ninive accepted the weight of woven cloth and metal pins when she wanted to run like a wild pony across the moors. For her sake, he could do the same.

Men wondered what deep purpose lay behind his return, but he had no plan, no intentions. In his heart he knew that Ninive was not his daimon incarnate in a maiden's flesh. But she held him to the human world. He looked at her now, standing with the other girls who served the queen. For a moment their eyes met, and he heard the cry of a falcon soaring above the headlands, and the hushed roar of the sea.

The long chamber where once the magistrates of Durnovaria had held their meetings was beginning to fill. Constantine sat on the south side with the chieftain whose lands lay on the Saxon border beside him. A half dozen of his houseguard muttered behind him, fists straying to their hips and then away when they remembered that they had been required to leave their swords outside.

A side door opened and he saw Guendivar, framed like an icon against the darkness of the passageway. She was mantled in gold, her pointed face framed by the pearl lappets of a Byzantine diadem. But the splendor in which she walked was only a visible focus for the penumbra of power, and men rose to greet her with a reverence that was more than formal. The queen ascended the dais and took her seat, and the two youths who had escorted her, one red as a fox, the other fair, took their places to either side of the carved chair. Eormenric looked about him smiling, but red Ceawlin gazed at the door with a face like carved bone.

The double doors at the end of the hall swung open. Tall men came through it. The flaming hair of their leader was dusted now with ash, but it was bright enough to set an answering flame ablaze in Ceawlin's eyes.

"*Waes hael, drighten. Wilcume!*" said the queen, who had learned a little Saxon from her hostages.

Cynric blinked, then brought up his arm in acknowledgment. He and his men wheeled and took their places on the northern wall.

Merlin let his mind drift, the point and counterpoint of complaint and accusation like the mutter of distant thunder. Behind Cynric he could just make out a darker head amongst the fair and brown. The Saxon leader stepped forward, gesturing, and a ray of light from the upper window touched the head of the man behind him with a gleam of bronze. That was no Saxon! Merlin stepped out from behind the queen's chair, extending other, secret, senses towards the stranger.

As if he had felt the touch, the bronze-haired man straightened and turned, and Merlin recoiled, recognizing, in a face that was a masculine reflection of Morgause, the grey gaze of Artor the king. Any other identity of form or feature might have been put down to their common inheritance from Igierne, but not those eyes, which had come to Artor from Uthir, who was father to him alone.

"Lady, as you have deemed, so shall it be. Eadwulf will bring his kinsmen back from the western bank of the river. We give up our claim to the land—" Cynric's voice grew louder, and the Dumnonian lords began to grin. "I call your *Witan*, your council, to witness that we of the West Seax have kept faith with you. In your hall my son has grown to manhood. You have taught him much. Now it is time for him to come back to his own land and learn the ways of the folk that he will one day rule. In exchange, I return to you the son of your king!"

As Medraut stepped forward, a whisper of amazement, of question, of commentary swept the hall like the wind that heralds the storm. Those who remembered the Pendragon were marking the resemblance that identified Medraut not only as Artor's nephew but as his son. The tablet-woven banding on his dark tunic was all Saxon, like the seax-knife that hung at his side. But the brooch that held his mantle was of Pictish work, and the pride of the House of Maximian shone in his eyes. He halted, and half a hundred glances flickered from his face to that of the queen.

Surely, thought Merlin, Artor must have told her—but for nine years Medraut had been hidden among the Saxons like a hound among wolves. It had been too easy for all of them to forget that one day he would return to hunt with his own pack once more.

If she was surprised, Guendivar gave no sign. Speaking softly, she turned to Ceawlin, and the eagerness burning in his eyes for a moment dimmed as he bent to kiss her hand.

"I will not forget you, lady," he said hoarsely. Then, as if she had slipped his leash, he bounded to his father's side.

"And Eormenric"—she turned to the other youth—"you have spent as many years among us as your father did when he was young. I will not keep you here when your companion has gone."

For a moment the fair lad's face flamed. "My father loved King Artor," he said in a low mice. "But my loyalty is given to *you*. If ever you have need of me, you have only to call." He bent his head, turned, and went out of the hall.

Cynric and his son had moved a little aside, so that Medraut stood alone. Would the queen welcome him? Would she spurn him? Would she hail him as nephew or son? His face had gone very white, and as he looked at Guendivar, something anguished flickered in his eyes.

Fragmented images fluttered behind Merlin's vision. He grasped for them, and for a moment glimpsed dark shapes battling beneath the hard light of noon. His spirit reached out for comprehension to the daimon who from childhood had guided him, and in the next moment he found he was staring at Ninive, standing solid and alive beside the queen. For so long he had fled the power of foreknowledge that had haunted his childhood. Now, when he needed it, the only meaning he understood lay in the fair face of one young girl.

Guendivar leaned forward, stretching out her hand. "Come, Medraut—I bid you welcome home. . . ."

VI

A Wind from the North

A.D. 513

"My lady, a man has come—from Gallia. . . ."

Medraut's voice was quiet, the northern burr worn smooth by his years among the Saxons. Guendivar dropped the ball of embroidery wool she had been winding. As it rolled across the floor, Medraut bent smoothly and scooped it up, handing it back to her with a bow. Since he had been so unexpectedly returned to them, he had become an accepted presence in her court.

The thin lad who had appeared so briefly at Camalot nine years before had never met her eyes. Now she understood why, knowing him for Artor's son. She was glad that the king had told her himself, and not left her to learn it from gossip, or worse still, from Cynric. If Medraut's birth troubled him, he no longer let it show. His mother had trained him well, the queen thought wryly—he certainly knew how to make himself useful among the women. But his silent appearances still startled her, and she was no closer to understanding him.

"With news?" It was three months since she had heard from Artor, and a wet winter was turning into a chilly spring.

"He bears letters, but he is no messenger—"

At the sardonic tone, Guendivar lifted one eyebrow, but to comment would be to admit weakness, and instinct and experience both told her that with this one she must always seem strong.

"Shall I receive him here, or make him wait for a formal audience?" she asked, waiting curiously for his reply.

Since Medraut's arrival, she had searched her soul, grateful that she had suppressed her first furious impulse to send the boy back to Morgause. He had not asked to be born. Certainly, she thought with some resentment, she could not conceive when the king was in Gallia, even if Artor had been potent in her bed. Medraut was Artor's only son; even with his ambiguous heritage, he could be Artor's heir.

"Not here—" Medraut gazed around at the domestic clutter of the Women's Sunhouse. "And yet, I think this man is one you will wish to bind to your service. His name is Theodoric, a Goth of the kingdom of Tolosa and a man of the sea. Dress richly, but meet him in the garden."

Guendivar nodded slowly. Whether or not Medraut had the instinct for kingship, he certainly understood how to manipulate men. She glanced at the angle of the sun.

"That is good advice. Just after noon, bring him to me there."

Guendivar was already waiting on the stone bench beside the lavender bush when Theodoric entered the garden. One forgot that for a hundred years the Goths had been part of the Empire, not always peacefully, to be sure, but living side by side with Romans, learning their ways and their laws. They were even some kind of heretical Christians, she had heard. Certainly this man, tall and weathered by sun and wind though he might be, was no barbarian.

"I am Theodoric son of Theudebald—" The Goth stopped before her, bowing.

The queen rose to meet him, extending her hand. "Praefectus Classis," she continued in Latin, "be welcome to Britannia. Has my husband given you letters to bring to me?"

"He has, and said that to deliver them safely should be my best recommendation to you. I parted from the lord Artor on the last day of February." From the case at his side he drew a tubular letter case and held it out to her.

"Truly?" she said, calculating, "then you have made a swift passage. In a moment I will read what he has to say of you, but for now you must tell me about yourself, and why you have come."

"Lady, I need a home." A flush stained the bronzed cheeks, but he met her eyes steadily. "The Franks have driven my people over the mountains and into Iberia. The Goths are carving out a new kingdom, but it is all inland, whereas I am a man of the sea. I know how to sail it, how to fight upon it, how to build ships and defend harbors."

"And Britannia has many miles of coastline, and enemies who attack her from the sea—" finished Guendivar. "Now I understand why Artor sent you."

He straightened, relieved, but not surprised at her understanding. *What,* she wondered, *did Artor tell him about me?*

"What remains of the Gothic navy waits at Aquilonia—five vessels with their crews and captains who will sail at my command. I offer it to you."

"Our most present danger is the Irish, who attack the coasts of Demetia at will. Make your base at Glevum—I will send to the lord Agricola, who rules Demetia, to provide you with supplies. With your skills and his resources, we may hope to dislodge the Irish who have settled there and discourage them from trying again. Does that sound well to you?"

"It does indeed," he breathed. "I will write to my men immediately, and my ship can carry any messages you may have for the lord Artor." He started to turn, then paused, staring at her. "But perhaps you will want to read the king's letter first. To take me at my own word like this—you are very trusting."

"Perhaps." She smiled. "Although, if I have second thoughts, I can always send riders after you. But I hope that my lord would not have left his land in my charge if he did not trust my ability to read men."

For a moment longer Theodoric looked at her. Then, once again he bowed, not the courteous inclination with which he had greeted her, but the full reverence he might have made at the court of an emperor.

"Domina, I came here hoping to find safe harbor. But I have also found a queen. . . ."

Guendivar felt her own cheeks growing warm, but managed a gracious nod. "Medraut—" she called. She had not seen him, but she suspected he would not be out of earshot, and indeed it was only a moment before he appeared. "Escort our new admiral and help him to whatever he needs."

When he had gone, she sat down on the bench once more, and with fingers that trembled a little, opened the leather tube and pulled out the vellum roll inside.

"My lady, I must write swiftly, for Theodoric wishes to catch the morning tide. He has a good reputation among the Goths, and seems a sensible man, but we here have no need for a navy. I give him to you for the defense of Demetia. Use him well.

"The Franks have marched more swiftly than I expected, despite the rain, and our supplies are getting low. Whatever you can send will be very welcome. The sons of Chlodovechus quarrel among themselves, but they can combine efficiently enough when they recognize an enemy. So far Theuderich, the eldest and most experienced among them, is still holding onto the leadership, even though he is not the son of Queen Chlotild, but of a concubine.

"Yesterday they brought us to battle, a hard-fought, muddy encounter that left no clear victor. We did not retreat—perhaps that may be counted as a victory. But it was costly. My nephew Aggarban was killed in the fighting, and there are many wounded.

"Riothamus still lives, but he is failing. Soon, I fear he will leave us, and I will have to decide whether or not to claim his sovereignty. I care for these people, and I believe that many of them have come to look to me with love and loyalty. But this is not my land. Last summer my journeys took me deep into Gallia, and there I found a town called Aballo, which in our tongue is the same as Afallon, the place of apples. And I closed my eyes, and saw the vale and the Tor so clearly I nearly wept

with longing to be there. And you were there, standing beneath the apple trees."

There was a break in the writing there, as if he had been distracted, or perhaps too overcome to continue. Guendivar found her own eyes prickling with unshed tears, and shook her head. *How can you write such things,* she wondered angrily, *and not come home to me?* Wiping her eyes, she picked up the scroll once more.

"You will have to tell Medraut about his brother's death. About the boy himself, I do not know what to say. I did not understand him that season he was with me, and I cannot imagine what nine years among the Saxons have made of him. I can only trust that the powers that protect Britannia had some purpose in bringing him to birth."

Once more there was a space. The writing that followed was smaller, and precise, as if he had been exerting all his control.

"You, my queen, are the one most wronged by his existence. If you, of your charity, will keep him by you I will be grateful, but if it seems better, send him away. I leave him in your hands."

There was a blot on the page, as if he had started to write *"I wish . . ."* and then crossed it out. Beyond that she saw only the scrawled letters of his name.

"I wish!" Guendivar repeated aloud, glaring at the page and wondering whether this was trust or desperation. Should she be honored or angry? Either way, Medraut was her problem now. She would have to make another attempt to talk to him.

Artor, Artor, you have been too long away. What will it take to bring you home again? She rolled up the vellum and slid it into its case once more.

Guendivar had intended to talk with Medraut that evening, but just as they sat down to their meal a messenger arrived. He was from King Icel, his news an attack on Anglia by raiders from the northern land that is called Lochlann in Eriu, and by the Romans Skandza. They had picked their way through the shoals of the Metaris estuary and struck southward through the fens, burning farmsteads and carrying off livestock, goods, and men. Icel did not precisely ask for aid—he had, after all, been given those lands on the understanding that he would defend them—but the implication that he would welcome some support was clear.

"Otherwise, he would have simply reported his victory," said Cai. "We must send a troop—enough men so they will know we have not abandoned them. I can raise some from my own country, and perhaps the Dumnonians—"

"Will send no men to aid Saxons, as you know very well!" Guendivar interrupted him. "And you are not going to lead them, whoever they are. I need you here!"

That was not entirely true, but Cai must know as well as she did that he was in no condition for campaigning. He did not protest her decision, and that worried her. In the past year he had grown short of breath, and his high color was not a mark of health. Cai refused to discuss his condition with her or with Merlin. To keep him from exhausting himself further was the most she could manage.

"The messenger will need a day or two to recover. I will think on what we may do."

The queen was still worrying over the problem that evening when Medraut knocked at the door of the accounting house.

For the first time, she regretted allowing Gualchmai to go to Gallia. Or Theodoric to depart for Demetia—but the Anglians would not have been impressed by a Goth newly come to Britannia, no matter how good his navy. And she dared not send a Dumnonian prince, who was as likely to encourage the Northmen to attack Icel as to defend him. She needed someone of unquestioned British background who could deal with the Saxons.

"They are saying," said Medraut as he entered, "that my brother Aggarban is dead."

Guendivar set down the tax rolls she had been pretending to examine. "It is so. He died from wounds taken in battle. I am sorry."

Medraut shrugged. "He was some years older, and left home when I was only five years old. I did not know him well."

There was an uncomfortable silence.

"Will you sit?" she asked finally, setting the scroll she had been pretending to read aside. "The nights are still chilly. I will ask Fulvia to bring us some chamomile tea."

"Let me call her—" There was a hint of indulgence in Medraut's smile. He indicated the table covered with scrolls and wax tablets. "You have labored enough this evening already." He rose and went to the door.

Guendivar kept her face still. In the past six years she had learned to recognize the subtle tension of manipulation. It was unusual to find such skill in a man so young, but she thought that constant practice had made her even more skillful at it than he.

"The Goth, Theodoric, brought letters from the king," she said when Medraut had taken his seat once more.

"—my father," he completed her sentence.

Guendivar lifted an eyebrow. Was that the way he wanted it? "The king your father has left it to me to decide whether to keep you here or to send you elsewhere." She watched Medraut carefully, uncertain whether the tightening she thought she saw in his face came from the flicker of the lampflame or from unease.

But if she had worried him, he covered it quickly—when he lifted his head she saw the skin stretched across the strong, graceful bones of his face as smoothly as a mask.

"Since he has abandoned both kith and kingdom, it is fitting that his son, like Britannia, should be in the keeping of his queen. . . ."

"Say, rather, that he has left both in a mother's care . . ." she corrected blandly.

"Oh, pray do not!" Medraut's tone was sardonic, but she could see that she had shaken him. "You forget—my mother is Morgause!"

Guendivar blinked. She was only too aware how Morgause had damaged Artor—for the first time it occurred to her to wonder how she might have warped her son. She thought, *I will be the good mother Medraut never had,* and suppressed the anguished resentment that Artor had never allowed her to be the wife she should have been.

Medraut was still watching her, and Guendivar gave him a

gentle smile. "Has your mother turned you against all women, then?"

He shook his head, lamplight sending ripples of flame along the smooth waves of auburn hair. The grey gaze that was so like Artor's held her own. But as she met his eyes, she realized that the expression there was nothing like Artor's at all.

"And has my father turned you against all men, leaving you to lie in an empty bed for so many years?"

Guendivar stiffened. Medraut's voice was very soft, his eyes hidden now by the sweep of downturned lashes so that she could not tell whether sympathy or irony glimmered there.

"That is not a question you may ask of me!"

"Then who can?" He straightened, and now it was she who could not look away. "Who has a better right to question what happens in King Artor's bed than you and I? We have a unique relationship," he said bitterly. "It was you, my lady, who chose to begin this conversation—you cannot take refuge in the ordinary courtesies now!"

Guendivar struggled to keep her composure. "It is clear," she said tightly, "that you do not want another mother."

"A mother?" He shuddered. "For that, you would have had to take me when I was born. But you were only six years old. Did you realize, my lady, how nearly of an age we are?" He reached out to her.

"What do you want, Medraut? What am I to do with you?" she said desperately, trying to forget that for a moment she had wanted to take his hand.

"Use me! Let me show what I can do, not as Artor's mistake or the tool of Morgause, but as myself, a prince of the line of Maximian!" he exclaimed. "Send me to the Anglians! Who else do you have who can understand them? They will not care about my birth, except to recognize that it is royal. There are stories of such matings in their own lore. With thirty men, or sixty, well-mounted, I could show them that the arm of Britannia is still long, even when her king is away!"

Guendivar could not fault his reasoning. But even as she agreed, she realized that it was not for his sake that she wanted him away, but for her own.

*　*　*

Medraut coughed as a shift in the wind brought the acrid reek of burning thatch. The black horse tossed its head uneasily and he jerked on the rein. The British had joined forces with Icel's men at Camulodunum and followed the trail of burnt farmsteads northward. And now, it would appear they had found the enemy. That same wind carried a singsong gabble of northern voices. He lifted his hand, a swift glance catching the attention of the British who rode behind him and the Anglian spearmen who marched with Creoda, a broad-built young man with ashy brown hair who was Icel's youngest son.

Creoda was the only one of Icel's children born in Britannia. He had been a boy during Artor's Anglian wars, brought up on his elder brother's tales of vanished glories. Medraut had not found it difficult to get him talking—he was much like the sons of the chieftains in Cynric's hall, enjoying the benefits of peace, but chafing because they had been born too late to be heroes. It was only when fending off marauders like these Northmen that they got the chance to fight at all.

Carefully they moved forward, the British on the road, the Anglians spreading out through the tangle of second-growth woodland where the old Roman fields were going back to the wild. Then the road curved, and suddenly the trees were gone. Beyond the young barley that the Anglian settler had planted in his home field they could see the burning farmstead.

Medraut yelled and bent forward, digging his heels into the black's sides. As the horse lurched into a gallop, he dropped the knotted reins on its neck, shrugged his shield onto his arm and plucked his spear from its rest at his side. He noted the bodies of the farmfolk without emotion, attention fixed on the foe. The raiders were dropping their booty and snatching up the weapons they had laid aside, but he had caught them by surprise. They were still scattered when the British hit them, stabbing and slashing with spear and sword.

The buildings were still smouldering when the fighting ended. Medraut drew a deep breath, grinning, exulting in the rush of blood through his veins. It had been like this when he had ridden with Cynric to break up a fight between two feuding clans of Saxons—the tension before the conflict and the exaltation after, as if he were drunk on a dark mead of war. Growing up in the hulking shadows of his brothers, he had sometimes despaired of ever becoming a warrior—but Cynric had trained him well. Though he did not have Goriat's height or Aggarban's heavy muscles, he had learned to make full use of the swift flexibility of his lean frame.

A dozen northern bodies sprawled in the farmyard, blood and mud darkening their fair hair. The rest, near forty in number, stood together by the well, their weapons heaped before them, glaring at the circle of Anglian spearmen who had caught those who tried to flee. Two of Creoda's men had been killed and several wounded; one of the British had broken a leg when he was pulled from his horse. But Medraut himself had not a mark on him, while three of the fallen had died at his hand. He was *good* at fighting—a gift he owed neither to father nor mother, but to Cynric's teaching and his own hard-won skill.

He grinned savagely, surveying his prisoners.

"Does one of you have the Roman tongue?" he asked.

A young man with hair so pale it seemed white in the spring sunlight straightened. Medraut had already guessed him to be the leader from the gold armring he wore.

"*Appeto Galliam*—" he said in rough Latin, using a verb which could mean either traveling to a place or attacking it, to indicate that he had been to Gallia.

"That I can believe!" murmured one of the British.

"*Mercator*—" the Northman continued. *As a merchant*—

"And that, I do not believe at all!"

"*Gippus, filius Gauthagastus regulus.*" The prisoner touched his chest. *Gipp son of Gauthagast. . . .*

"*Medrautus filius Artorius.*" He tapped his own breast, ignoring the little murmur of reaction from his men. "So, we have a king's son to ransom," he added in the Saxon tongue.

"A second son only," said Gipp in the same language. "You will not get much for me."

"Oh, I will get something—" Medraut smiled sweetly. "Where are the others?"

"The rest of you swine!" snarled Creoda when the prisoner did not answer.

"Gone by now, full-laden—" The Northman grinned. "They left us six days ago, but we were still hungry."

"This time, you have bit off more than you can chew," said Creoda, but the news had clearly relieved him.

Medraut nodded. "Who are your best seamen? They shall take your ship back to the North with word to your people. The rest of you will come with us to Camulodunum. Creoda, will you set up a rotation of guards?"

"Gladly! And send a messenger to my father." He favored Medraut with an approving smile. "You fight like one of our own, son of the Bear. We have done good work today!"

The Britons and their Anglian allies moved slowly southward, for some of the Northmen were wounded and could not go fast. But the weather had cleared and the roads were beginning to dry. With all their enemies accounted for, they could afford to relax.

On the third evening, knowing that the next day's march would bring them to Camulodunum, Medraut took a skin of ale and sat down beside his prisoner.

"Tomorrow we will come to Camulodunum," he said, offering the ale.

"A Roman town—who now lives there?" Gipp answered in the same tone. If he harbored fears for his future, he was doing well at hiding them.

"Anglians. The town was falling into ruin. Icel sent one of his chieftains to hold the place by the terms of his treaty with King Artor."

Gipp lifted an eyebrow. "I thought the Anglians conquered this land." He drank, and passed the skin of ale back again.

"Then why do I ride with them?" asked Medraut. "Artor defeated Icel's army twenty years ago. But by then, all the Britons had fled and there was no one to till the land. So Artor took the Anglians into his kingdom, to protect it from raiders."

"Like me. . . ." Gipp grinned. "They do not do so well, eh?"

"They have mostly settled the richer lands inland, not the coasts. Is this land much like your own?"

Gipp laughed. "It would be hard for a place to be more different. Halogaland is all mountains, with little pockets of pasture clinging above the narrow fjords. This land—so flat—" He gestured at the mixed marsh and woodland around them. "Seems very strange. But there are no rocks. A man could grow anything in this soil."

"Have you seen many lands?" Medraut wiped his mouth and passed the ale-skin back again.

"Oh, there are always kings who look for good fighting men. I marched with Ela when he attacked the Geats, after they took in the banished sons of his brother. He killed Heardred, the Geatish king, but Adgils and Admund escaped him. They say Beowulf rules there now, and he is a hero of whom there are already many tales. I think there would be little profit in following Ela now."

"It is profit you look for, not glory?" Medraut rested his forearms on his knees, considering the other man.

Gipp's high-boned face creased in a smile. "They say in my country that cattle and kinsmen will die, and only a man's fame live after. But I have won my name in battle, and it seems to me that so long as I live in this world I will need the cattle and the kin. I would not be sorry to settle down with a plump wife and a good farm. But at home there is little land."

"And that is why you think your father will not ransom you? Gipp shrugged. "A man cannot escape his wyrd."

"Well—" Medraut got to his feet, motioning to the Northman to keep the ale-skin. "Perhaps we will find some other use for you."

The bright, hot weather of June was smiling on the land when Medraut came back to Camalot. The fortress was full of men and horses—Guendivar had called the princes of Britannia to council, and their retinues sat drinking and dicing in stable and ramparts and hall.

He had stayed with the Anglians long enough to get Icel's agreement to settle Gipp at the mouth of the Arwe, north of Camulodunum, to hold the place for the Anglians as they held the whole of Anglia for Artor. But the Northman knew whom he had to thank for his good fortune. Medraut had not decided what use he might make of the warrior, but it never hurt to have the gratitude of a good fighting man.

Medraut was twenty-six years old. At his age, his father had already been king for eleven years. He himself had spent the equivalent years with Cynric, and what had they gotten him?

The sons of the Saxons are not the only ones who dream of glory, he thought ruefully as he gazed at the grizzled locks of the princes who sat at council in the great roundhouse with their sons behind them. *Where, in this empire Artor is building, is there a place for me?*

The queen had summoned the assembly to set the levies for this year's taxes. It was not going well.

"Eleven years! Next year it will be ten years since the king was sailing oversea!" exclaimed Cunobelinus, his northern accent striking with a painful familiarity in Medraut's ear. " 'Tis as long, surely, as it took the Greeks to take the city of Troy!"

"And will that be the end of it? Or will Artor, like Ulysses, be another ten years returning home?" Perctur echoed him.

"The seas that separate our shores from Gallia are neither so great nor so treacherous as the Mare Internum," the queen said tartly, "but even if it were so, when Artor returns he will find me as faithful as Penelope."

"My lady—no one doubts your fidelity," Eldaul of Glevum said gently, "only the need for it. The king of Britannia belongs at home."

"Oh, he may bide abroad for another ten years with my good will and conquer all the way to the gates of Roma," put in Paulinus of Viroconium, "so long as he does not require my taxes! Let the men of Gallia support his army if they desire his presence so greatly."

There was a murmur of agreement from many of the others.

"We have done well enough without him, these past years!" said someone at the other end of the hall. Medraut peered through the shadows and recognized the prince of Guenet.

Cunobelinus turned towards him, glaring. "But without the king, how long will the Pax Artoria be lasting? Drest Gurthin-moch has honored his treaty, but a new generation of warriors is growing up on tales of the riches of Britannia. How long will he be able to hold them? If he thinks that Artor has abandoned us, how long will he try?"

"The king has not abandoned us!" exclaimed Guendivar, two spots of color burning in her cheeks.

Perhaps not, my lady, thought Medraut, *but he certainly appears to have abandoned* you*!* She was very beautiful in her anger. He thought with distaste of his mother, who had also had to rule alone when Leudonus began to fail. But Morgause had lusted after power.

What do you lust for, Guendivar, he wondered, gazing at her, *or do you even know?* Last night he had dreamed of Kea, the Pictish slave who had been his first woman. Like the queen, she had been sweetly rounded, with hair like amber in the sun. At the time, he had thought her beautiful, but compared to Guendivar's radiance, her light was only an oil-lamp's flame.

"Artor asks for our taxes—for gold and for grain—" Peretur of Eburacum was speaking now. "And for the defense of Britannia we have never denied him—" His grim gaze swept the assembly, as if tallying those who *had* sometimes refused their support, even during the Saxon wars. "But I am loath to give up resources which, if the Picts break the Border, we will need ourselves!"

The babble of response was like the roar of a distant sea. Guendivar surveyed the assembly, cheeks flaming with anger, and rose to her feet, staring them down until silence fell once more. But when she spoke, her voice was calm.

"Clearly, there are many factors here to be considered, and we have sat long at our debate. Hunger is not the best counselor. Let us go out to the meal that my cooks have been preparing, and meet again when the sun begins its descent once more."

As he followed the others from the roundhouse, Medraut continued to watch the queen. Though her women had come out to escort her, she seemed very much alone, her brow furrowed with the anxiety she had been too proud to show in the hall.

Britannia may be able to endure without Artor, he thought then, *but if he does not return, what will happen to the queen?* His gaze followed her as she entered her own quarters, and he blinked, his vision for a moment overlaid with memory of the dream in which little Kea had lain in his arms.

"Medraut!"

At the shout, he turned, and saw the heir to Viroconium hurrying towards him. Martinus was a puppy, with an open face and eager eyes, but he might have his uses. Medraut paused, arranging his features in a pleasant expression.

"I hear that you fought wild savages from Lochlann last spring. What were they like? How many did you kill?"

With some effort, Medraut maintained his smile. Martinus' voice was both penetrating and loud; others were turning, younger men for the most part, second sons and chieftains' heirs. He saw Caninus of Glevum, who was a good fighter already, and the two cousins from Guenet, Cunoglassus and Maglocun. In another moment, a group was gathering, and Medraut grinned.

"They are fierce fighters indeed, but no monsters. If you like, I will tell you the tale. . . ."

Whatever he might say was bound to be more interesting than the political debates of their elders, thought Medraut as he led his audience to the shade below the palisade.

"You all know that we defeated the Anglians twenty years ago, and gave them lands in the east that our own people had abandoned, on condition that they should defend them."

"My grandfather says the king betrayed his own people, making that treaty—" said Marc'h, a lanky thirteen-year-old who was the son of Constantine. "He should have killed them all."

"Huh—*your* grandfather started the last Saxon war!" someone else replied.

"Perhaps—" Medraut cut in once more, "but then the land would have been empty, and these same Northmen you call savages might have come instead, and been much harder to deal with. The Saxons, and the Anglians, are not bad people— I have lived among them, and I know. They become more like us the longer they live in our land."

"They hold a quarter of Britannia," muttered Marc'h. "My grandfather says they will try to gobble down the rest of it one day."

Medraut shook his head. "Not if we are strong and stand together. Not if their kings see an advantage in being our allies. I fought shoulder to shoulder with Icel's son, Creoda, and now he calls me friend."

"The campaign—tell us—" came a babble of voices, and Medraut began his tale. He did not exaggerate, or at least, only a little. The men of Demetia who had ridden with him could disprove any claims that were too extravagant, after all. But he had learned among the Saxons that a man owed it to himself to claim his victories.

"And so I have the gratitude of both the Anglians and the Northmen!" Medraut allowed himself a small smile. "There is still glory to be won without ever leaving Britannia."

"The lord Peretur says that the Picts are sure to start a new war soon," said a young guardsman from Eburacum. "He says if the king does not come back soon, Britannia will be as it was in the time of the Vor-Tigernus, when the princes fought each other and left the land at the mercy of its enemies."

"It is true," Medraut said thoughtfully. "We need a strong king, who will put Britannia first. . . ." He stopped, seeing a sudden doubt in some of their faces, while others nodded agreement. Had he meant to hint at rebellion? He hardly knew himself, but the seed was planted now.

"And what if Artor does not come back? What if he and your brothers and all the experienced fighting men are killed by the Franks?" Martinus cried.

"We still have the queen—" answered Medraut. "During these past years, will any deny that she has governed well?"

"But she cannot lead an army—"

"Perhaps not, though I seem to remember that the queens of our people did just that, when the Romans were conquering this land. But she does not need to. I come from the North, where they still understand that the queen is the source of sovereignty. If the high king falls, or fails, it is for Guendivar to choose a lord to lead this land."

vii

Bitter Harvest

A.D. 514

The yearly levies of gold and grain were due at the end of summer, when the corn harvest was in. Each year since the king had departed, it seemed to Guendivar, the totals had diminished. Were the princes lying in their reports, or had Artor's absence really drained the fertility from the land? In the North, folk held that the soil's productivity depended on the queen. That was no help, she thought, staring at the smoke-stained plaster of the wall. How could the land be fecund when the queen was barren?

"Do you have the tally from Dumnonia?" asked Medraut from the other side of the room.

"Such as it is—" she answered. "According to this, there is scarcely a stalk of grain in Kernow, and hardly a fish in the sea." She leaned from her chair to hand him the scroll.

Putting another table in the room for him to use had made for cramped quarters, but Guendivar did not grudge it. Medraut had a sharp brain, and his mother, whatever his feelings about her might be, had trained him well. In the past year he had turned into an able assistant.

And now he was more necessary than ever. The queen felt her eyes filling with remembered sorrow. For the past year Cai had insisted on continuing to work even when it was clear he was in pain, and just after midsummer his noble heart had given way at last. She still missed his dour, steady support, but at least Medraut was taking on some of his labor.

"You cannot blame the Dumnonians for wishing to keep their harvest for their own use when they know that what they give us will go to support a war across the sea," he said then.

"Can't they see the need?" Guendivar exclaimed.

"To a farmer in Kernow or a shepherd in the Lake Country, Gallia seems very far away—"

"I'm sure the Armoricans thought the Franks were distant too," Guendivar replied tartly, "but now they are at their gates. It does not need a Merlin to prophesy that if the Franks are not stopped in Gallia, one day the cliffs of Dubris may see their sails."

"But not today—" repeated Medraut, "and this day, this harvest, is what the people see. They do not understand why their king has abandoned them. They cannot share his dreams."

"What can I do?" She shook her head despairingly. The changes had been slow, and small, but each day the king was away from his kingdom, the web of obligation and loyalty that had held Britannia together frayed a little more. "How can I make them understand?"

"It is Artor's dream!" he exclaimed, rising. "Let *him* persuade them. It is not fair to lay this burden on you!"

"At least this is something I *can* do for him," Guendivar said sadly.

"And this is something I can do for you . . ." Medraut replied.

Guendivar felt a gentle touch on her shoulder, and then his strong fingers kneading, banishing the tension that knotted the muscles there. She gave an involuntary sigh, leaning into the pressure of his hands. She had not realized how tightly she had been braced against the demands of each day.

"Is that better?" he said softly.

"Wonderful . . . where did you learn to do this?"

There was a silence, while he pressed the points that would release the tensions at the base of her neck.

"My mother also was a ruling queen, although, unlike you, she lusted after power. But after a day among the accounts she too grew stiff and sore. She taught me how to massage the pain away. In the evenings I would stand behind her, as now I stand behind you, while her harper played."

"She taught you well. . . ."

"Oh indeed." His voice grew bitter. "She taught me many things . . ." For a moment his grip was almost painful. She made a stifled sound of protest and he grew gentle again.

"What did Morgause do, to hurt you so?" Guendivar asked at last.

"Sometimes I think her first sin was to give birth to me. But no child hates its life. She was my whole world, then." He sighed. "And I believed that I was hers. I knew she favored me more than my brothers. She kept me always by her, directing my every step, and thought, and word. I loved her—I had no one else to love."

"Was that so bad? Or did she change?"

"Change? Not until it was too late for me." Medraut replied. "When I began to feel a man's urges, she took me to the Picts. There were a number of boys of my age there— they showed us a beautiful girl and said she should choose as her lover the lad who did best in the games. She had amber hair like yours," he added softly, "but she was wearing one of my mother's gowns. I know now that it was all arranged beforehand, but at the time I thought her a princess, whom I had won in fair competition with the other boys.

"And perhaps I would have!" he burst out then. "I was skillful and strong. I did well! But after that night, in which I discovered the joy that men find in women's arms, she confessed that she was only a slavegirl, and that she had been told which boy to choose. She wept in my arms, my little Kea, for by then she loved me, and I believed that I loved her, too.

"I begged my mother to buy her for me, but she said the girl was bestowed elsewhere. It was more than a year before I found out that my mother had already purchased Kea herself and ordered her strangled before we had even arrived back at Dun Eidyn."

"But why?" exclaimed Guendivar.

"The reason given was that she must never open to another the womb that had received my first seed! I think that my mother saw how I loved Kea, and feared a rival. . . . But by the time I found out what had happened, Morgause no longer cared whether I loved her. She had left me and whatever plot she had meant to use me in, and run back to her own mother at the Isle of Maidens. I came south, hoping to find better treatment at the hands of my father. But he has abandoned me too, just as he abandoned you!"

"Oh, Medraut!" she exclaimed, half turning. "I am so sorry!"

For a moment the knowing fingers stilled. "Poor little queen . . . so beautiful and wise. She cares for everyone else, but who will care for her?" He began to work again, stroking down along her arms, massaging the muscles of forearm and hand, especially the right, cramped from long hours with stylus and quill.

"Such a fair white hand—it doesn't deserve such labor—" He turned it over and began very gently to explore the contours of the palm.

Guendivar shivered. He stood very close, his arms curved around her. It seemed natural to lean against him, savoring the warm strength of the male body that supported her own.

"It deserves . . . to be kissed—" Medraut lifted her hand and gently pressed his lips to the sensitive center of her palm.

"Oh!" She pulled her hand away, still quivering from the jolt of energy that had passed through her body at his touch. "It tickles—" she stammered, stiffening.

Medraut said nothing, but the strong hands drifted back up to her shoulders, gentling her like a nervous mare, and then to her neck and scalp. She relaxed once more, the dangerous moment past.

"You spoke of a plot. What did Morgause plan? I know she did not intend your conception," she said then.

Again, for a moment, the clever fingers stilled. "Not my conception, but from the hour of my birth she raised me to be her puppet on Artor's throne, because he had stolen Igierne's love, and because she knew the princes of Britannia would never accept her as queen. Now, of course, she is the holy Lady of the Lake herself, and would never dream of disloyalty—"

He drawled out the words with bitter irony.

"And you?" Guendivar said softly.

"I was brought up to serve a queen. You are my lady now. . . ." Gently he stroked her hair. She sat, half-tranced as his hands moved down to caress her cheek, turning her head as he came around to kneel beside her, and reached to kiss her lips.

His mouth was sweet and warm. She trembled, feeling her blood leap in answer, and his hand tightened, drawing her closer. Now his lips claimed what they had only requested before. Guendivar stiffened, and he let her go.

"I am your father's wife . . ." she whispered.

"But not my mother—" he said thickly. "This, at least, is not incest."

She straightened, taking a deep breath to slow her pulse. "Soon, Artor will return. I will keep faith with him."

"But what if he breaks faith with you? What if he never returns?" Medraut's gaze held hers.

"He will come back!" she said desperately. "Help me, Medraut, I need you. But between us there can be nothing more."

Medraut sat back on his heels, his expression relaxing to its usual look of irony. "Lady, I will remember. . . ."

The queen turned back to her papers, though she did not see them, knowing that she would remember as well.

When the first chill winds of fall plucked leaves from the trees and gleaned the stubbled fields, the princes of Britannia went hunting. It had become Guendivar's custom, in the years of Artor's absence, to progress through the kingdom during the time between harvest and midwinter, allowing her household to enjoy the sport, renewing acquaintance with the chieftains, and collecting any taxes that were still in arrears. This year it was Dumnonia whose contribution was still lacking, and so it was that at the Turning of Autumn the royal household found itself at Caellwic, an old hillfort south of Din Tagell that Constantine used as a hunting lodge.

The stags were in rut already. The woodland rang with their bellowing. Men stopped when they heard that harsh music, listening, and Medraut recognized the excitement that pulsed in his own veins in the glitter of other men's eyes.

"Go—" said Constantine, who was prevented by a twisted knee from riding. "It is clear that until you have had your sport no one will have any patience for sitting in council. I only wish I could go with you!"

They set out early the next morning, guided by a little dark fellow called Cuby who reminded Medraut of the hidden people of the northern hills. Several of the riders had brought dogs with them, lean grey sight-hounds that strained at their tethers and curly-haired brachets that could follow a blood trail all the way to Annuen.

"A stag—you get now, while still has flesh—" The little man laughed softly. "Wears self to bone, rutting and fighting. This time o'year, thinks with his balls!"

"Like you, Ebi—" said Martinus of Viroconium to one of his friends.

The young man in question flushed. He had acquired a reputation second only to Gualchmai's for affairs with women, and since the latter's marriage, might even have surpassed him.

"And why not?" said someone else in a lower tone. "We must prove our manhood in bed if we are not allowed to do so in war!"

Medraut smiled without speaking, paying more attention to the tone than the words. The men who had come out with him were mostly of his own generation, sons of chieftains, or of men who had gone with Artor over the sea. He watched how they rode and handled their weapons, considering which of them he might want to add to the guard with which he had garrisoned Camalot.

They came down off the high moorland into a wooded valley and their guide held up a hand for silence. Medraut leaned back, gripping hard with his knees as his mount slid down the bank. Somewhere ahead he could hear the gurgle of a stream.

His pony threw up its head, snorting, and he reined in hard as half a dozen dark heads popped up from among the hazels. They spoke to Cuby in a soft gabble, and the guide turned back to the riders with a grin.

"They say there is fine deer in meadow downstream. You go carefully, bows ready, and they drive him."

One of the dogs whined and was hushed. The hounds pulled at their leashes, quivering, knowing that soon they would be freed to run.

"Very well," said Medraut. He turned to the other riders. "Mark your targets as you will, but the king stag belongs to me!"

He kicked his mount into the lead. They moved off through the autumn woods, dappled with the golden shadows of the turning leaves. The riders, wrapped in hunting mantles chequered in the earth tones of natural wool, seemed to blend into the branches. Fallen foliage deadened the horses' footfalls; only a soft rustle accompanied their progress, with the squeak of saddle leather and the occasional chink of steel.

There was a tense moment when Martinus reined his mount in hard and it squealed. Medraut rounded on him, frowning, and Martinus pointed to the black-and-white ripple of an adder winding away among the leaves. Martinus was notorious for his fear of serpents; hopefully they would not encounter another. Medraut sighed, and motioned him to move on.

Presently the trees began to thin. Beyond them he glimpsed the meadow, and the red-brown shapes of deer. He reined back and lifted a hand to alert the others, then loosened his rein. His mount took a few steps forward, paused to snatch a mouthful of greenery, then moved on. Through the veil of leaves he saw one of the deer lift its head, ears swiveling, and then, sensing only the random movements of grazing quadrupeds, return to its own meal.

Slowly the hunting party moved through the wood, men peeling off at Medraut's signal to tie their mounts to trees and ready their bows. They could see the deer clearly now, grazing at the other end of the meadow— seven soft-eyed does and the stag who was courting them, his flanks a little ragged, but his head upheld proudly beneath its antler crown. The old king of the forest he was, a stag of twelve tines who had survived many battles and begotten many fawns.

Ho, old man, thought Medraut, *you are looking for the young stag who will try to steal your does. But the creature that comes against you now will take not only your females but land and life itself! Beware!*

The does were grazing, but the stag stood with head up, nostrils flaring as he tested the wind. He was clearly uneasy, but the random movements of the horses had deceived him, and the scent he was seeking was that of his own kind. Medraut saw the edge of the wood before him and reined his own mount in. Moving slowly, he slid from the saddle, using the body of the horse to hide his own from view. With equal care he unslung his bow and nocked an arrow.

A two-legged shape flickered in and out of view at the other end of the meadow. Among the deer, heads jerked up. They began to move, alerted, but not yet alarmed.

Come here, my king . . . thought Medraut, *this way. Your life belongs to me!*

Again the half-seen movement. Now the wind must be bringing scent as well, for a doe jumped to one side. The others stiffened and the stag's heavy head swung round. In another moment they would flee. Medraut lifted the bow, his own muscles quivering with strain.

Off to his left someone sneezed. The deer exploded into motion. Medraut, his gaze fixed on the stag, turned as it leaped forward, awareness narrowing to the gleam of red hide. He felt the arrow thrum from between his fingers, saw it sink into the shining flank, then the stag flashed past him and crashed off through the trees.

He jerked the rein free and flung himself onto his horse's back. A grey shape hurtled past him, barking excitedly. From behind him, hunting horns sounded the chase in bitter harmony. Medraut dug his heels into the pony's sides and sent it after, lips peeled back in a feral grin.

The minutes that followed were a confusion of thrashing leaves and whipping branches. His shot had been a good one, but the stag was strong, and by the time blood loss began to slow him he was halfway down the valley.

Medraut heard a furious yammering of dogs and slapped his pony's neck with the reins. Through the trees he saw a plunging shape, red and brown as it passed through sunlight and shade. Five hounds had brought the stag to bay against an outcropping of stone. As Medraut pulled up, he heard hoofbeats behind him and saw Martinus on a lathered mount.

"Over there—" he shouted. "Keep the dogs to their work!"

Martinus nodded and urged his horse forward, sounding the death on his horn and encouraging the hounds with yips and cries. Medraut had dismounted and tied his own mount, and was working his way around the side, pulling the short hunting sword from its sheath. He heard other riders arriving, but none would dispute his claim. He eased around the tumbled rocks, calculating his approach.

The hart, wheeling to face the darting dogs, was oblivious to its danger. One dog was bleeding from a gashed flank already, and as Medraut crept closer, the stag's head dipped and it hooked another, yelping, into the air. Medraut darted forward, slashing at the tendon that ran down the hind leg, leaping back as the beast lurched, three legged, towards him.

For a moment he met the white-rimmed gaze, furious and disdainful even now. Then the antlers scythed downward in a wicked slash.

Medraut leaped sideways, aiming for the spot behind the shoulder where a swift stab could pierce upward to the heart. But the stag was faster. Twelve blades blurred towards him. He dropped his sword and threw himself forward, under the tines, then jumped, grabbing the beast's neck and jerking up his legs to avoid the striking hooves.

Overbalanced, the stag fell. Medraut, pinned beneath it, twisted an arm free to draw his dagger, stabbing. His body strained against that of the deer in a desperate embrace, his face jammed against the rank hide, until with a last spasm the stag gave up the battle and lay still.

"My lord! Lord Medraut!"

Dimly, he heard the cries. He struggled to sit up as men

pulled the carcass off of him. He got to his feet, amazed to find
nothing broken, though battered limbs were already beginning
to complain. The neck of the hart was a bloody mess, its eyes
already dull. He kicked the body and raised his arms, red to the
elbow.

"The old king is dead!" he cried, his voice shrill with release. "The victory is mine!"

In the eyes of the men around him he saw relief, and wonder, and a feral excitement that matched his own. They began
to cry out his name as horns belled victory. In that moment, the
forest, and the dead deer, and the shouting hunters were one.
He looked at them and felt a visceral jolt of connection, as if
the spirit of the stag had entered him. *They are mine!* he
thought. *This land is mine! I claim it as a conqueror!*

Bitter as memory, the music of the horns was carried by the
wind from the tree-choked valley to the bare high moorland
that looked over the sea. Merlin paused to listen, the sprig of
thyme forgotten in his hand.

"Medraut has made his kill," said Ninive. "Tonight there
will be venison for the table."

"I would that were all that Medraut brought with him—"
The words came from somewhere below Merlin's conscious
awareness.

"What do you mean?" asked the girl, her fair hair lifting in
the breeze.

Merlin shrugged, knowing neither what he feared nor from
whence the knowledge came.

Eyes narrowing, she gestured towards the plant in his hand.
"You said you would teach me. This lore of herbs and healing
I could learn at the Isle of Maidens. But you are the prophet of
Britannia—teach me how to *know.* . . . "

He spread his hands helplessly, letting the thyme fall to the
ground. Standing with her face uplifted to the sky, Ninive
seemed made of light, her pointed features one with the face of
the daimon that lived within his soul.

"How can I teach you? You *are* knowledge."

"When you look at me, what do you see? And what do I see
when I look at you?" She gave him a long, enigmatic look.

"What you cannot say, perhaps you can show—" she said softly. Then her voice sharpened. "Speak, O man of wisdom. In the name of your daimon I conjure you. How goes it with the high king in Gallia?"

Merlin felt the first wave of vertigo and gripped the shaft of the Spear with both hands, thrusting the point into the earth as if to root it there. Vision came and went in waves, so he closed his eyes, feeling the ashwood shaft in his hands become the trunk of a great tree mighty enough to uphold worlds. Supported by its strength, he relinquished his attempt to hold onto normal consciousness and let his spirit soar.

In the first moments, awareness extended, borne on the wings of the wind. Below him tossed the grey waves of the sea. Then vision began to focus; he saw hacked woodlands and broad fields trampled to mud where armies had passed. In the dim distance where he had left his body, a voice called his name. He knew that he answered, but not what he said to her.

There was the smoke of a burned village; the air trembled with the echo of battle. Awareness focused further; he saw the standard of the Pendragon and men in battered Roman armor locked in a struggle against big, fairhaired men in high-peaked spangenhelms with gilded figures of eagles glittering from their shields.

He saw Artor bestriding the body of Gwyhir, hewing Franks with mighty strokes until Gualchmai clove a way through the tangle to stand with him. Horns blared, and a wedge of cavalry bore down upon the fray, Betiver in the lead. The Franks fell back then, running towards the mounts they had left at the edge of the field. Betiver pursued. The long Roman lances stabbed and more blood fed the ground.

The scene changed then. It was sunset, and within a circle of torches he could see the body of an old man, wrapped in a purple mantle and laid upon a pyre. Artor took a torch from one of the soldiers and plunged it between the logs, then stood back, the flicker of light gilding the hard planes of his face, as the fire caught the oil-soaked wood and blazed high.

Men crowded around him. One held a cloak like the one that had wrapped the corpse. Artor was shaking his head, but they cast the purple across his shoulders. Others surged forward, shields on their arms, and knelt as the king, still protesting, was lifted. Cheering, they raised him on their shields. Merlin could see mouths opening in unison, heard the echo of their shouting in his soul—*"Imperator! Imperator!"*

Awareness recoiled in a whirl of purple and flame, and he opened his eyes, gasping in the red light of the dying day.

"The king—" he croaked, and coughed, trying to sort through the maelstrom of fading images. "What did I say?"

"Riothamus is dead," said Ninive in a shaken voice, "and they have acclaimed Artor as emperor. . . ."

The Isle of Afallon lay wrapped in the dreaming peace of autumn. Guendivar sat beside the Blood Spring, watching yellow leaves swirl slowly across the pool.

"He will never return, Julia," she said sadly. "I feel it in my heart. If they have made Artor emperor, he has his desire. Why should he return to me, or to Britannia?"

"If you can trust the sorcerer's vision," observed the other woman a trifle grimly. The years had changed Julia little, save for the white veil of a sworn nun that covered her cropped hair. "Every day, it seems, we hear a new tale. Some say that it was Artor, not Riothamus, who died."

Guendivar shook her head. "He is not dead. I would know. . . ."

"Because you are his wife?" Julia lifted one eyebrow. "He has never truly been a husband to you."

"Because I am Artor's queen," corrected Guendivar, "and the land itself would break into lamentation if he departed this world."

Julia snorted disbelievingly. "After ten years does the land even remember him? It is you, my dear one, who are the source of sovereignty. What will you do?" After the death of Mother Madured, the nuns had chosen Julia to lead them, and she spoke with authority.

"Theodoric has sent a ship to Aquilonia for news. I will decide when we know for sure—"

"If you have time!" Julia rose to her feet, shaking her head. "Artor has been too long away, and Britannia is humming like a hive. If he does not come back himself along with the messenger, he may find that the land has given herself elsewhere! But whatever happens, my queen, remember that there will always be a place for you at Afallon."

Guendivar tried to smile. Once she had thought this isle a prison, but now she could appreciate the power that lay beneath its peace. All the disciplines of the nuns barely allowed them to endure the energies that pulsed in the chill waters of the spring. She leaned over the water, seeing her own face as a design in flowing planes amid the spiral flow of the current. She dipped up water and the image dislimned, forming anew in the shining drops that fell from her hands.

Both women turned at the sound of a step on the stones. It was one of the novices, still nervous before the queen of Britannia.

"Lady, the lord Medraut would speak with you. . . ."

"He cannot come here," Julia began, but Guendivar was already rising.

"Tell him to join me in the orchard," she said, pulling the veil up over her hair.

The apples had been harvested, and the leaves were falling. Only a few wizened fruits, too small to be worth the effort to reach them, still clung to the highest boughs. But though the trees were bare, they were not barren, for with the new year they would flower and fruit once more.

Unlike me . . . the queen thought bitterly. She paced between the trees and turned, frowning, as Medraut shut the gate and came towards her. Lean and well-knit, with the sunlight burnishing his auburn hair, at least he did not remind her of Artor.

"The horses are ready. If we would reach Camalot before dark, we must go now."

"Why should I go back? If Artor does not return, I am no longer queen." Guendivar could feel the kingdom crumbling around her, or perhaps it was she herself who was drying up and flaking away. Medraut caught her by the shoulder as she started to turn.

"Guendivar!" His grip tightened. "You are the source of sovereignty! Britannia needs you—*I* need you! My lady, my beloved, don't you understand?"

She retreated, shaking her head, and he followed, still holding her, until her back was against a tree.

"Guendivar. . . . Guendivar. . . ." He pulled the veil from her head and, very gently, touched her hair. "You are source and the center, the wellspring and the sacred grove."

She stood, scarcely breathing, as his hand moved from her hair to her cheek. This was not the disguised seduction he had tried before. Gentle he might be, but there was an authority in his grip that she could not deny. She turned her head, but he forced it back again, and then he was kissing her, hard and deep, and she felt the power begin to leave her limbs.

"Artor is gone . . ." he murmured into her hair. "He has abandoned us, and without a king, the princes will tear this poor land apart like wolves. I can lead them, I know it, but only you can legitimate my rule!"

His hand slid down her neck, pushing the tunica from her shoulder to cup her breast, and she began to tremble, long-supressed responses flaming into awareness once more.

"Guendivar . . . Guendivar. . . . Marry me, and I will love you as he never could. I know how to serve a queen!" He bowed before her, hands sliding down her sides until he knelt, holding her against him, head pressed against the joining of her thighs.

"I am your father's wife . . ." she whispered, fighting to stay upright. If once he got her on her back upon the grass, she would have no power to stop whatever he might do.

And why am I resisting? she wondered. When had Artor ever come to her with such passion, such need?

"He has renounced the marriage, and you are no kin to me—" he said thickly. "Come to me, Guendivar, give me the right to rule. . . ."

"Not here . . ." she whispered. "This is holy ground. . . ."

Medraut leaned back a little, gazing up at her with darkened gaze. "But you will lie with me, won't you, my dearest? You will marry me?"

Guendivar shuddered, her body aching with need. It was too

late, she thought. She had no choice, now—she had already given too much away. Without volition, the words came to her. "When you are king. . . ."

The queen sat in her place in the round Council Hall, an image of sovereignty draped in cloth of gold. Medraut had taken his seat on the other side of the king's empty chair.

Soon, he thought, *it will be* my *chair!* As soon as the men he had summoned to his Midwinter Feasting agreed. . . . The blazing fire in the center of the circle flickered on faces sharpened by interest, glinted on the softness of fur-lined mantles and the glint of gold. The houseposts were wreathed with evergreen, set with holly and ivy and mistletoe.

To call them together had been a risk, he knew. It might have been safer to simply proclaim himself king. If Artor had left the Sword behind, Medraut could have proved his right by pulling it from the stone. His mother had explained the trick of it, and he was of the blood—twice over, he thought with a sardonic grin.

But he could call himself Basileus of Byzantium, or lord of the Blessed Isles, and it would mean nothing if no one followed him. He must be acclaimed by the princes of Britannia, or by enough of them to impress the remainder. Camalot was garrisoned with men he had chosen. He had sent word already to Aelle and Cynric and Icel, and knew that they would send him warriors when he called. But to rule Britannia, he needed the support of these men.

He gazed around the chamber, counting those of whom he was certain, and those he judged weak enough to be swayed. There were some, like Theodoric in Demetia and Eldaul of Glevum, whom he knew would accept no heir until they saw Artor in his grave. The invitations sent to them had all—so sorry—gone astray. Of the older men, he had only Cataur of Dumnonia, who had never been Artor's friend, with his son Constantine by his side.

But Martinus of Viroconium, newly succeeded to his father's seat, would stand behind him, and so would Caninus of Glevum, whatever his father might say. The boys from Guenet, Maglouen and Cunoglassus, though young, came of noble kin.

Where the sons were seduced by dreams of glory, the fathers might be persuaded by lower taxes and a more accommodating authority.

Medraut waited, poised as the hawk that hovers over the field, until all had taken their places, waited until the silence was becoming uncomfortable, before he got to his feet in an easy movement that focused their attention. He had dressed with care in a long tunic of Byzantine brocade dyed a crimson so deep it was almost purple. His black cloak was lined with wolfskin. Around his neck glinted a king's torque of twisted gold.

"Lords of Britannia, I bid you welcome. It is the queen who has called you here to council, as is her right. I speak in her name—" He bowed to Guendivar, who inclined her head, her features as expressionless as those of a Roman statue beneath the veil.

"And why does she—or you—summon us here?" Cataur called out in reply.

"To take counsel for the future of this island, for ten long years bereft of her king." He waited for the murmur to subside.

"Have you had word of Artor's death?" asked Paulinus of Viroconium.

"We have had rumors only. There was a great battle with the Franks, and many were killed. My informants saw a funeral pyre and were told that the Britons were burning their king."

The outbreak of response to this was sharper. Many here had resented Artor's rule, but he had also been much loved. Guendivar looked up abruptly at his words, for she believed the confused tale of Merlin's prophecy, that it was Riothamus who had died.

"Perhaps he is not dead"—he shrugged—"although I do not understand why, if Artor lives, he has not sent word. Perhaps they have made him emperor, and he no longer cares for Britannia." Medraut spread his hands. "My lords—does it really matter? He is not here! Is that the act of a lord who cares for his people?" he exclaimed.

"The season of storms is on us, bad for sailing," said someone, but the rest of the men were shouting agreement.

"Is that the way of a Defender of the land? The way of a

king?" Medraut continued, drawing more shouts with each repetition.

He moved away from his seat and began to pace around the circle. "Last year men from the North attacked the coast of Anglia. I led a troop of British warriors, and rode with Icel's son Creoda to defeat them. We parted in friendship, but do you think the Anglians did not notice that Britannia has no king to defend her? They accepted me only because I am King Artor's . . . kin."

Medraut saw eyes flickering towards his face and away again. They had become accustomed to him—time to remind them who he really was.

"I spent nearly nine years among the Saxons, and learned their tongue. After a time they forgot to watch their words around me. They are quiet now, but they have not given up their dreams of conquering the rest of this isle. For a decade the fear of Artor's name has held them, but a new generation of warriors is growing up who have not learned to respect British arms. Whether by fear or friendship, they must be fettered anew, and this can only be done by a king."

The fire wavered as the pressure inside the hall was changed by a gust of wind outside, as if to echo his words.

"And do you claim the kingship?" cried one of the Dumnonian lords.

Medraut took a deep breath. For this he had been born; he had been trained up by his mother to be her weapon against the king. Now that Morgause had renounced vengeance, to take Artor's place would be his revenge on her. And he wanted it, more than he had ever wanted anything, except perhaps for his mother's love, or Kea, or Guendivar.

"I do. I have the right, whether you count me as son or sister-son, and I have the will." His voice rang through the hall. "Artor wasted your sons and your wealth in a senseless foreign war. I will keep both safe in Britannia. He kept a tight rein on the princes of this land; but the Saxon wars are long past, and we can afford to rule with less central authority. There must be one man with the power, and the prestige, to deal with them. All these things I will do as your king!"

"What says the lady Guendivar?" asked Constantine.

Medraut turned to the queen and held out his hand. She rose to her feet, paler, if possible, than she had been before.

"Artor has abandoned us," she said in a low voice. "Let Medraut take the rule. . . ."

He bent before her, then straightened, standing of a purpose where firelight would veil him in gold.

"Medraut!" called Martinus and Cunoglassus, and after them a dozen others took up the cry. They shouted his name till the rafters rang, and when the acclamation died away at last, Medraut sat down in the great carved chair of the king.

VIII

BELTAIN FIRES

A.D. 515

Artor splashed through the icy waves, struggling to keep his feet against the surge, until the tide retreated behind him. A few more steps and the stony shore was solid beneath his feet. He sank to his knees, plunging his fingers deep into the swirled ridges of pebble and sand.

Britannia! For so long, as winter storms lashed the narrow sea, he had thought he would never get here. But this holy earth was truly his homeland—it spoke to him as the soil of Gallia could never do. He bent and kissed the stones.

The ground trembled to the tread of the men and horses that were struggling ashore all around him. As he straightened again, the mists thinned and he saw the pale glimmer of the chalk cliffs that flanked the harbor. For two months they had haunted him, seen first in the dream that had brought him home. Even now the images made him writhe: Medraut in the king's high seat, Medraut with his arms around Guendivar. At first, he had thought the vision some bastard offspring of his own fears. But the dream had the flavor of Merlin's power, and as Artor got his men into winter quarters after that last, triumphant battle, he had begun to believe it, even before Theodoric's storm-battered galley brought the news.

Medraut had proclaimed himself high king. He held Camalot and Londinium, and Dumnonia stood his ally. He had made his own treaties with the Saxons, and the rest of the Island was on the verge of civil war. And Guendivar had pledged herself to be his queen.

That was the blade that pierced Artor's heart. Until she betrayed him, he had not realized how much of his soul he had given to his queen. He lifted his head, trying to see through the mists. He had half expected to find Merlin waiting for him to come ashore. If the Druid knew enough to warn him, why had he not put a stop to Medraut's treachery?

"My lord! Did you fall?" Goriat's tall form bent beside him.

Artor shook his head, but the damp of the voyage had stiffened his joints, and he accepted a hand to help himself get up again. There was not much left in Goriat of the youth who had once served in the kitchens of Camalot, he thought grimly, except for the innocence in his eyes. He looked much like Gualchmai, both of them hard muscled and fair and taller than the other men, though Gualchmai's sandy hair was laced with silver now. Aggarban and Gwyhir lay in the earth of Gallia. Since hearing the news from Britannia, the two brothers who survived no longer counted Medraut as kin.

"Well, at least there's no enemy here to meet us—" Goriat squinted past the remains of the old fortress of Dubris towards the downs.

Artor nodded. No doubt that was why Merlin had shown him these cliffs in his dream. In the season of storms he dared no longer crossing, and Dumnonia and the lands the south Saxons ruled would be held against him. Only in Cantium could he hope to land unopposed, if Rigana and Eormenric stayed true.

He looked around him, shading his eyes as the pale February sunlight broke through the fog. Shadow shapes of boats darkened the shoreline. The strand was a confusion of horses and men. It was the warriors of Britannia he had with him—

the others had been left with Betiver in Gallia. Men fought best for their own land. The sorrow here was that the same might be said of both sides.

"Get the gear unloaded and form up the baggage train. I'll want to meet with troop commanders as soon as possible. We'll march on Cantuwareburh in the morning."

A day later, Artor was sitting in Hengest's hall. The beams were darker, the walls covered by embroidered cloths, but otherwise it was much as he remembered from Oesc's wedding to Rigana, some twenty-one years before. The year before Mons Badonicus, that had been, when Oesc was killed. Rigana's slenderness had become a whipcord strength, her features sharpened by maturity; in appearance, she seemed little changed. He did not think that she had mellowed, though she seemed to have her temper under better control. But Eormenric was grown to manhood, and Artor winced to see his father look out of his eyes.

Oesc, wherever he is now, has more reason to be proud of his son than I do of mine, he thought bitterly.

"Oh yes, Medraut has sent messengers," observed Rigana, as if she had read his thought. "Gifts as well. We smiled, and took them. Why not?" she went on. "There was no point in defiance until we knew your plans—" She untied a soft leather bag from her belt and plopped it in front of Artor with a musical clink of gold.

"What, did you think I still held Oesc's death against you?" Rigana added wryly. "It was Cataur and Ceretic who destroyed him. And the West Seax and the Dumnonians are Medraut's allies." She turned to her son, whose face had changed at the mention of Ceretic's name. "I know you fear to face your friend Ceawlin in battle, but this is the way of the world. When he thought it needful to avenge me, your father went even against Artor, whom he loved. . . ."

The king watched his own fingers clench on his drinking horn until the knuckles whitened, and forced them to release again. "If you will raise the men of your *fyrd* to follow me, under a good commander, I will be grateful," he said harshly. "But you, boy, stay home to guard Cantuware. This conflict has set brother against brother and father against son already. I will not ask you to fight against your friend."

Rigana's gaze softened. "I see you are still capable of mercy. Remember it, when you have the victory."

"Do you think I will win?"

"When the people see that you have come back to them, they will turn to you," she answered him, "save for those who have been driven so far they think no forgiveness is possible."

"You are talking about Medraut, and . . . the queen?" Odd, how he could not say her name.

"Consider this—Guendivar supports his cause, but she has not married him. Leave a way open for her to come to you. . . ."

Artor stared at her, thinking on the things she did not say. Rigana was the Lady of Cantium; she knew the queen could bestow the sovereignty of the land on the man who served her well. Perhaps Guendivar had not yet given herself to Medraut, but he himself had been no use to her either. He recognized now that it was one reason he had stayed away.

"She must hate me—" he whispered, knowing that until he was able to forgive himself, he could not forgive his queen. And until then, he had no choice but to press on with the bloody business of war.

The king's forces marched swiftly through the chill spring rains, taking the old Roman road westward towards Londinium. At Durobrivae their camp was attacked in the hour before dawn by tall, fair men whose sleek ships had crossed the estuary of the Tamesis. By the time they were beaten off, several wagonloads of supplies had been burned and a number of men killed. The one prisoner they took told them he was a Northman from the settlement Gipp had made on the coast of the Anglian lands, and then, laughing, tore off the bandage with which they had stopped his bleeding and died.

The art of making friends with barbarians, thought Artor grimly, was a gift his son seemed to have inherited. But he said nothing, and ordered his army to continue on.

There were several skirmishes before they reached Londinium, but the city was not held against them. There was no need. Medraut had already stripped it of all supplies. Even in Artor's youth the city had been decaying. There was little left of it now. Still, it was good to take shelter beneath such roofs as remained intact while the king's scouts tried to find out which way the enemy had gone. There he found Betiver's son by the Votadini girl who for nearly twenty years had been his concubine. To have the young man at his side was some small consolation for having had to leave Betiver with the rest of his troops in Gallia.

Thus, it was the middle of the month of Mars before word came that the rebel forces were gathering near Ambrosiacum on the great western plain.

Medraut stood before the Mound of the Princes, watching his father's army form up across the plain. They were armed, as were his own forces, but had not put on their helmets. Artor had called for a parley. Medraut wondered if it could possibly succeed. A chill wind rustled the husks of last year's grass and ruffled the new blades of green, its force scarcely checked by the ancient stones of the Giant's Dance, and he refastened his wolfskin cloak above his mail.

He had not done so badly, he thought, looking over his men. The South and much of the West had declared for him, and those few who resisted, like Eldaul of Glevum, had been overcome. But except for a few skirmishes, the rebels had not yet faced Artor's army, and the old king's reputation was worth a legion. It was Constantine who had insisted that they try negotiation now.

Medraut wondered whether he was confused by old loyalties or simply afraid. Artor's men might be veterans, thought Medraut as he watched uneasily, but they were *old;* experienced they might be, but their strength had been worn away in the Gallian campaigns. He told himself there was no need to fear.

The wind died, and Medraut looked over his shoulder, seized by the odd sense that the spirits in the mound were watching him. He smiled sardonically. They must be very confused. A war of Briton against Briton would be familiar enough, but behind Artor marched Jutes from Cantuware, while Saxons led by Cynric and Cymen and Anglians under Creoda rode in his own train.

The movement before him shivered to stillness. From Artor's army a horn blew shrill, to be answered after a moment from his own side. Constantine of Dumnonia stepped forward, his thinning hair blowing in the breeze. From Artor's side, the spokesman was Gualchmai, grim-faced and frowning, limping a little from some wound got in the Gallian wars. There was a murmur of disbelief from the Dumnonians when they saw him come forward. If the king had sent Gualchmai, it was not to negotiate, but to deliver terms.

Gualchmai halted, his thumbs hooked through his belt, surveying the enemy. Medraut flinched at the chill in his brother's blue gaze.

"So, we are standing together. If I had my will, I'd answer the boasts of your little prince with a good hiding, but I am bound to hear ye out, so say on—"

"My lord Medraut . . ." Constantine coughed to stop his voice from wavering, "requires that the high king give him the North to govern and recognize him as heir to Britannia."

"Fine words for a rebel!" growled Gualchmai. "My lord king requires first that Medraut return his lady and queen. After that, he may find the patience to receive your surrender!"

"Surrender?" Constantine tried to laugh. "When our army outnumbers yours?"

"We've beaten the Franks, who smashed every other army that faced them. D'ye think we'd have any trouble with yours?"

"It is a hard thing, when brother fights brother . . ." Constantine said piously. "And in any case, it is not for us to dispose of the Lady Guendivar—the choice of where she should go is hers."

The queen had been left in the care of a household of holy women who had settled at Ambrosiacum, and even Medraut did not know what she would do. Sometimes the aching tenderness with which he courted her gave way to visions in which he held that smooth white body splayed beneath him, victim of his desire. But he was too much his mother's son to dare to force her. He had felt her need for him—surely he was the one she would choose!

"Promise the prince a territory to govern and his place as heir, and we will disband," Constantine went on.

Let me have the North, thought Medraut, *and Artor will have to face Cynric and Cymen here.* . . . It would be good to get back to his own country. Once across the Wall he would be dealing with folk who had never really accepted the rule of Britannia. And beyond them waited the Picts, allies even more powerful than the Saxon tribes.

Artor nodded, and Gualchmai turned to Constantine with a sigh. "Let it be so."

But not for long, thought Medraut. Artor had not met his gaze, but in the grey light he could see the lines in the older man's face and the silver in his hair. He remembered how the stag had gasped out its life beneath his blade. *You are old, my father—and soon my time will come.*

"We'll drink together to seal the bargain," the Dumnonian replied, "and our lords shall swear to keep faith on the holy cross." Young Maglocun brought out a silver-banded horn filled with ale, and Father Kebi was pushed forward across the grass with crucifix in hand, eyeing the warriors around him like a wether among wolves.

On both sides, the men moved forward, the better to see. And at that moment, someone yelled and steel flashed in the sun. Every head turned. Medraut saw Martinus' face contort in disgust, and a flicker of black-and-white in the grass. The bare blade in his hand lifted, stained with red.

But a greater light was already flaring from the wheeling arc of Gualchmai's sword. "Treachery!" he cried, and then he clove Martinus through the shoulder and struck him down.

For an instant longer Medraut stared. The scene had shattered like a broken mosaic, horns blaring, men running everywhere. Then Cunoglassus pulled him back, shoving helm and shield into his hands. He fumbled to fix the straps, saw Cymen with his houseguard forming a shieldwall, and ran towards its protection.

In the years that came after, few could tell the true story of that deadly, confused conflict before the ancient circle of stones; a battle begun without plan and ending in darkness, with no clear victor. Folk knew only that more blood dyed the plain that day than had ever moistened the pagan altar stone. When it was over, the remnants of Medraut's army marched northward. From that time, news of the war came to the Britons of the South only as rumors that blended to create an imagined reality.

But to Artor, searching the battlefield with flickering torch in hand, it was all too real. Though most of the fallen came from the ranks of his foes, the toll among the men he had brought back from Gallia was heavy as well. He moved among the heaped bodies, recognizing here a man who had saved his life in Armorica, and there a fellow who had always been able to make his comrades laugh.

And near the hour of midnight, when the flesh grows cold on the bones, he found Gualchmai.

The king saw first the corpses, heaped in a distorted circle as if some dark elf had tried to construct a hillfort from the bodies of the slain. He had seen such ramparts before, where some brave soldier had stood at bay, but never so high. He was still staring at it when Goriat came up to him.

"Have you found your brother?" Artor asked, and Goriat shook his head. "Well, perhaps we should look there—" the king said then, indicating the heap of slain.

Wordless, Goriat handed Artor his torch and began to drag the bodies aside. They had fallen in layers—Icel's Anglians atop men from Dumnonia, and beneath them warriors from Cynric's band, all slain by the strokes of a sword. When Goriat had cleared a narrow pathway, Artor followed him to the center. Gualchmai lay there in a pool of red, the great sword still clenched in his hand. No single warrior could have killed him—it was loss of blood from too many wounds that had felled him at last.

"I used to dream of surpassing him," whispered Goriat. "But no warrior will ever enter Annuen with such a noble escort as these."

Artor nodded agreement, then stiffened as Gualchmai stirred. In the next moment he was kneeling beside him, feeling for a pulse beneath the blood-stiffened beard.

"Gualchmai, lad, can you hear me?" He cradled his nephew's head on his lap, stroking his brow. "Goriat, go for a wagon, bring blankets and water, run!" Gualchmai's flesh was cold, but his chest still rose and fell.

"Artor. . . ."

He could barely hear the whisper of sound. "Hush, lad, I am here."

"My fault . . . it was an adder . . . I saw . . . as my sword fell. . . . I have paid."

"Gualchmai, you must live," Artor said desperately. "I loved you and Betiver best of all in the world. Without you, how can I survive?"

Perhaps it was a trick of the torchlight, but he thought Gualchmai's lips curved in a smile. "The king . . . will never die. . . ."

When Goriat and the others arrived, Artor was still sitting with Gualchmai's head pillowed on his thigh, but on the king's cheek they could see the glistening track of tears, and they knew that the champion of Britannia was gone.

"My lord, what shall we do now?"

"Bury Gualchmai in the Mound of the Princes, and dig a grave for the rest of our folk who have fallen here," said Artor. From his eyes the tears still flowed, but his voice was like stone. "Where is the enemy?"

"The Dumnonians are scuttling westward like rats to their holes, but Medraut has gone north," answered Goriat. "They say he has taken the queen and the lady Ninive."

"Then north we shall go as well. Whether he flees to Alba or to Ultima Thule, there is no place on this earth so distant that I will not follow him."

By the day, the air rang with the sound of adze and hammer as Medraut's soldiers rebuilt the palisade of Dun Bara, the fort on the hill. Escorted, Guendivar paced the old earthworks, Ninive beside her. Battered and bruised by the pace of their journey northward, she had prayed only for its ending, but as her body recovered, she began to realize how small was the difference between prize and prisoner.

Beyond the half-built walls she could see a long sweep of hill and moorland and a bright glitter of water beyond them. It was the estuary of the Tava, they had told her. On the other side lay the dark masses of Fodreu. Even the Votadini lands, thought Guendivar as she refastened her cloak, would have seemed strange to her, but Medraut had carried her deep into the country of the Pretani, the Painted People, who had always been the enemies of Britannia. Wind and water tasted different here, and the soil was strange. Here, she was no longer a queen.

Ninive, on the other hand, had grown stronger with every step northward. "My mother was a Royal Woman of the Hidden People, the first folk to inhabit this land," she said, laughing, her fair hair flying in the wind. "I ran wild as a moorland pony until I was eleven years old. Then Gualchmai rode that way out hunting, as he had done when he met my mother and begot me. She was dead by then, and he took me to the Isle of Maidens, to Igierne. Only in this land have I ever been truly free!"

Guendivar shook her head, understanding only that when Medraut ordered her to choose one woman to come with her she had been wise to take Ninive. Had Merlin come north as well? Some of Medraut's men claimed to have seen a Wild Man beyond the flicker of their fires, but if it was the Druid, he had made no attempt to speak with her.

And why should he? she thought bitterly. *I have given him no reason to think I need rescuing. He waits for Ninive, not for me. . . .*

She shivered, and turned towards the roughly thatched hut they had built for the women while they worked on Medraut's hall. It was dark and had few comforts, but at least there was a fire.

That night, Medraut returned, with a band of laughing Pictish warriors, a herd of hairy black cattle, and a line of laden horses. Soon fires were burning and two of the cows were cooking, the large joints roasting over the coals while the rest boiled in crude bags made from their own hides.

For Guendivar he brought a straw-filled mattress and warm woolen blankets, and a mantle of chequered wool in shades of earthy green that he said was a gift from the Pictish queen.

"I am grateful," she said dully when Bleitisbluth, the smooth-tongued Pict who had become Medraut's shadow, had left them, "particularly since I am sure she has no wish to share her land with another queen. This is not my country, Medraut. How long will you keep me here?"

"Is it not?" He grinned whitely, and she realized that he had already had his share of the heather beer. "Pretani is just another word for Briton, and though this land never bowed to Rome, Alba and the south are all part of the same hallowed isle!"

"But these are Picts!" she said in a low voice. "They have always been our enemies!"

"The enemies of the soft southern tribes," he answered, "and the foes of Rome, not mine."

Guendivar could see that that was true. Medraut stood now in kilt and mantle chequered in soft ochre and crimson. Of his southern gear he retained only the golden torque. His bare breast was shaded blue with the sinuous spirals of Pictish tattooing, his brow banded with Pictish gold.

"I have endured the rites by which they make a man a warrior. At the feast of Beltain we will swear formal alliance, and I will make for you a wedding feast in the old way that our people followed before ever Christian priest came into this land."

As Medraut's hands closed on her shoulders she stepped backward, but the doorpost was behind her, and there was nowhere to go. She trembled as his mouth claimed hers, feeling even now, as his hands moved over her body, the traitorous leap in the blood.

"Lie with me, Guendivar . . ." he said thickly, his touch growing more intimate. "Open your womb, white lady, and let me possess you utterly. Then I will truly be king!"

"When we are wedded—" she gasped. "I am no use to you if men think me your whore."

For a moment longer he gripped her, until she wondered if the conflict between lust and logic would break him—or her. Then, with an oath, he jerked away.

"*Wise* Guendivar . . ." he said furiously. "You deny me with such reasonable words. But in half a moon I will have you, spread-eagled on the feasting table if need be, so that all men may see that you are mine!" He thrust her away and pushed through the cowhide that hung across the door.

The fire flared as it flapped shut behind him, and Guendivar sank to her knees, her breath coming in shuddering sobs.

"Help me, Ninive!" she whispered as the younger woman put her arms around her. "What can I do?"

"You want him, don't you . . ." murmured Ninive, helping her to sit down by the fire.

"Him?" The queen shivered. "Not now, not anymore. But a man's strength to hold me, that I do—Medraut has lit the fire, damn him, and I burn! You don't understand, do you?" She lifted her head to look at Ninive. "Have you never felt your flesh quicken at the touch of a man?"

The other woman shook her head, her great eyes dark and quiet as forest pools.

"Not even Merlin?" Guendivar asked then.

"The love of the body is not what the Druid wants from me. . . ." Her lips curved in a secret smile.

The queen stared at her, but she had not the strength just now to try to understand. "It does not matter. But if Merlin were here, I would beg him to carry me away. . . ."

"Is that truly your will?" Ninive said slowly.

"Oh, my dear, I have known for moons that Medraut is no true king, but where could I go? Artor may have sworn to retrieve me, but he will not want me back again. Still, I will not weaken him further by joining myself to a man who would destroy Britannia! Better I should die in the wilderness, or live a hermit for the rest of my days, than become Medraut's queen!"

"Eat something, my lady, and rest while you may," said Ninive, her gaze gone inward. "And in the dark hours, when the men lie drunk or sleeping, we shall see. . . ."

Sure that sleep was impossible, Guendivar obeyed, but exhaustion claimed her, and when she roused at last to Ninive's whisper, it was from a dream of the Isle of Apples and the sacred spring.

The hearthfire was cold and the doorflap had been thrust aside. Mist curled through the opening, and when she emerged, wrapped in the Pictish cloak, she could see no more than the snoring shape of little Doli, the Pictish servant whom

Medraut had set to guard her. Beyond him rose the bulk of the half-built hall. Then, as if he had precipitated from the mist, another figure was there, tall, swathed in a mantle, leaning on a spear.

He gestured, and Ninive took the queen's arm and drew her after, past men sprawled in sleep and drowsing horses, through the open gate of the fortress and down the hill into the waiting fog.

To Guendivar, it was as if they passed through the mists of the Otherworld. But by morning, her aching legs told her that they had covered many miles. They took refuge in a shallow cave, its entrance hidden by hawthorns whose buds were just on the edge of bloom. Guendivar had barely a moment to long for the Pict-queen's mattress before she fell asleep in Ninive's arms.

The next night also they travelled, though the queen's sore feet and aching muscles would not let her go fast or far. If Medraut had set the Picts to search for her she saw no sign of them, and trusted Merlin's woodcraft to keep their passage unknown. On the third day, he brought them horses—sturdy moorland ponies who could cross rough terrain without injury and would keep on going long after the endurance of a war-horse failed.

They moved south and east through the hills, Merlin pacing like a shadow ahead and beside them. His hair and beard were now entirely silver, but despite his age, he pushed on. Each morning there would be a handful of spring greens and some small creature, a hare or grouse or hedgehog, to cook over their little fire. Where Guendivar was sore and exhausted, Ninive grew lean and hardy, kirtling up her skirts and letting down her hair until she was no longer a royal lady but a woods-colt who could keep pace with Merlin.

On the fifth day of their journey, the pace eased, and they began to travel by day. They had crossed over into the lands of the Votadini, where the Picts would not yet follow. That night, Merlin asked her where she wished to go.

"Artor is on his way northward, though he goes slowly, trying to heal the destruction Medraut wrought as he passed.

There is hardly a family that this rebellion has not divided, a thousand sparks that must be stamped out before he can fight the real fire."

"I cannot face him!" Guendivar drew back, trying to read the dark eyes beneath Merlin's bushy brows. He walked now in the skin garments of a Wild Man, the only touch of civilization about him the rune-carved Spear. It seemed to her that from time to time he leaned on it more heavily; that the pace he had set for them during the past days was slower, but she did not dare to ask if he were well.

"If I could choose, I would return to the South, to my own country. Perhaps I could take refuge with the holy women at the Isle of Afallon."

"Do you not understand?" He shook his head. "The choice is always yours—you are the queen."

Guendivar stared at him, tears burning down her cheeks, her throat aching so that she could not say a word.

"But the time for decision is not yet upon us," he went on as if he had not seen. "We will continue south towards the Wall, and perhaps on the journey you will find better counsel."

The days lengthened towards Beltain, and the land began to bloom. Now creamy primroses appeared in sunny patches, and the first bluebells nodded beneath the leafing trees. The moorlands were starred with white heather and budding bilberry. Just so, thought Guendivar, the land had arrayed itself when she rode to her wedding, and wondered if she would ever be done with tears.

They made their way eastward along the shore of the Bodotria, and then turned south to follow the old Roman road. Travel grew easier and she lost count of the days.

And then, one evening as the sun began to sink behind the hills, she heard the faint throb of drums. She kicked the pony into a trot and caught up with Merlin.

"What is it? Is there war?"

He shook his head, smiling oddly. "It is the eve of Beltain. . . ."

"Do you know some warded spot where we will be safe through the dark hours?"

"My child, why are you so frightened? Have you forgotten everything you knew?" He picked an early hawthorn blossom from the hedge and laid it in her hand. "Do not fear—where I lead you we will be welcome."

They rode onward through the long spring dusk. Across the valley she saw three peaks in silhouette against the sky. The drumming came now from one direction, now from another, soft with distance. Ninive had made wreaths for herself and Merlin, out of primrose and fragrant herbs. She held another up to Guendivar, and the queen had already set it on her brow before she realized it was a hawthorn crown.

For a moment Guendivar wanted to throw it down, remembering the wreath that had held her bridal veil. But the air was full of a rich, green smell, and she was no longer the child who had been Artor's bride. *Let them do as they will . . .* she thought with sweet melancholy, *it does not matter what happens to me.*

It was almost dark, but Merlin led them unflagging onto a track that wound across the moor. The western horizon still glowed, but above them, stars were blossoming in the sky. They had come around behind the tall northeastern peak where the remains of earthen ramparts rose, and were approaching the space between the other two hills.

The drumming was much louder. A prickle of fear chilled her.

"Ninive—what is it? Where are we going?"

For a moment the younger woman paused. "Oh my lady, those are the drums of my own people! I did not know that any still lived in these lands!" She ran ahead up the path.

But Merlin took Guendivar's bridle and led the horse up around the curve of the hill, stopping once or twice to catch his breath before pressing on. In the fold between the middle and southern peaks rose a rocky bump, where a bonfire sent sparks whirling up to dance with the stars. Dark figures cavorted around it, clad, like Ninive, who had cast off her tunic and run to join them, only in wreaths of flowers. The dancers clustered around her, chattering in a swift guttural language Guendivar did not know, but as Merlin led her into the circle of firelight they fell silent.

She stared into eyes dark as Ninive's, memory whirling with fragments of fearful tales of the people of the hills. After a long moment, she realized that they were as frightened as she. Merlin spoke then, his deep voice rumbling like an echo of the drums, and the fear changed to wonder. Women pulled heather and covered it with skins to make a seat, and when she slid down from the pony, escorted her there. As the drumming began once more, a small girl shyly offered her a wooden bowl filled with a dark liquid that tasted like honey mixed with fire.

"What did you tell them," she asked Merlin, "to make them welcome me this way?"

He smiled down at her, his hair bright as a snowy peak in the sun. "I told them the truth—I said that I had brought their queen."

She should have been angry, but the mead had lit a fire in her belly, and the drumming was beating in her blood. She looked at him and laughed. If eating this food bound her to the Hidden Realm, perhaps she could forget Artor.

The dancing continued. Guendivar ate roasted meat and dried berries, mixed with other things she did not try to identify. There was always more mead when her bowl emptied, the fire's reflection burning across the surface like liquid gold. She grew warm, and pulled off gown and tunica until she was as naked as the dancers. Men and women jumped together over the fire and wandered off into the darkness, laughing softly. The sighs of their passion whispered in time to the beat of the drums.

In the heavens, the stars were dancing, wheeling across the sky in patterns ancient when the world was new. She thought it must be near midnight when something in the music began to change.

People were still leaping around the fire, but they were not the same. They had put on the skins of animals, or perhaps they *were* animals, coupling in the compulsion of spring. She blinked, peering through the swirling smoke, and could not tell. Merlin would know, she thought then, but he too had disappeared, or changed. The drumming had a deeper note, as if the earth itself had become a single vibrating skin. That beat throbbed in her belly, bringing her swaying to her feet. From some depths she had never suspected, a sound rose in her throat and burst free in a wordless cry.

All around her, people were joined in the night's ecstasy, exulting in the passion that she had never been free to enjoy—she, whose fulfillment should have renewed them all! Guendivar took a step forward, stretching her arms to the skies.

"Come!" she cried to the night, to the fire, to the earth beneath her feet. "Oh my beloved, in the name of the Lady, come to me!"

And in the moment between one breath and another, from forest and flame and shadow, He came.

Furred like a beast, like a man He walked upright, and the antlers of the king of the wood crowned His brow. Erect, He came to her and bore her away in His strong arms. Filling and fulfilling He served her, pressing her down upon the moist earth, and the passion that until now had lain potential within her welled up in response, and flowed out from her into the land.

Guendivar was awakened in the dawning by the singing of many birds. Warm wool wrapped her, but the grass against her face was chill with dew. She stretched, muzzily aware of a pleasant soreness, and opened her eyes. The Pict-queen's cloak covered her, and her head was pillowed on her folded clothes. She blinked again; the world around her was a delicate dazzle of light. Through the branches of the hawthorn she could see a translucent sky whose banners of cloud were beginning to flush with gold. But each leaf was outlined in its own radiance, and moving among them she glimpsed vortices of whirling light.

She sat up, and clearing vision showed her luminous forms that expanded, as if in response to her attention, until they were the size of children, staring back at her with shining eyes.

"We hail the Queen!" sang the sweet voices. *"We hail the Hawthorn Bride! The Lady has come to the land!"*

"I know you . . ." whispered Guendivar, looking back in memory at the girl-child who had played with the faerie folk in the woods of the Summer Country long ago. For a moment, her vision blurred. Prisoned within walls, surrounded by humans with all their blind needs, she had forgotten how to see. . . .

"We live between the worlds. Between sunrise and sunset we can fly from one end to the other of this Isle. Will you stay with us, Lady, or will you ride?" Bird song and faerie song mingled in a cascade of harmonies.

"The queen has come to the land, but the king still wanders—" she answered.

Merlin had tried to tell her what was needed, but she had been unable to understand. She looked from the bright spirits to her own flesh—it felt solid, but her skin had a translucent glow, as if she could see the pulse of power.

"Between sunrise and sunset, my fair ones, take me to Britannia's true king. . . ."

IX

THE TURNING

It was the evening of Beltain, and the sun was withdrawing westward, trailing tattered standards of flame. From the Wall, Artor could see the flicker of bonfires here and there upon the land. *Like detachments that have been cut off from their main force and must stand alone against the dark*— A very military metaphor for the fires of spring, he thought grimly, but his heart was a battlefield, with no room for anything but war.

Some of the fires burned in the old fortress of Verçovicium, where his army had made camp. It was a central location, and until he knew whether Medraut meant to strike southward through Luguvalium or Dun Eidyn, as good a place as any to wait for news.

Here, the Wall took advantage of natural escarpments, with a view of the open country to either side. The water of the loughs reflected the sky's conflagration in fragments of flame. There were fires there as well, where the folk of scattered farmsteads had gathered to celebrate the festival.

On this night, no army would move. In the fort, his men could safely drink as much of the local beer as they had been able to collect on their march northward, but liquor would not drown Artor's sorrows. Instead he had set out to walk the Wall.

It curved away to the eastward, climbing the escarpments and swooping through the dales, even now, when parts of it were crumbling, a mighty testament to the empire it had defended. As he walked, the king fingered a fragment of bronze he had found among the stones, an old military badge with the image of an eagle, wishing it had the power to call to his aid the spirits of the men who had set these stones, as the image of the goddess had raised the ghosts at Mons Badonicus.

He had done what he could to pacify the land behind him, swearing new oaths with the sons of King Icel, and fighting a series of swift and bloody conflicts with the rebel lords of Demetia and Pagus and Guenet. They were a flock of fighting cocks, each crowing on his own dunghill. How quickly they had forgotten the host of enemies that waited beyond the farm-yard wall!

This Wall, he thought, as his footfalls rang against the solid masonry. He peered into the shadow that was creeping across the northern lands. There lay the darkness that would extinguish the light of Britannia, where Medraut was gathering the wild tribes of the North. Their last defense was this slender line of stone.

Ahead, indeed, a section had fallen. Carefully, Artor clambered downward until he stood on the springy turf. The slope fell away before him, rising again to a pair of outcrops in stark silhouette against the fading sky. In the cleft between them he saw the sudden spark of a fire and started towards it.

Any one of his men who ventured thus into hostile territory, without orders and unsupported, would have been mucking out stables for a week, but Cai and Gualchmai were no longer here to scold him. Silent through the dusk, the king made his way forward, summoning all the woodcraft Merlin had taught him to move unseen. And in truth he did not think it was an enemy, but some shepherd who would not grudge a stranger the warmth of his Beltain fire.

That flame, burning in the lee of a sandstone boulder, was

the only light remaining in a darkening world. Artor closed his cloak to hide his mail and stepped towards it, wondering what they could be burning to make the air smell so sweet, as if the open moorland had somehow gathered all the rich scents of a woodland spring. He blinked at shadows laced with whirling sparkles of brightness that fled away at his approach until there was only one shape by the fire. As he drew nearer it straightened, light shining on a tangle of golden hair and glowing on the folds of a cloak striped and chequered in spring green.

Guendivar. . . .

Artor stopped short, staring. *A vision,* he thought numbly, *born of my need.* But no image in his memory matched this face that was both older than he remembered and as fresh as the hawthorn flowers that wreathed her brow. Would a vision have mud clinging to the hem of her tunica and leaves caught in her hair?

She is real! He could not even imagine how she came to be here. A flash of heat and chill together pebbled his skin.

"I bring a Beltain blessing from Britannia to her king. . . ." Her voice trembled as if the anxieties of humanity warred with the magic that still starred her eyes. He swallowed, remembering what reason she had to be afraid.

"What right have you to give such a blessing, who have betrayed both Britannia and me?"

Her cheeks grew first red, then pale, but her voice was steady as she replied. "The right of a priestess of Brigantia, whose land this is. I have not betrayed *her,* and what I give I have the right to take away."

"You have taken away my heart, and given another my bed and my throne!" Artor said bitterly, setting his hand on the hilt of his sword. "I should slay you where you stand!"

"Not your bed," she said in a low voice, "empty though it has been. The blade you bear is a Sword of Justice, which would refuse to touch me. You would do better to ask what gifts I bestow."

He let go of the pommel as if stung. His bed had been barren indeed, he thought in shame, but his soul was singing at the knowledge that Medraut had not lain with her there. "What are your gifts . . . Lady?" The words limped from his lips.

"Sovereignty. Potency. Power."

Artor believed her. She had never been so beautiful arrayed in silk and gold as she was now, standing by the fire in her smudged gown. And in that moment he knew himself an empty husk, unfit to serve her.

"Guendivar. . . ." The anger that had strengthened his voice drained away. Throughout this war that fury had sustained him. He had nothing, now. "I have tried to hate you," he said tiredly, "but whatever you have done, it was my sin and my failure that was the cause. Can you believe that little though I showed it, you have always had my love?"

"My dear—" she said with a tenderness that pierced his heart. "I have had your letters. Do you think I did not know? But you did not come, and I grew heartsick and confused, and did what I thought I must for the sake of the land. If there is blame, much of it must be mine."

He stood before her with bowed head and empty hands. "I have lived by the sword for forty years, Guendivar, and I am tired. My peace is broken, and my people tear at each other like wolves. I have nothing left to give. . . ."

"Did I not say it?" she said softly. "The gifts are mine. I am the Tigernissa, the Queen. Come to me. . . ."

Step by unsteady step, he made his way around the fire. She reached up to unclasp the penannular brooch that pinned his cloak and began to unbuckle the belt that held his sword. He stopped her, glancing around him, calculating the distance back to the Wall.

"We are warded by sentinels more vigilant than any of your soldiers," said Guendivar. "Take off your armor, Artor, and perhaps you will be able to see. . . ."

Piece by piece the king laid his garments aside, until he stood defenseless in that place where faith is the companion of despair. It did not matter whether he believed her. Love or death would be equally welcome, if they came in her arms. The queen had also thrown down her green mantle and unpinned the fibulae that held her gown, so that she stood dressed only in her hawthorn crown.

"Thus do I salute you, for you are the head of the people—" She stretched to kiss his brow.

Behind his closed eyes light flared, illuminating past and present so that he saw and understood the meanings and connections between all things.

Her hands moved down his shoulders and the blossoms of her crown brushed soft against his breast as her lips pressed the skin above his heart. "I salute you, for you are the protector of the nation—"

At the words, fire filled his breast, and a purifying protective tenderness that would dare all dangers, not from hatred, but for love.

Then Guendivar bent to his thighs, her fingers sliding softly along the track left by Melwas' spear. He drew in a sharp breath as her lips touched his phallus and he felt it rise.

"I salute you, for you are the Lord of the Land—"

Artor clutched at her shoulders, shaken by the raw pulse of power that leaped from the earth to flare through every limb, his stiffened member straining against her hand.

She tipped her head back, gazing up at him. "Oh my beloved, come to me!"

No man living could have resisted that command. The queen drew him down beside the stone, her white thighs opening to enfold him, and in her arms the power that filled him found its rightful outlet at last.

Conquered and conqueror, giving and receiving, very swiftly Artor ceased to distinguish between Guendivar's ecstasy and his own. And in the ultimate moment, when the entire essence of being was focused to a single point, even that blossomed in an expansion of awareness that included himself and Guendivar and the earth beneath them and all the hallowed isle.

Afterward, he and Guendivar lay beside the fire, wrapped in their cloaks against the chill they had not felt before. When her head rested thus, upon his shoulder, Artor knew there could be no wrong anywhere. If he had not been filled with joy, he could have wept for all the nights when they had lain separate in the royal bed.

"If we had a ship we could sail away to the Blessed Isles," he murmured against her hair.

She shook her head a little, nestling closer. "I think we have run far enough, you and I. It is we who must bring a blessing to *this* Isle."

"As you have given it to me. . . ." Artor smiled. "But what power brought you to me here?"

"Merlin took me from Medraut's fort. God knows what tales they will be telling—they must think that Ninive and I vanished into the air!" Her laughter faded as she told the tale. "But it was the fair folk who brought me to this place, though I hardly expected the High King of Britannia to be wandering alone on the moor."

"Not quite alone. There are something over four thousand men camped in the old fort—" He gestured towards the irregular line of the Wall, dark against the stars. "I had meant to pursue Medraut all the way to Fodreu, but now I do not know what I should do."

"Stay here," answered Guendivar, "where you have a source of supply and some protection. Medraut is raising the North against you—better to meet him on your own home ground." She began to speak of what she had learned during her captivity concerning the strength of the enemy and Medraut's plans.

"I suppose we should get up," he said finally. "My men will be wondering what has become of *me*."

"Need we go back quite yet?" Guendivar laughed a little, reaching up to kiss his ear.

To his delight, Artor's body responded—he had wondered if their loving would be a reproducible miracle. He kissed her, and matters proceeded from there, and this time, if their joining did not quite reach the earlier excesses of ecstasy, he was better able to appreciate the solid reality of the woman in his arms.

Merlin sat with eyes half-closed and his back against an oak tree, listening to his heart drum in his breast. Nearby, Ninive was building up the fire and preparing a framework of willow twigs to cook the string of trout she had caught in the stream. From time to time she would glance at him, frowning, but she had said no word.

She's afraid to ask . . . he thought grimly. *Well, that's no wonder.* What had begun as a shortness of breath on the journey through Pictland had become a general weakness, as if with every step the life within him was bleeding back into the soil. Three weeks had passed since Beltain, and they had scarcely gone the distance he used to run in a day.

He himself did not feel fear so much as amazement that the body which had endured so many years past the normal span of men was failing at last. *It could have chosen a better moment to go,* he thought then. But most men, he had heard, found themselves unready when their time came at last.

He had rescued Guendivar, and the faerie folk told him she was reunited with the king. Indeed, he had hardly needed telling, for the joy of their reunion had reverberated through the land. But the spirits spoke also of a mighty hosting in the land of the Pretani. He had dreamed of a fort above a river, where men fought and died. Soon, Artor would face his greatest battle, and Merlin would not be there.

When he closed his eyes, he saw the face of the daimon of his prophecies, wide-eyed with wisdom and ethereally fair. When he opened them, he saw Ninive, as bright of hair, but with fine skin browned by sun and wind, and anxiety clouding her dark eyes. She had gone back entirely to the dress of her mother's people, a woolen skirt whose ragged fringe brushed her knees, and a skin cape pinned at the breast by a sharpened bone. Barefoot, she could fade into the woods like one of the folk of faerie. She knew the wildlands as he did, the perfect companion for his wanderings, but could she become something more?

"My lord, the fish is cooked—see how the flesh flakes off the bones." Ninive knelt beside him, offering the trout on a dock leaf.

"I will try." He smiled. He picked up fragments of the trout with a delicate touch.

"I am thinking," said Ninive when they were done, "that if I were to leave food here for you, I could fetch help and bring you to some farmstead where you could rest. . . ."

He shook his head. "We have to go on."

"Not all the way to the Wall!" she protested. "It would be

harvest before we arrived, and you—" She broke off, looking away.

"Will likely not get there," he finished for her. "Do you think I do not know?" The face she turned to him was anguished, and he stretched out a hand already thinner than it had been a week ago. "My little one, do you care so much for me?"

Ninive gestured around her. "You have given me back my soul!" She took his hand and pressed her forehead against it. With his other hand, very gently, he touched her hair.

"I am ninety years old and had begun to fear myself immortal. In truth, I am relieved to find it is not so. In the forest, when a creature grows too weak to hunt food, death comes soon. I would tell you to leave me here—"

"I would not do it!" she interrupted.

"But I must ask something harder. Great forces are gathering against the king, and I cannot be there. I have dreamed of a future that fills me with fear. I must use the time that is left to me so that something will survive."

She stared at him, her eyes dark as forest pools. "What do you need me to do?"

"There is a place that I must find before Midsummer Day. It lies deep in the Forest of Caledon—" He gestured southward. "When we reach it, we will work a mighty magic."

Beltain, or perhaps the queen, had brought in the summer. Even along the Wall, flowers bloomed and grass grew tall, and on the moors the heather, weighted with an emperor's wealth of purple bloom, hummed with the song of bees. Now the days lengthened rapidly towards midsummer's epiphany.

Artor made good use of the time. New messages had gone out across Britannia, proclaiming that king and queen were once more united, and calling the warriors to a great hosting at Vercovicium. At this season the demands of the fields kept many on their farmsteads, but each day, it seemed, another group of riders would come jogging along the Military Way that ran below the Wall.

"You see, they are still loyal," said Guendivar, gazing down from the walkway of the fortress wall at the moving tapestry of men and horses below.

"It is your name that has brought them," Artor replied, putting his arms around her. "They know that the sovereignty of Britannia is returned to me."

She leaned against him, the warmth of his touch still filling her with wonder. It was now well into June, and the weather had turned bright and fair; the long northern dusk spread a veil of amethyst across the hills. In the evening peace, sounds carried clearly.

"What is that?" she asked, as a noise like distant thunder began to overwhelm the ordinary sounds of the camp below.

She felt Artor stiffen. He lifted his hand to shade his eyes from the westering sun, staring at the Military Way, where something was moving, dust boiling behind it in a plume. She turned to look up at him. Already the hard stare of the commander was replacing the tenderness in his eyes.

"A messenger," he said grimly, "who rides at too headlong a pace to bear good news."

Medraut had taken Luguvalium. The chieftains of the Selgovae, still resenting the taxes Artor had laid upon them a dozen years ago, had joined him in a swift drive southward, and Morcant Bulc of Dun Breatann, denying his father's treaties, had joined them. The main body of the Picts had not yet appeared, but their most likely route would be eastward through the Votadini lands. Artor had been aware of the danger, and ordered Cunobelinus to stay where he was and defend Dun Eidyn. But if Medraut held one end of the Wall and the Picts the other, the king's force would be caught in between.

The solution, obviously, was to attack Medraut first and destroy him. Artor got his men to Luguvalium in two days of hard marching and was preparing to attack the fort by the time Guendivar, following more slowly, caught up with him.

The wind carried a faint reek of something burning, and the air resounded with the yammering of crows. Guendivar gazed up at her husband, searching for words with which to say good-bye.

All her life, she had heard stories of Artor's battles, but she had never before seen him armed for war. The gilded scales of his hauberk gleamed in the sunlight and his mantle was of the purple of emperors. The big black horse stamped and snorted as he reined it in outside the little church at the edge of the town where he had taken her.

"Stay here, my heart—" he said, leaning down to touch her hair. "If we destroy them here, I will come for you, but if they flee, we will be pursuing, and you will be safer behind us." His shield was new, but the horse's harness and Artor's leather leg wrappings and the heavy wool tunic showed signs of hard wear.

"But how will I know—"

"If we win, I daresay someone will tell you." He laughed, his teeth flashing in the close-cropped beard. It was threaded with silver, but his hair still grew strongly. Her hands clenched as she fought the desire to bury her fingers in its thick waves once more.

"And if we lose—" His face sobered. "You must stay hidden and make your way south somehow. Do not fail me, my lady, for if I fall, only you can pass on the sovereignty."

"Do not say it!" she exclaimed. "I will not lose you now!"

"Guendivar . . . I will always be with you. . . ."

Behind him a horn blared and the king straightened, sliding the helmet he had carried in the crook of his arm onto his head. With nasal and side-flanges covering most of his face, he was suddenly a stranger. The stallion reared and Artor reined it around. The men of his escort fell in behind him, and then they were away.

The queen stared after them, and only when the echo of hoofbeats on cobblestones had faded did she allow the tears to come.

All through that endless day she prayed, kneeling on the worn planking of the church's floor, though she hardly knew which god it was to whom she addressed her prayers. About the middle of the afternoon, she heard a great clamor that gradually diminished until there were only a few dogs barking, and then, one by one, the voices of the people of the town.

Presently the old priest who served the church came back again.

"The king is safe, or at least he was an hour ago. But the

Perjurer broke through his lines and fled with most of his men, and our army has gone after him, save for a detachment left under Prince Peretur to guard you and the town. Let us praise the Lord of Hosts, who gives victory!"

At night the Forest of Caledon was full of whispers; the wind continuing its conversation with the trees. Merlin felt the vibration through the trunk behind him, just as it thrummed through the shaft of the Spear at his side. Sitting so, his thoughts matched themselves to the long slow rhythms of the forest, and the rustle of leaf and twig became the words of a dialogue between the Goddess who lived in the earth and the God.

As the journey continued, the Druid understood them ever more clearly. By day he clung to the pony Ninive had brought for him, riding by balance. At night, when the girl lay breathing softly by the embers of their fire, Merlin became a tree, drawing from soil and sky the energy he needed to go on. But the earth drummed with distant hoofbeats and the wind rang with the crying of ravens, calling their kindred to a great killing, and he dared not succumb to the forest's peace.

And each day the hours of twilight lengthened as the season turned towards the solstice, all powers drawing together to resolve the conflict that had unbalanced the land.

At the Isle of Maidens, Morgause woke from evil dreams. It lacked a week to midsummer, and the priestesses were preparing for the festival, but her nightmares had been filled with blood and battle. She saw Artor and Medraut facing each other in battered armor, fury stamping their faces with its own likeness, and felt the perspiration break out on her brow. In that confrontation she sensed some great turning of fate, and it filled her with fear.

She left her chamber, calling to her maidens. "Pack journey food and blankets. Nest and Verica, you will come with me."

"But Lady," they protested, "what about the sacred rites, the festival?"

"This year the Lady of Ravens is celebrating her own ritual," she said heavily. "I must be at the Wall by Midsummer Day. . . ."

* * *

"Midsummer Eve . . ." said Goriat, surveying the winding river and the bluff above it, where lights twinkled from the old fortress. "At home, the clans will be gathering to light their solstice fires, throwing flaming brands high into the air to make the crops grow, and carrying the torches through the fields."

"In the South, also," answered Artor.

He felt as if he were thinking with two minds, one part evaluating the site's military potential while the other appreciated the beauty of the scene. The fort stood on a crag with a steep escarpment. Below stretched flats through which a small river wound. The higher ground was astir with men and horses as the Britons settled in.

"How strange that this stream should also have the name of Cam," the younger man said then.

The king shrugged. "Britannia is full of rivers that turn and wind in their courses, and I suppose many of them must bear that name." He walked along the riverbank, his officers following.

"You must wish it was the one that runs near Camalot."

"Only if I were inside its walls," Artor answered with grim humor. "If I must attack a fortress, I am glad it is not a place of my own building. Camboglanna was strong once, but now it is in disrepair, and Medraut is not provisioned for a seige."

"He has trapped himself, then—" Goriat grinned.

Vortipor shook his head. "Not if the Picts arrive to relieve him. That's our danger. He can't outrun us, so he hopes to outwait us—"

"—Until he outnumbers us. I see." Goriat squinted up at the fort. "The old Romans built well. To see that ragtag of northerners occupying Camboglanna galls my soul! An attack uphill from this side would be difficult, and I don't suppose the far side is any better."

Peretur shrugged. "The Wall joins the edge of the fort on both sides and there is only one gate, still in good repair."

Goriat turned to Artor. "We'll have to winkle him out of there somehow, my lord."

Artor's gaze was still on the river—the gleam of late sunlight on the water shone like Guendivar's hair. *I have been fighting too long.* He sighed. *I want to take her with me somewhere they have never heard of warfare—perhaps the Blessed Isles.* But he had to fight one more battle. If he could win that one perhaps he would be done.

"I'll send a message. Medraut has run from me twice now. If force won't budge him, we'll see what shame will do."

They gazed up at the road that crossed the overgrown vallum ditch before the walls. Dark figures moved on the walkway above it, bows in their hands.

"I'll deliver it," said Goriat with a sigh. "We were brothers once. He might hesitate before ordering those archers to shoot me. . . ."

Above Camboglanna, two ravens circled, then swung out over the river and settled, calling, in the branches of a gnarled thorn tree.

Raven wings filled Merlin's vision with fragments of shadow. He clung to the saddle bow, drawing breath harshly, willing the wheeling world to slow. Over the tumult in his head he heard someone calling him—

"My lord, I have found the spring!"

He opened his eyes and found Ninive, a fixed point around which the world stilled to comprehensible shape and meaning. The ravens were at Camboglanna. Here, there were only the irregular flitterings of wren and tit, and the musical gurgle of a tiny stream.

Before him, the narrow leaves of young rowan trees moved gently in the breeze, their edges gilded by the westering sun. Below spread a hawthorn to whose twigs a few fading white blossoms still clung. Beyond them he saw a noble oak tree.

"The water flows from that outcrop of rock just beyond the trees—" Ninive danced back across the jumble of fallen leaves and mossy boulders. Through the tangle of branches loomed the side of the hill.

"It is the place. . . . The headwaters of the Cam," he muttered, nodding as he recognized each feature of the image that had haunted his dreams. "And the day—have we come too late? Tell me, what is the day?"

"By the calculations you gave me at the beginning of this journey, this will be the shortest night of the year," she replied.

He sat back with a long sigh. "Midsummer Eve. They will fight tomorrow by the river."

"Can you help?" asked the girl. "Will the water carry your power to Artor?"

"Can anyone turn fate?" he murmured. "Now, at least, I have a chance to try!"

He slid from the pony's back, and with Ninive and the Spear to prop him, made his way to the oak, whose knobbed root made a seat above the stream. There he sat, extending his senses to encompass every part of the wood around him, and waited, as at Camboglanna two armies were waiting, for the dawning of the longest day.

The first sunlight gleamed from the river and from the helmets of the men who stood beside it: Artor's army, in full battle array. Medraut could see them clearly. So could his men. They were talking about the damned letter. Did they think he could not hear?

He had burned the parchment, but the words were burned in his memory.

"You boast of your courage, but twice now you have run from my wrath. You boast of your right to rule, but the queen has fled you and returned to my bed. . . ."

Guendivar! Oh, Artor had known that would enrage him. In dreams he still held her rounded body in his arms.

The hateful words echoed in his inner ear—his mother's scolding voice, speaking his father's words.

"Like a greedy child, you have tried to seize your inheritance, and by doing so, forfeited all claim! You are coward and craven—tainted in blood and corrupt in mind."

And if I am, Mother, he thought in bitter reply, *I am what you and he have made me!* And still the accusations rolled on.

"And these things all men shall know for truth if you do not come out and face me, body to body and soul to soul!"

Ravens were circling in the air below, calling out to their goddess the tally of the slain. He had only to wait, Medraut thought furiously, and they would all be safe. But these bloodthirsty fools whom he commanded were chafing to avenge their defeat at Luguvalium.

"My lord," said Bleitisbluth, "the men are angry. The enemy has been shouting evil things. The Rome-king left a garrison in Luguvalium, and we outnumber them. Better to order our warriors to attack while you still can!"

The raven voices grew louder, blended to a single voice, calling to him. *Guendivar is lost to me,* he thought, *I must serve the Lady of Ravens now....*

"Very well—if they are so eager for battle, fight they shall!" Certainty came to Medraut like a spark kindling tinder, and with it a fierce exultation. He reeled off a list of chieftains, their order and numbers. "The remainder will form a reserve force, hidden here, with me."

Medraut watched from the gatehouse as his army rolled down to meet the waiting force below. The men of the North rode their sturdy ponies to battle, but they fought on foot, with shield and spear. The narrow flats by the river favored them. He had expected that Artor would not be able to use his cavalry to full advantage, and indeed, he could see that the king himself was fighting dismounted.

As the morning passed, the purple cloak was everywhere on the field, the pendragon floating above it as Artor's standard bearer strove to keep up with him. As noon drew nearer, the sun's strength grew.

He is an old man, thought Medraut, *and it's getting hotter. Soon, he will fail!*

From below came clouds of dust, stopping the throat and stinging the eyes. The only color was the crimson of blood, bright as the cloak of the goddess of battles in the pitiless radiance of Midsummer Day.

What kept Merlin upright was the Spear. He had taken his stand in the space between the oak, the mountain ash trees, and the thorn, just where the waters of the Cam emerged from the stone. His heart galloped like Artor's warhorse, vision pulsing in time to its beat. Increasingly he relied on inner senses, extending them through air and soil until his body no longer contained his awareness. He risked losing focus entirely, but his control would last long enough, he thought, for what he had to do.

"Cast the circle, Ninive—"

The girl's voice rose and fell as she paced sunwise around him, sprinkling the sacred herbs, chanting in the old tongue of her mother's people. She was weeping, but her voice stayed strong, and he had time for a moment of pride. Nine times she made the circuit, and with each circumnambulation the Druid's consciousness drew inward, trading the diffuse awareness of his earlier state for a more powerful and precise connection with the space immediately around him, as if he stood within a pillar of crystal bounded by oak and ash and thorn.

Then she completed the spell, and he needed his control no longer, for the magic upheld him. Ninive was a spark of light before him, sensed rather than seen.

"The hour moves towards the triumph of the sun, the longest day! I summon you, O Prophet of Britannia, to say what shall come to this land."

For a moment Merlin knew nothing. Then the daimon within him awakened and his mind reeled beneath the flood of foreknowledge.

"The Red Dragon gives birth to a Boar and a litter of little Foxes that between them shall tear and worry at the land. Men and women shall cry out and flee their rulers, and give their name to Armorica, for it is the princes of their own people that oppress them. And then the White Dragon shall rise from his sleep and devour them, from Land's End to the Orcades."

Immensities of time and space rushed before him; he saw strange armies marching across Britannia, steel roads and devastated forests and cities covering the land. He saw a crossed banner that circled the world. The images he saw he could not comprehend, and presently he waited in silence once more.

"When these things come to pass, O Prophet, where will you be?" A new question came.

"I will be Lailoken in the court of Gwendoleu, and in the court of Urien I will be Taliessin. I shall not leave this land, but ever and again I will shape myself as her need compels me. Going in and out of the body, my voice will be heard in Britannia throughout the ages." In vision, all those lives were clear before him, and Merlin laughed.

"The sun nears her nooning, master, and there is one thing more to ask. Say now what fate is twined for Artor the king!"

The vision that had spanned centuries folded cataclysmically inward, arrowing like lightning towards its goal. Merlin saw the bloody field of Camboglanna, and Artor, catching his breath as he leaned upon a broken spear. Goriat lay dead beside him, but his enemies were fleeing up the hill. Above them the God of the Sword and the Lady of Ravens hovered, invisible to mortal eyes. And then the air rang with the bitter music of warpipes, and from the fortress a troop of mounted men came riding, and Medraut sped before them.

The bean-sidhe *is wailing*—thought Artor, *that doom-singing demon that Cunorix used to speak of so long ago*. He wiped sweat from his eyes with the back of his hand and peered up at the fort, knowing already that it was something worse. The army he had faced was gone, but Medraut, whom he had sought in vain all through the battle, was coming out at last. *Now,* he thought despairingly, *when I am already tired*. But this was no time to stand swearing.

"Edrit, run—tell Vortipor to get ready!" he called to the warrior who bore his standard, and started to slog back to the high ground. Medraut had been clever to field a reserve force when the battle was almost done. But Artor had been clever too.

He heard a gleeful shout as the enemy sighted him, and struggled towards the line of willow trees.

On the other side, Vortipor waited with the best riders the British had. A boy was holding Artor's big black stallion, a descendent of the first Raven he had ridden to war. Edrit boosted him into the saddle and handed him a javelin and a horseman's round shield. Taking up the reins, he peered through the screen of branches. Medraut's troop had reached the bottom of the hill. They were losing speed as they spread out along the road.

He turned back to his men. "Has it been hot here, waiting? It was hot work down there too! But now it's your turn, my lads, and you are the veterans of Gallia. Keep your formation, and that rabble will scatter like bees from an overturned hive!"

Someone murmured, "But they can still sting!" And the others laughed.

They started forward, Vortipor taking the point and Artor riding among the men on the wing. As the rebels turned towards the river, the king's men burst through the willows, urging their mounts to full gallop as the slope lent them momentum.

"Artor!" cried the British riders. "Artor and Britannia!"

They were going to hit the enemy at an angle. The king wrapped his long legs around Raven's sides, dropped the knotted reins on the horse's neck, and cocked his arm, poising the javelin to throw.

He sighted on Medraut, then the point of the British wedge struck, and Artor was carried past him. Training ingrained to the point of instinct selected a new target; he cast, and a man fell. A spearpoint drove towards him; he lifted his shield and grunted as it took the weight of the weapon, shifted his weight and jerked as the horse moved, and felt the spear tear from the man's grip and clatter to the ground.

He thrust the shield outward to protect his body as he reached across his belly to grip the hilt of the Chalybe sword. *May the Defender be with me!* he prayed, and felt a tremor of eagerness shock through his hand. At the battle of Verulamium the god of the Sword had come himself to counter an alien magic, but this was a battle of men, and Artor dared ask only for the strength to endure to the end.

The black horse was fresh and knew its trade, wheeling to knock a smaller beast sideways so that Artor could finish the rider with a slash of his sword. Then another shape loomed up before him. He struck, and struck again. The sweat ran hot beneath his armor, for the sun stood high. After each blow his arm came back up more slowly, yet still he slew, seeing Medraut's mocking face on every foe.

The sun stood high, and all the wood trembled beneath the weight of its glory. The circle of power where Merlin stood was a dazzle of light. But his inner sight was filled with the image of Artor, fighting on while all around him men fled or fell.

An enemy sword cracked the king's shield; Merlin saw him lose his balance and tumble from the horse's back. In the next moment his opponent was downed by a thrown javelin. Artor struggled to his knees at the water's edge, shieldless, but still clinging to his sword. The king looked up. Medraut stood before him.

Merlin gripped the shaft of the Spear. "Is it time?" he whispered, and the rune-carved wood quivered like a live thing in his hand. In all the forest, there was no sound but the sweet music of the infant stream. "This is my will," he said aloud, "that my spirit shall neither sleep nor seek the Summerland, but continue to wander the world!

"I am the wind on the wave!" Merlin cried.

"I am the fire in the wood!

"I am the sun beneath the sea and the seed in the stone.

"Before time's beginning I was with the gods, and I will sing at its end.

"I am Wild Man and Witega, Druid and daimon—

"I invoke the land of Britannia to the aid of her king!"

The Spear whirled in his hand, and he plunged it, point downward, into the moist soil. Deep, deep it sank, to the roots of creation, but the wooden shaft was expanding, extending branches to embrace the sky. For an eternal moment, Merlin was the Tree, linking earth and heaven.

Then the world collapsed around him in a roar of falling stone. But the essence that had been Merlin was already shaping itself to root and branch, to soil and stone and the rising wind, but most powerfully to the winding waters at his feet. Swift as thought he sped southward towards Camboglanna.

X

RAVEN OF THE SUN

A.D. 515

Medraut was a faceless shadow between Artor and the sun.

"So, my lord father, you kneel before me! Will you admit you are beaten at last?"

The king squinted up at him, licking blood from a lip that had split when he hit the ground. His helmet had come off; the air felt cool on his sweat-soaked hair. It was a little past noon.

"I kneel to the earth, whose power brought me down," he said evenly. "Are you going to let me get up, or do I have to fight you from my knees?" They were getting wet; he looked down and realized that he had fallen in the shallows at the edge of the stream.

Medraut slowly lifted his sword. *He's tired,* Artor observed, but he himself was exhausted. Perhaps it would be easier to fight from here. Or to let Medraut kill him. They were surrounded by the dead and dying. He had lost his army, he thought numbly, and Britannia.

The river ran purling past his foot, sweet and clear. When

346

Medraut still did not answer, the king scooped up a handful of water.

His first thought was that he had not known he was so thirsty. He dipped up more, and felt his tissues expanding like parched earth in the rain. With the third mouthful, he sensed the triumphant surge of Merlin's spirit making him one with everything around him. The cool sweetness of water, the solid strength of earth, the dry heat of the air—he felt them all with an intensity that was almost pain.

A movement that would have been impossible a moment before brought the king to his feet. Medraut jumped back, staring.

"Thank you . . ." Artor whispered, but it was not his opponent to whom he was speaking. He swayed, and Medraut started forward, sword swinging high.

A smooth twist brought the king on guard, bringing up the Sword of the Defender two-handed to deflect Medraut's blow. The clangor as the two blades met echoed across the vale. Artor's knees bent slightly, the great sword drifting up to hover above his right shoulder.

"Why did you do this, Medraut? Why did you try to destroy Britannia?"

His son looked at him uncomprehending. "I wanted to rule—"

Artor shook his head. "The land cannot be ruled, only served."

Medraut's mouth twisted and he lunged. "You left her! You left *me*!"

For a moment the king hesitated, the truth of that accusation piercing more deeply than any enemy sword. Then strength surged up from the soil once more and he knew that he was still the Lady's Champion.

Artor leaped back, sword sweeping down and to the side, knocking his son's weapon away and spinning him so that for a moment they stood with shoulders touching, as if they met in the dance.

"I was promised everything, and then betrayed," hissed Medraut. "I came to you, since my mother had cast me aside like a tool she no longer wanted to use. And you banished me to the barbarians and *forgot* me! I've had to fight for my life, my name. . . ." He whirled away, the rest hanging unspoken between them—*for Guendivar.* . . .

"Surrender and you shall rule the North," said Artor, his breath coming fast.

"I could win it all yet, *Father.* . . ." Medraut advanced with a series of flashing blows that kept the king busy defending.

"Not while I live!" Artor knocked the younger man's last stroke aside with a force that sent him reeling.

"You will die, at my hand, or the hand of time—" answered Medraut, panting. "The heirs of Britannia are young foxes, eager to gnaw out their own little kingdoms, and that will be the end of your dream."

Instinctively Artor settled to guard, but his mind was whirling. He bore the Sword of the Defender, but what could a dead man defend? He looked up at the mocking face of his son. Men called Medraut the Perjurer, but surely Deceiver would be a better name, sent to tempt him to despair. And yet the power of that impossible moment of connection with the land still sang in his veins.

"Oh Medraut, is there room for nothing in your heart but hate?"

"You took the only thing I might have loved!" Medraut cried out in answer, and ran at him with wildly swinging sword.

Artor retreated, using all his skill to fend that blade away. The boy was a good swordsman, but he was battering with berserker fury as if he meant to obliterate, not merely kill. Forty years of experience kept the king's weapon between him and that deadly blade. It was those same battle-trained reflexes, not Artor's will, that halted Medraut's charge at last with a stop-thrust that pierced through hauberk and breastbone and out the other side.

For a moment they stared into each other's eyes. Then Medraut's features contorted. His weapon slipped from his hand, and Artor felt the weight of the boy's body begin to drag down the sword. He stepped back, and the blade slid free as Medraut fell, the bright blood—his son's blood—staining the steel.

The air rang with silence.

"Father. . . ." A little blood was running from Medraut's mouth. The king knelt beside him, laying down the Chalybe sword, reaching to ease off his son's helm and smooth back the hair from his brow as if he had been a little child. Medraut's eyes widened, meeting his father's gaze unbarriered at last, shock transmuting gradually into an appalled understanding.

Then he twisted, hand clutching at his side. "It is not *my* blood," he whispered, "that will consecrate the ground—"

He convulsed once more, thrusting the dagger that had been sheathed at his hip up beneath Artor's mail. It seared along the old scar where Melwas had wounded the king long ago and stabbed upward into his groin.

For a moment all other awareness disappeared in a red wave of agony. When it began to recede, Artor looked down and saw that Medraut lay still and sightless, his face upturned to the sun.

Oh, Lady— thought the king, *is this your sacrifice?*

He could feel the warm seep of blood across his thigh and the beginnings of a deeper agony. Slowly he lowered himself to the earth beside the body of his son, vision flashing dark and bright with each pulse, fixing on the pebble that lay beside him. A glowing spiral spun within the stone. Artor's fingers closed upon its solid certainty.

This is the king stone . . . the heart of Britannia. It was beneath my feet all along.

His hearing must be going too, he thought then, for his head rang with strange music . . . like Gaulish battle horns. . . .

Guendivar gasped and reached out to Peretur for support as pain stabbed upward through her womb.

"My lady, what is it? Are you ill?"

She tried to straighten, staring round at the men who had come with her to the marketplace. Blood and dust and sunlight filled her vision; she saw an old fortress on a hill.

"Camboglanna . . ." she whispered. "Artor has been wounded!"

As the words articulated her inner vision, she was aware of a great surge of mingled grief and exultation that seemed to rise from the very soil.

"Lady, the king told us to guard you here!" said Peretur in alarm.

She shook her head. "The battle is over. If you want to keep me safe, then follow, for go to him I will!" She started towards the stables, and after a moment the men came after her.

To Morgause, the moment was like a shadow on the sun, a shudder in the soil. She stood swaying in the road, suddenly finding it hard to breathe. Luguvalium lay a day and a half behind them. To left and right rose the outriders of the moors. Ahead, the Wall marched over the first of the crags, and brown dust stained the sky.

"What is it?" cried her priestesses. "What do you hear?"

"I hear a calling of ravens," whispered Morgause. "I hear the groans of dying men. The blood of kings soaks into the soil. We must go quickly, if we are to get there in time!"

"In time for what?" asked Nest, hurrying after her, but Morgause did not reply.

Ninive stood weeping before the tumble of earth and stone where once a cliff had been. Oak and ash and thorn had disappeared beneath the landslip, and with them all trace of the Druid who had used her aid to perform his last and greatest act of magic, but from beneath the rubble, the little stream still trickled, singing to the stones.

Merlin had accomplished what he intended, but had he saved the king? She knew only that there had been a great shift in the fabric of reality. What would he want her to do? Ninive dried her tears and stood listening, and it seemed to her that in the whisper of the wind and the gurgle of the stream she heard his voice once more.

She picked up the bag in which she had carried their food, and began to follow the course of the Cam south, toward the Wall.

Consciousness returned slowly. Artor drew a very careful breath, wondering how long he had lain wounded for his body to have already begun to learn ways to avoid the pain. He could feel the wound as a dull ache in his lower belly, but his flesh held the memory of a throbbing agony.

People were talking in low voices nearby—someone must have survived. He must have wakened before, already fevered, for he had thought that Morgause was there, and Betiver. The king opened his eyes and blinked, recognizing a Roman hauberk and curling dark hair threaded with grey.

"My lord! You are with us again!" Betiver turned and knelt beside him, his fine features bronzed with campaigning and drawn with strain.

"And so are you," answered Artor. "Old friend, what are you doing here?" He had been unconscious for some time, he thought, for his wound had been bandaged, and he was lying inside some roughly repaired building in the fortress.

"We could get no news—" Betiver said helplessly. "I thought you might need me. I came as swiftly as I could—dear God, if only I had come in time!"

"You did." The king's gaze moved around the room, seeing only Betiver's men. "We won. . . ."

"The field was already yours when I got here," said Betiver. "My men have scoured it, seeking survivors. A few of the rebels got away. Vortipor is alive, though wounded, and a few others—pitifully few."

Artor drew a long sigh and winced as his belly began to ache again. "I saw Goriat fall . . ." he said.

Betiver nodded. "Morgause has gone out to look for him. We were grateful to have someone so skilled in leechcraft join us," he added with reluctant appreciation. "It was she who dressed your wound."

"My poor sister. She has lost all her sons . . ." said Artor. *And so have I,* he thought then, and the tide of grief that followed bore him once more down into the dark.

Once, as a child, she had been told the tale of Niobe, who had boasted too loudly of her children, and seen them taken by the gods. Now, thought Morgause as she searched the field of Camboglanna, she wept Niobe's tears.

The dead lay scattered like chaff in a newly reaped field;

ravens stalked among them, gleaning their share of the grisly harvest. Selgovae and Saxons lay sprawled together, Dumnonians and Demetians, men from every corner of Britannia; in death there was no distinction between Medraut's rebels and those who had stayed loyal to Artor. This was not like the Saxon wars, when Britons had fought invaders from across the sea. There could be no winner in such a conflict as this had been, no matter which side claimed victory.

She had found Goriat early on. With him, she mourned Aggarban and Gwyhir and Gualchmai, but in a sense, she had lost them all a long time ago. The grief that kept her creeping from one body to another, turning them to peer at contorted faces, had been born when her youngest son left the Isle of Maidens, cursing her name.

That longest of days was beginning to draw to an end by the time she discovered Medraut. Betiver had said that his body had lain next to that of the king, but after Artor was taken up, the corpse must have been moved by the men who had served with the king in Gallia. It had not only been moved, she saw now, but hacked and slashed in posthumous vengeance so that without Betiver's description she would not have known which wound had been made by the Chalybe sword.

She carried water from the river and bathed the body as once she had bathed her child. They had stripped Medraut as well as mutilating him, but she could still see that her son had grown into a beautiful man—fair in body, at least, if not in soul. Cleansed of blood, his face bore a familiar sneering smile.

"And whose fault was that?" she muttered as she covered him with her veil. "Surely you were my most successful creation, a weapon aimed and sharpened which has finally struck home." He had pierced her to the heart as well.

"Is this all my doing?" Morgause gazed around her, shivering despite the warmth of the sun. "Ah, Medraut, even now I cannot hate you without hating myself as well!"

At the Isle of Maidens she had been kept too busy to think about the past; now it overwhelmed her. If she had had a blade, in that moment she might have executed her own self-judgment, but the fallen weapons had already been collected.

A raven fluttered to the ground nearby, its beak opening in a groan; in a moment two more followed it.

"You shall not have him!" Morgause exclaimed, and in their cries she heard an answer.

"I shall have all of them . . . from my bloody womb they are born, and in blood they return to me. Weep, my daughter, for all slain sons, and for all the mothers who will mourn them—weep with Me!"

The lamentations of the ravens rang around her, but the wail that rose from her belly to her breast to burst from her throat was far louder—an ululation of mourning that echoed from the escarpment. Hearing it, men crossed themselves or flexed fingers in the sign of the Horns, looking over their shoulders.

But Morgause, when that cry had gone out of her, felt her own burden of grief a little lessened, knowing she did not mourn alone. Presently she heard the creak of wheels as men came with the cart to gather the corpses for the funeral pyre.

"Treat him with honor," Morgause said harshly, as they bent to take up Medraut's body, "for he came of the blood of kings."

"Lady, will you return to the fortress?" asked the troop leader. "They said that the king has awakened and is in pain."

The king . . . she thought numbly. Artor still needed her. She would have to live, at least for awhile.

"He is still alive?" Guendivar slid down from the horse and staggered as her muscles cramped from the long ride. Torchlight chased distorted shadows across the yard of the fortress. It was after midnight, but she had insisted that they continue without stopping, desperate to reach Artor.

"The king lives," said Betiver, "but—"

She stumbled past him up the steps of the praetorium, where the roof had been repaired with rough thatching. An oil-lamp cast a fitful light on the sleeping man and the woman who sat by him. At Guendivar's step, she rose, and the queen stiffened, recognizing in the drawn features a reflection of Medraut.

Morgause stepped back abruptly, as if she had seen that moment of recoil. "You will wish to be with him. There is no more I can do for now." With a rustle of draperies she left the room.

The queen sank down upon the bench and took Artor's hand. It was warm, as if within, the solstice fires still burned. She laid her own fingers, chilled by her ride, upon his brow, and saw the flickers of pain that moved beneath his dreaming fade, and the firm lips within the curling beard curve in a little smile.

Presently his eyes opened. "I dreamed I was in Demetia . . . the Irish campaign. But you are here. . . ."

Guendivar nodded. She had been with him in Demetia too, but not like this, her soul seeking his like a homing bird.

"And I am here"— Artor grimaced —"for awhile. . . ." She started to protest, but he shook his head. "I always expected to die in battle, but I had hoped for a clean kill."

"It is only the wound fever," she said desperately. "We healed you before!"

"Well, we shall see. . . ." His voice trailed off. "God knows, now that we are together at last, I want. . . ." His eyes closed. She bent over him in panic, but it was only sleep.

She set her arms about him, calling on the goddess who had filled her at Beltain, and presently there came to her, not the exultant sexual power that had awakened the king's manhood, but a brooding, maternal tenderness—Brigantia, comforting her fallen champion, her most beloved child.

Through the remaining hours of darkness, a little longer than the night before, Guendivar dozed, cradling her king in her arms. When the light of morning began to filter through the thatching, she heard voices outside and, looking up, saw Ninive. As the young woman entered the room, Artor stirred.

"You were with Merlin—" said the king. In the strengthening daylight, Guendivar could see all too clearly how the fever had already begun to burn his flesh away.

Ninive nodded and came to the foot of the bed, looking like a wood spirit in her tattered cape, with leaves still caught in her hair.

"We were in the Forest of Caledon. He wanted to come to you—"

"But something happened. He touched me during the battle. What did he do?" the king asked harshly.

"Age came on him suddenly, as it does, in the wild . . ." Ninive said with difficulty. "He used the last of his strength to make a great magic. And when it was over I felt him all around me, as if he had not gone away, but become present everywhere in the world."

"Perhaps it must be so," Artor murmured then. "It was ever the way for the prophet to go before the king. . . ."

Later that morning, when the king had slipped once more into uneasy sleep, Guendivar consented to walk out into the sunlight and take a little food. They had set up a rude table and there was some thin ale and barley bread and hard cheese. Presently, she was joined by Ninive and Morgause.

"How bad is the king's wound?" asked the girl.

Guendivar fixed her eyes on the broken gate, through which she could see the edge of the bluff and the gleam of river beyond, as if she could bear to hear the answer but not to read it in the older woman's eyes.

"Bad enough, if the blade has only penetrated the layers of muscle that sheathe the belly. But if it opened the gut . . ." Morgause shook her head. "There is nothing I can do."

Guendivar turned. "You are the Lady of the Lake! We must take him there," she said desperately. "The Cauldron healed him before!"

Morgause stared at her as if, sunk in her own sorrow, she had forgotten who she was.

"Could he endure the jolting of a horselitter for so long?" asked Ninive, looking from one to the other.

"He will die if he stays here," Morgause said slowly. "Perhaps, if a coracle would float this far upstream, we could take him by water part of the way."

"We will do it!" Guendivar stood up suddenly. "I am the Tigernissa, and even Betiver will obey!"

"You are the Tigernissa, queen in the realm of men," said Morgause, something kindling in her face that had not been there before, "as I am the Hidden Queen, the White Raven who reigns in the country of the soul."

"Among my mother's people I might be counted a queen as well," said Ninive, "though the forest is where I rule."

"With three queens to care for him, surely Artor will be healed!" exclaimed Guendivar, and in that moment, when the sun shone so brightly on the hills, she could even believe it true.

As the coracle began its journey downriver, Morgause saw two ravens lift from the old thorn tree and fly away before them. On the next day, there were a dozen, and after that, always at least that many, circling the boat and flying ahead or behind it.

Guendivar would stiffen when she saw them, as if to defend the king, though the birds showed no signs of hunger. The warriors who paced them along the bank had another interpretation, and said that Lugos and the Lady of Battles had sent their birds to guard their champion. Ninive said it was Woden, who had given Merlin his Spear.

But Morgause remembered how Artor had found the head of Brannos in the White Mount at Londinium, and claimed the old king's place as Guardian of Britannia. It was said that the ravens had come to him that day, recognizing their chieftain. Perhaps it was the ravens of Brannos that followed Artor now, but whether they escorted him to death or to greater glory she could not tell.

At first some of the men waded with the coracle as it floated down the river, easing it over the shallows and clearing obstructions. But presently the water became deeper, and needed only an occasional dip of the boatman's paddle to keep the king moving smoothly towards Luguvalium. Always, while the other two rode with the warriors, one of the queens sat with him, singing, and laying cloths cooled by the waters of the river upon his burning brow.

Morgause could sense Artor's pain even when she was not beside him. The infusions of white willow she gave him did little to dull it. She had fed him a stew of leeks and caught their scent from the wound. She was sure now that there was a perforation there, and putrefaction in the belly, and when delirium set him babbling of old battles she was almost glad.

Before the Cam reached the Salmaes firth, they turned aside into the river that flowed north from Voreda, and moved upstream, towing the coracle where necessary by ropes pulled by men on the shore. Each night was just a little longer, and it seemed that the king's strength ebbed with the lessening of the sun's power. He was still fighting—she thought sometimes that was why he so often dreamed of war—but more and more often, consciousness fled entirely to give his tortured body a few hours of uneasy rest.

When they came at last to Voreda, they paused to construct a horselitter, and began the final part of the journey into the hills.

Morgause took a deep breath. Always, in the great hills, there was a living silence, a mingling of wind in leaves and the voice of waterfalls, or perhaps it was the breathing of the mountains themselves that she heard. Overhead, a raven rested on the wind. They had halted in the shade of a stand of birches to breathe the horses just before the last rise, and in the quiet, that hush filled her awareness.

The heavy warmth of the lowlands had sapped strength of mind and body, but Morgause felt new vigor flowing into her with every step she took into the hills. As she walked back along the line to check on Artor, it seemed to her that surely he must be the better for it as well. And indeed, she found him awake, staring around him with fever-bright eyes.

"Where are we?" he whispered.

"We are just below the circle of stones on the brow of the hill."

The king nodded. "I remember."

"Beyond the next turning the trail runs downward. Soon we will see before us the Lake and the Island."

"I do not think I will ever come there—" said Artor with a sigh.

Morgause took his wrist, and felt the pulse flicker like a guttering candle flame. Guendivar and Ninive had dismounted as well, and seeing them talking, came to join her.

"What is it?" asked Guendivar, bending to smooth the sweat-soaked hair back from Artor's brow. "Is there more pain?" Morgause could hear the effort it took to keep her voice even.

"Oh, my beloved," he breathed, "it is beyond pain. The

sinews of my being are withering, and each step frays them further. I cannot go on. . . ."

"My king," Betiver said desperately, "we are almost to the Lake!"

Ninive took Morgause's arm. "Lady, let him wait in the circle; perhaps he will draw some strength from its power. Cannot we run ahead and bring the Cauldron here?"

Ninive had been a priestess at the Lake, thought Morgause. She was her granddaughter, heir to her power—perhaps the Goddess spoke through her now.

"The circle of stones . . ." echoed Artor. "I can feel it calling. Sister, if you have forgiven me for the wrong I did you by my birth, let me rest there. . . ."

"My brother," she asked, "can you find it in your heart to forgive *me*?"

He shook his head a little. "Our son's blood cancelled all debts, Morgause."

"I will go," she said softly, though her voice shook. "Wait for me, Artor! Wait for me!"

As she started down the trail, she heard his whisper behind her— "I will . . . if I can. . . ."

Artor lay upon the breast of the mountain, embraced by the open sky. He could sense the strength of the stones like a royal guard, he himself at their center, and the hill on which they stood surrounded by mountains, and this land of lake and mountain itself the still center of the circles of the world.

They had wished to build a shade above him, but he would not have it. He needed the light. He breathed more easily here than he had in days, but he had no illusions about his condition. From time to time the dark shape of a raven moved across his field of vision. *Soon,* he thought, *I will come with you. Be patient for just a little while.*

In his lucid moments it had gradually come to him that his disintegration had progressed too far for even the Cauldron to heal. Its power was to restore the natural order, and Nature's way, for a body so wasted as his, was to let the spirit go.

The kingdom he had ruled from Camalot was ended, and who would guard Britannia now? He twitched restlessly, remembering the young foxes of Medraut's prophecy. What would come to the land if one of them should try to set himself above the others, brandishing the Chalybe sword? Even the priestesses of the Isle could not guard it against a determined attacker—

He must have moaned, because suddenly Betiver was leaning over him. "My lord, do you need water?"

Artor swallowed. "The Sword—bring it here. . . ." He closed his eyes for a moment, until he felt the familiar ridges of the hilt beneath his hand. He tried to grip it, amazed at how little strength remained in his fingers. But even that was enough for him to feel the current of power.

Defender . . . he prayed, *what is Your will for this blade?* and, in the next moment, trembled beneath a flood of images as he understood what he must do.

Guendivar's hands were cool upon his face, lifting him, and he felt a little water from the skin bag dribble across dry lips. He looked up at Betiver.

"Take the Sword down to the Lake's edge, and with all the power that is in you, throw it in."

"Artor! It is the strength of the kingdom!" exclaimed Betiver.

"It is—it will always be—so long as it does not fall into evil hands! Take it and go, and tell me what befalls!"

When Betiver had departed, Artor lay back again, waiting for his racing pulse to slow. His frame seemed hardly solid enough to keep the gallop of his heart from carrying him away. His body was an empty vessel being filled by the sunlight, or perhaps it was the fever that was burning away his mortality as the dross is burned when the Goddess puts on her smith's apron and purifies the ore in the fire.

Artor's skin is so transparent, thought Guendivar, *he is like a vessel filled with light. . . .* She had always known him as strong and, in his way, attractive; now, with flesh wasted to reveal the pure line of bone, he was beautiful. *And I am going to lose him.* Her stomach churned with the ripple of fear that had become all too familiar since the battle on the Cam.

He seemed to be sleeping, but she could not be sure. Through the link that had grown between them since Beltain, she sensed that for much of the time he lived in the dim borderland between sleep and waking—or perhaps it was the borders of the Otherworld. She had talked to him often on this journey, not knowing whether he could hear her, but there was still so much to say.

"I have missed so much," she said in a low voice. "Children, and the comfort of your arms through the long years. I weep because I could not give you a true son to carry that sword after you were gone. But to no other woman was this blessing given, to rule beside you as your queen. And if the kingdom we tried to build must fall, still, we tried, and for a little while at least we kept back the dark."

Gently she stroked his hair. "If you must leave me, I think I will go south again, to Afallon. Would you like to come with me, my love, so that one day we may lie together upon the holy isle?"

She heard a footstep, and looked up as Betiver came up the hill. He was empty-handed, and she frowned. Had so much time passed?

"And see, here is Betiver back again," she said then, and Artor opened his eyes, so perhaps he had been listening after all.

"Is it done?" asked the king. "What did you see?"

Betiver was staring at the grass. A muscle jumped in his jaw. "The wind on the water, and a splash. What more could there be?"

"The Sword going into the Lake!" said Artor with a strength that made everyone turn to see. "For you have not done what I asked! Go once more, Betiver, and obey my command, if I am still your king."

Ravens rose in a black cloud, carking with angry voices as Betiver started back down the hill. Several flapped after him, winged shadows of Artor's will.

Guendivar and the warriors sat in silence, waiting for his return. And yet the time seemed still too short for a man to have climbed down to the Lake and back when Betiver came again.

"Betiver, I trusted you!" The king's voice thinned with sorrow. "For five and twenty years you have been with me, closer than kin! Will even you betray me at the end?"

Betiver stretched out his hands, his cheeks glistening with tears. "My lord, wait for them to bring the Cauldron, and heal you, and take the Sword back again! Or if you must leave us, do not deprive us of the only hope we will have! You have named no successor! How shall we choose a true king, if not by the Sword?"

"You are all my heirs!" the king said strongly. "Everyone who hears my story! And it is not by arms that the heritage I leave you shall be defended. . . ." Artor's head moved weakly against the pillow. "You must find hope in your hearts, not in the Sword. . . ." He tried to speak again and coughed. Guendivar saw he did not have the strength for more.

"Betiver," she said with the steel she had learned in ten years as regent for the king, "I command you to do Artor's will, in the name of the love you bear for me. . . ." His eyes lifted to hers, and she saw the desperation go out of them, replaced by a grief as deep as her own.

"Lady," he answered in a breaking voice, "my son also lies among the dead on Camboglanna's field."

His steps were slow as he started down the hill towards the Lake once more.

Morgause sat in the bow of the boat, swaying as Nest poled them towards the shore. The Cauldron was cradled in her arms. Ninive crouched before her, holding the bag that held the medicines and other gear it had taken them all this while to find, for they might have to spend some time on the hill before Artor could be moved again.

We have the time . . . Morgause affirmed silently, turning on her seat to gaze up the hill. *He is safe in the circle. He will live till I return. . . .*

Beneath its wrappings the Cauldron quivered against her belly, as if she held something living. For so many years she had desired it and, seizing it, had herself been possessed and transformed by its power. But for more than a dozen years she had served as its priestess, handling it only with the prescribed and warded touch of ritual. This intimate contact dizzied her.

Brigantia be with me, she prayed. *Let me work Thy will!*

A movement on the shore caught her eye and she leaned forward, staring. "Nest, turn the boat," she commanded suddenly. "Toward the little beach by the boulder."

Betiver stood at the water's edge, holding the Sword. Even from here she could see that he was weeping.

"What are you doing?" she cried. "Is Artor—"

"Oh, Lady, he commanded me to throw it in!" Betiver called back, his face working.

The boat rocked as Morgause stood up. Before Artor, the women of her blood had been the Sword's keepers.

"Stop! You must not—" she began, but Betiver was already drawing back the blade, whirling it up and around behind him.

For a moment, at the height of his swing, the Sword seemed to hover, blazing in the light of the sun. Then it flew free, soaring above the water in an arc of flame. Morgause lurched forward, felt Ninive clutch at her legs at the same moment as the Cauldron leaped from fingers that no longer had the power to hold it.

The Cauldron spun across the water like a silver wheel, the Sword drove downward. Where they met, Light flared outward, blinding the senses. But as Morgause fell back, it was not the afterimage of Sword and Cauldron that remained imprinted behind her eyelids, but that of a goddess, reaching up from the waters of the Lake to embrace the god. . . .

Artor jerked back to consciousness, gasping. *I am dying!* he thought, but his pain-wracked body still imprisoned him. It was the world that was whirling, to settle at last into a new configuration, and he understood that the perfect balance for which he had been striving since first he drew the Sword from the Stone was at last attained.

"Guendivar!" He reached out to her. "Do you feel it? It is done!"

She caught his hand against her breast, and he felt her heart beating almost as wildly as his own. He grinned as a warrior does at the end of a battle fought past the borders of desperation, and beyond hope, won. In her face he saw a reflected wonder.

"Help me to move—" he said with sudden authority. "Set me with my back against a stone."

The queen nodded, and men came to lift him, grim understanding in their eyes. They set him against one of the boulders that marked out a rectangle at the eastern edge of the circle, its face worn smooth by the centuries. It made a royal seat, he thought, for the death of a king.

Artor took a deep breath, and let it slowly out. The cold stone warmed against him; a vibration travelled down his spine and into the depths of the earth, then fountained upward. And now he could hear it—the stones were singing, crying out in recognition of his sovereignty. Could not the others hear? He coughed, and coughed again, feeling the bonds that held soul to body fray.

Guendivar knelt beside him, weeping.

"My love . . . my love . . ." he whispered, understanding now so many things. "We cannot lose each other. I will never be far away from you. When my body sleeps in the earth, my spirit will watch over Britannia. . . . Watch with me, my queen, until we are joined once more. . . ."

She took his hand, and Artor smiled. He was aware of voices—Betiver and Morgause and Ninive, panting from their swift climb, but he could not find the strength to speak to them. He let his eyes close.

Through his eyelids he could still see sunlight; his other senses seemed to sharpen. The borders of his body could no longer hold him; awareness expanded outward through earth and air and water. Beyond the surfaces he had always accepted as reality, he perceived the real Britannia, the true country of the heart that no matter what evils passed in the world of men would always endure. This was his kingdom. Why, he wondered, had it taken him so long to understand?

To Guendivar, the light that had filled Artor's face seemed slowly to fade. But the radiance all around her was growing. Blinking back tears, she looked up from the emptied body, wondering where he had gone.

From Morgause came an anguished cry, and as if that had

been a signal, the ravens rushed upward in a glistening dark cloud. Three times above the still body the black birds circled, calling out in grief and triumph. Then from their midst Guendivar saw one Raven rise and wing southward, its feathers turning incandescent in the sun.

Epilogue
Rex Aeternus

A.D. 1189

"They say that you know all the Breton tales," says the king. "Can you sing of King Arthur as well?" He taps a leather-bound book on the table before him. "Here are the *Lais* of Marie, that she dedicated to me. I have read the *Brut* also, and Geoffrey's *Historia,* when I was a young man. And I have heard very many songs of the jongleurs of your country. You will be hard put, I warn you, to find anything that I have not heard!"

The bard inclines his head. He is old, but seems strong, with a pair of dark eyes beneath bushy brows. He is a very big man.

"Lord king, I know many tales that no one has heard, of Artor, and other things." In the light from the pointed window, his beard glints silver against the dusty white of his robe.

"Hah!" says King Henry. "Sit, then, for I've a fox that gnaws my vitals, and a good tale may help me to forget the pain." He has filled the castle of Chinon with beautiful things. The stool to which he gestures the bard has a seat of red leather and feet carved like griffons' claws.

365

"That was how King Arthur died," says the bard. "Stabbed in the belly by his son." He speaks the French tongue with the deep music of the Celtic lands.

The king gives him a sharp look. "My sons have done the same, both Richard, who fights me, and John, who intrigues with that viper Philippe Auguste while smiling and praising my name. But you surprise me," he goes on, sipping more wine. "Mostly the Bretons say that Arthur never died, but sleeps in the Western Isles, or in a cavern in the hills, or in the vale of Avalon. The Welshmen, too, especially when they are preaching rebellion."

"Those who speak of Avalon come closest to the truth," rumbles the bard. "He is buried there."

"Now how did that come to pass?" Henry pulls his robe more closely around him and leans back in his carved chair, one eyebrow raised.

"The battle of Camlann was fought in the north of Angleterre, near the Wall," says the bard, "not in Cornuailles, as so many say. And when Arthur was dead, his body was carried south by Queen Guenivere and buried in Inis Witrin, which is the Isle of Avalon."

"Indeed?" The king cocks his head, willing to be amused. "Say then, if you know so much, what manner of man was Arthur, and how old he was when he met his end?"

"A big man, like you, and fifty-five years of age when he died. He too quarreled with churchmen for the good of the land, and dreamed of an empire in Gaul."

Henry frowns. "I have passed him, then, for I am fifty-six. I wonder, do you mean to threaten or to flatter me?"

The bard shrugs. "Arthur walked the earth, and loved greatly, and strove greatly to make good laws and keep the peace and preserve the land from her enemies."

"So also have I," the king replies, more softly. "But you take the magic from the story, telling it so!"

"Is it not a greater wonder that this same history should still be recounted some six centuries after Arthur died, and in every country of Christendom?" the bard answers more softly still.

King Henry shakes his head, laughing. "You will never make your fortune telling such tales to mortal kings! We prefer to believe that Arthur lived in an age of marvels, and avoid comparisons!"

"But what if it were true?"

"If it could be proved, you mean?" Suddenly the king grasps his sinewy arm. "Who are you, to know such things?"

For a moment the bard considers him. Then, very gently, he smiles, and Henry finds his grip loosening. "I have been called by many names. I am a Wild Man in the wood, and a bard in the courts of kings. I am a wanderer upon the roads of the world, and the prophet of Arthur. And you yourself can prove the truth of my words—"

He leans forward. "The abbey at Glastonbury burned five years ago, and the monks are still rebuilding. Command them to dig deep between the two pyramids in the churchyard. They will find there a coffin hollowed from a log of oak, and in it the bones of Arthur, and at his feet, Guenivere, with a leaden cross that gives their names."

"That would settle the Welsh!" exclaims the king, then sobers. "They claim Arthur as their Defender, but so do the English, and we Normans likewise, for my grandson bears his name. These days, he belongs to everyone. Why is that, do you suppose?" Henry says then. "Why should he matter so?"

"Because he loved Britannia . . ." answers the bard. "Because for a little while he kept her safe against the dark." He sits back, considering the king.

"I tell you these things so that you may know that such deeds can be achieved by mortal men. And yet what the Welsh and the Bretons tell you is the truth as well. Arthur's spirit never departed—neither to Heaven nor to the Otherworld. He watches over the Hallowed Isle. . . ."

People and Places

A note on pronunciation:

British names are given in fifth-century spelling, which does not yet reflect pronunciation changes. Initial letters should be pronounced as they are in English. Medial letters are as follows:

SPELLED	PRONOUNCED
p	b
t	d
k/c	(soft) g
b	v (approximately)
d	soft "th" (modern Welsh "dd")
g	"yuh"
m	v
ue	w

† PEOPLE
CAPITALS = major character
* = historical personage
( ) = dead before story begins
[ ] = name as given in later literature
Italics = diety or mythological personage

*Aelle—king of the South Saxons

Aggarban [Agravaine]—third son of Morgause

*Agricola—prince of Demetia

*Alaric II—king of the Visigoths

(*Ambrosius Aurelianus—emperor of Britannia and Vitalinus' rival)

(*Amlodius—Artor's grandfather)

Amminius—one of Artor's men

ARTOR [Arthur]—son of Uthir and Igierne, high king of Britannia

(Artoria Argantel—Artor's grandmother)

Beowulf—king of the Geats in Denmark

BETIVER [Bedivere]—nephew to Riothamus, one of Artor's Companions

Bleitisbluth—a Pictish chieftain

Brigantia/Brigid—British goddess of healing, inspiration, and the land

*Budic—a grandson of Riothamus, lord of Civitas Aquilonia

CAI—son of Caius Turpilius, Artor's foster-brother and Companion

*Caninus [Aurelius Caninus]—son of the prince of Glevum, ally of Medraut

CATAUR [Cador]—prince of Dumnonia

Cathubodva—Lady of Ravens, a British war goddess

*Ceawlin—son of Cynric and grandson of Ceretic

Ceincair—a priestess on the Isle of Maidens

(*Ceretic [Cerdic]—king of the West Saxons)

*Chlodovechus [Clovis]—king of the Franks in Gallia

*Chlotild—queen of the Franks

*Conan—lord of Venetorum

*Constantine—son of Cataur, prince of Dumnonia

*Creoda—son of Icel of Anglia

*Cuil—a brigand

*Cunobelinus—warleader of the northern Votadini

*Cunoglassus—a prince of Guenet, ally of Medraut

Cunovinda—a young priestess on the Isle of Maidens

*Cymen—Aelle's eldest son

*Cynric—son of Ceretic, king of the West Saxons

*Daniel Dremrud—son of Riothamus

Doli—a Pictish warrior in the service of Morgause

*Drest Gurthinmoch—high king of the Picts

(*Dubricius—bishop of Isca and head of the church in Britannia)

*Dumnoval [Dyfnwal]—lord of the Southern Votadini

Edrit—a young warrior in the service of Aggarban

Eldaul the younger [Eldol]—prince of Glevum

*Eormenric—son of Oesc, child-king of Cantuware

*Feragussos [Fergus]—king of the Scotti of Dal Riada

*Gipp—Norse founder of Gippewic in Essex, Medraut's ally

GORIAT [Gareth]—fourth son of Morgause

(Gorlosius [Gorlois]—first husband of Igierne, father of Morgause)

Gracilia—wife of Gualchmai

GUALCHMAI [Gawain]—first son of Morgause

GUENDIVAR [Gwenivere]—Artor's queen

*Guenomarcus—lord of Plebs Legionorum

Gwyhir [Gaheris]—second son of Morgause

Hæthwæge—a Saxon wisewoman

(*Hengest—king of Cantuware, leader of Saxon revolt)

*Henry II—king of England

*Icel—king of the Anglians in Britannia

IGIERNE [Igraine]—Artor's mother, Lady of the Lake

Johannes Rutilius—brother-in-law to Riothamus, Betiver's father

Julia—a nun from the Isle of Glass, Guendivar's companion

(Kea—a British slave girl among the Picts, Medraut's first woman)

Father Kedi—an Irish priest at the court of Artor

Leodegranus [Leodegrance]—prince of Lindinis, Guendivar's father

(Leudonus [Lot]—king of the Votadini)

Maglouen [Maelgwn]—a prince of Guenet, Medraut's ally

(*Magnus Maximus [Maxen Wledig]—general serving in Britain who was proclaimed emperor 383–388)

Marcus Conomorus [Mark of Cornwall]—son of Constantine

Martinus of Viroconium—an ally of Medraut

Maxentius—a grandson of Riothamus

MEDRAUT—fifth son of Morgause, by Artor

Melguas [Meleagrance]—an Irishman born in Guenet, abductor of Guendivar

MERLIN—Druid and wizard, Artor's advisor

Morcant Bulc—heir to Dun Breatann

MORGAUSE—daughter of Igierne and Gorlosius, queen of the Votadini

(*Naitan Morbet—king of all the provinces of the Picts)

Nest—a priestess on the Isle of Maidens

Ninive—daughter of Gualchmai by a woman of the hills

(*Oesc—grandson of Hengest and king of Cantuware, Eormenric's father)

*Othar, Ela, Adgils, Admund [Othere, Onela, Eadgils, Eadmund]—King Ottar of Sweden, his brother Ali, his sons

Adils and Eadmund
Paulinus Clutorix—lord of Viroconium
*Peretur [Peredur]—son of Eleutherius, lord of Eboracum
*Pompeius Regalis [Riwal]—lord of Domnonia
*Ridarchus—king at Altaclutha and protector of Luguvalium
Rigana—widow of Oesc, Eormenric's mother
*Riothamus—ruler of Armorica
*Theodoric—a Gothic admiral in the service of Britannia
*Theuderich—king of the Franks, son of Chlodovechus and a
    concubine, and one of his successors, along with Chlo-
    domer, Childebert, and Lothar (by Queen Clotild)
Uorepona—the "Great Mare," high queen of the Picts
(Uthir [Uther Pendragon]—Artor's father)
Verica—a young priestess on the Isle of Maidens
(*Vitalinus, the Vor-Tigernus—ruler of Britannia who brought
    in the Saxons)
*Vortipor—son of Agricola, prince of Demetia

†
PLACES

Afallon [Avalon]—Isle of Apples, Glastonbury
Alba—Scotland
Altaclutha—kingdom of the Clyde
Ambrosiacum—Amesbury .
Anglia—Lindsey and Lincoln
Annuen [Annwyn]—the land of the dead
Aquae Sulis—Bath
Armorica—Britanny
Belisama fluvius—River Ribble, Lancashire
Bodotria aestuarius—Firth of Forth
Britannia—Great Britain
Caellwic—Kelliwic, Cornwall

Caledonian forest—southern Scotland
Calleva—Silchester
Camalot [Camelot]—Cadbury Castle, Somerset
Camboglanna [Camlann]—fortress of Birdoswald, the Wall
Camulodunum—Colchester
Cantium, Cantuware—Kent
Castra Legionis—Caerleon
Cendtire—Kintyre peninsula
Civitas Aquilonia—Quimper, Brittany
Clutha—River Clyde
Demetia—Pembroke and Carmarthen
Domnonia—Cotes du Nord, Brittany
Dumnonia—Cornwall and Devon
Dun Bara—Barry Hill, Perth
Dun Breatann—"fortress of the Britons," Dumbarton Rock
Dun Eidyn   Edinburgh Rock
Durnovaria—Dorchester, Dorset
Durobrivae—1. Rochester, Kent; 2. Water Newton, Cambridge
Fodreu—Fortriu, Fife
Forest of Caledon—Caledonian forest, southern Scotland
Gallia—France
Giants' Dance—Stonehenge
Gippewic   in Essex
Glevum—Gloucester
Guenet [Gwynedd]—Denbigh and Caernarvon
Isca (Silurum)—Caerwent
Isle of Glass (Inis Witrin)—Glastonbury
Isle of Maidens in the Lake—Derwentwater, Cumbria
Lindinis—Ilchester, Somerset
Lindum—Lincoln
Londinium—London
Metaris aestuarius—the Wash
Mona—Anglesey
Plebs Legionorum—St. Pol de Léon, Brittany

Pyrenaei montes—the Pyrenees
Sabrina fluvia—the Severn River and estuary
Segontium—Caernarvon, Wales
Sorviodunum—Salisbury
Summer Country—Somerset
Tava—River Tay
Tolosa—Toulouse
Urbs Legionis (Deva)—Chester
Uxela fluvius—River Axe, Severn estuary
Venetorum—Vannes, in Brittany
Venta Belgarum—Winchester
Venta Siluricum—Caerwent, Wales
Viroconium—Wroxeter
Voreda—Old Penrith, Cumberland

DISCOVER THE KINGDOM
OF KING ARTHUR
by award-winning author
DIANA L. PAXSON

THE HALLOWED ISLE
THE BOOK OF THE SWORD
AND
THE BOOK OF THE SPEAR
0-380-81367-X / $6.50 US / $8.99 Can

THE HALLOWED ISLE
THE BOOK OF THE CAULDRON
AND
THE BOOK OF THE STONE
0-380-81759-4 / $6.50 US / $8.99 Can

Available wherever books are sold or please call 1-800-331-3761
to order.

DLP 1100

New York Times Bestselling Author

RAYMOND E. FEIST

The Riftwar Legacy

"Feist brings a new world alive."
Portland Oregonian

KRONDOR: THE BETRAYAL
0-380-79527-2/$6.99 US/$8.99 Can

KRONDOR: THE ASSASSINS
0-380-80323-2/$6.99 US/$9.99 Can

and, coming soon in hardcover . . .

KRONDOR: TEAR OF THE GODS
0-380-97800-8/$25.00 US/$37.95 Can

The realm's most sacred artifact must be protected at all cost.
For if it falls into malevolent hands, darkness will
devour the light . . . and evil will rule.

Available wherever books are sold or please call 1-800-331-3761
to order.   REF 1100

THE PENDRAGON CYCLE
by Award-Winning Author
STEPHEN R. LAWHEAD

TALIESIN
70613-X/$6.99 US/$9.99 Can

A remarkable epic tale of the twilight of Atlantis—and of the brilliant dawning of the Arthurian Era!

MERLIN
70889-2/$6.99 US/$9.99 Can

Seer, Bard, Sage, Warrior…His wisdom was legend, his courage spawned greatness!

ARTHUR
70890-6/$6.99 US/$9.99 Can

He was the glorious King of Summer—His legend—the stuff of dreams.

PENDRAGON
71757-3/$6.99 US/$8.99 Can

Arthur is King, but darkest evil has descended upon Britain in many guises.

GRAIL
78104-2/$6.99 US/$9.99 Can

The ultimate battle for the heart and soul of a king.

· ·

Available wherever books are sold or please call 1-800-331-3761 to order.

PEN 0800

Bestselling Fantasy Author
Janny Wurts

GRAND CONSPIRACY
0-06-10546-6/$6.99 US/$9.99 Can

On the world of Athera, two half-brothers gifted of Light and Shadow defeated the Mistwraith. But its revenge left them cursed to life-long enmity, stirring war and deadly intrigue.

Also by Janny Wurts

FUGITIVE PRINCE
0-06-105468-2/$6.99 US/$9.99 Can

SHIPS OF MERIOR
0-06-105465-8/$6.99 US/$8.99 Can

WARHOST OF VASTMARK
Ships of Merior, Vol. II
0-06-105667-7/$6.99 US/$8.99 Can

And in trade paperback

THE CYCLE OF FIRE TRILOGY
0-06-107355-5/$16.00 US/$23.50 Can

Available wherever books are sold or please call 1-800-331-3761 to order.
JW 0101